Way of the Moon Bear

Way of the Moon Bear

Joseph E. Green

Copyright (C) 2017 Joseph E. Green
Layout design and Copyright (C) 2017 Creativia
Published 2017 by Creativia
ISBN: 978-1979399333
Cover art by Cover Mint
This book is a work of fiction. Names, characters, places, and incidents are the product of the author's imagination or are used fictitiously. Any resemblance to actual events, locales, or persons, living or dead, is purely coincidental.
All rights reserved. No part of this book may be reproduced or transmitted in any form or by any means, electronic or mechanical, including photocopying, recording, or by any information storage and retrieval system, without the author's permission.

Contents

1	Backwards	1
2	Eyes of Crimson	12
3	Noble Enforcers	20
4	The World Unfolding	29
5	Come Forth, the Evil	51
6	Heavy Conversations and a Shift in Direction	59
7	In Search of Sea-Thieves	66
8	The Sentient Maze	74
9	Slay	87
10	Relentless By Name	95
11	Two Heads and Two Sides	103
12	Answers and Apologies	110

13	The Unwelcome Drum	116
14	Fearful Suspicions	136
15	Dead Discipline	145
16	Knowledge Avarice	163
17	Forwards	170
18	The Holhouettes of Favarly	181
19	Troll Crusade and the Crystal Messenger	192
20	Free Life if Only for a Second	202
21	Lay-Vau's Tomb	222
22	The Lone Olash	227
23	One More Fellow	239
24	Dreams for Spirits	247
25	Fighting for the Sun	259
26	Loved Ones Lost	285
27	Words Like Wildfire	308
28	Victims of Voodoo	319
29	Detachment	332
30	Girl of Importance	347

Chapter 1

Backwards

The birth of existence, the growth of life and the awakening of advancement – all momentous factors that once unravelled through time. Reality flows across the same course, forever-changing and evolving, like a river eroding away at conventional perception, breaking away to create a new trail for everything to be carried along. There is no one constructor of protocol, nor is there a decider of fate. All things come to be seemingly on their own accord, but whether these things are orchestrated by time itself is unknown. One thing pre-dates the next, over and over until history is ripe with a collection subsistence, affecting the world and shaping it for better or worse. Forms of being that call themselves Men and Women come and go as though they carry importance, but all are specks beside the other creatures that populate the dirt, air and waters. However, humanity once made a name for itself amongst the most majestic of entities, securing their place above all else, if only for a moment. They became the artificial bearers of all – holding time in one hand and reality in the other, as though they had the capability to bend it to their will. Arrogance and avarice had helped them climb to the top, but it quickly betrayed them and became their catalyst. Their wish had become true, humans *did* stand out above all else for the most part. Unfortunately, it was never supposed to be. Their hunger for knowledge and power soon hit a dead end, preventing them from surpassing what it meant to be human, as their comprehension was never designed to stretch beyond what their minds and souls could let them. Before long, they reverted back to their true, animalistic ways, spilling blood and provoking death to rivals. Humanity's hatred spawned war, and their wars sparked division, forgetting that they would always share the same world, no matter how hard they fought. In their search to become divine, they realised that the only thing they could create was turmoil. Ages cluttered with anguish eventually halted growth and advancement, yet existence continued, holding humans in a never-ending cycle of inevitable doom. Although time continued to unfold, reality was trapped at a standstill, bound to the actions of the Earth's destroyers. As punishment, the worldly tools and equipment capable of real progress were torn from their grasp, costing them whatever fulfilling destinies they had in store. All was lost. Everything had now been designed to stop and oppress, thwarting what could have been and forbidding reality from ever catching up with its ongoing counterpart. If only they knew that it would only take one person to seek out answers – to discover the price they had all unknowingly paid – to regress their actions and start anew, but second chances don't come all too easily. For thousands of years, humanity lived on in secret torment, confined to the lower life forms which surrounded them, with just subtle hints towards an untapped potential. Unlike the other creatures, humans created kingdoms and castles for those elected to then govern over the rest. They scattered far and wide, claiming areas for themselves, breaking connections further and devoting their interests solely to the one piece of land they lived on. Their disconnection from each other generated opposing views, ideals and religions. Ground-breaking discoveries struck fear in the uneducated, sprouting an unhealthy obsession with the new and enlightening, in hopes to become greater than the other countries and clans around them. They were embarking on the exact same destructive path as before, except this time it was between themselves. The world had sadly become nothing more than a host for trivial conflict and tension, which passed on through endless generations. New life was then created and forced to continue their predecessor's lives of nothingness, as though it was their duty to do so. Life had become a paradoxical mockery of itself. From the moment a child opened their eyes, they were destined to take everything as it was and be doomed from the start. How was a boy expected to fare in such a world? No child would ask of any of it, but it was the people next in line that were born – they would continue to carry the weight of all existence. However, burdens came in all shapes and sizes, and not all were designed to be merely held in-hand. With the help of time, the container for life's problems had finally reached its tipping point, and things that would challenge humanity and its definition were ready to shift and change as it poured. The greatest burden of all was soon to be adopted within the palms of a boy. Whether or not he was prepared to change the fate of the world was left for him to decide.

The eyes were said to be access to the soul. It was a beautiful idea, although it made people overlook their literal purpose, which was to see and observe. The first second of perception feeds directly to the mind, so that a proper reaction can be decided in regard to what was just seen. The ability to simply see something for what it *was* rather than what it *meant* could easily make for a dangerous and frightening experience, especially when that person was merely a child, and their memory had been stolen from them. The moment young Greenwick reopened his eyes from an involuntary slumber, he was reserved the right to be alarmed. His eyelids slowly pulled apart to reveal a large, twitching nose, connected to a furry snout. The heavy sniffling from the wet nostrils was the reason he had woken up in the first place. On the contrary, to finally match the peculiar noise with the equally-strange sight was anything but closure. The boy connected with the beast's black, beady eyes, trapping him in fear. It was made apparent to Greenwick that he was currently laying on the floor, outdoors, in the middle of a forest during the day, with an extraordinarily large bear standing over him, observing his body whilst casting a huge shadow over it. The majority of the creature's head was round and fluffy, making it difficult to figure out where its skull actually stopped. The bottom half of its head made way for its wide, salivated jaws, armed with long and pointy teeth that could have torn the boy apart almost instantly. Its face as a whole though seemed gormless but curious, like a dim-witted brute that didn't really know how big and domineering they were. Greenwick dared to turn his head left then right to look at the fat paws at either side of him. If the teeth weren't able to rip him to shreds, the long, hook-like claws would have certainly done the trick. At first he was too scared to get up and run, but the moment the bear let out a quick grunt, his frozen state of fear transformed into a heated escape. The boy scurried backwards from under the looming body of hair and scrambled to his feet at incredible speed, without a moment to waste on looking back. He galloped through and over bushes, weaving in and out of a crowd of trees, listening to the bear's heavy steps and breathing between his own. His shock prevented him from screaming at the top of his voice. His heart raced around inside of his chest, beating rapidly as a wave of numbing adrenaline coursed through his veins. The rustles and stomps behind him increased in volume, indicating that the bear was gaining on him. At last, he felt the need to do a quick look back to see how giant the beast actually was. Its chunky body rippled as it ran towards him, and drool flung from its mouth when it growled. Whilst Greenwick faced the wrong way, his foot smacked into an unearthed root, causing him to fly and roll uncontrollably for several feet, before eventually hitting a tree, concussing him slightly, but by the time he got back up, the bear was stood in front of him on all-fours, no longer trying to get as close at first, until it noticed the bleeding cut on the boy's head. The intimidating animal plodded towards him. "Stay away from me!" he screamed, holding his arms above his head in fear. The bear was taken back by surprise for a moment, then tried to walk to him again. "Back! Get back!" he cried. For some reason, the beast seemed confused by the child's response. It leant back and dropped its hind legs to sit down, creating a deep thud on the soil and a small cloud of dusty dirt. It was a big, wide blob of a creature, but it no longer seemed as bloodthirsty. Greenwick stared at it for a while and noticed more of an adorable side. "What's happening?" he asked himself which unintentionally caused the bear to get back up and walk forward again. "No, I said stay away!" he put his hands out in front and made a pushing action with his arms in an attempt to shoo it. The brawny thing hesitated at first, but ultimately ignored the boy's requests and stretched out closer and closer until its head was in his face. The child was once again frozen in place, hoping that he wasn't about to be eaten. He closed his eyes to accept whatever the outcome was set to be, but to his surprise, the bear licked the fresh cut on his forehead as though it was concerned. After cleaning the wound, it sniffed him again continuously whilst grunting. Wick's panic had diminished slightly, giving him the courage to raise his hand and place it on the bear's fur. There was no reaction, so he began to stroke it vigorously in confusion. "Why aren't you trying to hurt me?" he wondered as the beast sat back down. It was a unique way to wake up. The more he thought about it, the quicker he realised that his memory had been compromised. He had no recollection of anything from before he woke up on the floor. All that remained were faint voices but he couldn't hear any actual words other than the screaming of his own name. He had no idea where he was or what he was meant to be doing, and the strangely domestic bear wasn't helping him piece things together either. Nothing made sense. He hoped he was trapped in some sort of dream, but it felt all too real. "What happened to me? Why can't I remember anything?" he whined. The bear didn't seem to enjoy seeing Wick in despair, so it walked at him again. "I told you to stay back," he said sternly whilst scratching his head, before walking around in circles in hopes of regaining his memory. After a while, he'd left the bear in the distance, causing it to run over and catch up to him. "I mean it, leave me alone!" he moaned. His head filled up with countless questions but he couldn't answer any of them, making his heart beat even faster than before when he was being chased. The baffling situation was all too much, and the boy's legs collapsed, forcing him down to his knees in misery. The worried brute didn't enjoy watching the poor child cry, so came in for another face lick as well as a nudge from the snout. "Stop it," he blubbered. "Where do

I go?" Suddenly, the bear pulled Wick's collar using its teeth, like it was trying to lead him in a particular direction. "Get off of me!" the boy sighed, but it continued to yank and tug whilst grumbling. "I'm not letting a bear take me anywhere," he huffed and stood back up, shaking his head at the ridiculousness. He started to march through the woods spontaneously, expecting to eventually reach civilisation. Perhaps other people could have provided him with answers. Before he could gain much distance though, the bear pulled on him again, this time by his baggy sleeves. "What? Fine, I'll go *this* way instead… but I'm not walking with you," Wick muttered. Whether he liked it or not, the beast persistently tagged along, keeping an eye on the direction they were heading in. The boy walked with haste, praying that he'd be left alone, but the bear had twice as many legs as him so keeping up wasn't a problem. They may have been travelling together, but Greenwick refused to consider the scary animal a companion. At the same time though, he couldn't help but think how it could be so domesticated and friendly.

After what felt like hours, they finally reached some sort of village. The tatty, wooden houses were surrounded by large logs, joining together to create a barrier for the civilian's protection. A watchtower was placed on each corner of the walls, all sporting a bland, grey flag with strange patterns on them. It was all meaningless to Wick. Even if he once knew what they meant, there was no point dwelling on it because at that moment, he had no idea. He cautiously strolled out from behind the trees and into the open, but so did the bear. "No, you have to stay here! You're going to frighten everyone to death!" he stressed whilst pushing the heavy dope back into the cover of vegetation. It backed up, confused with the request, then tried to move again. "No, no no! You need to stay put. Do you understand?" Wick scoffed. He walked back out into the open then turned to make sure the bear wasn't following. "Good. Now stay… stay. Lay down. Yes, that's perfect," he ordered. The bewildered creature did the best it could to follow his instructions, shifting from side to side with a dumbfounded face, then slumping down into a large bush so only his nose poked through. Wick ran over to the large entrance of the village but was stopped by two armoured guardsmen. "State your business, little one," they demanded.

"Oh, I'm lost. Well, not just that... I-I can't remember anything. I need help-".

"You can't remember anything?" one of them interrupted.

"I woke up in the middle of the woods and there was a big- I mean, I've just lost my memory".

"You just lost your memory, aye? Sounds like some sort of sorcery to me".

"I don't even know what that means".

"I see. So, where are your parents then?"

"My parents? I don't know if I even have any," Wick murmured, forgetting all about his potential Mother and Father that could have been out somewhere, looking for him. "Ah, well have you travelled far to get here then?" they asked.

"A few hours maybe".

"I bet you went out into the woods to play and hit your head or something. Don't worry, I reckon your parents live right here in Whonestead. There's no other towns around here so they have to be here. Go on in, take a look around, I'm sure they'll spot you in no time," they smiled whilst moving out the way of the entrance. Wick quickly ran into the town square but he wasn't recognising any of it. There were small houses scattered around with thin glass panes for windows. The paths were simply made of dirt, and the rest of the ground was occupied by grass. He walked over to a well and leant against it as he looked around. He noticed a large number of people dressed in simple clothing made of cotton. Whonestead was seeming like a rather poor area to him, as his own clothes didn't seem to match everyone else's. He looked at himself in the drab reflection of a tavern window and saw how black and curly his hair was as it dangled down over his ears. His white, long-sleeved shirt was connected to a brown, sleeveless jacket by brass studs, with a high-waisted belt helping hold it all together. There wasn't much to his trousers – just simple, grey leggings wrapped around his lower half, and his boots strapped up all the way to the top of his shins. His own outfit wasn't necessarily outstanding, but it was definitely different to the plain blouses and tunics that everyone else was wearing, making him feel as though he wasn't actually from Whonestead. The most striking accessory on his body however was the necklace he hadn't had chance to notice until then. With simple string keeping it attached, a little wooden bear totem dangled from it, reinforcing there was some sort of connection between himself and the actual bear. The carvings were simplistic but beautiful enough for Wick to gaze at it for a moment, but he soon broke out of the trance. Searching for answers was more important, so he asked a group of civilians ahead with little hope or faith. "Hello? Can anyone help me?" he said with a sweet and innocent voice. They were hard at work fixing a badly broken building. The remnants of what was once a roof were covered in large scratch marks, and the walls were burnt and windows smashed. "What is it you want? We haven't got time," a grumpy woman sighed.

"What happened?" he asked.

"Dragons. Either a couple of Flockflys or something a bit bigger like a Yimlam," an exhausted man groaned.

"There's dragons around here?"

"Aye, but only the small ones," he replied. Wick looked at the destructive capabilities of the apparently small dragons and dreaded to think what a larger one could have done. He'd never seen one in person, but seeing the damage one had left behind made him somewhat less scared of the bear, knowing that there were much deadlier things in the world to worry about. "So what was it you wanted? We're busy," the woman said.

"This will sound odd but… do I look like I'm from around here?" Wick asked.

"Do you look like you're from around here? What sort of question is that? I know for a start you're not from Whonestead. I would have seen you around before… it's a small community. What's all this about?"

"I'm just trying to find out where I belong".

"Well that's a strange thing to say". Wick zoned out from her yammering and looked over to the village entrance. The two guardsmen had ran away screaming for some reason. Before long, more people started to shout and wail as they ran to their homes or towards any tools they could use as weapons. To his regret, he watched on as the intruding bear lumbered into the village without a care in the world. It was looking for the boy but in the process, struck fear into the whole of Whonestead. People either ran out of its way or towards it to attack. "I told you to wait!" Wick complained as it reached him. Pitchforks and scythes made their way to the two of them. "Look out, boy! It's a bear!" one villager yelled. Wick couldn't be bothered to explain everything to them. Even if he wanted to, they were all too loud and riled up to listen. Instead, he ran back to the unguarded entrance, knowing that the bear would follow him. Their only chance of escape was to head back into the forest, but the angry mob were hot on their trail, throwing stones and farming tools at them, uncaring of the fact that they could have hit Wick. They hurried frantically into the woods, listening to the decrease in screaming from behind. Neither of them were willing to stick around to see if they were being hunted through the forest, so made sure to keep running until they were at least half a mile away from Whonestead. Wick stopped to catch his breath, prompting the bear to do the same. "Well done, I was asking them for help, stupid bear!" he panted between gasps. His confused associate hung its head in shame and avoided eye contact. "That's right. You *should* feel guilty". He wiped the sweat from his head and walked on at a steady pace. "Now where do I go?" he mumbled to himself. Right after he finished speaking, the bear attempted to answer by tugging on his sleeve again. "Stop doing that. I'm not going anywhere with you". Just then, it began to rain heavily out of nowhere. Not even the cover of trees could prevent them from getting wet. The droplets were fast and aggressive, breaking though the branches and soaking them both in the matter of minutes. All they could do was press on, hoping that it would eventually stop, but it was shaping up to be an overnight ordeal.

There was no shelter in sight and they had been walking for an hour straight with their soggy hair covering the majority of their view. The ground had become rather sloppy and thick with oozing mud, covering Wick's boots up to the ankles. "It's not stopping," he moaned, provoking the bear to pull at his clothes again. "Oh, fine!" he shouted, giving in to the animal's wishes again. It wasted no time and started to run ahead without him unexpectedly. After getting to a certain distance, it turned around and grunted at him, as a way of telling him to hurry. "Okay, okay. I'm coming". Greenwick ran and followed from behind for yet another tiring hour, but he was glad that he had done, for the bear had found them a small cave to take refuge in, which was perfect as the sun was starting to take its leave. They both raced to be the first one inside, excited to be free from the infuriating downpour. Wick dropped to the floor, uncaring for how hard the ground was. He was happy he able to relax after a long and arduous day. The bear shook his fur, sending his smelly, wet aroma everywhere. "Disgusting," he said whilst laying in the line of fire, getting even more drenched from the bear's rigorous shaking. It may have been tense being in one another's company, but they put everything aside for the time being to enjoy the shelter, though there was still a few things Wick couldn't help but think about. He reflected on the spontaneous day, replaying it all piece by piece in his head whilst the wall of rain outside created an ominous yet soothing background noise. So much had happened that he couldn't bring his feelings to words. There wasn't a lot he could do with the absence of memory. Over and over, he asked himself the same questions of identity and belonging, not knowing if people were looking for him, or if he was completely alone. He didn't know how he could have lost his memory, but he hoped it was accidental and there wasn't something bigger at work that did it to him purposely. The only voice he recalled in his head was that of a male, calling his name. He assumed it could have been his Father. Even so, it only made him wonder about the whereabouts of his Mother, so for the time being, he considered only having a Father tied to the situation. Then there was the matter of the friendly bear. The only explanation he had is that they may have known each other well before his mind was erased, which would have explained the necklace. Even if that *was* the case, he still didn't feel entirely safe around it, even after it lead him to a safe cave. There were too many mysteries at once for his young head to ache about, so he finally emptied his brain the best he could for the time being. The bear laid down next to him. It could have gotten closer but it knew that Wick wasn't feeling comfortable enough yet. The two of them rested in the darkening shelter as night dimmed into establishment, taking over the daylight and consuming it whole. The beginning of Greenwick's journey was so abrupt, he didn't realise the importance of it, or the fact that he was even travelling towards anything in particular. The loss of all recollection was an evident hurdle, but it would turn out to be an interesting advantage in the future. All he could do was wait and continue to go about his days. Knowledge of the world and the roads he would have to take were waiting patiently to be discovered. All he had to do what let go and allow fate to carry him in the right direction – fate being in the form of a four-legged woodland giant.

Chapter 2

Eyes of Crimson

Greenwick opened his eyes the morning after the cave slumber and jumped up in fright, forgetting about the bear at his side. "Oh, you," he groaned, looking over to the snoozing bulk and recalling the events of the day before. He wasn't lucky enough to be trapped within a dream. His troubling companion and lack of memory were as real as the pain he felt internally. He rubbed his dry, aching eyes and staggered out of the cave to take in the fresh outdoors, hoping that the beautiful scenery would at least ease his worries a little. Unfortunately, the day was suffering from a mundane gloom after the heavy rain that invaded the ground overnight. Water dripped from leaves and birds shook their soggy feathers the best they could on the neighbouring twigs, but all drying efforts were futile as more dark clouds entered the sky, roaming around and threatening to douse the land in more tiresome wetness. The potential downpour didn't stop Wick from leaving the cave however. It was the perfect chance for him to leave the sleeping bear and continue his search for answers alone, not having to worry about hiding a dangerous animal the size of three men wherever he went. He took one final look back to make sure he wasn't being followed and made a hasty exit into the thick, slippery forest. The boy didn't mind being alone, especially during the safety of daylight. The woods felt seemingly endless to him though, with a lack of wildlife occupants, but the loneliness only gave him closure, knowing that there weren't any threatening creatures lurking around. No matter how long he walked for, there was bound to be an end, or at least a break in the trees eventually, so the only plan he really had was to trudge along until he crossed paths with civilisation. For the first few hours, the only noises he could hear were the squishes of his footsteps, the rustling of passing bushes, and the hundreds of overlapping bird calls. The lack of distractions allowed him to reflect on things, although there was only so much he could question and think about before he was just repeating the same issues he had from the previous day. The worst part of all was the fact that he remembered less and less as time continued to push, even though the portion he *could* remember was already minuscule anyway. Before long, all was lost. He'd been lucky in some respects, being able to dissect and save his name from disappearing, but he would have happily sacrificed his identity in return for answers to the more burning questions on his mind. A part of him simply wanted to move on, knowing that there wouldn't be a way to restore what was missing, so there'd be no reason to dwell on what technically no longer existed, but on the other hand, he knew he'd feel incomplete for the rest of his life, unable to obtain even the slightest bit of closure.

An interesting noise in the distance eventually broke his cycle of mental torture and shifted his interest towards the source of sound instead. At first, it sounded like chaotic screams of pain, but after creeping closer for a look, it was made clear that the yelling was simply merchants attempting to sell their goods. Twenty to thirty stalls clumped themselves together in the middle of a field to create a large square, each selling unique items at varying qualities. Silk tradesmen had travelled far from distant desert lands in hopes to sell their fine materials, desperate Easterners shoved dragon hide in customer's faces, praying that they wouldn't know how fake they were. Other stalls sold vibrant fruits and vegetables that most people hadn't even seen, looking delicious and intriguing. The boy's stomach cried in agony the second his eyes connected to the juicy foods. He had no form of currency, but he checked his pockets thoroughly anyway just in case. For all he knew, he could have been a rich child, but alas, he was as poor as he'd dreaded. He was too scared to beg as well, in fear of getting into conflict with unfriendly sellers. Most of them seemed to have travelled great distances with their products, so none of them were bound to give their goods away for free, not even to a starving boy, alone in the wild. He looked at their angry, desperate and sleazy faces which only confirmed his judgement and speculations. Greenwick had two options – steal, or starve. None of the merchants had noticed him walking over to blend into the crowds, rubbing his sweaty hands nervously. His head only reached the men and women's waists, so he was well-hidden and remained inconspicuous, as though he was simply lumbering around with parents. Whonestead had provided a sense of community, but the market provided a sense of diverse culture. It was a rare instance of differing cultures coming together as one, but even the market was war and conflict in itself. People blabbered between themselves in their native tongues, dealing snide glares over to oppositions. The entire square was intense and hostile, as though one small disagreement could had led to explosive riots and outrage. Thankfully, the larger kingdoms of the world had sent authoritative figures to keep their watchful eyes open for escalating arguments, illegal goods and theft. Wick hadn't noticed the guards though, and so obviously lingered around the food stalls like the robbing novice he was. The raw hunger had taken over his innocence, squashing down his morals and ethics, and replacing them with the rabid necessity to eat. At last, a chance to snatch and grab stood before him. The owner of a fruit stall was busy negotiating prices to a customer in a different language, allowing Wick to sneak over and swipe an oddly-coloured apple. He turned around and walked away instantly, stuffing the fruit inside of his jacket awkwardly whilst pushing his way through the crowds to get to a safe distance. Before he could relax and act casual, a woman purposely bumped into him, knocking him to the floor and causing his loot to roll out across the floor. She stood over him unimpressed with long, dark hair trailing down the sides of her serious face. Her outfit was like nothing Wick had ever seen. She wore a white

Knight's suit of metal armour, with golden chainmail poking out between the openings, as she held a sharp and scary helmet in her heavy gauntlets. The most striking feature of all were the irregular spectacles she had clasped tightly to her head, concealing her actual eyes which only made her emotions and expressions all the more mysterious and terrifying. They were handmade, seemingly by an incredibly skilled crafter way ahead of their time. Intricate, gold side-shields covered the eyes even more by going across both sides of her head, which then connected to the leather straps and braces that wrapped around her ears tightly, making them more like goggles. The most ominous part was the round, glass lenses, stained blood-red, allowing her to hide all kinds of death stares behind them. "You should be more careful, little thief," she said in a calm but cold manner. Wick couldn't help but gawk rudely at her eye accessory. "What are those?" he asked in amazement, forgetting for a moment that he was actually in a great deal of trouble. "My craftsman made them for me. He calls them, *spectacles*. I call them, *none of your business*, what's it to you? Are you going to try and steal them like you did that fruit?" she rudely answered.

"I only took it because I was hungry".

"I'm tired, yet you don't see me sleeping on a bed".

"I'm sorry, I won't do it again."

"I know, because you're coming with me".

"Can't I just leave? I'll give the fruit back and explain myself".

"Do you know what we do here in Magmalia when we catch thieves? We tie the hands together and burn them. The bubbling flesh merges everything into one big, messy clump".

"I don't want that! It not my fault!" Before he could explain himself better, she took his arm and pulled him from the market to a secluded dirt road, leading towards the large city of Magmalia. "I'm sorry, I'm sorry! Please, just let me go!" he cried.

"Criminals are only sorry when they're caught. You're obviously a foolish child who knows nothing of the world if you dare pester around *these* lands," she jabbed.

"I lost my memory, I don't even know where I am in the world".

"Strange boy," she said to herself. Wick began to wriggle around and struggle but her grip was tight and had started to bruise his wrist. "Get off me, I don't want to go with you!"

"You don't have a choice," she cackled.

"Help! Somebody, help me!"

"Ha, no one is going to oppose me. To oppose me is to oppose the law... just like you did when you stole that fruit. Do you not know what I stand for or who I serve?" she chuckled at his stupidity whilst pulling him effortlessly across the floor. "I don't care! Get off! Help!" Just then, the bear jumped out from the trees at their side, knocking her over into the mud. The heavy armour protected her from harm and allowed her to spring back to her feet with a sword at the ready. The blade was swift and elegant in shape. The boy had no idea what sort of affairs he had stumbled upon, but was thankful for the bear's unexpected rescue. The beast tugged him by the sleeve again, and this time, Wick happily obliged. The Knight adjusted her odd eye-wear and ran after them. The bear was large enough for the boy to climb on top of and sit on its back as they continued to escape. They passed the market, knocking over stalls and sending people's precious goods up into the air in a frantic barge-through, but the woman was close behind, jumping over debris and moving between the confused bystanders. The ones that were vigilant enough to notice the stampeding beast didn't need to be told to move out of the way. It didn't take long for the whole market to escalate into disarray. The boy's pursuer had all the more reason to catch him after demolishing civilian's livelihood in the matter of seconds, but no matter how angry or desperate she got, her legs could only move so fast. She wasn't the sort of person to give up easily though and calculated a new strategy almost instantly upon noticing a horse tied up on a nearby fence. After cutting the restraints, she jumped on and galloped as fast as possible. Wick and the bear were well into the forest at that point, but they could see her manoeuvring the horse with great skill across the cluttered floor, whereas the heavy battering ram of an animal that the boy was on simply, but messily, pushed its way through everything that dared stand in front. "Faster,

faster!" he yelled as the crazed lady gained on them. Neither he nor the bear were properly looking where they were going, and after a manic death chase, their speedy flee turned into a clumsy plummet. The two of them had reached an unseen cliff edge that emerged from behind a set of dense bushes, preventing them from stopping and saving themselves a fall. Instead, they dropped for ages and flailed in the air uncontrollably, unable to obtain any sense of direction, until finally reaching the bottom with two separate impact sounds – with one being much louder than the other. The horse-riding Knight had finally caught up with them, but she was too late, their bodies were thirty feet down at the bottom of the cliff, slopped heavily into the gloopy marshlands that rotted the area. The two escapees had survived the unplanned descent with help from the deep, grimy muck cushioning their fall. It took them a moment to collect themselves and to make sure they were still alive, but both were unharmed. Wick looked up at the angry woman. He could tell she was scowling even though there was a hefty distance between them. She looked on and let them go, having no intentions of getting her prideful armour covered in thick slime. They were no longer her or Magmalia's problem, but the dangerous terrain ahead of them was punishment in itself. She turned around and clopped back through the forest to return the horse and inform her Captain of the day's events, with the intention of leaving out the parts where she failed, whilst the boy's next dilemma was to traverse the swamp without drowning in ooze.

Wick and the bear had found themselves in the infamous, Marsh of Magmalia, not knowing how far it stretched on for. Their bodies were covered in mud from top to bottom, but it dried and became crispy on their faces rather quickly. Wick was lucky he only had the top of his head covered in hair. The poor bear had irritating dirt stuck all over it. There wasn't much they could do about their messy appearance so they just focused on getting out. At first, the boy figured that the best thing to do was to keep heading in a straight direction, but he soon noticed his furry saviour heading a different way. "I've had enough of you trying to lead the way. I can't take guidance from a bear," Wick complained. Of course, the beast didn't reply, and continued in the direction it felt best, expecting the boy to keep up. "Listen to me, I mean it. Where are you trying to take me anyway?" he continued to moan. At long last, his curiosity got the better of him and he gave into the seemingly fixated way of the bear, just so he could finally see what all the fuss was about. "I don't know where you're wanting to go but I suppose it'd be best if I just let you get there. Maybe I'll find out a little more about what happened to me… and maybe you'll stop having to tug on my sleeves too". He couldn't believe how the failed theft of one fruit had led them knee-deep into a disgusting swamp, but he was grateful for being saved from the woman. The bear's loyalty had been falsely regarded as foolery, and his compassion was at first perceived as fixation. To jump in and save his life after it had been left behind to sleep in the cave, been told that it was being stupid, ordered to stay away and leave him alone, he felt as though the bear must have had an unbreakable relationship with him before he lost his memory, so the boy was willing to regain it in case his assumptions were true. "Hey, bear," he called, making it turn around and look him in the eyes. "Thank you for saving me earlier. Maybe I was being too harsh at first… but it's because I was confused. Do you understand me?" he explained. To his surprise, the bear walked over to him and licked his face over and over. "Alright, alright. Let's get moving," he giggled. Perfectly timed with the glimmer of happiness, the stormy clouds finally collapsed under the weight and let loose onto them for the second time in the space of two days, transforming the boy's mood back to his usual state of depression, as though each drop of water that ran down his face carried with it a reminder of just how much trouble he was in. His faith in humanity had been spoilt by the lack of understanding from the people of Whonestead, and the harshness and cruelty from the Magmalian Knight. If they were unable to visit other places in the future without causing a fiasco, Wick felt little use in trying. His first experience of punishment and pain with the red-spectacled woman had scared him greatly, but he kept his fear inside and focused on getting as far away from her as possible. The way ahead had just been made all the more difficult due to the rain, and his mental miseries added extra weight for him to carry. No matter what though, his new acknowledged friend continued to lead in the mystery direction as he trailed behind, still dying of starvation. He could have attempted to eat one of the many differing fungi sprouting around, but it was too much of a risk. Instead, he tried his best to not think about food and followed the pathway that the wide and heavy body in front of him was making, no longer accompanied with a simple beast, but with a caring guardian.

Chapter 3

Noble Enforcers

The central city to all was known by many names. Some called it, the Heart of all Heroes, others knew it as, the Home of Opportunity, but its most popular name was, Mighty Magmalia, and mighty it was. Whilst other cities and kingdoms wallowed in the contained struggles of their walls, Magmalia was famous for intruding in multi-national affairs with only the intentions of uniting and aiding others. Sincere honour and affection was in short supply in the world, so their help was welcomed in the majority lands. The only motive coming from opposing factions was their reluctance to be helped and protected. Their pride and refusal to be assisted usually turned them into enemies of Magmalia, as though it was merely impulse for them to reject positivity. In the beginning, the kingdom was small and unknown, but soon grew rapidly with every new supporter. Men and women from different corners of the world with the ability to put aside their differences eventually came together to create an alliance of saviours, with the sole purpose of bringing peace across the Earth. They no longer carried their former identities that were once determined by their race and ethnicity – all were Magmalian from that point on, regardless of prior differences. In a world full of such pain and torture, the central city was almost too good to be true, but word travelled fast, and more people seeking harmony joined the cause. Five centuries later, and Mighty Magmalia had become the largest of kingdoms, controlled by eight different rulers, representing the different areas of the world, with a total of five Queens and Three Kings. However, all eight of them had passed the responsibility of security and conflict to their elite nine-person team of Paladin Knights. The figureheads of the land wanted to keep their hands clean from orders of extermination and execution to focus on the more peaceful elements of ruling, whilst the Knights ruled over themselves, never having to discuss their matters with their Kings and Queens, allowing them the freedom to keep not only their kingdom safe, but the world as a whole safe from whatever evil they could abolish. The Paladins answered only to their superior, Captain Asieda Hockmunn. Other than his obvious commands, he worked well as a leader with the other eight Knights, unafraid to run through the thickest of dilemmas side by side with them, rather than delivering orders from the comfort of his headquarters. Greenwick had no idea of the kingdom he had passed on his travels, nor did he know the authority vested in Paladin Troyori Quait, known to him simply as the fierce woman with the peculiar red spectacles. If he had known of the famous Magmalia and the power they possessed, he wouldn't have dared steal food from the outskirt markets. Quait had returned to the castle in the middle of the city, after failing to capture Wick and his bear. The structure was mostly white, just like the majority of other buildings in the city. It was built wide as well as tall, giving it the ability to house such a large quantity of soldiers, guardsmen, royal families, and other important figures to the kingdom. Being a Paladin meant that she and her brothers and sisters in arms resided at the tallest point of the castle, as a symbol of watching over the whole city, allowing them to gaze across and look at the precious land they all served to protect. The mainland was surrounded by huge, mountainous walls, creating a large circle that wrapped around for miles. Whilst most natural land was engulfed in forests of trees, Magmalia was a forest of flat-roofed buildings. The people below got on with their lives with no problems, grateful for such a unified benevolence. Most materials and resources passed through the walls as it was only natural for the largest of communities to thrive in the trade and transfer business, making the vast majority of occupants wealthier than what outsiders could have ever imagined. Everyone was happy and they had good reason to be, but it came at a price. Most of Magmalia's civilians had never left the comfort of the kingdom, preventing them from knowing how the world truly functioned beyond the safety of their homes. They believed the whole world lived in harmony just as they did, with no idea of how hard the Paladins worked to keep them safe. The Knights were trained to be humble though, and told to keep their matters and affairs away from the public to maintain a false microcosm of serenity. Just like the other eight Paladins, Troyori had to abide by these rules, all for the sake of the citizen's wellbeings. It was cruel in its own right, but they had a compelling reason to do so. They would've rather provided Magmalia's people with an embellished world of peace rather than haunting them of the everyday struggles beyond the borders. Their ultimate goal was to one day create just that, but they were happy to bend the truth up until that point, fully confident that they would achieve their objectives one day anyway. Fundamentally, it was nothing more than a gamble that the Knights had to play for the sake of their people.

Troyori made her way indoors, still in full armour apart from the helmet she hated to wear, as it would tamper with her special goggles. She walked through the many pristine corridors and towards her Captain's private base of operations, passing a few of her fellow comrades that acknowledged one another with a quick beat to the chest with their fist. The door stood before her, but before knocking, she figured out the best way of wording what had happened at the market to prevent her from sounding incompetent. Once she felt confident enough, she knocked three times and awaited a response. "Who is it?" Captain Hockmunn's muffled voice seeped through the door. She stood up straight in respect even though she wasn't in the presence of onlookers, simply by force of habit. "Paladin Quait, Captain. I'd like to discuss the events of my guard duty," she snapped.

"You may enter," he commanded. Troyori swung the door open and marched in, before placing her hand on her chest as a salute. Hockmunn did the same back, then prompted her to relax. The Knight was outfitted in a more casual variant of the armour, consisting mostly of chainmail whilst he was indoors, which wrapped around his strong, chiselled physique as though it was all part of his skin. He had short, black hair and a well-groomed beard, stressing to his Paladins and himself that appearances were everything. He was equipped with a face that could switch between friendly and serious in the blink of an eye, so Troyori stayed vigilant and responded to him in the right ways, knowing how his mind and personality worked after their long time together. He leant in front of his desk, giving Quait a casual vibe to her relief. He was evidently softer on her than the other Knights, but they kept it to themselves in case it tarnished both of their reputations. "We've spoken about your helmet, Quait. You either wear it, or you relieve it to the armoury... you can't just carry it around all day," he chuckled.

"Yes, apologies, Captain. It's just...".

"Just what?"

"If I don't possess the complete set of armour, I don't feel like a complete Paladin. If only I could wear the helmet without it becoming a hindrance to my eye-wear, Captain".

"Oh, Troyori, you've always been the most profound. Please, ease your stature... you have permission to speak freely," he laughed.

"Thank you, Captain".

"So, I heard about the disaster that happened at the markets today. I was told it was a boy... riding on a bear? They harassed the merchants and destroyed their stock? Oh dear".

"That's correct".

"What do you think their motives were?"

"Well, I'd caught the child stealing food, then before I knew it, the grizzly bear had tackled me to the ground and escaped with the boy, demolishing the stalls in the process".

"So you're saying this bear was trying the save the boy?"

"As much as I'd have hoped it to be a coincidental attack, the fact that the child proceeded to ride on its back makes me think they were well-acquainted prior to the attack".

"So it *was* just a child. We can rule out a deliberate attack of terrorism I hope?"

"I believe so".

"The only issue I have with this is how an animal could be so... so, domesticated? Especially when it's a giant bear," he sighed with a snigger whilst scratching his head. "So, what happened next?" he asked.

"Oh, well... I chased them on horseback through the North-East portion of the forest... and then they reached the cliffs".

"Did they escape?"

"They fell... but I believe they both died," she lied, as it was easier than telling her Captain that a child managed to escape her clutches. "Quait," he sighed.

"Yes, Captain?"

"You're the youngest of our order. I can imagine there's a great deal of pressure to succeed in difficult circumstances... but lying to your Captain is no success at all. You wouldn't be lying to me right now would you?" he asked whilst coming forward in interest to her upcoming response. His serious side had taken over, so it was best for her to be honest before she missed the chance for redemption. "I'm sorry, Captain. I feared if I'd let them escape, I would be painted in a colour I refuse to associated with".

"Good. I'm glad you told the truth. We had scouts search the area and we saw pretty evident footprints belonging to a small boy and a bear. If you feel the need to lie to save your reputation, then your reputation must mean a lot to you, and I respect that to some degree. Just don't lie to me again, understand?"

"Yes, Captain. Sorry, Captain".

"I will keep our discussion between ourselves. I wouldn't want this to affect your status as I know how much of a valuable asset you are to the other Paladins".

"Thank you, Captain. I appreciate-".

"That's why I'm placing you in charge of surveying our newest member, Paladin Vousa Falk".

"I'm sorry?"

"The tenth Knight of our circle has been chosen, and I know you'll watch over him well".

"With all due respect, Captain, yourself or Paladin Soa are usually the ones in charge of evaluation".

"I simply wanted to give you the opportunity to become a greater Paladin and see over the training of our next Knight. To achieve ten Paladins is a momentous occasion. Besides, you lied to me, so consider this a form of punishment," he taunted.

"Then I will accept your offer and see it through with rigorous effort, Captain," she snapped, almost turning into a different person whenever her career was at stake. "Excellent!" Hockmunn praised. "You're free to go," he instructed.

"Thank you, Captain," she said before taking her leave. As soon as the door closed, she let out a huge, overwhelming breath of air and wiped the sweat from her brow. After getting her head back together, she travelled downstairs to the armoury and tossed her unwanted helmet without concern for where it landed, then headed back up to the living quarters to discuss matters with her Paladin members that weren't assigned to any duties that day.

The room was made up of nine beds, soon to be ten, all accompanied with a private chest for personal clothing and items. The other half of the room consisted of arm chairs, surrounded by a large, cosy fireplace. The castle as a whole was carved majestically with marble features, but the dormitory was perhaps the most elegant area of it all, besides the royal chambers. It was the only place they had in the world where they could relax and be themselves, so they valued their time there as though it was payment to their services. Paladin Soa slouched in his chair like it was slowly swallowing him, with a glass of wine in his hand. He was the oldest of the Knights, and his lack of energy made it apparent that he would have had to retire soon. His face was withered and wrinkled and the majority of his hair had done. Quait barged into the room and took a seat beside him without asking. "You're looking displeased," he stated.

"Nonsense, *you're* the miserable one, Soa," she replied whilst snatching his wine from him to take a gulp. The two of them sank down in front of the fire and sighed. "This is about the new Knight isn't it? I'm no longer surveying newcomers. Too old now... less patience," he explained.

"But why me?"

"The Captain must see some potential in you. It's obvious that you're already one of his favourites".

"Yes, well perhaps you should try harder then, maybe you could become favoured as well".

"I no longer crave acceptance. My presence has left its mark, there's no more effort inside of me".

"Don't let Hockmunn hear you say that".

"Well that's the thing... I think it's time that I resigned before I push my luck".

"You can't. The Captain is happy now that there'll be ten of us. If you left, we'd be back down to nine".

"That doesn't affect my opinion. No matter what good news appears, I'm still ageing," he exhaled. Quait shook her head, but accepted his answers. Soa had served Magmalia longer than most, yet never held interest in becoming Captain, allowing Hockmunn to fill the seat when the time came. The old man had been a part of the action since before Troyori was born, either preventing or fighting in a number of conflicts. The kingdom was indebted to his years of service, but he wasn't one to search for recognition. "So, when is it you're thinking of quitting?" she jabbed.

"It's difficult to say. I'm still needed with Western command... those Slayer soldiers are trying to push towards the cities. Then there's the matter of Tbrok, who has broken our alliance between us and his Trolls of N'tur Grung. We're still trying to figure out why he'd be so quick to break away from us".

"You know what Trolls are like… they're stubborn and sporadic. It's probably for the best".

"But there's a chance they're uniting with our enemies instead".

"You worry too much. Knowing Tbrok, he was probably just tired of being ordered around by us humans".

"Still, it's one of many matters that are preventing me from leaving. Once all this dies down, I'll be gone".

"I'll be sad when you leave… but it'll be a lot more cheerful around here at least," she joked.

"You've always been a great woman to be beside. I can tell that you'll be working your way up the hill of recognition soon. To that I say good luck… but just be careful of those around you. Your likeability might make you more enemies than friends," he warned.

"Thank you, Soa. I'll see to it that this kingdom maintains its order," she smiled. Just then, the newcomer stumbled in, wearing a complete suit of armour including the helmet. He stood in the doorway to salute both Quait and Soa, before rudely walking between them and the fire. "Paladin Soa, Paladin Quait I presume. I am Vousa Falk and I will be under your watchful eyes for the next year," he announced.

"Yes, yes, you don't have to wear your helmet indoors you know. Also, it's not me, just Quait," Soa moaned. Vousa unclasped his helmet and pulled it off clumsily. His blonde hair was long and tied back, and his face seemed young and confused. Like most others, he couldn't help but stare at Troyori's red lenses. "How old are you, Vousa?" she asked, knowing that he'd be caught off-guard whilst gawking at her eyes. It took him a worryingly long time to snap out of it, but eventually he readjusted his upright stance and continued to act professional. "I'm twenty-seven, Paladin Quait… may I ask about that *thing* in front of your eyes?" he asked.

"Excellent, I'm no longer the youngest member… and no you may not. All I will tell you is that they help me focus, and that's all you need to know, is that understood?" she hissed. Soa sniggered to himself. He enjoyed listening to Troyori having to repeat her answers to everyone's inevitable questions regarding her spectacles. He also remembered back to when he asked about them himself, and how she almost bit his head off. "Understood, Paladin Quait," Vousa stuttered.

"Excellent. That will make our time together a lot less awkward," she joked with a serious face. Even though her tutoring hadn't officially begun, she was quickly getting the hang of ordering someone below herself. At first, she rejected the idea of taking over for Paladin Soa, but with just one small taste of command, her opinions on the matter had flipped over completely. Paladin Falk had a tough time ahead of him with Troyori watching over. Training someone that was responsible for the fates of the world's largest kingdom was bound to be rough and demanding, as they were expected to be the best of the best, meaning that Vousa would have already come from an outstanding career within the ranks of Magmalia's warriors. Even with an honourable record greater than most, the way of the Paladin still had the chance of breaking the most resilient of people.

Chapter 4

The World Unfolding

Both Greenwick and the bear remained exhausted from the swampy trails they had endured several hours before. The rain was still lingering and Wick's boots squelched with every step. The open world was no place for a boy – a boy with no idea of where he was, what to do or where he belonged. The traumatic shock that came with the unfolding events prevented him from breaking down and crying. Instead, he wandered on almost emotionless with the bear guiding him, as they made their way into a sticky, humid forest, with a pathetic wave of misty rain floating down onto them. The overgrown tree maze profusely refused to let any light in from above, as though the sun's rays were poison to the soil they both stood on. The roots arching over from the ground were more like walls rather than simple tripping hazards, and the uneven ground meant that they were often clambering up and down. The elevations were like mountains for him, but molehills for his four-legged guardian. It was unclear as to how big the forest was and where they would end up, but Wick kept his head down and gazed at his own feet as well as the paws beside him that plodded along. The mundane slumping unfortunately grounded to a halt as Wick noticed the paws had stopped moving. The concerned beast's head swooped upright and its eyes were focused on the distance. "What is it? What's wrong?" he asked whilst clinging closer. The bear grunted and pushed Wick into a deeper area of the forest. At this point he was stumbling backwards still questioning, but of course the bear couldn't elaborate. A stumble too many led to Wick dropping to the floor as dramatically as a falling tree. The bear left him in the bushes whilst he scurried off, as though he had to go and find something. Twig snaps and rustles could be heard which explained the bear's sudden concern. It roared and growled whilst cautiously looking left to right, though nothing could be seen but the infinite trees and bushes. The rustling then suddenly stopped, but he was still on high alert, scanning the area. Just at that moment, a rugged man jumped out into the open with a spear, forcing the bear into a spontaneous fight. "Rargh!" the man shouted whilst dodging and weaving the claws of his rival. He tried to scare the creature but it refused to back down. They circled each other slowly and intensely, with the occasional twitch and attempt of attack. The man thought that if the bear felt obligated not to let him pass, then he'd have no other choice but to kill it. He whacked the angry beast on its shoulder with the blunt end of the spear, causing it to stumble. Over and over, he hit the bear, weakening it until it couldn't stand back up. It was at that point, the man stopped. The spear was turned to its more deadly end, inches away from ending the animal's life. "Don't hurt him!" screamed Wick as he forced himself through the fierce bushes, causing the man to jump. He continued to hold the spear with one hand whilst aiming a tomahawk in the boy's line of sight. Relieved to see a mere child, but confused at the same time, he lowered one of his weapons. "It's a bear, child. Besides, it wouldn't back away!" he tried to explain as a means to justify killing, unknowing of the two's companionship. The man sported a scraggly beard and messy, dreaded hair. His clothes were just as rough-looking as his face, as both were cut and wrinkled slightly. His uneven fingerless gloves were weaved into the ends of his long jacket sleeves and his trousers were ripped at the bottom, only reaching three quarters down, showing off his bruised shins. His boots had seen better days as well. They looked like they were made of ancient hide from an animal that went extinct long, long ago – so old that they could crumble and decompose at any moment. His tired and weary features was a deceitful excuse for his opponents to use, for they would end up underestimating his actual strength and agility. His fighting skills made it clear that he was a master of survival, but whether he was good or evil at that point for the boy was unknown. "He's my only friend," cried Wick. The bear grunted and barged past the man whilst he let his guard down. He didn't retaliate but instead watched on in astonishment when the unlikely pair comforted one another. He'd seen many animal-human relationships such as cats and dogs, but for a bear to befriend a boy, it was beyond any conventional understanding, or any form of sorcery he had knowledge of. Greenwick wiped his tears away as his sniffling came to an end. His protective accomplice grunted angrily at the bewildered man then escorted the boy back on their walk. The man stood and watched them walk away, confused for a while, but then decided to walk swiftly behind them in seek of answers.

"Ahem, e-excuse me, child?" the curious man nagged from ten feet behind them. Whenever he got too close, the bear would swing its head around and growl. He should have considered himself lucky that the beast was too busy transporting the boy, or else there would be another fight. "She doesn't want to listen to you," Wick huffed in defence, also not in the mood to talk to someone who tried to stab things before asking questions. "*She*? I can tell from here that he shares the same traits as us, young man," he responded.

"You're a *he*? Sorry," Wick gasped, looking across to the large, grumbling animal. Their pace quickened in hopes that the man would go a separate way, but travelling with a large, scary creature was bound to gain the surprising eyes of passers-by. "My name's Yewki. I'm just intrigued is all," he blabbered.

"I don't talk to strangers anymore. It's already gotten us into enough trouble already," Wick sighed.

"That's a rightful policy, boy… but you seem perfectly fine talking to a wild bear? That's stranger than me trying to ask you questions, don't you think? We're the same species at least. I can't be that much of a stranger, surely".

"You can ask us from a distance".

"Pardon?"

"I said, you can ask us from a distance!" the boy shouted, keeping his ears perked, listening to the squishy footsteps behind him which soon sped up and got louder, indicating that Yewki had tried getting closer again. After a roll of his eyes, Wick nudged his companion. The two of them turned around and directed their flames of hatred at the man's face. "I'm sorry, I couldn't hear from a distance," he lied.

"Oh, right," Wick said, pretending he didn't realise it was all a ruse to get near. The bear prodded the boy with his nose and they continued their walk. Yewki was allowed a couple of feet closer at that point, simply because they had given up telling him to get away. "So, are you two performers from afar? Because we don't get many acts like yours around here," he asked.

"It's not a performance. Go away," Wick moaned.

"So you just chose to befriend a giant grizzly?"

"I don't know, now go away!"

"What do you mean, *you don't know?*"

"It means I can't remember anything," Wick muttered.

"You hit your head?" Yewki asked, instantly wondering if his own head had been hit, looking over at the unorthodox situation walking in front of him. "I don't know. I just woke up on the floor and this bear seems to be my friend, like I'm supposed to know him," Wick sighed.

"Does he understand you and I?"

"I'm pretty sure".

"Does he talk back?"

"Not that I'm aware".

"Good. So it's only half-odd". The three of them walked on a little further into the thicker areas of forest. The daylight was vacating quickly, and the looming branches blocking the sun weren't helping. The only positive for them was that the moody drizzle of rain had stopped. For some strange reason, Yewki didn't mind being sidetracked by the duo. They had moved a hefty way from where they had met, and he was no longer moving towards the destination he was aiming for. He seemed to have no time to waste explaining his own motives and continued to interrogate the tired child. "So, where is it you're going exactly?" he pondered out loud. After a large, weary exhale, Wick answered, "I don't know. The bear's leading the way".

"Remarkable. And how do you know he's leading you somewhere safe? How do you know he's leading you somewhere particular at all? What if-". Before he could ask a hundred more questions, the beast turned around and ran towards him, knocking him over into the sloppy mud. "I think you should leave us alone now," Wick spoke for the bear. The startled man stayed down and raised his arms in surrender, lacking the breath in his lungs to respond with actual words. He sat in the dirt and watched them turn to specks between the trees, preparing himself for an alternate approach. His curiosity wasn't done with them yet. Thankfully, he was an incredible tracker, and following the large footsteps was all too easy.

After hours of walking, hiding and sneaking, Yewki stopped and crouched behind an old stone wall. The boy had stopped, but the bear was trying to pull him by his sleeve. Ahead of them was a small, charred building that had fell victim to a fire. Black wooden beams pointed where the roof once was and soot buried the surrounding grass and soil. The walls were noticeably once a grey clay, but had cracked and burnt into an ugly mess of materials. Wick felt no significance to the demolished structure, but the bear clearly did. "I'm not going in there!" the boy complained whilst being pushed and pulled. Yewki hurdled over the mound of stones and attempted to intervene. "I knew he was dangerous!" he announced, then pulled his spear from his back straps. "Don't hurt him!" Wick cried again.

"He's trying to move you to that scorched house… that's not normal. Run to me, boy… I'll protect you".

"No! You, Yewki-man; I don't need your help. Adults have done nothing but try and stop us and you're no exception! And you, stupid bear; I'm not going into that burnt down place. Don't you see? It's destroyed, broken, no more. I don't know if it was your home or what, but it's gone! All gone, Moon!" Wick's hurtful words struck a particular nerve in the bear's body, causing him to stop tugging and sit down to face the building. He regretted losing his temper almost instantly, but he didn't dare touch his fur for comfort. Yewki crept up and dragged the boy away slightly. "So, he's called *Moon*?" he asked.

"What? I don't know," Wick whispered.

"You just called him *Moon* when you shouted at him".

"I did? I didn't even notice".

"The fact that you didn't pick up on it shows that it must be second nature for you to call him that. His name must be Moon".

"Wow. I wonder why he's called that," Wick gawked. The name seemed ominous yet elegant, odd yet fitting, and a possible title was better than none. Finally knowing what to call him suddenly gave the bear more of a sense of identity in Wick's eyes, and the more he said the name in his head, the more it felt normal. His lack of memory was relieved slightly, but it only created more branches of questions on the tree of mystery. Whilst the two humans thought about it, Moon stayed sat down, looking over to the crispy house as though it had value in his heart and soul. "Do you not feel the same way as the bear- oh, *Moon*?" Yewki questioned.

"No... and I don't know if I should or not. All I know is that whatever I said to him has made him realise something," Wick murmured.

"Try your hardest. Think back. Was this house your own? Did you live here with Moon? Surley that necklace has something to do with this".

"There's too many questions to count. Wait, why am I still talking to you?" Wick gagged, tucking his necklace on the inside of his shirt in annoyance. "Just give me a chance, please. It's gotten pretty dark and I'm assuming neither of you know how to get a fire going. Unless that bear can breathe flames like a dragon".

"Fine. But if you try to kidnap me, kill me or steal from me, I think Moon will probaly devour you," Wick huffed, finally giving in to Yewki's constant pressure, but only because of the heated moment and the engulfing night sky. Before he could move along with the man, he wanted to apologise to Moon who was still deep in a woeful trance. He strolled up to him slowly with his arm out. "M-Moon?" he called, using his name for the first time intentionally. To his surprise, the bear turned his head with a sudden delight upon properly hearing his name. After only managing to get halfway through saying how sorry he was, Wick was bumped to the floor gently by his furry friend and was met with licks and sniffles. There was no doubt about his name anymore. Moon was just happy that Wick had remembered at least one thing, but it was a humbling bonus that it was regarding him. "Extraordinary. He must be really special to you if that's the only thing you remember," Yewki smiled warmly. Moon broke out of his burst of happiness after hearing the intruding man speak then ran towards him roaring. "No, no, no, Moon! He's on our side!" Wick panted, jumping in between the two former fighters. The tension radiated back and forth from them both. "I'm just going to make a fire for your child friend, okay? Then I'll be on my way. He doesn't have fur like you. He needs warmth for the night," Yewki stressed, dropping his spear to the floor. After a few seconds of thought and hesitation, Moon walked to him slowly without taking his eyes off of him, then picked up the spear and began chewing and scratching on it. "Moon! That's not very nice," Wick gasped.

"No, no, it's quite alright. If destroying my spear makes him feel safer then let him get on with it I guess," he sighed, failing to mention how long it had taken him to design and carve it. He walked away to gather fire wood as an excuse to be alone and mutter angrily to himself whilst Wick stood and took a second glance at the broken old house. No matter how hard he tried, no memories were pulled from it, and he didn't want to try too hard searching for answers in case he unintentionally started to make things up. The troubled and lost mind of a young boy could have easily blended dreams and ideas with past time memories if he wasn't careful, and that wouldn't have made anything easier. For the time being, he was happy and serene with just knowing the bear a little better. Although, there was still the matter of *why* he was called Moon. "The clouds are clearing up. We should be alright starting a fire here in the open," Yewki stated on his way back to them. "Ah, I see you've made quick work of my spear. I suppose we could throw the remains of it onto the fire too," he scorned.

"Do you want me to help with anything?" Wick asked.

"Not really, I can manage. But you could tell me your name if you feel comfortable with that".

"It's... I think it's... Greenwick," he hesitated.

"Pleased to meet you, Greenwick. Alas, I already spoilt my name on our walk here didn't I," he sniggered.

"You weren't walking with us... you were following us. You've already told us your name, but you can move on to the important things... like why are you trying to help me?" Wick awaited an answer but Yewki kept his mouth closed whilst setting up the fire to try and construct a sentence in his head. "I'm just a traveller... and there's nothing more to it really," he finally said.

"I'm sure there's more than that".

"There's a few things I may have left out, yes... but it's nothing for the ears of a child".

"I've let you stay with us. The least you could do is answer properly," Wick whinged as he folded his arms. Yewki sighed then lowered himself to his knees to get closer to the pile of wood. "All you need to know is that I'm not going to hurt you, or Moon".

"So you're just here to ask us things and start a fire?" Wick complained. The only thing Yewki had managed to ignite so far was the boy's desire to know more. However, it didn't take the man much longer to give up and spill a little more information, as though he only enjoyed the novelty of being shrouded in mystery. "I'm on an important quest at the moment. Don't worry, neither you or Moon have anything to do with it," he revealed whilst getting the fire going successfully, showing that he was obviously used to living in the harsh outdoors. "So why are you so interested in us then?"

"Because it's not every day you see a child alone with a domestic grizzly bear. This world has been uncovering some particularly strange things lately. New and potentially dangerous things have stepped forward from the depths of shadows and into the light of society. You'll have to forgive me if I was easily provoked by the existence of the two of you in the circumstance you're currently in. Do you understand?"

"I think so... but if Moon and I have nothing to do with what you're talking about, why have you put aside your quest? You said it was important". Yewki ignored the question for a moment and looked around to avoid eye contact, but he soon came around, remembering that it was only a boy he was talking to and deep feelings and excuses meant nothing to someone he'd be saying goodbye to shortly. "It's because I'm delaying my orders for as long as I can. The bear attack was unexpected... but it was a blessing in my eyes. It gave me an excuse to get lost from my duties. Even if it *was* just for a few hours". Wick copied Yewki and sat down beside the growing flames. Their skin soaked in the heat like water on sand. It was a much-needed surge of warmth for Wick, especially after lacking even an ounce of peace for the past few days. The two of them sat in the comfort of their seclusion, forgetting their worries and troubles for as long as possible. They didn't know each other, but the fire was incredibly welcoming, seemingly spreading an aura of tranquillity within its light. The mud and wet grass up until that point had frozen Wick's feet stiff, so to be able to stick them close to the crackling blazes gave his spirit a second wind. The spontaneous shifts and pops amongst the heap of wood broke Yewki out of his daydreams, allowing him to focus his mind on the boy in front of him. He recalled saying that he'd leave the two of them be after starting the fire, but he was hoping they'd forgotten. So far so good. The warmth was too enjoyable for him to leave. He looked behind Wick's head and noticed the bear sat in the cold dark, looking up to the sky without moving the slightest bit. "I see why he's called Moon," he alerted Wick, nodding his head over towards the frozen beast. The boy got up and ran over to him, but no matter how hard he pushed or pestered, Moon didn't want to move. "What are you doing? Why won't you move?" Wick began to panic. The most he could do was lift one of his paws but when he let go, it just flopped back to the ground. Finally, through the worry and confusion, he looked at the bear's head and how it pointed up to the night. The only thing of interest besides the dazzling stars was the moon itself, shimmering brightly like a gaping hole to the heavens. Moon was somehow mesmerised by his orbiting counterpart. It was unknown how far the sky jewel was from Earth, but Moon's connection meant that it didn't matter. His black, beady eyes were pulled directly towards it, if not into it, as though it had swallowed his consciousness and his body sat waiting for its return. "Does he do this every night?" Yewki wondered.

"I've never seen this happen. This is the first time we've slept properly outdoors so it's the first time I've seen him with look at the moon. We've been taking refuge underneath shelters every other night," Wick stammered. The only way for them to test if it was a frequent occurrence was to wait for the night after, but Yewki knew he'd be outstaying his welcome in the eyes of Moon. The urge to see what would happen the following evening was too strong and was worth challenging the bear for. Suddenly, Moon shuddered and started to look around. "What was that?" Wick asked hopelessly, knowing that there couldn't be an answer back from him. Yewki tried his best to offer a possibility instead. "Well he doesn't look confused. This must be normal for him," he figured. Upon hearing the man's voice, Moon got back to all-fours and grunted in his face. "Ah yes, the fire is lit. Perhaps I should be on my way as I promised," Yewki said in an exaggerated sulk, hoping that he'd be able to stay for a while longer. "Wait. I mean… well, you don't have to go just yet… not if you don't want to," Wick said, giving into the obvious guilt trip. Moon wasn't pleased and followed him closely. Once they sat back down, the bear plopped his large body between them both to act intimidating and to remind Yewki who was in charge. Being unable to voice his opinion like the humans did was proving to be annoyingly tiresome. All he could do was look and point with his nose with the occasional grunt or roar. No matter what though, communication came second and the boy's safety came first. "Why was he staring at the moon like that?" Wick asked himself.

"So, you have a domestic bear which seemingly understands us and sits down for a nightly stare at the moon? Anything else about him you're not telling me before I end up surprised again?" Yewki chuckled.

"Not that I know of".

"The others won't believe me when I tell them. Mind you, with the things that have been happening lately, it probably wouldn't seem too out of the ordinary".

"What others? Are you all on important quests?"

"There's a number of us, yes. Doing separate things that come together for a bigger cause I guess is the best way of putting it".

"What's so important then?" Wick asked, tired of Yewki constantly beating around the bush. Moon looked over at the man the same time the boy did. After the infinite questions he'd asked them, it was only fair for him to be a little more open. Although, what he was about to speak of shouldn't have concerned a mere child. "There is... a man, roaming the world in search of power-".

"What kind of power?" Wick interrupted.

"While most people would consider power as the ability and wealth to rule over anything they wanted, this man searches for something... different. For what was once thought to be a myth has been confirmed as very, very real. He knows this, but so do I... and now I race towards it in secret, in hopes to stop him stealing it," he explained, being as unbearably vague as possible. "If you need to hurry then I suppose you should stop wasting time with me," Wick said. Yewki cracked a nervous smile and looked around awkwardly, knowing that the answer would paint him as both gentleman and coward at the same time. "Well you see, I have a friend who is rather old. He's like a Father to me. He taught me respect and compassion, for that's what he gave me when I was younger. Seeing you walk alone with Moon made my instincts take over. My concern followed you here... and I just wanted to make sure you're okay. But... it was also a distraction. The fact is, I know what I have to do in the days ahead, but I'm struggling to bring myself to it for... personal reasons. I know I shouldn't have been wasting time here with you but... I don't know. My personality and my quest has conflicted my will," he elaborated. Moon tried not to look too interested or sympathetic, but he had listened to everything Yewki had said. Unfortunately, his stubbornness and concern of people interfering still prevented him from feeling calm and relaxed. He refused to fall to sleep in fear of Yewki killing the two of them, even though the beautiful fire was amplifying his tiredness and making his eyes blink slowly and close for extended intervals. "It's okay. I guess we don't have to talk about that anymore. Well, not if you don't want to," Wick suggested.

"Why thank you, child. That keeps my troubles at ease-".

"But you can tell me about all the adventures you've already been on. Have you ever seen a dragon? How far have you travelled? What weapons can you use?" the boy asked rapidly.

"Oh, well, let's see... yes, dragons are rather common in my line of work. If I'm not using them for transport then I'm running away from an enemy one. In terms of how far I've travelled... well, I've mostly been around the West and some of the North... but a little bit of everywhere really. It's hard to explain the distance I've travelled because I can't convey how large the world is".

"Is there much to see?"

"More than what your imagination could ever comprehend, child. Exclusive terrain and weather, races of people you had no idea existed, creatures of dreams and monsters of nightmares. There is evil to the far West that no one deserves to be tangled up in, but there is also a handful of noble kingdoms too. The only problem is that they're scattered, and malice seems to outweigh them all in number. It's the devotion of people like myself that prevent what disasters they can, as we travel around and defend. If this world wasn't large and full of beauty then I wouldn't be so inclined to speak of it with such passion... but what's truly mesmerising is that there's still so much to explore and uncover. So many legends and mysteries too. But like I said, this world is under threat by things we once knew as fable and folklore. New and scarier things are happening the more the Earth's secrets are uncovered, and our enemies seem to be able to keep up with it all, as though they're the ones that orchestrate them". Yewki didn't mind explaining the ruin of the world to a boy that would never be affected by it. Towns, villages and cities usually kept to themselves whilst a select few put themselves forward to keep danger at bay, allowing the civilians to live their lives safe and sound. If only the masses knew what jeopardies laid outside the borders of their walls and fences. Different customs, different world views and beliefs, different abilities and practices – all things that were never needed to be known for the millions of people that kept their communities to themselves. The sort of evil that Yewki spoke of though was threatening all ways of life, so it was up to him and the rest of Earth's various securities to stop that from happening. The world was bigger than what one small boy could dream of, especially one that had no recollection of their past. Yewki's words fed into Wick's brain with emotional impact. The thought of an exciting life of quests and travel was exactly the thing he craved. Not even the notion of perilous entities held back his drive. "It sounds incredible!" he cheered loudly, waking Moon up who had accidentally dozed off. Yewki laughed to himself as he prodded the fire with a stick. He had certainly sold it to the boy, but Yewki knew Wick's young, playful mind would easily exaggerate the good and diminish the bad. "I'll be honest, it *is* a life of wondrous journeys… but it comes at a price," he stressed.

"What price?"

"Your life," he explained, looking Wick in the eyes before continuing. "The moment you accept the weight of the world's problems on your shoulders, you have to be prepared to die carrying it. It's not something you seek out for fun. People who choose to sacrifice a life of peace usually have a reason to. Whether it's a vendetta… or an unquenchable urge to help, no one puts themselves forward in hopes of pleasure and success. It's not a greater life… but it ensures that everyone else can live theirs with greater potential".

"Then I want to help! Just as you've helped me keep warm tonight," Wick begged.

"Not a chance".

"Well you can't stop me".

"I suppose… but I know someone who will," he teased, looking over to Moon. Wick slumped forward and rested his head in his hands in disappointment. "You're just a child. You should be lucky you have nothing to be worried about," Yewki continued.

"I have no worries? All I remember is my name and this bear's. I have no home, no family and I haven't the slightest idea of what to do or where to go. I have no ties or bounds… what better reason to follow you and-".

"No, Greenwick. Do you forget your age? You look like, what, twelve… thirteen? Even if you had the most valid reason of all, I'm saving you from a world of disaster".

"And what's *your* reason to be involved with *that man's* search for power?"

"Because it is a quest assigned to me and that's all you will know about my life. Now I think it'd be best if I go now. I underestimated how easily influenced you'd be. That's my fault for helping a poor boy that's been torn from his Mother and Father," he complained and stood up to take his leave. Moon got to his feet too in case Yewki tried anything. "Don't go!" Wick pleaded. "I don't how much more of this torment I can take," he explained in regard to being alone with the bear, forever moving around with no purpose or end goal in mind. Yewki knew the importance of his mission, but he'd also feel slightly responsible for the boy's fate if he left. "Okay. Seeing as though I've diverted this much on my journey, it'd be best if I continue in this direction. There's a long dirt road a few miles from here which takes cargo wagons to and fro. If I can travel with one of them then I can make up for lost time. I'll stay the night, but tomorrow I must be on my way… if that's okay with your bear?" Yewki said, but Moon just looked at him blankly, instantly hating the idea and all that came with it. "Please, Moon," Wick begged. The bear exhaled and grunted to himself then laid back down and looked at the fire. "I'll take that as a yes," Yewki supposed, sitting back down slowly, still somewhat afraid of Moon.

They gained what rest they could in the cold open, until the sun's irritating light pierced through their closed eyelids, waking Wick and Moon up at around the same time. They peered over to the ashy remanence of the fire, completely dead with not even the slightest bit of smoke exerting the black logs, looking not too different to the burnt house across from them. Even though they'd only managed to collect five hours' worth of sleep, it was enough for them to feel refreshed. It took Wick a while to remember about Yewki, as though there was a chance he had dreamt the whole evening. He got up and scanned the area but there was no sign of him. "I guess he's already gone," he sighed to Moon, hoping he could have said farewell. The emptiness and loneliness quickly returned, but he was unable to complain because he understood the importance of Yewki's departure. "I see you've finally woken up!" the man applauded, making himself known from between the trees. "I thought you had already left," Wick said with a sigh of relief. Yewki chuckled as he got closer, carrying a couple of small woodland creatures in his hand. "I couldn't leave without feeding you. I found some berries and vegetables... then I lured some rabbits with them, so I got those too," he smiled as he poured the food on the floor, along with the two dead animals. Wick glared at how lifeless they were and scowled at the thought of having to eat them. "Maybe Moon can have the rabbits?" he suggested, hoping that he wouldn't have to eat them himself. "But, I got them for you and I," Yewki whined.

"We can have the vegetables can't we?" Wick subliminally begged. Yewki looked down at the meat he'd struggled to capture and how he'd looked forward to cooking them on a fire, but before he could do anything else, Moon lunged in and shoved them both in his own mouth. "Well I suppose we'll be fine with just the berries and vegetables," he moaned.

"Just the vegetables," Wick prompted.

"Why?"

"Moon's already eaten the berries".

"What... when? Oh, never mind," he chuntered. The three of them ate up to regain their strength. Wick didn't care about the dirt taste, or the fact it was almost too hard to crunch and chew. The feeling of sustenance dancing around his deprived tongue was all he focused on, making the most tasteless of things feel like meals fit for Kings. Yewki and Moon exchanged death stares whilst eating. His precious rabbits were being torn apart and chewed up by the bear, and his furry mouth was stained purple from the berry theft. Once they'd filled up their stomachs, it was time for Yewki to head off. Moon no longer had a desire to lead Wick anywhere in particular, so they followed the man for as long as they could, as Wick felt much safer in his presence. "It's funny how things have turned around," Yewki said.

"What do you mean?" Wick asked.

"I was the one following you yesterday. The bear hated it... but yet here you both are, following me".

"Yes, well, we had every right to be apprehensive of you. Every other person that's tried speaking to us has gotten us into trouble".

"So is it safe to say you trust me now?"

"I suppose... but I don't know about Moon".

"Well thankfully for him, I'll be leaving you two soon. The dirt road I mentioned is up ahead". Wick didn't respond and kept his thoughts to himself. He didn't want Yewki to leave and nagging him to stay would have been selfish. Before he had the chance to feel sad about it, Moon's head raised up out of nowhere whilst his sniffing became frantic and wild. He felt the presence of other people, just like he had done the day before when he detected Yewki. "What is it?" Wick whispered. Yewki turned around and noticed the bear's alert stature. "Heads down, now" he ordered, pulling out a concealed sword from the inside of his long jacket. Wick was surprised but Moon was angry. Neither of them knew he was even carrying yet another weapon. They looked ahead through the trees and saw a handful of poorly dressed men and women with strips of cloth covering their mouths and noses, and dark paint slapped across their eyes and brows. "They're a bunch of bandits... waiting for wagons to go by to steal from," Yewki examined.

"That's right," a bandit laughed from behind them. Wick, Moon and Yewki quickly turned around, startled by the secondary group of sneaky thugs. There was four of them, all carrying terribly old daggers and knives. Including the other bandits near the road, there were eleven in total. "Give us that sword and whatever other shiny things ye got," one of them demanded.

"If you want this sword you're going to have to kill me for it," Yewki warned.

"You wanna be brave? That's fine, we'll just whistle over our friends down there by the road, then we'll beat you all to death and take what we want. That bear's fur will look nice on me don't ya think?" they intimidated. Wick began to panic. He was more scared at the fact they had threatened Moon and was less concerned about his own health and well-being. The bear noticed Wick's nervousness and it made him furious. He stood up on his back legs and roared, causing the bandits to take a few steps back. "Whoa, he's a biggun, isn't he?" one of them chuckled anxiously.

"Yes… and he'll crush you all at once if you don't leave us alone," Wick said.

"Oi, you lot, come over 'ere! We've got a bear that needs skinning," another bandit called to the other group. Before long, the three of them were surrounded by all eleven thieves. It was an intense ring of death, but Yewki seemed relaxed with the outnumbering. He leaned over to Wick and told him to stay between him and Moon, then raised his sword. All the bandits ran inwards at the same time with their weapons leading the way. Wick curled up on the floor and covered his eyes with his hands, but after a while, he created a gap to peek through. He saw Moon standing tall, whacking villains left and right with his huge paws. On the other side, Yewki was cutting the rest of them effortlessly. Both bear and man were working together to protect the boy, putting aside their touchy relationship and focusing on the task at hand. Yewki fought incredibly well, proving that he was taking it easy on Moon with the spear. He moved out of the way of incoming stabs and slices then tripped the thugs over onto each other. Any that were foolish enough to get back up and try again were met by his harsh blade. Moon was ragging one around in his mouth whilst stomping on the rest. He flung them all over then chased away the ones that could still walk. Whilst he was occupied, one managed to creep up behind him, prepared to stab him in the spine. Wick noticed and tried to get his attention, but Moon couldn't hear anything besides his own roars as well as the screams of his victims. The boy then turned over to Yewki, but he was in the middle of a scuffle with two bandits jumping all over him. Wick had no choice but to try and save the bear himself. He ran and leaped onto the thug's back and hit him on the head over and over with a sudden surge of confidence. The bandit span around, trying to shake him off, but Wick was clasped on tightly. "Leave my bear alone!" he grunted before biting his enemy's ear. After a squelchy crunch and a loud cry of pain, Wick was finally thrown off. The bandit held his bleeding ear with one hand and charged at the boy with his knife. His deathly eyes were as wide open as his mouth and he snarled like a crazy dog, prepared to kill Wick without hesitation. Just as he reached him, Yewki's tomahawk span through the air and penetrated the bandit's skull, sending his freshly dead body flying to the floor from the sheer force of the throw. Wick turned around and saw Yewki catching his breath, surrounded by the fallen, with his sword covered in their blood. Moon had finished scaring away the rest and reunited with the boy to see if he was okay. "I'm sorry you had to see all of that, Wick," Yewki panted.

"It's okay," Wick lied, still shaken up by the fight. Yewki hoped it didn't have to come to what it had. He knew the sort of impression blood and death had on someone so young. "Let's move on," he said with haste, in hopes of sparing the boy from anymore trauma. They left the bodies to bleed in the soil and marched over to the dirt road, only to see another corpse at the hooves of two horses. It was a passing cargo wagon that had seemingly been attacked by the bandits they'd just fought. Yewki examined it quickly then got on one of the horse's backs to take control. "You can't just take that man's cart!" Wick gasped.

"He's dead, boy. I need it, you know I do," he replied, grabbing the ropes, seconds away from whipping them to get moving. "You're going just like that?" the boy whimpered.

"How else should I leave?"

"I don't know". Yewki was trying to move along abruptly. He felt responsible for the bloodshed that would inevitably scar Wick's mind. He thought that if he left in a hurry it would increase his guilt, but it would at least rid the boy of any further horrific instances, as though the only danger in Wick's way was that created by Yewki. Getting on with his quest would mean he'd no longer be tied to him or the bear and perhaps in time, he could forget about them. He couldn't bear to think what would happen to them once he left, but he felt that it was surely safer than bringing them along with him. "Goodbye, both of you. You two have been incredibly unexpected. Take care of the boy, Moon… and look after your bear, Wick," he said before commanding the horses to proceed. "Wait, you can't just leave us here. What if more bandits come? We don't know where to go," Wick worried whilst running alongside the cart. Yewki tried to ignore him and bit his lip. "I want to go on adventures with you! I want to see the world. Please, Moon and I have nothing," he continued to nag. Eventually, Yewki stopped but he didn't look happy or accepting. He grumbled to himself whilst Wick caught up to him. "I was lying, it was all a lie. There *is* no adventure, I'm just trying to get away from you. I thought that danger would put you off, but evidently not. There is no world of wonder. Forget I said anything and leave me alone," he said sternly.

"It was all a lie?" Wick mumbled.

"Yes. Goodbye for the last time". He continued on his travels but Wick didn't chase after him that time. He stood still and watched on as the cart increased in distance. Moon came up to him for comfort and sniffed his face, but the boy was too busy with his thoughts. Almost five das with no home, no family and no hope was more than enough for him to miss Yewki before he had actually gone. Even though he told him he'd lied, Wick still enjoyed the stories, not just the quality time with an adult. No matter how much the bear tried, the boy needed a

Father figure who not only knew how to survive, but who also cared. They could have bumped into anyone on their travels. They could have met more killers and more danger. Stumbling across Yewki just by walking through a forest had too much fate at play for Wick's liking. His young, child heart demanded adventure with thanks to Yewki's tales. After a quick reflection, impulse took over, and the boy ran for the wagon cart again, catching Moon off guard and forcing him to keep up with haste. "We're coming with you!" he shouted, causing Yewki to halt again. Wick continued to run until he got to the side of the horses, then looked up to Yewki with a famished stare, hungry for a life worth living. "I don't care what's real, I still want to go with you!"

"Listen, Greenwick... I wasn't really lying about the things I said. I thought if I told you it was all fake, you'd be disappointed and you'd forget all about me... but perhaps the truth will sway you aside instead. What I do... what I'm setting out to do... it's incredibly dangerous, and I can't bring a boy into it, plain and simple".

"I knew it wasn't a lie! There was too much passion in your voice. I don't care for what could happen, it's all the more reason for me to come and find out for myself!"

"You don't understand. Danger is best avoided, not faced head on without fear. I wish I was still an innocent child like yourself. Years of calamity turns you into me... and you don't want that, I assure you".

"You saved me... *and* Moon".

"I was only doing what I should have. Those bandits had it coming".

"No, not just that. You saved me... ever since you followed Moon and I, and started that fire for us," Wick explained with a crack in his voice and a tear in his eye. Yewki thought about how Wick had still come running to the cart even when he said that everything was a lie, even though it wasn't. For the boy, the adventurous life was a secondary factor. Wick ran to the cart solely because Yewki was the sort of person he needed to be with. He sighed, then shook his head slowly. "I know how important it is for you to find shelter... to find someone to take care of you both... but it can't be me. I'm sorry".

"But why?"

"I have no time to fulfil my duties *and* look out for a boy and his bear! I'm not the one".

"You're the only one! Who else is going to? I can't hunt, I can't kill. I don't even *want* to kill!" Wick whined. Yewki knew that rejecting the boy's wishes was essentially killing him. They were a hundred miles away from safe accommodation, and his mission couldn't wait any longer. He gritted his teeth and clenched on the steering ropes tightly to contain his anger. "I'm on my way to a port. I have a planned voyage with an accomplice of mine. The surrounding town is a safe place. I can take you as far as there and then I'll be continuing my journey at sea, without you," he exhaled. Wick smiled as wide as possible and cheered to himself. It was the best result he was going to be able to get from Yewki, so he took it without a moment to lose and ran behind to climb into the wagon. "Oh, well… I think you'd be safer by my side on the other horse, boy," Yewki exclaimed.

"I can't leave Moon alone in the back," Wick enlightened. Yewki had almost forgot about transporting the bear also. It was lucky there was a wagon for him to clamber onto, but before he'd do such a thing, Wick had the strenuous task of convincing him. Moon avoided eye contact by looking down, like a child stripped of their favourite doll. Except, the bear was stripped of his leadership and was being forced to follow someone they hardly knew. He was well aware that they would both benefit from being with a survival expert, but a man who lives a life full of threats only drew conflict. Wick was safer in the hands of his own kind, and ultimately, the boy's safety was Moon's greatest concern. Difficult choices were bound to bombard them sooner or later so it was about time they encountered their first one. The bear lugged his big body into the cart and laid down. Wick didn't have to say anything to him luckily, but he could tell Moon was grouchy about the whole thing. "Thank you, Moon," he smiled whilst joining him in the wagon. He huddled up for a cuddle, but the bear was having none of it. "Are all ready?" Yewki sighed.

"Go, go!" Wick screamed happily. The enduring near-week of depression, pain and turmoil was slowly being left behind. The boy was ecstatic to finally see the end of his strenuous travels. Moon often forgot that Wick was a human that required the comfort of other people. He could survive in the wild and live a fulfilling life, but the boy wouldn't stand a chance, especially without human supervision. It was for the best, whether he liked it or not. The bumps and rumbles bounced them up and down continuously, but they welcomed it as though its annoyance was nothing compared to what they had already experienced. Things were finally getting better. Perhaps they could finally live comfortably in hopes of never having to sleep outdoors again. Only time could provide the answer, but Wick was happy to wait and see whilst relaxing atop the warm, soft body of Moon.

Chapter 5

Come Forth, the Evil

Troyori Quait stood with the newest of the Paladins, Vousa Falk, in the busy streets of Magmalia. She had started him off with simply keeping an eye out for wrongdoers – something that was near enough unheard of within the city walls. Paladin Soa was inside the castle, discussing matters with Captain Hockmunn, whilst the other six Knights were scattered across the neighbouring lands on their various duties. Falk felt somewhat undervalued, as though Quait and the Captain had forgotten the effort it took for him to become one of them, but the hours of pointless surveillance was orchestrated simply as a calm starting point for him and Quait to bond, in a work environment free from trouble or distraction. The paths and wagon roads were overflowing with lively characters, moving around from one place to the other all day long. Those who had a spare second to look at their surroundings would notice the two Paladins, and stare at Troyori for as long as possible. She was used to the confused faces people dealt and often stared back at them to intimidate them further. "Do you ever get tired of people staring?" Vousa asked.

"At what? My armour or my eye-wear? Because if it's my armour and what it stands for, no, I don't mind their admiration. If it's my eyes then yes, that grew beyond tiresome years ago. But these people have every right to be curious. They've never experienced the great outdoors like you and I, therefore the slight change from what is deemed, *normal*, or a refusal to conform is bound to grab their attention," she explained.

"People fear what they don't know".

"That is correct. But these people should be lucky, they've been spared the horrors of this world".

"At the expense of men and women like us," he said proudly.

"Tell me, Falk, where were you stationed? What horrors have you seen?" she asked him whilst beginning to stroll through the streets. Everyone moved out of their way, as though they walked with ease against a strong current. Vousa kept his head down as he recalled his years of service as a simple soldier. "My Father was a carpenter over in the South side of the city. His plan was to teach me so I could continue the business, but it wasn't for me. My perception of the world was limited within Magmalia, and whilst most people wouldn't care, I did… so I became a soldier. At first, I watched over the streets just like we are now, but the longer I served, the higher my rank became. After five years being a part of the Magmalian army, I had become a commander in my own right, leading a battalion of my own. We fought hard against Elal, the Matshi, the Slayers, all oppositions thrown at us, we were never defeated… but again and again, more waves replaced the ones we destroyed. I've lost all my warriors, one by one. They fell by the hands of our indestructible foes. It was like having a family and outliving them all. That's why I wanted to become a Paladin… because if there's one faction strong enough to keep evil at bay, it's the Magmalian Knights," Falk told her.

"We all have our motives," Quait responded.

"And what's yours?"

"Well I'm not originally from this kingdom. To put it simply, the Slayers killed my parents and I joined the Magmalian army for revenge," she answered. Vousa was slightly disappointed with her quick summary. He'd spilled his heart out telling his story that he expected the same back, as well as a reason for her spectacles, but she wasn't the expressive type. "Chances are I fought alongside you in the wars before you became a Paladin yourself then," he said.

"Maybe so, but you wouldn't have been able to recognise me from the past. My appearance has... changed," she sighed, referring to the equipment covering her eyes. They shared an awkward moment of silence, then Falk spoke up. "Well, no matter," he assured.

"Sounds like you were a valiant warrior, Vousa".

"Thank you, Paladin Quait".

"You just have to be aware that being one of us means more than just being a skilled swordsman. Paladins try their hardest to *prevent* wars, not start them. You'll have to think like a true custodian, baring the health of the kingdom as a first priority. Every thought, every move... it's with Magmalia in mind".

"Yes, Paladin Quait. I aim to-".

"Just call me, Troyori," she requested.

"Oh, okay".

"You'll soon be sharing a living area with me and eight other Knights... You need to see us all as friends as well as team members. We're your new family now".

"Thank you, Troyori," he said, letting out a slight smile. He was worried that he wouldn't be accepted into the group, but no matter his feelings, the other Knights would have to respect him for his prior contribution to the land. Their walk together had broken the introductory tension in the air. He only hoped that he could loosen himself in front of the others as quickly as he did with Quait, but it was only because she knew what it was like to be looked at differently and judged. With still a few hours left of their surveillance duties, they were forced to end early upon the sound of large horns blowing from the castle. Troyori turned and ran without a moment of hesitation, causing Falk to follow. "What's going on?" he asked.

"The castle is under attack," she gasped.

"But threats never make it into the city... and you're saying they've made it all the way to the castle? Is this a test?"

"I wish it was," she groaned whilst leading the new Knight towards his first conflict as a Paladin, whilst also being a first for her in some respects as well, seeing as though enemies had never attacked inside of Magmalia in her lifetime.

Quait led the way up the spiralling staircases and through chaotic passages and hallways, all whilst evacuating the people they happened to run by. They had no idea where the attacks were taking place, as the castle was so big, but luckily, Paladin Soa was on his way to find the two of them. "Quickly, this way," the old man panted, waving his arms over to gain their attention. "They're heading towards the Royal Chambers," he elaborated.

"Weapons at the ready from this point onwards, Vousa," Troyori ordered, whilst she and Soa unsheathed their blades. "But I haven't been issued a sword yet!" Falk stuttered.

"Find a way around it," she huffed, unable to waste any more time. They continued their race to save the Kings and Queens, following the noise of battle cries and metal clanging together. After a few more sets of stairs and a frantic sprint, they saw a large group of masked killers, making quick work of the many guardsmen in their way. The three Knights charged at them ferociously to avenge the fallen. Quait and Soa slashed their swords across the narrow corridors, whilst Vousa improvised with his fists due to his lack of weapon. Eventually though, he was able to steal the blade of his enemy and struck them down with it, all in the same amount of time it took the other two Knights to defeat ten each. "Keep up, Falk," Soa warned, showing the younger generation how it was done. Another handful of adversaries lurked around the next corner, ramming down doors and seeping into the Royal Chambers. "We must stop them now!" Troyori roared. The trio ran at them together, pinning them against walls and cutting them in half one by one. The survivors had managed to barge through the fortified doors and threatened to kill what King or Queen they could get their hands on. "Help me move this!" Soa demanded, as he pushed a large cabinet across the floor, blocking the gaping doorway. More enemies came at them, but he and Falk defended the entrance whilst Quait stopped the other menaces from harming the royals in the large, golden hall. She jumped across tables and chairs, landing feet first with her sword pointing down to the heads of her foes, catching the eyes of the remaining enemies. "Paladin vermin!" one of them growled.

"Face me all at once if you dare," she taunted. Fortunately for her, they were all foolish enough to do so, and stormed at her from all angles. Her body span after every motion and slash of her blade, ensuring that she fought from all angles. She was outnumbered greatly, but she remained alert and exploited weak points in their incoming attacks, giving her the upper hand, as though the more people she faced, the greater her chance of victory. After a few more rotations, all were defeated, leaving only a few to fight for their lives on the floor, covered in their own blood. Soa and Falk had finished barricading the doorway and joined back with her, only to see she was already done killing. Before they could applaud themselves, a dying enemy tried to crawl away using only their arms, but the involuntary coughing and spluttering of blood gave him away. Troyori stood on his legs to keep him in place, forcing him to cry out in pain, but his agony soon transformed to a disturbing cackle. "Who sent you?" she grunted, pressing down harder with her heavy, armoured foot. "I'm not telling you anything! I'm going to die anyway," he laughed whilst struggling for air. "We've done what we set out to do, and that's all what matters," he continued.

"And what was that?" Soa asked.

"To deliver a message. A declaration of war to Magmalian scum like you!"

"Look at yourself, bound with your head to the dirty floor like the vile creature you are. Your message means nothing to us! Magmalia grows by the day… it only becomes stronger".

"That's where you're wrong. Magmalia *does* grow by the day… but it only makes you more vulnerable. The more people you unite with, the greater number of opponents we have. Grouping more and more people against us only ensures a larger extermination in the end. Keep growing… that's what we want!"

"And how do you propose you bring an entire kingdom down when you can't even storm a castle successfully?" Quait asked.

"I know you," the dying man exclaimed with a smile. He tilted his head and squinted as his life left his body. "You must be the Crimson Paladin. You're our greatest obstacle... but you'll suffer soon enough," he said before bursting into laughter again. Quait frowned and raised her sword above him. "Not by *your* hands," she muttered before stabbing him in the chest, pinning his dead body to the ground. Just then, Captain Hockmunn crashed along the balcony above them, throwing two remaining enemies off the side, sending them to their deaths. "You've been stalled!" he alerted.

"What?!" Soa gasped.

"King Brudress and Queen Elepine have been killed!" he shouted. The Knights had to stop for a moment to take in the news. They weren't used to a loss, especially at such a personal level within their own land. Two of the eight royals had been murdered whilst the Paladins were distracted. It was certainly a memorable first day for Vousa. The Magmalian Knights were spoken of with such commendation and respect that the notion of them ever failing was absurd, so seeing them defeated took the newcomer by surprise. In the five hundred years of Magmalia's existence, there had only been a handful of invasive conflicts, and it was the first of them all which carried with it the death of not just one, but two royal figures. The Paladins were preparing for their polished image to be tarnished for the first time in their lives.

"How did such a large number even gain access to the city?" Vousa asked.

"They must have been coming in disguised as traders and merchants... frequently, but in small quantities. That's the only way, surely," the Captain guessed.

"This is preposterous!" Soa bellowed.

"They somehow knew the Kings and Queens were in this room together. The collective meetings are once a month... how would they have known about this?" Quait wondered.

"We can rule out luck, that's for certain! There is a devious plot at work here, and I intend on finding *all* of the missing pieces!" Soa shouted again.

"Paladin Garjian Soa, lower your tone at once! Screaming won't help us here," Hockmunn ordered.

"Yes, Captain," the old man acknowledged with a grumble whilst grinding his teeth together and tensing his body to prevent further eruption. "What do you propose we do?" Vousa worried.

"We await the backlash of our joint failure. The remaining royals will no doubt reconsider our right of command, but all we can do is ensure them that it won't happen again… because it won't," the Captain said.

"I suspect someone on the inside," Soa said to himself.

"You think so?" Hockmunn asked.

"Our unparalleled strength is evident… our only weakness would come from within ourselves," he explained.

"I'd hate to think so, but I suppose we shouldn't rule it out". Amidst their pondering, a soldier ran into the room, struggling to catch her breath. "Paladin Hockmunn, we have an urgent report from our Western scouts," she informed.

"Proceed".

"There has been frequent skirmishes working its way down the coastline. It eventually stopped at Port Duracia… but it's been turned to rubble".

"What did they look like?"

"There were said to have been masked men… like t-those ones," she said whilst pointing to the dead bodies around them in horror. "We're not the only place they attacked then it seems," Quait sighed.

"What business do they have at the harbours?" Soa moaned.

"I don't know, but I plan on finding out," the Captain stated before vacating the room in a tantrum, leaving the others surrounded by pools of blood. All but Troyori seemed bothered at the sheer amount of blood on the floor, instead she bent down to examine the man she'd had a short interrogation with. His clothing didn't tell her anything, but the infamous dragon-shaped branding on his hand did. "Of course, I should have known they'd be Slayers," she scowled. Never before in history had their enemies made such a lasting and haunting impression on them. Things were changing, faster than any of them could comprehend. It was as though evil had been given a boost in power and force, breaking the Magmalian Knights' streak of maintaining the upper hand, leaving their limits no choice but to be pushed to breaking point, now that their opponents were challenging enough to disgrace the kingdom's flawless reputation.

Chapter 6

Heavy Conversations and a Shift in Direction

Wick and Moon rested in the wagon, allowing Yewki to be alone with his thoughts. They had travelled twenty miles without any trouble. However, they were still only halfway to the port that Yewki had mentioned, so they kept their eyes peeled in case of another bandit ambush. Wick rummaged around the crates and sacks at his side, hoping to find food but the closest he got was handfuls of wheat. He picked at them and flicked them off the cart to entertain himself, too scared to ask Yewki any questions, as it was obvious he was trying to forget about his unwanted passengers the best he could. Unfortunately for Yewki though, there was a dreadful lack of distractions on the long and straight road, leaving him with no choice but to start a conversation with Wick to break up the unbearable nothingness. "So, I'm assuming you've never been to a port before?" he asked to get the ball rolling. His deep voice made the boy jump and drop the rest of the wheat between the cracks in the wagon floor. "No. I'm not sure what one is… but you said that you'd be journeying by sea, so I'm assuming it's a town where boats stay when they're not sailing".

"Near enough. You're a clever boy. The one we're going to is called Port Duracia. We'll be getting close to the curving coastline soon.

There's several ports and harbours all the way up it but Duracia is the best".

"Why's that?"

"Because it has the least crime".

"Oh," Wick mumbled, before climbing and sitting on the wagon's barriers to get slightly closer to Yewki. He held on tight as they passed over the uneven ground and looked ahead, wondering if he could see the coast through the trees. "The friend you're meeting there; is he a sailor?"

"Luckily. He's the one leading the voyage. It's a good thing I have him on my side... there's not many people I know who'd be willing to go where we're going".

"An island of monsters?" Wick's imagination guessed.

"Somewhere within the waters actually. In the middle of the Veranic Ocean". The more Yewki spoke about the names of locations, seas and oceans, the more Wick's perception of the world expanded, creating a map inside of his head of all the places he was learning about. "You're going somewhere beneath the water? I'd say it's impossible but what do I know," the boy gasped.

"Don't worry, it *is* as ridiculous as you think. No one has ever been... not that we know of. Even if I manage to find it, I don't know what to expect inside. All I've been told is that it's a living labyrinth that can alternate at will".

"This is all too much. I thought I'd be able to accept anything you say. How can things like this exist? How can there be a maze under the water? How can it be... alive?"

"I told you this world is full of wonders didn't I? But as fascinating as it may sound, I could just be heading towards my own death".

"Let's say I believe you – why do you need to go there?"

"Well this is where things get even more unbelievable". Wick prepared himself for a heavy portion of bewilderment and leant forward. Yewki took a deep breath then began to explain the best he could. "The world has its history written down by the people living within its accumulating ages. We can read back at the alliances, formations, the discoveries and the wars of each year, each decade, each century and in some cases, we can look as far as a millennia. The further you look, the scarcer our knowledge of the past becomes, until you have to question what was real and what's legend. What lies within the heart of that maze is older than any other historical account, making its existence unknown to the whole world... except for a small number of people. I'm fortunate to be one of those people, but the enemy happens to be another. What he wants could give him incomprehensible power to do as he pleases, so it's up to me to take it first and stop him before he stops me... because no mortal should ever be allowed to wield it".

"A weapon?"

"In Eastern history, it's been mentioned as the Key of Energy. In Western history, it was once known as the Sun Binder. Its protector still lives to this day, and thankfully, he's been kind enough to shed some light on its mystery. He told us that the artefact is called the Day Relic".

"Incredible. So there's some sort of ancient tool that's been kept secret for thousands of years? Wait, you said its protector is still alive... how?" Wick wondered. Yewki couldn't help chuckling to himself at Wick's lack of knowledge. "Greenwick, do you believe in life after death? Spirits and the realms they travel between? I haven't even begun to tell you about the soothsaying Shamans either. Don't worry, there's a few things I'm still too stubborn to understand... but trust me when I say this. Spirits are very real and very powerful. Most of them are just as concerned about the well-being of this Earth as we mortals. The Day Relic's protector is a form of spectral entity. That's why he's been able to provide me with such an extensive knowledge – because he's the only one old enough to properly know of its existence," he answered sternly. Wick held his thoughts in for a moment to ponder on them. It was a lot to get his head around, especially all at once without any prior experiences to back up as supporting evidence. His verdict had to be fabricated with nothing but Yewki's words. Being young meant that he was still uneducated about the world, but even every day men and women were kept in the dark regarding such deep matters. Wick was dealt a shocking truth that most adults would be too stubborn to accept, even with a vast knowledge of all things. "I-I don't know what to say, Yewki," he muttered.

"That's okay. Perhaps it's best that you're left to think about these things-".

"It just all sounds too extraordinary to be real," he blabbered.

"You don't have to believe me if you don't want to. I imagine you'll never come close to encountering any of it, just like most people. I can leave you in Port Duracia, you can grow up and you'll probably forget that we ever met". Wick wished he could follow Yewki further than the port and see all the miraculous things for himself. It was unbearable being restricted to teasing descriptions. The way things were heading, Wick was destined to become another speck in the grand scale of humanity, worrying about food, shelter, money, laws and the politics of cities and kingdoms, just like everybody else. However, a simple bird was prepared to challenge the fates of all aboard the wagon.

"How long until we get to the port?" Wick sighed, wanting the journey to last as long as possible before they parted ways. "We'll be at the coastline any minute now. We'll be passing a few harbours on the way, but it's Duracia we want. You start at the bottom of the coast, then the further you travel, the better the conditions get. I don't like these sorts of places but that's just my preference... but I know you'll be safe," Yewki assured.

"What do you propose I do when you abandon me?"

"I'm not abandoning you... I'm leaving you in more capable hands".

"And who's hands are they?"

"I don't know yet. There's plenty of inns. I imagine you could keep Moon in a stable whilst you help on the docks loading and unloading cargo. If not, there's plenty of other jobs you could do".

"I have to work?"

"Well yes. If you want someone to take you under their wing, you'll have to earn your keep. It'll be tiring at first but you'll get used to it. Who knows, maybe you'll work your way up and become a sailor. You want to go on adventures? There's no better way than embarking on the high seas".

"Stop trying to make everything sound better than what it's going to be".

"Well it's better than how you and Moon have been living so far isn't it? If you don't want to work then you can beg on the streets... but I don't think they'd allow a bear to loiter around in public". Before Wick could respond, a hawk swooped by Yewki to make itself known, causing him to stop the wagon. Moon woke up from the jolt and looked around, worrying that something was wrong. The bird flew by again and Yewki reached out and snatched a small roll of parchment paper from its talons. He unravelled it and read the message in his head. The further he read, the sadder his expression became, as though his face was slowly melting. He crumpled it up and stuffed it into his jacket in anger, then started moving the wagon again at a quicker speed. "What was that?" Wick asked.

"Quiet for a moment. I'm trying to think," Yewki hissed. He closed his eyes to help him figure out the best course of action regarding the contents of the note. "It seems I was lucky to delay my visit to Duracia... because it's been under attack," he sighed. "An accomplice of mine delivers messages of importance using birds. She's notified me that an unknown party has laid waste to the majority of the town... and a large ship invaded the harbour and destroyed the other boats... all of them," he continued.

"Who would do such a thing? What about your friend?" Wick panicked.

"I have to assume he's dead," he grunted whilst gripping the ropes tighter. "The enemy I told you about, he must be sailing across the Veranic Ocean from the same port as I. Whether or not it was intentional and they knew it would slow me down is uncertain. What's most shocking is the fact he had a ship with him with such destructive magnitude it wiped out all others. He's been busy recruiting it seems".

"Now what?" Wick pestered.

"I have no other choice… I have to change the plan and sail from a different harbour. What's troubling is that I must stay well away from Duracia, meaning that the only ports available to me are those swimming in villainy and scum". Yewki commanded the horses to increase their speed again, knowing that his secondary plan was going to waste precious time. After the rushing air and passing trees, they reached the edge of a cliff, giving them a spectacular view of the entire coastline and the many ports littering them. The fresh breeze hit them like a chilling breath as the sun's reflection glimmered in the sea, bouncing off the waves and into their eyes. Fishing birds soared above them, squawking and calling to each other in a desperate and never-ending search for food. They could hear the sound of the wind carrying the aggressive waves towards the cliff face, sending them crashing into the rocks continuously. It was a miraculous sight, but they had no time to sit around and enjoy it. Yewki carried on the journey in search of a path for them to break off of for access to the ports below. "I think we'll continue on foot. If anyone recognises the wagon then it'll just make our lives more difficult," Yewki said, ushering Wick and Moon to get off. The bear dropped off the back, causing the wood the creak in relief, no longer having to carry the weight of him. Wick jumped off after him and helped Yewki untie the horses to set them free. They were moments away from seeing how the coastal civilians would react to a big grizzly roaming their streets, but that was the least of their problems. "Don't get excited, but you're going to have to come with me on the ship," Yewki moaned.

"Really?!" Wick wheezed.

"I can't leave you and Moon where we're going… it's full of misdeeds and violence, so I'm going to have to keep you with me a little while longer. We find a ship and you stay on it and don't interfere, understand?" Yewki said, hating the sound of his own idea. He had no time to escort Wick anywhere else safe, needing to set sail as quickly as possible. "We understand. Don't we Moon?" Wick giggled.

"I mean it. The only reason you're coming with me is because it's the only way. I planned to continue sailing West after I retrieve the relic and inform my associates. I could perhaps leave you in the care of one of them".

"Of course, yes, thank you! So, how are you going to get a new ship to sail on?" Wick chattered giddily.

"Well, there's not going to be many people daring or foolish enough to help… and all our options are bad options… but Curga Harbour is our best bet," Yewki said with apprehension. He led Wick and Moon down the steep cliff pathways towards the hub of horrors, praying that they wouldn't bump into any troublesome townsfolk.

Chapter 7

In Search of Sea-Thieves

A hundred seagulls squawked one after the other, rudely talking over the folksy melodies playing below them. The strange wind instruments accustom to Curga Harbour made Greenwick's visit an interesting one. The sea breeze blew violently but the salty men and women living there dressed in short, thin clothes as though they didn't feel the cold. They either grew used to the chills or drank enough bourbon to keep them warm, which explained people's slurry vernacular. "Keep your valuables close," Yewki murmured as they passed through the busy markets. Fresh fish and bottles were shoved in their faces as they passed through the tunnel of stalls. "Oi, mate, looky this… fresh eels!" a smelly desperate man declared.

"Fresh mullet, fresh squid, get it 'ere!" a large round woman squealed.

"Come on, lad! Have a taste of this," another man chortled, prodding an old smoking pipe in Wick's face. The whole trip turned from fascinating to uncomfortable in the matter of seconds. The three of them stayed close to each other to prevent harassment as much as they could, but Moon was catching the eyes of everyone. "Nice fur, can I 'av some?" a woman asked, waving sheers in the air. The bear sped up and shook his body in irritation, as though parasites had invaded his skin. Once they managed to get out into the open, they could appreciate the town for what it was. Although the people were obnoxious, the harbour was a delightful fiasco to witness. Countless crewman ran back and forth the docks, carrying and throwing crates, tubs and barrels to and from the ships. Wooden cranes creaked as they swung side by side lifting heavier items on board whilst people shouted directions below with obscure hand gestures. They were just as loud as the seagulls above them, but the noise was part of the entertaining atmosphere. Endless taverns awaited the thirsty sailors a footstep away from the docks. It was hard for Wick to tell which buildings were houses and which were pubs, for everyone seemed to be drinking in every window he looked through. Yewki turned around and noticed a large group of people following and touching Moon. "Hands off the bear," he warned.

"How much ye selling him for, ay?" one voice popped out from within the crowd.

"He's not for sale!" Wick shouted, tugging Moon away only to be followed again. The group of people increased the deeper they got into the town. "Unless you have a ship for us to sail on then we do not want your company. So make yourself scarce, you horde of salty sea creeps!" Yewki threatened. The men and women mumbled as they walked away, finally giving up and leaving the three of them in peace. Yewki strolled into the least busy and quietest tavern he could find in the street, which was still busy and loud to some degree. The people inside jumped in the air, screaming and knocking over bottles at the sight of the bear whilst numerous swords swooshed out of sheaths. "It's okay, he's a pet!" Wick assured.

"Get out of 'ere. Ye scaring me customers!" the landlord screamed. They tried another tavern down the road, leaving Moon outside to hide in the stables full of displeased horses.

Even without the four-legged beast at their side, locals still stared at the evident outsiders with drowsy eyelids and drunken sways. Yewki kept one hand on the hilt of his sword as they sat and scanned the room. "So who are we looking for in here?" asked Wick.

"No one in particular. Just someone who looks like a sailor," Yewki explained.

"What else?"

"They need to look brave".

"Ah, I'm flattered, me lads!" a croaky voice belted out to the side of them. Both Wick and Yewki swung their heads to the left in confusion to see a hunched man in his late forties sat on the next table all by himself. He whipped out a crooked grin, showing his assortment of gold and rotten teeth hidden behind his messy moustache and beard. "If you're looking for a bear, we've sold it," Yewki lied.

"Aye, I did see ya bear before ye stashed it out back... he's a beauty, but I ain't fussed about him," the raggedy man clarified. He stood up revealing his torn dark green coat and droopy scarf. His greasy hair draped out of his tattered feathered hat as he took it off and placed it on their table, just before taking a seat with them. Yewki didn't find his presence appealing, and upon closer examination of the hat, he pieced together the man's vocation. "I appreciate your interest but we require the assistance of those who won't try and rob us," Yewki snarled to Wicks surprise. "Ah, ye got it all wrong, laddie! I crave adventure just as much as possessions," the repulsive man cackled.

"That wasn't funny, but at least you don't try and lie about what you do".

"Thank you".

"That doesn't mean it was a compliment, nor does it mean we will sail with you". Yewki began to stand up from his seat to leave but the man pushed him back down into his seat. "You dare?" Yewki grumbled, trying not to make a scene. "I'm sorry, I'm sorry... it's just that... well, don't be mad like," the man nervously apologised whilst pulling a familiar scroll from the inside of his coat. "How did you get that?" Wick gasped.

"He's a no-good Sea-Thief, he's probably been stalking us since we arrived!" Yewki complained.

"That is true, yes... when I saw yous in the markets, ye caught me eyes! I could tell you were here for something important. I'm just nosey is all," the thief responded. Yewki snatched his scroll back from him and shoved it back in his jacket whilst checking if anything else had been stolen. "I'm presuming you read it then?" he sighed.

"I can't read well but I know what it's about. I say it can't be real, but it's not worth missing out on in case-".

"Oh it's the real deal alright, but I'm not finding it with the likes of you so forget it," Yewki interrupted.

"Is he always this stubborn, boy?" he smiled to Wick.

"Tell you what, point us in the direction of actual explorers and honest adventurers and I'll pay you a little if it means you'll leave us alone," Yewki suggested.

"You must've never been to Curga Harbour before, poshy. You won't find any spruced sailors 'ere. There's brave ones... but that's because they steal for a living," the man laughed. "I have the best ship here! And it's yours to direct, under my supervision of course," he continued.

"Why would you want to help find something that's potentially dangerous?" Yewki queried.

"I already said... me and the lads love adventuring... but obviously if there's untouched relics involved, we could be in for some big money," he explained.

"The Day Relic is for me to take," Yewki warned.

"That's alright. Don't wanna mess with that stuff really... but if there's other treasures down there then they belong to me... considering that scroll isn't complete baffle".

"How can I trust that you won't try and take the Relic from me if we find it?" The man paused for a few seconds before reacting to the question. He raised his eyebrows, smiled and stood up on his chair. "My name is Captain Cut-Throat Jibar, and I swear to the Sea-Thieves of old that I remain a man of my word 'till the moment of quest's end!" he proclaimed whilst Yewki tried to pull him down and shut him up. "Take the blood of my little one and join me in the sacred oath of my people, ladies and gentlemen!" he carried on, raising his little finger in the air ready to cut it with his knife. "No, okay I believe you!" Yewki wheezed, before the entirety of the pub could sing along with the crazy cut-throat. Jibar sat back down with glee shining off his face. "Aha! You won't be disappointed, laddie" he chuckled, rubbing his dirty hands together.

Wick helped Moon out of the stables and caught up with Yewki, who was trying to keep up with Jibar's excited pace. "How much did you pay for that bear, Captain?" a shipmate asked as they made it to the docks. Jibar didn't correct him because he was too giddy to climb on board and embark. "He's a member of the crew and you won't be taking his fur, understand?" Yewki informed the confused crew member. An average sized ship floated in front of them, equipped with strange gear and weaponry. Thick nets and jaggedly-pointed javelins coated the entirety of the hull, along with large cannons poking out of each of the gun ports. "I've never seen a boat like this before," Wick gawked.

"What kind of Sea-Thieves are you?" Yewki asked. Jibar bowed as he escorted the three of them on board. The ramp bent and wobbled with the weight of Moon, so they didn't waste any time to reach the deck. The banisters and masts were plastered with chunks of burnt wood and ash. The sails on the other hand looked only days old, as though they had recently been replaced. "Me fellow crew, please welcome... ah, what are ye names?" Jibar pondered.

"The boy is Greenwick, the bear is Moon... and my name... is Yewki," he anxiously answered. Wick noticed the Captain's subtle confusion the moment Yewki revealed his name. He was also puzzled himself as to why Yewki was so hesitant to disclose his identity. "Please welcome the brave young master, Greenwick, the astonishingly loyal and ferocious, Moon... and Yewki," Jibar continued. He raised his arms in the air to pay respects to his pride and joy of a ship. "And I say to you newcomers, welcome... to the *Dragon Breaker!*" he cheered with another bow. "That explains a lot," Yewki said to himself. Before they knew it, the whole ship broke out in a deep-voiced verse;

"*Oh-sea-thieves-come-in-many-forms,*
but-none-were-born-as-brave-as-us,
Raiding-ships'a-bygone-age,
so'we-catchin'-those-who-fly-above!"

Jibar laughed and coughed at his famous introductory serenade. "Do they catch dragons?" Wick inhaled.

"That we do, lad!" the Captain rejoiced before pointing him to all the ruthless equipment, all specially designed for different species of dragon. "I've never even seen a dragon," Wick told him.

"Aye well the sea is ripe with 'em. People use dragons to send cargo long distances... so we bate 'em in, net them up and take what we want! It's like fishing in the skies," Jibar explained with pride.

"There won't be any dragon breaking during *this* voyage," Yewki told them.

"Aye, but what if we see a big Glogspike? Or a Panchergeist?!"

"I don't know what type of dragon they are, nor do I care".

"Very well then. Let's just hope they all come out when ye sleeping," Jibar muttered. They wasted no more time with niceties and got on with the mission. Crewmen climbed all over the place, lifting and lowering pieces of the ship neither Yewki nor Wick knew the names of. The three of them stood back and watched the sailors work as one whilst the Captain yelled commands without pausing for a breath. Soon the sails covered the masts for the wind to give them gentle nudges and the anchor had been risen. There was no more time left for Yewki to reconsider, meaning that the journey was happening for definite. He looked back at Curga Harbour hoping that he would never have to return.

Six hours had passed and the land they left behind was no longer visible. They were truly at sea with the wind behind them. Wick and Moon kept themselves entertained by watching everyone work around the ship, whilst Yewki sat alone below deck next to a stack of barrels, with empty hammocks swooping back and forth above his head. He kept to himself with his troubled head contained and away from others, but his deep thoughts were disturbed when Jibar climbed down the stairs. "Here ye are," he said, beckoning Yewki to follow him. "Come with me". The two of them walked into the Captain's quarters where the walls were full of differing dragon teeth and claws. "Take a seat," Jibar pulled out a chair for Yewki and they both sat opposite each other at either side of the desk. "It's my name isn't it?" Yewki assumed confidently.

"I thought it be best we spoke in here away from ya kid," Jibar told him whilst leaning forward.

"He's not my son but-".

"Yeah so I'm guessing ye haven't told him about who you are? I mean, I certainly wouldn't if I were ya. I may not seem like the smartest man to you... but I know a great deal about what's been going on the past few years. You'd be surprised how much news and information we unintentionally collect when we're raiding cargo".

"So you know much of the Relic of Day?"

"Aye, and I know certain people's plans if certain peoples get 'old of it. We thieving folk may be menaces... but we don't want what that man wants, that's for sure".

"That's good to hear. Although there's still more you don't know, and I intend to keep it that way".

"Well there's no need to be rude about it... but that's fine by me. Just don't get me ship in trouble".

"I'm ahead of him, I think we'll be okay".

"You think? Y'know, if I knew ye name before we agreed on this trip I probably wouldn't 'av pestered ye so much!"

"Yes well I guess the greed that comes with being a Sea-Thief gets you in all sorts of predicaments. Promise me you won't discuss any of this with the boy... I wouldn't want him to see me differently".

"Aye, so long as you're unlike the other one seeking this relic". Jibar stood back up and escorted Yewki out of his cabin, unbeknown to both of them that Wick had been listening in on the conversation from behind the door. Wick acted normal and sat down with Moon, pretending he had been well away from the door the whole time. Yewki smiled at him as he looked up so he gave him a quick smile back. Jibar stood in the middle of the boat unravelling Yewki's scroll. "How did he get it again?!" Yewki gasped, patting his overcoat and feeling foolish for letting the Captain swipe the parchment twice. "Right lads, we've got at least a four-day journey ahead of us which'll take us Westbound across the Veranic Ocean; everyone's personal favourite… but alas, there will be no eyes in the sky as we sail. We keep our eyes focused on the sea. It says 'ere that there will be a doorway into the water but we don't know what that'll look like. The coordinates are mushy but we'll have 'em deciphered in no time!" Jibar educated the crew which was followed by a manly cheer across the whole ship. Wick's unorthodox life as a young adventurer had literally set sail. His lack of memory made him unable to compare with what a normal child his age should have been up to, but he didn't care. Although he felt blessed by being a part of something big, he couldn't help but think about Yewki and his vague conversation with Jibar.

Chapter 8

The Sentient Maze

Five days had passed since The Dragon Breaker's voyage began. Although they sailed mostly smoothly across the ocean, the three passengers hadn't grown any more used to the sickening movement of the ship. Wick and Yewki's stomachs whined all day long. The slop of indescribable mush they consumed twice a day seemed to eat away at them instead, whilst Moon was fed spare dragon bait, consisting of slabs of mouldy meats. Their daily diet explained why the crew were as thin as the ropes they tugged and tied. Captain Jibar scampered back and forth across the deck, babbling and grunting with haste. Nothing exciting had happened since they embarked so the irregular fast movement caught everyone's eyes. "What's happening? Everyone's moving around," Wick asked Yewki.

"It looks like they're panicking," he replied. Volumes increased and crew members doubled their speed, often bumping into Moon's obstructive body. Yewki chased after Jibar in search of answers, "What's going on?"

"You lot are gettin' off me ship, that's wot!" The Captain shouted. Yewki set his eyes on what everyone else was staring at and gulped. A monstrous hole had opened up in the water, spiralling rapidly which was slowly dragging the vessel to its doom. "Is that a-".

"A whirlpool! And am turning this ship round to a safe distance," Jibar interrupted.

"But what about the relic? We can't give up now, we should be close to the entrance!"

"The entrance? Yer lookin' at it, laddie!" Yewki looked back at the whirlpool, thinking of any way Jibar could be mistaken. "Not a chance. How?" he demanded a plausible answer before diving into the sea swallower. "Can ya think of another doorway into the water?" The Captain quoted. "We've been doing ten mile loops around these coordinates for the past day and a half, and there's been no doorway in sight so this has to be it". The two of them didn't notice Wick stood at their side, but he had heard the whole argument. "I don't even know if I can swim," he said.

"It's okay, you're not coming with me, you're staying on the ship," Yewki assured.

"No he's not," Jibar ordered.

"Pardon?"

"The boy's going with ya. I'm potentially sacrificing my men so ye can sacrifice one of yours!" he elaborated. Yewki scratched his head with rage. "Don't let Moon follow me in," Wick requested. Yewki shook his head not knowing what to do. The importance of the relic clashed with the responsibility of the child. "Now or never, laddie!" Jibar shouted as the ship began to turn around. Four crew members dived into the water and began to swim towards the whirlpool as though they had a death wish. "Agh! Why is this boy destined to stay by my side?!" Yewki growled whilst kicking the floor. "You stay by my side, understand?" he commanded Wick. Yewki was just as nervous as the boy. They held hands and stared down into the sea, almost reluctant to take the plunge. Moon noticed them from a distance and made his way to them but Jibar ordered his men to restrain him. "We will wait ten hours and no more!" The Captain warned.

"Ten hours? But it's a maze, we might-". Jibar pushed Yewki off the side of the ship before he could finish his plea, unwillingly dragging Wick down with him. The Captain's cackling laugh and the gushing wind was all they could hear as they plopped into the sea. Yewki hoisted Wick onto one of his shoulders to assist his swimming. "Are you okay?" he asked. Wick nodded as he coughed up salty water. "Kick your legs," he prompted. They could feel the increasing force of the whirlpool pulling them in the closer they got. They had no time to prepare or calculate, but even if they did, their heads consisted solely of fear and anxiety. "I'm sorry for dragging you into this," Yewki screamed as they began to rotate around the hole. The entire ride was torturous and frightful, spiralling uncontrollably, knowing there was no way to climb back out. Back on the boat, Moon pushed and shoved his way through grappling arms and nets. "We don't want to hurt ya, we just don't want ya chasing after the lad!" Jibar assured the bear, but he refused to listen. In a final attempt, Moon burst out of the pile of men and pushed straight by the captain, knocking him to the floor. "No, you silly animal!" Jibar yelled but it was too late. The bear flung himself overboard which resulted in a heavy splash. He struggled to swim but the strong pull of the whirlpool soon ensnared him. Wick and Yewki were deep underwater at this point not knowing which way was up, as though the surface had completely vanished and they were trapped in an infinite space of water. The panic for air had kicked in which didn't bode well with being lost in the water. No entrances of any sort could be seen at first glance, not even the previous men that had jumped in could be seen. Luckily, Wick noticed a reflective oval ring the size of a doorway, seemingly floating undisturbed. He pointed to it so Yewki wasted no time to inspect, dragging Wick behind. To their surprise, the ringed entrance followed them around like eyes on a portrait, as though it was intended to be perceived as two-dimensional from all directions. They swam right to it, unconcerned whether or not the ring was dangerous, as they just wanted to breathe again. Yewki pushed one arm through the ring which seemed to consume his limb. The rest of his body followed behind along with Wick. Just before his head was engulfed, he spotted a lifeless Moon bubbling away in the open, but Yewki had yanked Wick in completely before he could react. The two of them gasped manically and laid on the floor on the other side of the portal, soaking wet and on the verge of passing out. The air was welcome in their lungs, soon greeted with exhales of relief. They had successfully made it to the magical maze but there was another problem to overcome before they could begin their search. "Moon!" Wick bellowed as he leaped head-first back through the ring. He kicked his legs as hard as he could through the water towards the sinking bear, followed by Yewki. They both pushed and dragged Moon through the entrance, hoping he was still alive. All they could do was stare worryingly at the soggy beast. "Why did you follow me?" Wick blubbered.

"He's foolishly loyal," Yewki shook his head and sighed.

"We need to do something, please!"

"Push him onto his back". It was no easy task for them lifting his heavy legs up and swivelling its body from its side to a face-up position. Yewki raised Wick onto the bears belly and told him to stomp, pushing the water in Moon's lungs back out. Moon clambered onto his paws startled and confused, knocking Wick onto the floor. "Easy boy, you're okay," Yewki said softly as he stroked him. He grunted and thudded back down to catch his lost breath. "You almost died!" Wick yelled. Yewki walked several paces ahead. The walls, roof and floor were all creamy white and slightly painful for the eyes gaze upon for too long as the adjustment from dim to bright light was straining. The moment he turned the first corner, reality kicked in. He looked ahead in awe at the many branches of corridors leading deep into the heart of the maze. "You both have five minutes to catch your breaths," Yewki warned. "You're going to be breathless either way when you see what's ahead".

Countless twists and turns led the three of them through the endless routes with no relic or hope in sight. At least four hours had passed since they picked their starting path. There were no visible indications on the walls pointing in valuable directions, only the odd scratch left behind by previous adventurers. "How long do you think we've been down here?" Wick asked.

"I'm not sure," Yewki responded bluntly.

"Shouldn't we have been keeping track of our path so we can retrace our steps if we get lost?"

"We were lost the moment we entered that cursed whirlpool. Even if we remembered our way back to that portal we'd still be trapped in the water".

"But what if that's our only way out?"

"It's not".

"How do you know?"

"Because it was an entrance, not an exit!" His loud response echoed through the tunnels. Moon growled at Yewki's sudden aggressiveness. "I'm sorry, Wick. I'm just angry at myself. You shouldn't be here at all, but here you are, completely lost in this never-ending labyrinth." he confessed.

"Jibar wouldn't have let me stay on his ship anyway, so it's not your fault".

"But why were you on that ship in the first place? Because I dragged you with me". Wick didn't respond and kept his eyes focused on his footsteps. The near-dead silence provided him with a previously unheard noise from below. He listened carefully to the strange bangs and scrapes which seemed to come from multiple directions. "Can you hear that?" he asked. Yewki stopped and put his ear to the floor as Moon sniffed around. Wick placed his ear to the walls to discover that the noise was all around them. "Everything's been moving this whole time," Yewki sighed.

"Who's controlling it?"

"An *Iwa*," he answered.

"A *what*?" Wick gasped, but Yewki was too troubled to go into depth. The noises were suddenly accompanied with rumbles and dust leaked from cracks in the roof. "Let's go!" Yewki ordered as he ran full speed in an attempt to escape the quakes. Wick and Moon followed close behind, noticing bricks shifting on their own in the corners of their eyes. Water began spurting out of crevices, slowly rising to their knees, making it harder for them to run efficiently and smoke fogged their view. Pathways ahead had become sloped causing them to slide down with the gushing water and into another area of the maze. The frantic panic continued when they noticed the walls narrowing. Yewki pushed Moon ahead, as he needed to get by first, being the widest of the three. An open area could be seen ahead but the closing corridor walls were soon brushing against their shoulders. Thankfully, Moon had made it through but all he could do was look back and hope the others would too. Their bodies were forced to waddle sideways as they squirmed the rest of the way. Yewki finally heaved himself out and into the large room but Wick was still incoming. He stared forwards at Moon as both walls pushed on his chest and back. "Come on!" Yewki screeched, yanking Wick's arm the moment he could reach out for it. A fraction of a second stood between the boy and the thunderous slam of the two walls meeting, but what mattered was that he'd made it. Before they could reflect on what had just happened, several skeletal entities jumped from behind pillars, armed to the teeth with ancient tools and weapons. The skulls were not human, as though they had traded their heads with a variety of beasts, but had kept their bodies. Large fangs drooped from their upper jaws and their leaf skirts rustled violently like predators about to pounce from behind a bush. "What kind of magic is this?" Wick panted.

"This isn't magic," Yewki murmured. The bone soldiers jerked as they stepped forward. Yewki pointed his sword towards them but it didn't slow down their intimidating march. "We've come for the Relic of Day," he answered. The skeletons snarled and readied their weapons, unable to speak back. "And we're not leaving without it!" he continued. Drum beats vibrated around the room with no source and slowly increased in pace as the soldiers used the banging sounds to move and attack. Yewki fought all of them at once, slicing at vulnerable points such as the necks and legs. Moon slapped the bones to pieces but they began reconstructing themselves once the pitch of the drum altered, and the fight started all over again, but with double the ferocity. Wick noticed one of the skeletons still shattered on the floor with a crack in its skull. "Their heads! You need to break the heads!" he shouted whilst picking up rocks from the ground. Yewki and Moon persisted to crush the skulls they could as Wick provided a stone artillery from behind, knocking off a few heads himself. The drum beat stopped as soon as the last smash was made and the once animated bones lay still just as they were intended to. The three of them finally had a moment's peace to look around and evaluate the room. Their way in was sealed indefinitely until the maze changed again, and there was now only three corridors for them to choose from as opposed to the usual endless choices. "This must mean something. We have the choice of three," Yewki thought aloud. Each tunnel had a symbol above it, all similar but different at the same time – a sun surrounded by a differing number of light rays, chiselled into the stone. "That sun has a few rays, that one has many, and that one has barley any at all," he continued, completely stumped. The puzzle was evidently unkind which proved that the relic must have been close.

Two hours had gone by with no progress to the puzzle. The three of them walked back and forth with no new ideas in mind. "This is ridiculous," Yewki moaned.
"We must be missing something," Wick exhaled and sat down on the ground with his head in his hands.
"At least we have all the time in the world".
"But Jibar said ten hours".
"I'll be honest, even if we manage to retrieve the relic in the allocated time, how are we going to get out of here? I'm sorry but all we can do is hope there is an exit portal because no plan in our heads can help us escape an infinite space that shouldn't even exist in the first place".
"You knew all this but you still came down here to find it?"
"My options were get it myself and hope for an exit, or let the wrong hands find it and hope there isn't one. The world is not worth such a gamble". Just when all hope was lost, Moon had spotted carvings on the floor. He persisted to grunt and scratch at it for attention until the other two realised. The possible answer was on the floor all along but it was too big for them to notice. "A sundial?" Wick muttered and tilted his head.

"Yes," Yewki said whilst stepping back. "But it's missing the dial". The room strangely provided natural light through a small hole in the wall behind them. "Maybe *we* need to be the dial, and we use our shadow," Wick suggested. Yewki quickly stood on top of the carvings to see where his shadow would point. Although the light source beamed at an angle, Yewki's shadow faced directly forwards on the floor in a supernatural way. "Midday!" he cheered. "Midday is the brightest – the sun's prime". They charged together to the tunnel which had the most light rays illustrated. "I had a hunch but the shadow indication proves it!" Moon and Yewki ran in without hesitation but Wick took a closer look at the symbol. "Come on, Wick!" Yewnin beckoned. He ignored him and continued to gaze upon the chisellings with new findings. "There's space for more rays on that sun," he explained.

"But that sun has more rays than the others so it must be the right way," Yewki disagreed.

"That symbol has four, that one has eight, and this one has ten. Just because it has more than the others doesn't mean it has the most. What if we're missing a pathway?"

"But there's only these three". Wick didn't say anything back, instead he pointed up to the roof directly above the sundial. A near-missed fourth symbol had been insulting their intelligence for the past couple of hours. "Oh, that one has twelve rays," Yewki muttered.

"How do we get up there?" Wick asked.

"Maybe we don't have to". Yewki picked up a bow from one of the fallen skeletons and sharpened an arrow to the best of his abilities then aimed directly upwards. "I hope this works," he said to himself whilst pulling back on his bow before releasing the arrow, which stuck perfectly into the chiselled sun. The symbol glowed bright yellow as the three pathways closed shut. They spent a moment waiting for something to happen but nothing occurred. "We must have gone wrong somewhere, and now we're trapped!" Yewki whined. Before he could feel completely defeated, the floor beneath them opened up, dropping them into yet another area of the maze. They fell onto their faces one by one, happy that they were no longer trapped in the room but unhappy at their ever-growing list of bodily aches and pains. The maze looked different to before. Instead of enclosed tunnels, they stood in the open, surrounded by mossy stone platforms floating around and moving slowly. Mist shrouded their vision and lack of light made things worse. "I hope this is the final hurdle, I don't know how much more of this I can take," Yewki complained. They walked to the edge of where they were and looked down to see a thousand more floating platforms. Their disgusted faces stuck as they looked up to see the same thing above them too. "Where do we start?" Wick asked.

"At this point, it's anyone's guess".

"I've been thinking".

"Yes, Wick?"

"What if the maze doesn't want us to take it? What if whoever is protecting it wants to keep things the way they are?"

"Would you be surprised if I told you I know who its protector is?" Wick didn't answer, instead he remained gob-smacked, confused and astonished. "He wants me to take it and keep it safe".

"If that's the case, why is the maze still trying to kill us?" Wick asked.

"Because unfortunately we must still prove our worth, just like every other mortal who dares enter this place and claim it. The fate of the world is still in his best interests… but that doesn't mean he's *not* a savage". A peculiar humming sound began to fill the air, buzzing closer and closer to them. They looked as far as the fog would let them but there was nothing visible that matched the noise they heard. Moon slouched his shoulders and lowered his head, afraid of what was coming. After a nervous search, Yewki spotted a figure in the distance hiding behind a wall. "It's one of the Sea-Thieves, there!" Yewki pointed for Wick to see. The two of them waved their arms and shouted over to the man but he didn't respond. A more thorough look revealed that he was cowering and placing his finger over his mouth. "Shush," he whispered, but his platform was too far away for Wick and Yewki to hear. Moon perked his ears up to figure out what the man was trying to say, then nudged them, unable to successfully get across his desire for them to be quiet. "What's wrong?" Wick asked, trying to figure out what Moon wanted, but it was no use. "We should group up with him," Yewki suggested whilst clambering and jumping across platforms. Wick and Moon made their way across at a slower and clumsier rate. The Sea-Thief shook his head frantically but Yewki was too busy looking at his footing. "Where's the others?" Yewki asked upon arrival.

"No, go away!" the man whispered with desperation in his voice.

"What, why?"

"They'll hear you!" he whimpered, grabbing Yewki by his overcoat and shaking him back and forth. The humming suddenly turned into a gargling grunt but still nothing could be seen. "No, no, no! They've found me again!" he cried, running away in a panic. A deep boom hit the ground behind Yewki, startling him, although it was only Moon hitting the ground after the leap across from the previous platform followed by Wick. "Everyone be quiet," he mimicked the frightened man's plea.

"What's out there?" Wick muttered.

"I don't know". The man had made it to the end of a platform, seconds away from jumping only to be greeted by a hideous unknown insect twice the size of Moon. Its body was hairy and its pincers drooled with sticky spit. All six of its legs were tipped with sharp crooked points. The man screamed as the blood filled his lungs from the creature's deathly attack to the stomach. Another bug scurried its way from underneath the platform and fought for a bite of its own. "We need to move," Yewki ushered, now aware of what the consequences of being noisy were. They turned to go back the way they came only to be stopped by another giant insect blocking their way and ready to pounce. Moon dragged Wick by the collar with his mouth, out of the way of its attack. The spear-like legs left cracks in the floor which shook the entire platform. The creature let out a snarly war cry, calling its siblings for dinner. The three of them wasted no time to run and jump down to a lower area, uncaring of the big drop. Yewki hit the ground and rolled, quickly getting to his feet to catch Wick in an attempt to break his fall. Moon on the other hand landed heavily, knocking pieces of the floor loose which floated away. The bug's numbers had tripled and so did their pace. Neighbouring platforms began crashing into each other as a result of the large monsters jumping across on them. Each clash sent bricks and rubble flying all around them which was another obstacle for them to dodge. Yewki turned for a moment to fire an arrow but to his surprise, it pinged straight off the insect's hard shell of a body. With their stamina decreasing and their legs taking the toll of numerous leaps, they couldn't run any further. Before they knew it, forty bugs surrounded them in a circle of death. They could feel the platform lowering due to the immense weight on board. "Let's hope where we need to be is at the bottom of this place," Yewki said between his panting. The creatures knocked and smacked into one another as they closed in, all wanting to get the first taste. Moon had his nose on the floor, sniffing through a crack. Wick looked through the hole to see another, much smaller platform below. The bear didn't have to be asked as he jumped up and down, slamming his front paws to reveal a weak point in the ground. Yewki snatched two stones beneath his feet and scraped them together as hard as he could, for he had a plan of his own. The bugs all dived inwards at once, each hoping to be the first to devour. The sparks Yewki created between the two stones ignited the dry moss, spooking the creatures backwards. Unfamiliar with such a bright light, they collectively squealed as the crackling blazes damaged their many eyes. The fire followed and branched off across the numerous trails of moss, weakening the entire floor further. Moon dealt the ground one last blow creating a hole for the three of them to fall through, leaving the insects on the platform which had finally reached its breaking point. Moon landed on the lower platform first, providing a cushion for Wick, but Yewki hit the edge hard and rolled off. He gripped on with one hand and dangled as all the bugs dropped past them and into the mist below, screeching loudly as they fell to their deaths. Wick and Moon pulled him up to safety and shared the small amount of ground they had. All three of them were injured to some degree, but none more so than the bear. He licked his left paw as he struggled to put pressure on it. "Are you okay?" Wick asked softly, stroking the bear's fur. Yewki held his bleeding head and asked if Wick was alright. Luckily there was nothing more than scrapes and bruises between the two of them. Suddenly, the platform began to move as though someone was controlling it. Other clumps of stone moved out of their way but they still ducked their heads just in case. "I see another one of those portals," Wick gasped.

"We're being led to the exit?" Yewki asked rhetorically.

"But we didn't find the relic".

"Maybe there was no way out until we defeated those insect guards – that was the challenge". The portal stood right in front of them, glowing and enticing them in. Yewki went first to make sure the other end was safe. They found themselves in a room brighter than daylight and warmer than the hottest summers. Glowing rays glimmered and twinkled in their eyes as they squinted to see ahead. The immense heat didn't take long to make them sweat and itch away at their slowly burning skin. The drum beats from before accompanied the moment they laid their eyes upon the legendary Relic of Day. It was shaped like the hilt of a sword, but lacking both blade and pommel. Its colour mesmerised the human eye – glowing sunset orange wrapped around the perfect white and silver object. It rested peacefully atop a pedestal made of pure light energy, surrounded by various animal skulls. Wick noticed an unknown lettering on the wall beside them made up of jagged lines and crosses. "What does that say?" he asked.

"*Those who seek...the light.* Hmm, *those who seek the light... will embrace its might*," Yewki brushed his hands across the engraved text then continued, "*Those who mistreat what's mine... will never shine*". The two of them soon became more hesitant to pick it up. "This maze is no longer a safe place for this artefact. Although it was a valiant defence against miscreants for a millennia, human desire and resilience has grown and evolved," a third voice made itself known, causing them to turn around to face the portal they came through. A bald man stood wearing sleek leather garments, equipped with feathers and shiny gems. To Wick's surprise, he had no physical weapon, and the man's face looked similar to Yewki's. The man walked forward lifting and pinning the three of them against the walls without even moving a muscle. Yewki stayed quiet the entire time with sickening distraught on his face. "We're sorry we tried to take the relic… but we needed it!" Wick spluttered with an invisible force pushing on his chest. The man turned to look at the boy, "You think I'm the relic's protector?" he grinned. The Relic of Day glowed brighter the closer the man's hand reached out for it, begging to be held in the palm of a mortal. "I'm here to take it for myself… so no, I am not its protector. I intend to be its wielder," he explained whilst grasping the powerful device with both hands. His body shuddered and his eyes glowed bright as the light within bound with his soul. His disturbing smile grew whilst the seemingly painful procedure engulfed him whole until there was nothing but a white speck of light remaining which soon vanished too. The three of them fell from the walls the moment the stranger disappeared, followed by the entire room rumbling in agony as it began to darken. "Who w-was that? I think the protector is mad at him for taking it," Wick shouted.

"No, he's mad at *us* for letting him," Yewki sighed, completely dumbfounded and sedated towards the impending situation. The drum beats increased as the room collapsed in on itself, spinning both solid material and light in circles, similar to the whirlpool. Everything spiralled itself inwards until there was nothing left in existence – just a dark void of emptiness.

Chapter 9

Slay

Clouds had flooded the once clear skies above the Dragon Breaker and their formations were anything but natural. Wind twisted around an ever-growing ball of light that had appeared from thin air in the centre of the clouds, constructing a portal bigger and greater than the ones from before, surrounded by jolts of lightning and unexplainable wisps of surging energy. Out came Yewki, Wick and Moon alive and well, falling straight down as though a god had spat them out from the heavens. Thankfully the sea was there to catch them but it was still a big drop and a painful splash. "Wick?!" Yewki called out, but only Moon surfaced, struggling to keep his head above the water. "Get to the boat, I promise I will get the boy, but if you try and stay afloat you're going to drown!" he commanded. The bear didn't want to leave for a head start but he knew Yewki was right. Wick had broken from underneath the water luckily still conscious and climbed on Yewki's back barely able to propel himself without assistance. As they swam, they noticed the yellow beam of light coming from below the sea and into the cloud portal they'd just fell from. Looking back ahead, they saw and heard fighting aboard the ship, with an enemy ship circling it. The other vessel was much larger and covered in high quality materials and weaponry. The flag waved a symbol Wick had never seen before, featuring red and gold colours and a dragon. Fire had broken out and explosions of splintering wood burst from both boats as the sound of cannon fire rumbled through the air. Yewki screamed for a fishing net but it was hard to gain the attention of the battling shipmates. On board, Jibar led his men in an all-out war with a relentless army that had been tailing them since they'd departed. Large shadows swooped over the deck followed by the unique roars of fast, purple dragons with overly long tails. "Three… no, they have four Colliser dragons, lads!" Jibar announced. "Javelins, focus fire above! Mobile cannons, go for their abdomens! Let's show em why we're called the Dragon Breaker!" he cheered. Several crewmen had begun pulling Wick, Yewki and Moon up the side of the ship in their fishing net, with cannons blasting off next to their heads. They ducked and cowered until they were safely on board only to be ten feet away from more threats. "Get to the lower level and stay there," Yewki ordered Wick.

"I want to help!" he cried.

"A battle is no place for a boy". Yewki fought his way across the deck protecting Wick as Moon limped behind them dodging arrows. They noticed Jibar chopping his way through soldiers and kicking them overboard. "You've been missing a great fight, lads!" he bellowed over to them.

"He stole the relic from us," Yewki explained.

"So we're fighting them for nothing?"

"We're fighting so we don't die!" Yewki pointed down to the trap doors but Wick ignored his requesting gesture. He wanted to know who the bald man was that grabbed the relic, but Yewki was trying his hardest not to provide any details. There were explanations blatantly hidden and brushed aside, and Wick being left out made him want to know even more. One Colliser had been taken down which knocked half of a mast and sail into the water with it whilst the other three squirted short bursts of fire across the ship. The enemy soldiers were wearing thin but their ship still had plenty of cannon balls to deploy, and a surprise up their sleeve. Out of nowhere, a flash of white filled everyone's eyes as though a bolt of lightning had struck nearby. The mysterious relic thief floated slightly above the deck of the Dragon Breaker whilst both opposing sides stood still in a stand-off formation.

The Day Relic was clear in his hand and the enemy soldiers cheered and bashed their weapons against the floor upon recognition. The man looked puzzled but he tried his best to compose himself whilst he aimed his spare hand to the wooden planks beneath him. An abrupt stream of light energy shot out of his palm, burning and leaving a perfect hole on the deck. He shot again, this time at a mast, sending it sideways and snapping off completely. A warm glow surrounded him as he continued to clumsily blast the power of daylight across the ship. "You're lucky I must learn to control my new abilities, Yewki, or else I would end you myself right now," he shouted. Yewki looked down at the ground and scowled before answering back, "That was not yours to take, you fool!"

"If that *is* the case then come take it from me!" the man threatened. Jibar looked to Yewki, waiting for him to attack but he didn't move and looked back at the ground. "He won't fight you because he has a heart, unlike ye," the Captain insulted. Wick stepped forward. "Leave my friend alone!" he cried, holding a broken sword that he'd picked up off the floor. The man began to laugh as he lowered his powerful hands, "He's your friend… but for how long? If he had the audacity to turn his back on family, imagine what he'd do to those he calls *friend*," he teased.

"Yewnin, don't," Yewki pleaded. Wick had finally pieced everything together – the man was Yewki's brother which was why he was careful not to mention anything about him. "He's your brother?" Wick muttered, feeling slightly sick at the thought. "Get below deck, boy. I'll explain everything to you soon, I promise. I've already put you in harm's way enough as it is," Yewki sighed.

"You didn't tell him? Ha, you truly *are* ashamed to be associated with me aren't you? Surely it should be the other way around!" Yewnin waved his arm from left to right sending out more scorching light. "Tell me, boy… where's your Mother and Father? Why did they leave you? Most of all, why has my brother dragged you into this mess?" he asked Wick but he didn't answer as he was too busy thinking about the questions and how he could have known. Jibar stormed his way towards him. "Come forth ye sick freak, let me put you out of ya misery," he taunted.

"I will not flatter myself as I believe I am a man of honesty. I will not fight you because I know I have a chance of losing on this occasion, it's true. My preservations will be mistaken for cowardice I'm sure... but I need time to study this relic and unlock its true potential," Yewnin confessed. Blow horns of war came from the enemy ship, telling the Collisers to retreat and make way for two of a different species. "Chuck dragons aren't a good sign," Jibar growled to himself, looking up at the large, muscular orange beasts.

"Now you must *really* get inside," Yewki said whilst glaring at Wick. The fear in both men's faces convinced him to do as he was told. Moon followed him after giving Yewnin a death stare. "I don't even want to know why you have a bear on board," Yewnin chuckled. "I *would* say we can fight properly another time, but I don't want any of you to survive," he explained. The two Chucks flew low, allowing their individual pilots to jump on deck. A man in his early thirties and a younger fighter in his mid-twenties landed gracefully, both wielding two swords. Before Wick fully closed the trap door, he took a glimpse of them both. Their attire followed the colour scheme of their ship's flag which emphasised their importance. They didn't care for helmets like their fellow soldiers, for they were far too skilled to benefit from them. Neither of them spoke, but both of them grinned menacingly. Yewnin vanished in a similar way to how he did inside the maze, leaving both sides to carry on with their fight. Both warriors span their swords rapidly and tumbled acrobatically towards the crowd of Sea-Thieves without a care in the world. Their swords moved faster than the blink of an eye, and neither of them came close to being inflicted. A wave of fifteen men dropped to none in a matter of seconds as they worked together in perfect harmony, like a dancing duet of death. Jibar and Yewki were next on their kill lists. Their efforts increased to stay on par with the more prestigious fighters, but it was still easy for them. Jibar and Yewki struggled to cover their bodies from the four blades that felt more like a hundred. "Javelins, cannons, keep firing on their ship!" Jibar ordered, taking his attention off of the swords for a second too long which resulted in a sneaky dagger to the leg and a stab through the belly. "Argh!" he barked, jumping backwards to pull the sharp metal out of his stomach. Yewki was pinned, ducking and blocking with every heartbeat. Jibar needed to fulfil his plan before both of them were slaughtered, but the fight was requiring most of his concentration. "Strike a Chuck above their ship!" he managed to let out, although it came at a cost when his chest was sliced, knocking him to the ground. Yewki jumped over to protect him whilst he got back up, taking on both of them at once. Their attention shifted when the dying cry of a Chuck passed by. The dragon crashed into the enemy's vessel causing severe damage after numerous weak points had been created with cannon fire. "Your ship will crumble soon if ya don't leave! How are ye gonna get home if it does? This one has no masts left, and I have plenty of javelins left for your dragons so don't even think about escaping on this or those!" Jibar laughed. The older warrior whistled for the remaining Chuck to pick them up which Jibar didn't consider in his plan. "Take down the other one, quickly!" he yelled, but the dragon strafed across the deck with its wide radius fire blast. Jibar and Yewki jumped down into a small hole left behind by enemy cannonballs to escape the scorches the best they could. Unfortunately, Yewki's arm was caught in the fire, burning it slightly. The two warriors fled, sharing the Chuck to fly back to their ship. Another horn blew which summoned two large green aquatic dragons to surface slightly. They were chained to the front of the vessel which gave the ship an unfair boost of speed as they began swimming. They wasted no time to make their escape before the Captain could order anymore cannonballs at their fragile ship. Jibar climbed out of the hole and helped Yewki out afterwards. Both of them looked across to see the nearly destroyed boat take its leave before the two swimming dragons blew clouds of steam, covering their getaway. "Water dragons – Bogahaggons, two of em. That explains how they travel so fast at sea. That's cheating," Jibar hissed.

The aftermath of the great sea battle left the Dragon Breaker badly damaged with parts still ablaze. Surviving crewmen limped along the deck assisting the fallen and putting out fires. Jibar staggered left and right holding his abdominal wound with his hand. "That could 'av gone better," he grumbled.

"I'm presuming you're used to the occasional failure, Captain… but this isn't the sort of failure you can put behind you. We have seriously jeopardized much more than what your careless mentality can fathom," Yewki expressed with disappointment. Jibar took a seat on the deck surrounded by his fallen crew, not repulsed by their bloody bodies. "Av lost more men than I can care to count. I know full well wot the repercussions will be now. If ye considered ya mission important then perhaps ye shouldn't have accepted the help from a *horde of salty sea creeps*, as you so kindly put it," he jabbed, referring back to when Yewki warded off the civilians of Curga Harbour. "Wow, you really *were* stalking me, weren't you. I'm sorry… I appreciate your help. I never thought it be possible to respect a band of Sea-Thieves but you've proved to be honourable men where and when it matters," Yewki apologised humbly. "Out of curiosity, Jibar… did you plan to steal the relic from me if I'd gotten it?"

"Aye, well… I guess we'll never know now will we," he smirked. Wick slowly opened the hatch and gasped at the carnage above, letting himself out nervously to walk towards Yewki. He noticed Jibar's leaking red stomach, "Are you okay?" he asked.

"I hope so," the Captain smiled. "One of those Slayers had at me but it'll take more than a slice to take me down".

"*Slayers?*"

"The worst news Yewnin could have for us, but the most beneficial allegiance he could have made for his cause," Yewki interrupted. "We encountered two of the three brothers – Hundo the Wise and Rowdun the Woundless, sons of the Slayer King, Zamanite the Relentless. They fear nothing but the war god they worship. The Slayer Kingdom believe they were put on this Earth to rid it of the weak, so that only the strongest prevail, which would in turn reward them with immortality in the afterlife. Although their beliefs have always been disturbing, the last couple of decades have been more about ego and killing for sport," he explained. Jibar yanked the dagger out of his leg, which was encrusted with the royal Slayer emblem – a fire-red dragon surrounded by gold and onyx. He looked around at his poor ship and examined the unmistakable cuts on the wood left behind by the sleek blades of the Slayers. He sighed, finally breaking his light hearted streak. "Ye know how they choose their next King? Well, the death of their ruler usually means the oldest Prince takes over… but the throne is open to anyone so long as ya a citizen of the kingdom and ye achieve a never before seen feat of slaying… their King is whoever has the greatest kill. They're sick and twisted, and 'av long lost the meaning of life and the purpose of living. If someone as reckless as maself is saying something like this then I hope that gives ye an insight of how formidable they are," he spat as blood left his mouth whilst clenching his fist. "Can't someone stop them?" Wick asked.

"They're practically untouchable," answered Yewki. "Hence why one of them is called, *Woundless*. We're lucky to be alive". Wick didn't feel the need respond as he saw the pain in both men's eyes. He was too young to have to stress about the concept of deadly threats and war, but the innocence of childhood had to wait, or be left behind entirely. Unfortunately, Yewki had more than just the Slayers to worry about. He leant over the side of the ship and looked to the horizon thinking about how his own brother could be the cause of an upcoming great evil. All the years of apprehending him, he had blocked out who he was to make things easier, but things had finally gotten too extreme. They grew up together with same childhood and with the same blood in their veins. He was unsure if he could truly stop him as he imagined their future encounters. The notion of having to be prepared to kill his younger brother haunted him more than the notion of the imminent apocalypse he was orchestrating. Wick had troubles of his own. Yewnin sparked memories in his shrouded head like why his parents would leave him and where they could be now, if they were alive. He also wanted to ask Yewki more about Yewnin but he didn't want to make things any more uncomfortable. The once jolly vessel was silent and full of troubled thoughts for the first time. No one cared for plans and voyage destinations as the ship floated in the middle of nowhere, waiting for the waves to take them to shore as the yellow beacon of daylight faded from the sky the moment dusk transitioned to night.

Chapter 10

Relentless By Name

Forests segmented many lands across the Earth like fortress walls. The secluded, far North-West land was no exception – Emmrin-Rashmada was home to the infamous Kingdom of Slayers. Their surrounding forest was surprisingly fruitful and lush in comparison to the land itself, which was named after their legendary god of murder. The forest on the other hand had no name, but it was one of the most feared due to the fact that the most dangerous kingdom waited on the other side of it. The lack of people brave enough to venture inwards in fear of encountering the Slayers explained why the forest was left nicely untouched. Beyond the trees and towards civilisation stood the extremely long city walls, charred black metal and covered with thorn-like spikes. A bed of coal and soot lay at the bottom of them which added to the kingdoms list of unappealing features. A sickening smog forever blew across Emmrin-Rashmada from the constant dragon fire. Although, the land was not known to be home to many species of dragon, instead they were captured and enslaved there from different parts of the world and forced to follow the Slayer's commands. Puddles of blood were just as common as puddles of water inside the kingdom. A never before seen hybrid of dark wood and jagged metal structures made the whole city bleak and ugly. Homes and supplies would often be fought over as negotiating prices was a thing of the past for them. Savage civilians would kill one another for the pettiest reasons as though the only law they abided was to slay. It was like living in the wild, having to kill to survive amongst predators. It was the opposite of the Mighty Magmalia that focused on loyalty and justice, which was why they were avid enemies since the birth their nations. Royalty never worried too much of the decaying state of their city whilst comfortable inside their castle, which was overly sized and created an everlasting shadow over the streets below. There was no mantle of responsibility towards the people as King, nor a concern for the city's economy, only the desire to be above all else whilst killing for what they believed in. The life of a Slayer was ultimately a competition, and the whole world was their arena. The castles interior was draped in red, gold and black with trophies left behind from past conflicts. It was home to the most zealous and deadliest Slayer family to date as well as an overkill amount of guards sworn to serve and protect.

Hundo and Rowdun sat in one of their many dining halls, surrounded by the finest dragon meat. They barely ate for their appetite had gone, knowing that they were soon to be called upon by the King. "It was your fault," Rowdun scoffed.
"I did the right thing, you kook," Hundo scoffed back, dropping his knife and fork on the table.
"Is that what you're going to tell Father? You failed because it was the right thing?"
"There's more to it than that". Hundo slammed on the table. Rowdun rolled his eyes, showing no respect to his older brother. The King's elite guards entered the room. They didn't have to say anything – the Princes knew what they wanted. The two of them were escorted up a dozen flight of red stairs topped off with golden banisters. They were both nervous, praying in their heads for mercy as their heart rates increased. The guards opened the doors to King Zamanite's quarters where he stood facing the stained glass windows. They both bowed to their knees and stayed there awaiting their Father's wrath, but instead there was a drawn out silence. The crackles and popping of wood in the fireplace increased the tension in the room for a good minute.

"None of you wish to talk?" he asked. "Are you apathetic... or just pathetic?"

"We're sorry, Father," they answered at the same time.

"Your failure tarnished my reputation with Yewnin... do you think I deserve that?"

"No, Father," they said again in sync.

"Since when do Slayers flee? Since when did the Wise become *unwise*?" Zamanite asked patronisingly. Hundo lowered his head even more. "Our ship was on the verge of sinking, we even had to repair it as we sailed from risk of leaks. I deemed it too much of a risk to stay aboard the scum's vessel in case we were left stranded," he explained.

"You think I care for your well-beings? I care only for our kingdom's victories... I thought that was what you both believed too".

"Father, my selfish act to make it back home was merely because I wish to become King one day. How do you expect me to do so when I am stranded at sea and left to die?" Hundo explained with a crack in his voice, knowing that he was risking stepping out of line. "That is not my concern... if you fail to survive then your fate as future King is decided," Zamanite smirked. Hundo stormed out of the room, followed by angry grunts and noises of smashing pottery. The King shook his head in annoyance whilst Rowdun's anxiety doubled being the only person in the room with him. "I never planned to make him King... he's too wise for his own good. You on the other hand, Rowdun, I expect you to lead this kingdom one day so that I can transcend to the immortal heavens in peace, knowing that I have one son to be proud of," he revealed whilst sitting down at his desk. "Thank you, Father," he stuttered.

"You may leave," Zamanite prompted. Rowdun stood up with relief and opened the door, but paused before fully leaving the room. "Father... what about Eck?" he asked.

"Well yes of course *he's* your only competition... but Ecklethorpe is still young, so your head start shouldn't leave you with anything to worry about now should it?" the King answered. Rowdun closed the door behind him with much to think about. The third and youngest brother, Ecklethorpe lacked a subtitle next to his name. It was something a Slayer had to earn and then persist to resonate with, like a trait which would define them as a warrior. Hundo was a strategist and always knew the best possible plan of attack, Rowdun was untouchable in battle and had never seen his own blood, but although Eck was strong willed and efficient for his age, he was still too young to be given a label – the seventeen year old would have to wait. Rowdun didn't like any of his brothers. None of them were taught to love, but the Woundless was the most putrid of the three. Eck on the other hand looked up to Hundo, but compassion and appreciation was affecting his relentlessness – something Zamanite was passionate in passing on to his children.

Hundo slumped in his armchair smoking his pipe, staring at the various paintings on the wall, each retelling a famous moment in Slayer history. He wished for his legacy to be illustrated and framed one day, wearing a crown and holding the head of a deadly creature, unaware of Zamanite's refusal to ever make his dream a reality. The unhealthy yearning to be the greatest filled all three of the Princes' heads with fragile egos and distorted perceptions of reality, as though the only thing that mattered in life was fighting to the top. Their strong beliefs made them stubborn and unconcerned about other global issues which was useful seeing as though they were the cause of most problems. Their allegiance with Yewnin, a non-Slayer, was unheard of, but the King's decisions were never challenged or questioned. He was relentless in more ways than one, and not only did it resonate inside of him, it poisoned his son's hearts and souls the same way. Hundo often thought of killing his Father in the ultimate act of Slaying dominance, but he still had many years to train. In the meantime, he taught Eck how to fight, as well as leading missions alongside Rowdun. "What did Father say?" Eck asked, startling Hundo and crumbling his day dreams. He coughed on his pipe and turned to face his brother, "He said nothing," he sighed.

"Nothing?"

"Nothing important at least". Hundo wanted Eck to see him as a strong and bold character to respect so he didn't go into detail about Zamanite's disappointment. Hundo felt the hatred heavily from Rowdun and his Father, so he made sure Eck appreciated him because no one else would, in case the time came that he needed assistance. "I wish I could join you on your adventures," Eck sulked.

"A few more years". Rowdun entered the room and took a seat at the other side of the room, pretending he didn't notice his brothers, subtly rolling his eyes to himself instead. "How many did you kill today?" Eck asked. Hundo paused to think for a moment, "Probably around twenty-five. The soldiers did most of the work, we were a last resort," he answered.

"Well I killed thirty-two," Rowdun chimed in. Hundo shook his head to Eck causing him to snigger. Rowdun leant back on his chair to get a better view of them. "What's so funny?" he huffed.

"You always lie," Eck giggled. The Woundless jumped out of his chair and charged towards them both with a great scowl. "You weren't there, tiny… so stop trying to tarnish my reputation," he warned.

"You sound just like Father," Hundo coughed on his pipe again.

"I bet I would kill more than you if *I* was allowed to go!" Eck whined in Rowdun's face.

"Big talk from the teenager with no title. You shouldn't even be in here… these are *our* quarters, so get out". Rowdun pushed him over and stomped back to his chair. He played with his knife on the table, hoping for and thinking about a future encounter with Yewki, whilst Hundo sat back and dreamt of being the next King of death. Eck had ran out in such a hurry he didn't bother to close the door. He had no Mother to run and cry to because her life had been left a mystery to him. Eck had no memories of her, and no one else spoke of her. He had burning questions regarding her name, where she was and what she was like, but he didn't dare ask. It was as though her life was purposely stamped out of existence to forcibly grow his independence, which wasn't an uncommon practice.

Eck was no stranger from storming out of the castle. At least five royal guards would follow him against his will as protection though, but it was the furthest he could get away from family affairs. The courtyard wasn't good enough of an escape, he felt most comfortable in the midst of the city, which was ironic due to the sporadic bloodshed. A regular street would be drowning in loud merchants, boasting their low prices and deals, but the only screams and shouts were that of arguments and pain. It was not what Eck concentrated on, or thought about at all. Eck remained thoughtless and empty whilst trying to lose himself in the congested streets. He would be given stares of fear or anger depending on the person's views towards the royal family. Zamanite's family rule dated back at least one hundred years. Since then, the kingdom had started to die and the barbaric laws of the Slayers were taken all the more seriously, leaving families and rival bloodlines torn in half figuratively and literally – like a mouldy blood stain on the land that never washed out, but grew all the more rotten as the years went by. Money wasn't a concept that the people believed in. Their wealth was their kill count, and their collections of stolen possessions that they pillaged on dragon back, claiming resources and materials as their own the moment they'd lay eyes on it. Whilst most kingdoms would have harbours and docks for goods to come in and out of, the only ships that sailed were that of the royal family. Cargo would move in the air by the Dragon Port, being the first and only of its kind in the world, consisting of a bombardment of flying beasts, picking up and dropping things off. It truly was the cruellest land of all, sucking the life out of the rest of the world by using its dragons as leeches. Eck would enjoy watching the chaos at the port when dragons would crash into each other and men would fight for a place to land. The disorganisation was entertaining for a young adult but problematic for the actual adults risking their lives and their dragons, all for stolen food and resources. "Perhaps you should consider stepping back a few paces, my Prince," a royal guard suggested to Eck, as he etched his way closer into the action, completely ignoring them. Dragon tails swooped so low it created a gust of wind in his face but he didn't care about the danger, only the spectacle. A grubby toothless drunkard noticed the royal guards invading the port with Eck and began gathering the attention of others. "Look, the Princes are trying to ruin our livelihood!" he croaked. Eck noticed his guards intervening with the man, aiming their spears towards him, so he intervened himself to eradicate the confusion, "No, I'm just here to watch," he explained.

"Shut it, runt," the man spat.

"How dare you speak to the Prince in such a way!" a royal guard shouted, knocking the man to the floor. Bystanders gathered round and whispered between each other as they waited for the audacious man to be executed. "My Prince, the honour is yours," the guard informed, handing him his dagger whilst the others pinned the man down on his knees. Spectators began chanting their own opinions until there was just mashed-up babble. Eck's escapism had been cut short and his normal life of killing had leashed him back to reality. "I don't wish to kill today. I came here only to collect my thoughts," he proclaimed, dropping the dagger on the floor and walking off. The whole crowd fell silent and gob-smacked including the guards as they tried to catch up with the Prince. "My Price, I don't think your Father would be best pleased with your actions, or rather, *lack* of action," a guard warned. Eck didn't respond, he was too angry to think about the repercussions. He journeyed back to the castle in hopes of a stress-free evening.

The cold night had come and all drama had ended for just a moment, until screams and cries filled the corridors close by to Eck's room, where he sat up in bed startled, alarmed and prepared for the worst. There was no knock on the door, only a shove followed by Zamanite, two guards and the man from the port. "How can you sleep easy knowing you have unfinished business, boy?" the King hissed. Hundo and Rowdun ran into the room to get a good view of the show. "Please, spare me!" the bloody man whimpered.

"Take it," Zamanite ordered, waving a sword at Eck. "Take it!" he roared, throwing the sword on the ground. Eck scurried down to pick it up and aimed it at the blubbering civilian. The two of them looked at each other in the eyes. The man was tearful and sorrowful but Eck maintained a neutral composure. "He doesn't dare," Rowdun chuckled. As soon as the Woundless finished his sentence, Eck had sliced the man's throat, "I have killed dozens of people, and this man is no exception!" Eck yelled with a lump in his throat, feeling compromised in front of the whole family. His young spirit was still learning the fundamentals of keeping in line. The innocent teenage mind battled with the traits his Father expected, so he would often snap and transform into a murderous maniac when feeling challenged. It was a dangerous conflict of polar opposite characteristics, and only time would tell which side of him would dominate. Blood spilled all over Eck's bedroom and a grin curled up on Zamanite's face. "You're a disappointment... but there's still time for redemption," he muttered. Rowdun and Hundo followed the King out to leave Eck alone with the dead body staining his floor. He no longer felt like sleeping, but he was tired on the inside – tired of being looked down upon like the black sheep of the family. The only way for him to prove everyone wrong was to leave behind his apprehensions and focus on being the killing machine his Father desired. At that point, he was truly following in his manipulated brother's footsteps.

Chapter 11

Two Heads and Two Sides

King Zamanite the Relentless arched over a large table within his private quarters, observing a greatly detailed map. Huge areas of land and islands were covered with markings to keep note of all the locations the Slayers had control of. From East to West, North to South, the map was littered with big and small symbols, as well as the odd line which showed the paths his soldiers moved in. It was full of intricate strategies built up from centuries of war and misdeeds, and it was the King's duty to manage everything and ensure the best outcome for his kingdom. Worryingly, the giant land of Magmalia was covered in polluted Slayer markings more than anywhere else. The grandest and noblest of places was also carrying the greatest of all infections, which over time would puss and boil into fruition, destroying Zamanite's largest obstacle in the way of complete domination. If his spy within the Paladin circle continued to do their work, the next few years would bring the biggest downfall the world would ever see, and Zamanite would be the greatest ruler that ever graced the land of Emmrin-Rashmada. Before he could get too engrossed with the map, one of his elite guards entered. "My King, Yewnin has returned and requests your presence," they announced.

"Very well," the King responded with a monotone voice. He made his way down the many stairs and towards a large room. To his surprise, Yewnin had already let himself in and awaited his arrival whilst sitting on a large, round table. The room was covered in gold and ornamental flames. The table was worn but sturdy, as it served many Slayer Kings faithfully since the dawn of their kingdom. Yewnin leant forward in his chair, holding something tight in his hands. "Only the Slayer King and his highest officers may sit at that table," Zamanite huffed. The rude guest didn't seem to care and continued to stare at his possession, resting his forearms upon the sacred table. "I apologise, your majesty," he finally responded, breaking out of his trance. "The Day Relic, I have it," he continued whilst waving his prize in Zamanite's face. The relic glimmered beautifully as the King gazed upon it. "I'm well aware. My sons, Rowdun and Hundo informed me. I hope they served you well on the high seas," the Relentless said.

"Of course, I must thank you for your services. Destroying those harbours was no small feat… your soldiers are certainly talented. And providing me with such a large vessel is something I will never forget. Your services are honourable, unlike other kingdoms in this vile world. Although, I heard that your sons failed to destroy my brother and that measly ship he sailed on… now he could be anywhere," Yewnin expressed.

"Well, you could have destroyed them yourself".

"No, I needed time to train with the relic. Even so, before I knew it, I was transported to the middle of nowhere. I could feel my body shift from the Veranic Ocean to an… *impossible* place," Yewnin hinted, not feeling comfortable with telling Zamanite where his body was moved to when he vanished on the Dragon Breaker ship.

That day, against his will, his body and soul had been dropped in front of a burning house in the middle of the night. The flames were wild and monstrous, blazing high above the roof of the building and bursting out of broken windows. The wooden structure began to collapse in on itself as two boys in their teenage years ran out of what was left of the doorway. They dragged one another out of the way of falling debris and growing fires. The youngest one tried to run back in, but the other boy pulled him back and held him tightly. There was something precious inside of the house that both of them cried over, but only one of them was foolish enough to try and go back inside. They struggled and pushed one another until they had broken apart, allowing the seemingly suicidal of the two to jump into the deadly house without hesitation. After a daunting wait, the older boy ran in after him. Yewnin watched on at the events unfolding as though he already knew the outcome – like a story he had heard or been a part of, but more like a memory from an age ago. A few minutes passed, and the boy that entered last was dragging the younger one out, as he was unconscious, failing to obtain what he had gone back in for. "Wake up, brother!" the older boy wailed to his sibling. His brother's legs were covered in horrific burns but he wasn't dead, as he eventually let out a cough and began to groan in pain. Yewnin looked at his own bare legs and how they were covered in scars left behind from the blazes of his past. The youngest boy was actually him, so not only had Yewnin moved location, he had moved through time, only to observe his own repressed memories from an external point of view. The other boy was of course Yewki, his older brother. He had rescued him from the fire, but their brotherly love and loyalty didn't last long after that night. Suddenly, Yewnin had awoken upon the floor, as though the haunting reminder was just a dream, but his body had indeed transported, and onto a random field far from civilization nonetheless. The scorching heat of the sun pressed down on his face, as though the Day Relic amplified his connection with the great day-bringer in the sky. He thought that the relic was responsible for the forceful recollection of past memory, but he didn't know why.

"What do you mean, *an impossible place?*" Zamanite asked.

"It's not important," Yewnin lied. "What matters is that I have had time with this amazing tool… time to study and observe," he continued.

"And?" The King asked.

"I have learnt to welcome it into my soul as one with me. I can equip it at will and use its unparalleled power as I please. Great beams of light can be summoned from my hands, my feet are unshackled from the forces of gravity and I can travel through the air like a winged beast," he gloated.

"Impossible," Zamanite scoffed.

"The trust you placed in me to find this relic, the promises I spoke of... and after all that, you choose not to believe me?" Yewnin sniggered whilst levitating slightly above the ground as his eyes glowed yellow. The King took a step back to observe the mad man's use of the Day Relic and smiled like a giddy child. "The most unimaginable force of power the world has ever seen... all contained within that one artefact. The Slayers would benefit greatly with such a tool of destruction," Zamanite cackled. Yewnin dropped back to the floor and shoved the relic inside of his cloak with a troubled face. "You wouldn't be planning on taking it from me would you?" he asked.

"Not at all".

"Good, because it is not made to be held by mere men. It would consume you whole". Zamanite didn't appreciate the belittlement and thought about killing him where he stood, but their allegiance wasn't yet resolved and they still had plans to see through before he could take action against Yewnin's audacity. Their joining of force was tense and sometimes dysfunctional, but the King stood by it and looked towards the greater picture and the end result, for that was the only thing stopping him from slicing Yewnin's throat right there and then. Instead, he clenched his fists and bit his lip, then took a big exhale. "You know, we Slayers don't usually form with outsiders," the King warned.

"Now, now, Zamanite... remember our agreement".

"The fact you feel on par with the likes of me is outstanding. So naive". Yewnin had no need to reply because he knew full well that he was the furthest from naive than anyone else in the kingdom. He had no time to argue back, as he lacked the patience to explain how primitive the Slayers were compared to him.

After their greeting, they both went for a seemingly friendly stroll, but in reality, they wanted to kill each other. Zamanite escorted

Yewnin to the most sacred area of the kingdom, in hopes that he would be foolish enough to disrespect the King in front of the great statue of Emmrin-Rashmada, giving him an excuse to demolish his body and take the relic for himself. The Slayers were certainly savage, but their admiration and fanatic worship for their god brought out their creative side. Before them stood an incredible two-headed dragon, made of pure gold with red rubies for eyes and showered in other various gems and stones. Its huge wings wrapped around, casting a shadow as the metal gleamed in the sunlight. Both heads were identical, and their expressions were also the same. The only difference was that one head was raised higher than the other. "Behold our ruler, our mighty god, Emmrin-Rashmada," Zamanite applauded.

"Fancy," Yewnin muttered.

"One body, yet two minds. Notice how the left head, Emmrin, stands taller than the right, Rashmada. Emmrin shared his vessel with his counterpart as a symbol of balance, but Rashmada saw his extension as a parasite. He wanted to rid himself of Emmrin so that he could do as he pleased, and after a while, Emmrin wanted the same, but he wasn't as vocal about it. Both wanted their version of good, and both wanted to eradicate their version of bad, but they couldn't do so with different views. It shows that order and chaos cannot coexist… and one *has* to dominate. It's unknown as to which head symbolises order and which head symbolises chaos… all we know is that Emmrin was the victor and Rashmada did as he was told from then on".

"They wanted to destroy their own duality, rather than reach an agreement? No wonder you Slayers are so-".

"Relentless?" Zamanite grinned. "Man obtained the loyalty of Emmrin-Rashmada by fulfilling his requests. Their order was to rid the world of the weak so that only the strongest could ascend to greatness. We take our place in the heavens thanks to our compliance to the Great Dragon… and we end anything or anyone that gets in our way," he elaborated. Yewnin could tell that the King was trying to make a comparison with the two of them and Emmrin-Rashmada. Both wanted to be the leader and both wanted to control the other, but only one of them would be successful. Zamanite looked at Rashmada's lower head and thought of Yewnin, whilst Yewnin did the same about him. "So Emmrin shows strength and dominance, and Rashmada is a constant reminder that there will always be a greater competitor that stands in your way?" Yewnin wondered.

"Exactly. And it is our goal to reach the end of the line – to encounter our greatest competitors in hopes to die honourably alongside our god, on par with his excellence. In the meantime, we prove our worth by being the greatest threat the world has ever seen... and our job would be much easier with the Day Relic," the King murmured. Yewnin laughed and shook his head before walking away. "I couldn't care less about your need for bloodshed, but at least we seek the same outcome," he replied, then ordered two guards to lead him to the main gates, leaving Zamanite alone with the shining statue. "I take it we're going ahead with our next phase?" the King shouted across to him.

"Indeed. It's time to gather up the Shamans," Yewnin shouted back. Young Ecklethorpe had been nearby listening in to the conversation. It made him sick knowing that his Father would stoop to the likes of working with the outsider. Suddenly, Rowdun the Woundless crept up behind his younger brother and threw him out of the shadows by his neck. "Father, Eck was spying on you again," he laughed. Zamanite turned his nose up at Ecklethorpe who was sprawled out at his feet, then sighed with a scowl. "If the only thing you're good for is snivelling around like a slug then perhaps I should have made *you* my Magmalian spy," Zamanite scoffed.

"Forgive me, Father. I just don't trust that man, Yewnin," the teenager stuttered.

"Neither do I, but I don't expect him to trust *me* so it's only fair".

"But what of the risks?"

"There are no risks on our side. He's the one throwing himself at those dangerous artefacts and uncharted territories, we merely reap the benefits. And trust me, the Relic of Day will be mine the second he slips up. They'll come a time very soon where I assign you, sons of mine, as his bodyguards. You'll be there when he falls and you will retrieve the relic for me, do you understand?"

"Yes, Father," both Rowdun and Eck said.

"Inform Hundo and get out of my sight". The brothers ran back to the castle, allowing Zamanite to stand alone with the magnificent statue. He had a lot to calculate in terms of the destruction of Magmalia. His spy would soon have to thin the herd of Paladins to increase the chance of victory – all the King had to do was give the order, but for the time being, he just wanted to be by himself with nothing to think about but the love he had for his god.

Chapter 12

Answers and Apologies

There was another six days of isolation and slop consumption before the voyage finally came to an end, when the shattered Dragon Breaker reached land at long last. The distance they travelled mainly consisted of drifting as the last mast standing barely pushed them along. They had found themselves in the land of Dewhills, where forests were plenty and the majority of mystical Shamans resided. A river branched off from the open sea which was where the three adventurers parted ways with the Sea-Thieves. They had kindly given them two small boats to sail down once Yewki gave them all of his money. He and Wick brushed their oars through the relaxed river, with the second boat tied with rope closely behind for Moon to sit in. He looked in the water at all the fish, tempted to jump in to fill his incredibly empty stomach. Wick and Yewki were hungry too, but they wanted to push on to their destination before sundown. Wick looked at the beautiful blossoming trees to his side and thought of the bear. "Do you think Moon would prefer to be set free? I can't imagine he enjoys being on boats," he wondered.

"Set free? If he wanted to leave he would. Look at him, the cuddly giant needs you," Yewki chuckled. It was awkward for them to make much more conversation due to Yewnin being on both of their minds. Yewki knew Wick would have questions so after an agonising hour of silence, he finally gave in and attempted to explain. "Before I go into detail, I just want to know what you think of me," he prompted. Wick's heart rate increased in preparation for the awkward discussion they were about to have. "Well, I don't know much. You left me out of grown-up talks and I noticed you tried to tell me as little as you could," Wick answered.

"So what do you think of me?"

"Well I used to think you were an honest warrior who I happened to bump into, but now I don't know anymore. Now you seem more like a liar". Yewki accepted Wick's response because it was true, but he couldn't help but sigh. "Just to be clear, I would never try to hurt you or Moon, okay? The thing is, some people see me as a threat because of who my brother is".

"And who *is* your brother exactly?" Wick moaned.

"Well, Yewnin didn't used to be how he is now. He was loyal and full of spirit. He was just as much my best friend as he was my little brother. We lived together… until our parents died".

"How did they die?"

"It was an accident… but he blamed himself for it. Then after a few years… we went our separate ways. He spent most of his time travelling to ancient libraries and raiding tombs, fixated on mysticism. Over the grieving years, his drive turned into poisonous intrigue, and searching for knowledge led to the slaughtering of hundreds of Shamans".

"Knowledge on what?"

"On bringing our parents back from the dead". Yewki faced away in case he'd shed a tear. "At first he wanted to fix his mistake, but the deeper he dug, the more secrets of the world he uncovered. He soon left his desire to make things right behind along with his old self… now he's a different person, but the hard part is that he has the same face as my brother".

"What does he want?"

"He knows so much about how the world works spiritually, it's inhuman. In terms of his plan, right now it looks like he just wants to become some sort of god… that's surely why he took the Relic of Day.

His reasoning as to why is still unclear to me, but the fact that the Slayers have chosen to work by his side must mean that a great amount of death will come into play eventually". Yewki slumped his head down, "He was in so much pain... so much despair... but now whatever he's learnt has corrupted him. It's sad to think we were alike at one point". He wiped tears from his eyes as subtly as he could. The story of his brother brought back memories of happiness and how it would never be the same. It was horrifying for him to know that it was ultimately good intentions that drove Yewnin mad. Wick surprised him with a comforting hug which both of them seemed to need. "Just don't keep things from me anymore," Wick pleaded.

"Well is there anything else you want to know?" Yewki asked. Wick thought hard for a moment about things he didn't quite understand, but the list was rather endless. He decided to ask just one more thing so that the whole boat ride wouldn't consist solely of annoying questions. "So who *was* the Relic's protector in the maze?" he said. Yewki begged for any question but that, for even the thought of answering made him nervous. "You'll most likely meet him soon, when we join up with my friends. I'll be honest with you, I hope he doesn't show... because he's going to be furious," he answered.

"Is that where we're going now, to meet your friends?" Wick gulped. He was anxious thinking about meeting accomplices of Yewki, especially when one of them was supposedly angry at their failure. "Yes, but I use the term, *friends,* lightly for the most part". They continued to row as the sun turned orange with the arrival of dusk. "We still have quite a way to go until we get to them. Luckily, the Dragon Breaker was heading in a Westerly direction so it didn't throw us off too far when we arrived here in the Dewhills".

The summer heat kept them warm despite it being so late in the day. The river had escorted Yewki into familiar terrain just like he hoped it would. He explained to Wick how the Dewhills used to be home to an amazing race of chemists ahead of the curve. Although the majority of their structures had eroded away through war and time, Yewki used to visit one of the few remaining buildings high up in the hills, home to an incredibly smart man; Piea Fellow, who carried the last bloodline of Western chemists. Once Yewnin began the killing of Shamans, Piea tracked Yewki down to make sure the brothers weren't working together. Yewki provided information on Yewnin like no one else could, proving him worthy of joining Piea's cause. He soon discovered that the chemist's mission was bigger than just the two of them, as he introduced him to others from around the world. Men and women of all races and species had banded together to form a secret council with the sole purpose of preventing global catastrophes. It was the reason why Yewki knew the Dewhills so well, because their base of operations lay within the Fellow ruins of old. "It kind of reminds me of how I met you. Piea dragged me into his world, and I'm doing the same to you," Yewki smirked to Wick.

A thin fog floated just above the grass and through the trees on either side of the river. It was calming to gaze upon along with the pink clouds above, but their ride was coming to an end and night time crept around the corner. Yewki steered them towards an old embankment and climbed out first to check the area for threats. He then pulled Wick out of the boat and waited for Moon to collect the courage needed to jump out of his. The clumsy bear fell into the water but quickly clawed his way out and onto the grass, where Wick and Yewki stood and laughed. He shook his fur right in their faces, spraying them with the cold mist, but the fun turned into awe when Yewki looked across to the opposite side of the river. "Wick, look," he muttered, pointing over the water towards an elderly woman. She was marked with white clay lines on her cheeks and chin, and her ears drooped with heavy hoops hanging from them. "Is that a Shaman?" Wick asked.

"Yes! It's nice to that they are still roaming these parts… although their numbers are now scarce". They both felt her ominous and divine-like presence as she raised her wooden staff. "We must bow in respect," Yewki prompted, and so they did, with Moon even joining in and lowering his head. The Shaman got on with collecting water with her bucket, then walked back into the trees behind her. "That was a wonderful sight indeed," Yewki smiled. Shamans were incredibly spiritual people with a proficient understanding of the Earth. They spent years learning the art of divination until they could feel the world through their souls, like placing an ear on a chest to listen to a heartbeat. There was an element of soothsaying but it wasn't as simple as telling the definitive future. Masters could connect themselves to all organic life at once, calculating possible outcomes depending on what they could feel happening around the world. The Slayers were famous for kidnapping Shamans for that purpose alone, giving them the edge in war and conflict. It was extremely unethical, as they would usually be slain once they had fulfilled their purpose, treating them like nothing more than a non-renewable source of power. There was no doubt that the Shamans were dying out at an alarming rate, and things became worse the moment Yewnin started to devour their knowledge too. There was a sense of jealousy within him, knowing that he would never connect to the world as easily as the mystic masters. Someone couldn't become a Shaman over time – they were chosen from birth by the world itself, and Yewnin disliked missing out on such a blessing. Yewki reflected on the good and bad side of divination – how Shamans helped create peace around the world, and how Yewnin used the knowledge gained from it to destroy.

Both he and Wick were mute whilst their heads filled with depressing thoughts as they walked. The forest hike was rigorous and hilly. They often had to pull themselves forwards using trees, in fear of falling back down the steep slopes. Moon's sharp claws helped him cling onto the gooey soil with ease but he still trailed behind, keeping cautious to prevent any slippages. Their legs thanked the heavens as the ground began to level out at the top of a hill. "Just a few hours out now I believe. I want to get there before the bear holds us up with that weird, moon-stare thing," Yewki panted, rolling his eyes at Moon.

"I feel like a burden," Wick sobbed out of nowhere.

"Hey, don't be a fool," Yewki stopped walking for a moment to place his hand on Wick's shoulder and Moon looked across with sadness in his eyes. "You're doing something important and I got in your way. You were too nice to leave me and now you're paying the price," Wick sniffled.

"The same outcomes would occur if I was on my own. Besides, you and that bear have helped me as well as kept me company. Just remember... everything happens for a reason. Perhaps I was meant to find you". His urge to ditch the boy with someone else had left his mind for the time being, as though he and Moon were now a part of the team. Their forced teamwork in the maze had built on their friendship, and it was something they both felt, but neither of them had spoken about it until that point. "But what significance do I carry?" Wick moped.

"Well you have a strangely domestic bear for a start!" he sniggered.

"But what about me? What's so important about me? Maybe you were meant to just find Moon".

"Well even if that *was* the case, which I doubt it is, he'd refuse to leave your side, so you'd have to come along. You have a necklace with a miniature version of him on it. The two of you are as important as each other, I'm sure. Also, I'm going to assume you should keep it around your neck at all times. I don't know what it is or what it means, but it clearly signifies a connection between you both. I'd be worried that something would happen if you were torn from it". Yewki looked back at the bear and how their relationship had grown whilst both looking after the boy. "I just wish I could remember everything," Wick exhaled.

"I'm sure it's- oh no, not now!" Yewki groaned as he noticed the bear sitting down to begin his favourite part of the evening. The two of them tried to push and shove Moon, but his heavy lump of a body wouldn't budge. He stared up into the night sky, staring at the pearly white circle above through a break in the clouds. Wick and Yewki gave up and sat down to rest, letting him finish his ritual-like gaze before they pushed on with the final few miles.

Chapter 13

The Unwelcome Drum

It had gone past midnight for the three of them and their draining walk had eaten away at the majority of their energy. Thicker fog seemed to have rolled in from nowhere and insects began to make their diverse noises. Wick was slumped forward on the bear's back, struggling to stay awake, but the sudden jolt of Moon halting woke him up. "Are we here?" he asked. Yewki scanned the nearby hills and trees then turned to the two of them. "Yes, we're here," he announced. He picked up the pace, recognising more and more of the environment. To Wick, he looked like a predator sniffing out prey, but in reality he was finding the entrance to the underground hideout. "Here we are, hurry," Yewki pointed. He scampered into a tight hole like a rabbit, followed by Wick. Moon wasn't as eager to enter however. He sniffed and looked around, not entirely convinced that he would even fit. "Come on, boy," Wick hollered. The bear began to squeeze inside with help from Wick tugging on his neck fur. His large rear soon became an issue whilst his back legs flung dirt into the air as he pushed. With an almighty heave, the disgruntled beast forced his way completely inside, which left the muddy entrance permanently wider. He shook his dirty fur and caught up to Yewki who was halfway down the shaft. The narrow pathway soon grew larger into a full corridor for them to properly stand in, and the muddy floor had died down which revealed a brick path. The more they walked, the more the underground pass seemed more like a buried building. The tunnel soon turned to reveal a small open area, and the heat from a central fire quickly reeled them in. A man, two women and a strange male Troll sat around the flames. They were too deep in discussion to notice the three of them enter the room, but Moon's not so quiet footsteps soon boomed and echoed, gaining their attention. "Don't speak, boy," Yewki muttered.

"What?" Wick asked stupidly, followed by a swift yet gentle smack around the back of the head by Yewki. "Well that's certainly new," the man said with a deep croaky voice as he walked warmly towards the visitors. As he got closer, Wick examined his features. Like everyone else in the room, he was draped in terribly old clothes and fur. His shoulders were broad and his beard swung close to his waist, with the rest of his hair hidden under a thin, ripped hood. The man's right arm was missing and he walked with a limp. "Yewki! Ah yes, I'm glad you're not intruders," he shook his hand. "You *are* Yewki, yes?" He tilted his head with a squint. "Of course!" Yewki reassured.

"It's been what, eleven years? Forgive me for not truly recognising you," the man laughed as he put his hand on Yewki's shoulder. Wick tried not to stare too much at the man's missing arm but he was disrupted anyway when the man looked down at him with tired eyes and a weary smile. "Is this your son? My, you *have* been busy," he asked.

"No, no!" Yewki stammered, "It's not so simple, but I shall explain later".

"Disappointing," the man smirked. "So, let's not delay. What's your name, boy?" he asked, but Wick's lips were sealed. "Don't listen to Yewki, you can talk," he smiled.

"Greenwick," he said nervously.

"Nice to meet you, Greenwick. I'm Piea Fellow," he shook his small hand and quickly averted his eyes to the bear. "Such a beautiful creature you have here," he rejoiced, stroking Moon's fury head.

"The boy calls him, *Moon*. Again, I shall explain later. Or at least try".

"Delightful," Piea grinned as he gestured them towards the fire. The others were still deep in discussion when they came to sit down on the stone benches. Moon sat behind Wick. He was the most tired of the three and his paw still ached from the week before. "I'd usually eat bears," the large Troll grunted.

"Don't change the subject!" one of the women growled.

"The two women there are Thene and Lall. Thene is from the South and Lall is from the North. The smelly Troll is Tbrok," Piea informed.

"Where is he from?" Wick asked.

"He lives in Caverns-Colossal, but in terms of where he's actually from, we're not sure. He's so old, he's forgotten". Tbrok overheard them talking about him. He aimed his long nose in their direction which revealed his gruesome, old, grey face. One of his pointy ears had a chunk missing, as though it had been chewed off. Piercings covered his lips and cheeks, with beads and random dangling objects jingling and shaking as he moved his head to speak. "I'm not old!" he gargled.

"Compared to them you are. Rest assured, you're still young next to *me*," a sudden wispy voice came from the middle of the huddle. Piea looked towards the fire. "And that's Batehong". Wick was confused as he tried to look around the flames. "He's a spirit of fire," Yewki enlightened. They boy's incertitude turned to surprise, for what he thought was a simple camp fire turned out to actually be a member of the group. "I wouldn't advise getting too close to shake his hand," Piea joked. Wick was too amazed to laugh. The ugly Troll was enough to catch his eye, but the talking fire was even more of a wonder. "You're looking tired, Yewki," said Lall with the intent to insult. The two women sniggered to each other like giddy children. Both of them were dressed like experienced fighters, trained in diverse disciplines from opposite stretches of the world. Lall was slim with short hair and wore a breechcloth made of cow hide, wrapped onto her body with a leather belt, accompanied by flaps dangling down, reaching her sturdy leather shoes. There was an odd glove at her side made of the same material as her clothes, covered in holes and scratches which indicated that a bird of prey would often land on it. Thene looked a little more peculiar. Her facial features didn't match that of a traditional human – not one that Wick had seen before anyway. She wore a thin, grey woollen jacket and leggings coated with metal plates for protection.

Strangely, she wore no shoes, but her feet looked as rough and rugged as hands. Yewki sighed in response to the rude ladies. "We may not all get along, but if we feel obligated to come together, to discuss the future then please, it'd be incredibly helpful if we all stayed friendly and put aside our personal feelings". Lall rolled her eyes and scoffed, but the others nodded. Wick didn't have to be told about Yewki's past relationship with Lall, it was evident that there was once something between them which turned from good to bad. "I agree," Piea raised his voice, "Yewki is right. Our relationships, whatever they are, we need to leave them outside".

"We should feel lucky Lay-Vau hasn't turned up at least, or things would be much worse," Thene extended Piea's truce speech. Everyone grunted and nodded with relief. "We should get on with this," Tbrok rubbed his hands together sarcastically, knowing that their discussions would be tiring and mostly consist of bad news.

The adult's conversations seemed to never end. Wick didn't have a strong enough attention span to listen completely. Weary from the long journey and unable to contribute to the conversation, he fell to sleep on Moon. "I'm at the end of my wits with your brother," Thene complained to Yewki.

"I've known you since you were a boy, just like the one by your side. I hope you don't take offence by this but I don't think you're strong enough to stop him yourself," Piea shook his head. Yewki tried not to get too annoyed. Everyone's negativity towards his duty was getting too much for him. "Yewki is not some sort of merciless Slayer. I can imagine it's difficult for him to come to terms with what he must do," Tbrok pitied him but it only offended him more. He felt useless around the group of prestigious characters. "If we all have to uphold our duties then you have no excuse to be so hesitant with yours," Lall growled as she punched the bench stone she sat on. Yewki stood up in anger. "Batehong. You've stayed awfully quiet. Do you have any insults for me too?" Everyone stayed silent awaiting the fire's response. "See here… there's a young man out there who thinks he's doing the right thing. He thinks he's destined to save this Earth. Frankly, he's delusional… and I think we can all agree that he's too far gone. This audacious killer, foolish enough to challenge life itself has to be stopped. Unfortunately for you, he happens to be your brother. You said yourself that you should be the one to end his conquest," Batehong said.

"Go on, say it," Yewki prodded.

"I'm worried that you will try and reason with him and bring him back to sanity… but he won't waste a second to silence you. If you can't stop him then we need to assign someone else to handle this. I'm sorry, Yewki," he continued.

"None of you have the right to handle my brother," Yewki raised his voice.

"Oh my, you still care for him don't you?" asked Thene.

"Of course I do!" his voice cracked slightly. "Do you think it's easy for me to see my younger brother change so rapidly, so scarily into a monster?" He turned away to shed a subtle tear. Piea stood up to comfort him. Yewki was practically a son to him. "Maybe at first you thought you could do this. Now you've seen him in action you can't come to terms with it. The Yewnin that almost killed you at sea is not the same Yewnin you grew up with".

"I just saw his face, it was so surreal. He wanted me dead but I just wanted to comfort him", Yewki shed more tears. "No one is challenging your strength or loyalty. We can assign Thene or Tbrok instead. Now that we know he's working with the Slayers, we might *all* need to help. This is bigger than we first thought," Piea assured. The two of them sat back down and Yewki wiped his eyes. "I'm sorry everyone, truly".

"No matter," Tbrok mumbled with a nod.

"The last few days have been long," Yewki raised his eyebrows and smirked.

"I feel sorry for the boy! Dragging him into this," Lall scowled.

"I almost left him be, but I just couldn't. He would have been taken or killed by the many dangers out there, you don't understand because you're heartless," Yewki argued.

"Trust me, he's in more danger with you," Lall fought back. They all looked across to the snoozing boy. He twitched and shuddered in his sleep as his mind was engulfed deeply in strange dreams.

Wick was back in the labyrinth. The Day Relic was in front of him but he couldn't touch it. He could hear unclear whispers behind him, but there was no one around. Suddenly, Yewnin appeared in front of him and snatched the relic. The labyrinth broke away and Wick was flung into an infinite space of grey. Yewnin held the Day Relic in his hand as its power seemed to absorb into his body. His eyes shined bright and fire grew from below. Wick ran but couldn't move, and the fires quickly consumed him. He saw Yewnin burn full forests to the ground in the blink of an eye and the Earth began to crumble as lightning struck distant mountains. Wick panicked, unable to move or wake up from his dream. "Don't worry, it's not your fault," mysterious whispers flooded the air. He turned around and saw a fat, middle-aged man laughing. He was dressed in old leaves and bones. His necklace consisted of sharp, pointy teeth from a mixture of different creatures. The man's eyes glowed just like Yewnin's when he consumed the relic's power earlier in the dream. "You didn't know what you were getting into. But you have to be punished on behalf of Yewki's failures," he continued.

"I don't understand!" Wick cried.

"It's just the rules I'm afraid". The spectral man began to walk towards Wick with no regard for personal space or boundaries. "No! Why? I don't want to be punished!" Wick panicked. The man disappeared and reappeared right in front of him. "Just bang the drum, and I won't!" he smiled then turned into a ball of light. Wick woke up and jumped. He accidentally woke Moon up but he soon closed his eyes again and dozed off. None of the adults noticed him wake up in dismay as they were still discussing important matters. Wick scrolled his eyes to the left. He had to look twice at a random worn and dirty drum. It was small and wooden and looked like it could rip if it was hit slightly too hard. Small rodent skulls dangled around the lid. Feathers and straw poked outwards around the base. Wick forgot about the important conversation going on and interrupted. "Where did that drum come from?" he asked. No one else tried to look too surprised or worried, but deep down they were sickened. "Ah, at last. The final member has arrived," Piea applauded.

"Greetings, Lay-Vau," said Lall. Wick expected the drum to magically respond just like the fire did but there was a dead silence. Piea noticed Wicks puzzled face. "Lay-Vau isn't very sociable, but he acknowledges how important this meeting is. He knows he can be dangerous so he's kindly kept himself within his drum". Lay-Vau's drum seemingly listened to the discussions but of course never spoke. Yewki leant over to Wick. "Don't touch the drum," he stressed. The command seemed random and out of nowhere, but he knew it must have been important for Yewki to say it. Unfortunately it only made him more curious about the instrument. The more he stared, the more silent everything around him became. He soon felt a pulling sensation towards it as though it was wanting to draw him closer. He remembered the strange man in his dream mention the banging of a drum. He played his dream back in his head, the fear of being punished and the scary man. He thought to himself, "Was *Lay-Vau*, the man within the drum, the person from his dream?" Wick refused to go back to sleep and tried not to stare at the drum in the meantime. "We're sorry for not protecting the Day Relic as we promised," Yewki said with angst towards Lay-Vau's drum.

"*We?* No, *you* let Yewnin take it!" Lall shouted. "I think I can speak for everyone else here when I say this; you failed, we didn't".

"Now, now, Lall. What did we say earlier?" Piea attempted to mediate the tension.

"No! We've all risked our lives have we not? The Earth's lands are vast and dangerous, we've all had our share of long travels and conflict, yet Yewki is the only one to fail," Lall grumbled, finally losing what patience she had left. "Lall, please".

"No, Piea. Do not fight for me," Yewki interrupted. Wick was used to seeing Yewki as the strongest person in a group, but he seemed small for once as the wise and angry people around him pushed his morale deep underground. It shed Yewki in a different light than what Wick was used to, and he empathised him for it. Moon was woken by the squabbling and walked away into another room. "The bear is right. I think we're due for a break," Tbrok exasperated. Yewki wasted no time and left for another nearby room as well. Batehong's flames dimmed and everyone began to move. Piea put his hand on Wicks shoulder. "Come with me, I'll show you around," he smiled. Piea guided Wick through the many corridors and rooms in the sunken temple.

Everything was old and struggling to stand in one piece. Wood was rotting and stone was cold and cracked. Wick didn't want to look too disgusted because he was aware of how much respect the old building deserved. Piea had told him that they were all inside of an ancient temple, and how it was once the home of his ancestors, when the Fellow family had a great impact in the weapons and explosives trade. The Fellows believed in peace and knew that it was imperative to protect, and protection came in the form of blacksmithing and chemistry. The temple symbolised their peaceful and spiritual side, to emphasise what kind of people they truly were, in the hopes that they weren't labelled simply as weapon forgers and dealers. They believed that their knowledge of explosives soon had to be used and provided to those in need, rather than sticking to their tranquil origins. The temple held vital details in craftsmanship and chemical concoctions written down, which soon became a grand library. "The Fellows were protective of their information. Their power soon invited challenge. Enemies would die for this information," Piea explained as he showed him around the maze of bookshelves. "As a last resort, they dug deep tunnels below the temple that would explode and collapse. It would bury the temple... as though it never existed".

"I'm assuming the enemies fought back too hard," said Wick.

"Yes, obviously the temple has been sunk and forgotten. These old books are incredibly outdated and are practically useless now, but it's nice to walk around what was once such an important establishment.

Now we use my ancestor's home as a meeting point to discuss important matters, far away from evil ears," Piea smiled and flicked Wick's ear. Thene entered the room, cradling a near-empty bowl of fruit in her arms and aimed it towards the two of them. "They say I'm a fierce warrior, but I'd much prefer people to know me for my kind hospitality". Thene's smile stood out among the rest. Her red hair and eyes contrasted greatly against her pale white skin. The Olash race were easily recognised by their fiery features as well as their near-flat noses. Their smiles stood out the most simply because it was their biggest feature. Wick picked the largest fruit he could to comfort his hunger as much as possible and Piea took two for himself. His need for twice the amount of food was affirmed as he had the excuse of old age on his side. They both scoffed away as Thene took a piece for herself. "Thank you," Wick let out.

"It's the least I can do. I feel sorry for you, being looked after by Yewki," she smirked.

"I think I would be dead without him". Wick began to fortify Yewki's strength which seemed to be overlooked and long lost by the others. "You may have been dead alone yes, but how many times have you almost died whilst in his company?" she asked. Wick had no response. "These journeys, these battles, it's not for you my child," she continued.

"Yewki has been teaching me. How to fight and stay alive! He's told me about the relic and what his brother plans. I see how much it hurts him, so at this point, I just want to help... he's the one who saved me after all. I'm returning the favour," Wick explained.

"You sound like clever boy, Wick. Surely you realise, he didn't save you from anything. He brought you into a life much worse than what it already was for you".

"I don't care if it's more dangerous with him, he takes care of me and Moon so I'd rather live like this than live alone".

"We understand your attachment to Yewki – I too have admiration for him. We just don't want to see a child in the middle of all of this chaos," Thene said in a calming voice.

"She's not wrong. Thene could take you to her village. You would be very safe there. Your bear would be welcome too I'm sure," Piea reassured. Wick swallowed the last of his fruit. "I'm sorry, but I want to stay with Yewki". He saw the disappointment on both the adults' faces. They couldn't bring themselves to use force, but they wished they could. "If that's what you want, child. But you're welcome anytime," Thene hid her sulk behind a warm smile momentarily then left. Piea handed Wick his second piece of fruit. "Here you go. Don't eat it now, mind. If you're going with that nomadic klutz then you need all the food you can get," he playfully sniggered. Piea saw Yewki emerging from the dark corridor and into the room. The cackling old man soon shut up and left him to talk with Wick. "We will see you both back in the hall shortly," Piea prompted as he waved, before left to catch up with Thene. Yewki waited for Piea to walk far enough away for him and Wick to talk in absolute privacy. "You should have accepted Thene's offer. But I'm happy that you stood up for me," he sighed whilst yanking Wick by the shoulder for a brief sideways hug. "I hope you're going to share that apple by the way". Wick stuffed the fruit up his sleeve and shook his head and the two of them chuckled. Their momentary happiness was stopped in its track as, out of nowhere, the air became cold, followed by a returning voice. "Hit it," it muttered.

"What?" Wick asked.

"I didn't say anything," Yewki proclaimed.

"Hit it!" the mystery voice spoke again. Only Wick seemed to hear it. The voice blew through the wind as though it was right next to him. "Again, he said, *hit it!*" Wick panicked.

"I hear no voice," Yewki stressed, looking around.

"Your punishment awaits!" the voice laughed. The word, *'punishment'* struck Wick through the heart. He tied the voice with the man from earlier, from his dream. There was no mistaking the connection between the dream, the voice, the drum and Lay-Vau. "The drum, boy. The drum!" The voice bellowed inside of Wick's head. He held his hands to his ears but it was no use. "You hear a voice?" Yewki asked.

"It's the man in the drum, I swear!" Wick yelled.

"What is he saying?" Yewki gasped.

"He says I must be punished! I need to hit the drum!" Suddenly, bookshelves began to fall. The two of them had to move out of the way and towards the exit. "Go! Quickly!" Yewki commanded. Paper flew out of books and more bookshelves creaked as they fell like ancient trees. He escorted Wick to the exit first to assure his safety, but as soon as Wick cleared through the doorway, the door slammed shut behind him. Bookshelves barricaded the door and stopped Yewki from leaving too. It was exactly what Lay-Vau wanted. Wick looked back at the blocked door and shook it violently. "Wrong way!" Lay-Vau laughed. An invisible force dragged Wick by the legs and down the corridor. His cries for help echoed but it would've taken a while for anyone to reach him. The floor before him began to rumble. Bricks pried themselves from the ground like the pulling of deep-rooted teeth and flew by his head. The stones that once made up the corridor floor were now constructing themselves into a wall behind him, then moved towards him, ushering him forward against his will. Wick pushed against the possessed barrier but the force was too strong. He reluctantly slid towards the hole that the animated bricks had left behind until he had no choice but to fall. The hole spat him out conveniently into the main hall below. Lall and Tbrok were startled by the sudden thud of Wick's body, also causing Batehong to brighten in surprise. "Now, I can't make you hit the drum, that's just the rules, but you're gonna have to for your punishment," Lay-Vau confessed. Tbrok and Lall ran towards Wick. "Tell them, if they touch you, they'll die!" the invisible menace ordered.

"Don't touch me! You'll die," Wick coughed. The two of them halted and stepped back in fear and confusion. "What's happening?" Lall screamed.

"It's just the rules," Lay-Vau whispered.

"*It's just the rules!*" Wick mirrored in pain. He struggled back onto his feet, not knowing what to do, then felt a tug on his neck. He looked down to see his precious necklace snapped off and on the ground. He didn't hesitate to grab for it, but it soon began to fly around the room, forcing him to chase it, unable to get close. "Come on, you need to be faster!" Lay-Vau chuckled. "It's not nice having something important taken from you is it?" The mysterious necklace landed on the stone benches. Wick slapped his hand down fast but missed. Again, the necklace landed but he was too slow. "Tell me boy," he muttered as the necklace landed on an object once more. "You ever heard of Voodoo?" Wick didn't respond and slammed his hand down one last time in anger, but the necklace moved out the way to reveal the drum. The impact sent a wave of sound throughout the entire temple. As his blind rage died down, he realised the mistake he'd made. The drum was hit – it was punishment time. Voodoo wasn't a word he recognised but he instantly felt like it was as a threat after watching Lay-Vau being released from within the instrument in all his glory. Wick felt like he was sleeping again, but he knew he wasn't as the pain was all too real. Lay-Vau's humongous body loomed over the cowering boy. He looked and dressed just as Wick envisioned him from the dream, but with a wider, more sinister smile. "You summoned him!" Thene screeched as her and Piea entered the hall, both wielding their weapons. "Now, now... it's *my* fault. I made him bang the drum," Lay-Vau smirked.

"We knew it was too much of a risk to seek your aid," Piea growled.

"I still would have come without an invitation, don't flatter yourselves. This little group meeting concerns me doesn't it? More than anyone else here!" Lay-Vau turned and frowned at Yewki as he scurried into the room out of breath along with Moon. "Please," Yewki begged, raising his hands, but Lay-Vau stood closer and interrupted. "My Relic is gone!" he laughed sadistically. "You let him take the one thing I exist for. Would you like it if I took your heart?" he asked. Wick had no idea what was going to happen. A part of him was furious for being left in the dark about important things. "Why don't I ever get told about stuff like this?! What's happening?" the confused boy bleated.

"I told you not to hit the drum!" said Yewki. Lay-Vau closed his bright eyes slowly, looking as though he was sifting deep into the boy's aura. "I can feel your confusion, child. You're too young for all of this but yet here you are". He opened his eyes and tilted his head in a condescending way. "Oh… the poor thing doesn't have a clue what voodoo is. Yewki, I knew you were a stupid man but inviting a child to your quest? You just want to see him die in your care, is that it? Some sort of twisted, morbid curiosity wishes you to doom the life of such a young sapling?" Yewki had no response to the taunt. He was too ashamed to think of a comeback. Lay-Vau was now in charge. The drum began to beat itself with a slow, rhythmic tap. "It'd be a waste if this boy died with such little education, don't you think?" He looked around knowing the group wouldn't actually answer – he knew he had them all in the palm of his hand. "Son, voodoo is amazing! Beautiful!"

"I don't think it is," Wick muttered as he looked at the others and their completely paralysed bodies, frozen in fear and despair. "You can't *know* something that you don't know! Or didn't you know that?" Lay-Vau swung his head back and laughed. "Voodoo is great! There's no leader, it can heal your friends… curse your enemies," he chortled whilst turning to look at the group. "We can exist in the physical *and* the spiritual world at the same time. You know what a spirit is?" He walked through a solid stone bench as though his body was suddenly made of air. Wick didn't care too much for his words, as he was too frightened to function. "Why don't you answer? I know you can talk at least". The spirit grew larger than any normal man could, striking even more fear into the eyes of the innocent. "Spirits are evil," Wick blubbered.

"Is that what you think?" Lay-Vau spat.

"You're providing the evidence to prove it. Please stop," Piea intervened calmly.

"Does that boy even know how important that relic was to me?" They could sense the stress and anguish from his voice alone. "It wasn't his fault," Lall had plucked an ounce of courage to contribute once Piea had spoken back. "I know, but I'm making him a martyr. That boy doesn't even know what sort of peril you've brought him into," Lay-Vau hissed, lifting Wick into the air without touching him. The spirit's body began to spark flames all over. "I'm what you call an *Iwa*. An Iwa is a lesser spirit powered by voodoo. Most men and women seek aid from us, or guidance. We're a symbol of good luck and prosperity... but abuse us and we can quickly become the opposite. It's rather ironic, we can heal the sick yet I find myself moments away from polluting your blood".

"Punish me as you wish instead, I beg," Yewki surrendered. The sly Iwa laughed some more. No one knew how to intervene, they just stood with their weapons close by. "What good would come from harming someone who has already lost the will to live?" Lay-Vau smirked. Wick pitied Yewki's exposed emotional state. "Even so, you weren't the one who summoned me. Rules are rules!" the intimidating voodoo master continued. Yewki swung his sword out of his sheath. "Don't you dare punish the boy," he threatened. Lay-Vau wasn't fazed by the sudden sword as he floated his way even closer towards Wick. Yewki looked at the others for help but their heads lowered, knowing the rules of voodoo. "Anyone touches me and they're dead," Lay-Vau stressed as he pointed his finger to the group, whilst staring intently at Wick. Moon grunted and ran towards him, but Batehong bent his flames in the bear's direction to block him from intervening. "He would kill him and you, bear," the flames warned. Moon wanted to jump through the fire but he acknowledged the warning. "No!" Yewki screamed.

"Live with the notion of ruining this boy's life. In my defence, you had ruined most of it yourself," he snarled at Yewki. Wick ran towards the nearest exit but Lay-Vau just followed behind with no sense of hurry. The doors slammed and locked before Wick could leave. "I can't just stand here," Yewki exclaimed.

"We have to. No power can stop an Iwa," Thene sighed. Lay-Vau finally grabbed Wick by the head. A dark green glow exited his fingertips and entered the boy's eyes. He screamed but couldn't move or do anything about the transferring curse. "Give me back my Day Relic and I may just fix this for you," Lay-Vau whispered. Wick collapsed to the floor as Moon tended to his side. Yewki marched towards the Iwa. "What did you do to him?!"

"Get away from me, fool".

"Tell me!"

"I gave him the power of voodoo. Not a simple conventional curse I confess... but you must understand how angry you've made me!" Lay-Vau knocked Yewki to the floor. Everyone but Wick and Yewki stood together and armed their weapons, knowing that they could do no harm, but hoping desperately for the end of the child's torture. "You only came to punish one of us, didn't you?" Tbrok croaked.

"Indeed. I wasn't even listening to your conversations... I couldn't have cared less".

"Well you've done what you came here for, now leave," Piea demanded.

"The Relic of Day brought me light and warmth. And now it's gone". Lay-Vau raised his hand and consumed Batehong whole. "Compensation," he elaborated on his actions whilst taking the life from Batehong's flaming embodiment. The room soon darkened as Lay-Vau disappeared instantaneously along with his drum. Tbrok began to spark a fire as the others looked around for Wick, with Moon eventually being the one to find his unmoving body with his inate sense of smell. The beast whimpered and nudged Wick until he woke back up. "Tbrok, quickly!" Yewki begged. A fire began to glow which slowly revealed Wick sat up against the doors with Moon licking his face. "What's happened? What did he do to you?" Yewki ran and grabbed him. "I feel like a sickness has hit me hard in my head and heart," Wick trembled and cried.

"Voodoo can't be consumed within a mortal vessel," Thene explained.

"What's going to happen to me?" Wick stammered. No one answered at first because no one knew. Yewki looked at the others for an explanation, expecting it to be a waste of time trying. "No one knows," he wept as he sat by Wick's side. His body felt as though it died every time he gasped for air. He treasured the short moment of life that filled his lungs until the next deathly exhale. His vision became blurry from time to time but he had to keep his eyes open. Every time he closed them he saw the dastardly face of the Iwa. His body felt like it was on fire until the moment of ultimate intensity, where the heat would then turn to incomprehensible cold. The words and sentences coming from the others echoed inside of his head along with the sound of the drum. The wrath of Lay-Vau had struck the entire temple. Although everyone was scared, they stayed focused and concerned on the matter at hand, even if they only understood a miniscule portion of what actually happened to Wick's body.

When midnight had passed and the early morning had crept, everyone was still completely awake and alert, excluding Wick who had been enduring the voodoo for over four hours. He couldn't sleep, but his body felt like a corpse. Conversations were put aside for the rest of the night as tension built. Piea and Yewki threw books and parchment around frantically as they looked for anything that could help Wicks curse, but none of the old chemistry notes came close to a cure. Moon had picked the boy's necklace up from the floor and passed it over to him, but he received no comfort from it as his body was full of painful distractions. "This is the end of the line, Yewki," Lall screamed, finally breaking the silence. "I'm taking the boy from you".
"No, I will take him to my village," Thene intervened.
"He's not going anywhere!" Yewki screamed with his hands full of paper scrolls.
"This didn't have to happen. The poor boy... and my dear friend, Batehong!" Tbrok cried. Moon stopped his whimpering momentarily and charged at Yewki, snarling and showing his teeth which was enough to stop Yewki's constant page turning. "Even the bear blames you," Lall pointed.
"I'm sorry, Moon. I gained your trust and promised to help protect him... and I've failed". The angry bear pushed him down to the ground with ease. Instead of trying to clamber back up, he stayed on the floor in shame as Moon walked back to Wick's side. "He said he gave him the power of voodoo... and we know he can't contain it in his human body," Piea attempted to begin a group brainstorm.

"He said he would pollute his blood," Thene contributed, causing Piea to gasp. He limped over to Wick and began looking around at his body. "Did you get any cuts from your fall through the roof?" he asked. Wick moved his arms and legs, scanning for any wounds whilst the others gathered around him uncomfortably as though they were spectating a freak show. After rolling up his sleeve, which was anything but a grand reveal, Wick's face dropped along with everyone else's as he revealed a small gash. The cut wasn't the issue, rather the disturbing colour of his blood. "Black blood," Lall trembled. The thick oil-like liquid trickled down his arm. He was too horrified to scream and shout, instead he gawked at the small, inky puddle that was being created on the floor. "I'm going to die aren't I?" Wick wallowed.

"We won't let that happen to you, child," Piea answered. "There are remedies for poisons".

"That's a curse, Piea," Tbrok spat. The Troll didn't have the same level of sensitivity around children that the others had, and it didn't help that he was completely defeated after the loss of Batehong. "We need someone who knows voodoo... a Shaman perhaps?" Lall suggested.

"The Shaman are in hiding. It could be too late by the time we find one... we don't know the severity of this," Piea said as he stroked his beard. Wick shivered relentlessly as Tbrok picked him up and positioned him closer to the fire. "We need help from someone... look at him," the Troll shook his head in remorse. Yewki's sad face turned to grimace and then back into sorrow. He sighed before speaking, knowing he was in no position to help anymore, but the boy's life was first priority. "I know a man... a Wizard to be exact".

"Wizards are more scarce than Shamans, you can't know anyone of such rarity," Lall denied.

"No, it's true. His name is Seffry. Now, I know magic and voodoo are different, but if anyone knows more than us, it's him".

"Yewki, magic is a dead discipline. Are you sure this man is a true Wizard?" Thene questioned.

"I promise you. I just can't promise he can fix it completely. I know where to find him. It's a rigorous distance for such a short amount of time we may or may not have… but it's our only hope". The group lacked trust in Yewki, but they had to put the child's health first. "If Lay-Vau gave him the power of voodoo then he can heal the sick just like an Iwa. He could learn how to use his abilities to heal himself. It would be keeping him alive as fast as it would be killing him. It's not a real fix but hopefully it can keep him alive long enough to find how to rid himself of it," Piea agreed.

"I wish I was available to escort you, Yewki. If we all didn't have dilemmas of our own to deal with then tonight would be the last time you'd ever see that boy," Lall complained.

"Make this right," Piea placed his hand on Yewki's shoulder.

"I know I don't deserve the company of this kind-hearted child. As soon as I revert the curse he's all yours, Thene," he accepted. She nodded and smiled subtly with excitement. Wick had no choice but to begin growing used to the new, invasive feelings in his bloodstream. Every beat of his heart hurt and his ears rang to no end. It was unclear as to how long it would take to adjust, and how long he had left until his body completely rejected the voodoo. Despite everything that had happened to him, he still respected Yewki. "I must be off," Tbrok informed out of nowhere as he dragged his heavy legs to an exit. The others were aware of his important mission so they followed him to say their goodbyes. "No, stay there, you must rest," Thene ordered Wick as she noticed him struggling to get to his feet. Thankfully, Moon supported him like a crutch. His legs were weak but he managed to walk with the assistance. "I want to say bye to the Troll", he stated, trying to keep his mind off of his current health. The group were surprised to see him walking but they respected it. "You must rest as soon as I've left. Promise me that," Tbrok pleaded.

"I'll make sure he does," Yewki answered for Wick. The Troll lacked any response and led the way as the band of warriors followed. "How many do you have in your fleet?" Thene asked.

"One hundred and thirty," Tbrok replied.

"Will that be enough soldiers?" Lall challenged.

"For the last time, woman – they're not soldiers, they're Trolls! Soldiers are people trained to fight, but we're *born* to fight," he wittily proclaimed.

"Where is he going?" Wick muttered.

"He's been assigned with stopping my brother," Yewki said as he looked down at the floor. Wick knew how much that quest meant to him but he acknowledged that a seemingly careless Troll would fare better for the task. "Where is your army?" Wick asked like the typical child he was, seeping with questions and curiosity to keep his mind distracted as the shock of overwhelming pain pressed down on his poor body. "Oh, miles and miles away from here," he answered.

"What if you don't stop him in time? It's going to take you ages to reach the other Trolls". The Troll was taken by surprise. He looked down at his own fat, impractical legs. "Does it look like I walked here?" he chuckled. They entered a large chamber where a fat, blubbery dragon lay sleeping. Wick was in awe. He'd never encountered such an odd-looking dragon before. "What is that?" he asked.

"A Jevetin, lad," Tbrok answered as he mounted. The brown dragon woke up and stood up slowly on its measly legs whilst its wide mouth yawned. Thene jumped onto the back along with the Troll without request. "I don't want you to underestimate Yewnin. The Day Relic is in his hands which means he's transcended into something much stronger than a simple warrior... and if he has the Slayers beind him, it won't be easy. I want to help," she answered before anyone could even ask. Tbrok accepted the offer with a smile and a nod. "Goodbye and stay safe," he shouted in regard to the group, but mainly at Wick. The Jevetin struggled to take off with its small wings. Its flab wobbled as it raised from the floor and took flight. A large hole in the roof allowed them to exit, and the group waited and watched them leave as the wind from the flapping wings blew in their faces. Yewki was secretly hoping Lall was going to leave too because he had no more patience left with her. Lall on the other hand wished she could take the boy. As the group made their way back to the main hall it was evident that Wick was struggling. "Here, let me," Yewki said as he picked him up to not only help, but to reassure Moon that the child was still in safe hands. "Now you must rest," he told Wick.

"We all must," Piea interjected. "You must leave for the Wizard first thing tomorrow". They were strangley calm, but it was for Wick's sake, to make sure the severity of the curse didn't frighten him too much. If the boy was refraining from screaming and shouting, the rest of them had to as well. If one thing was apparent, it was his strong will, and the adults had to play along and not make a big deal out of it, even though Wick's life would never be the same again. It had been a long day for everyone. It was near impossible to sleep at all, let alone comfortably with the reflections of the evening playing in their heads over and over, accompanied with the different thoughts and feelings they had on the matter. Trauma had struck all that night with no remorse, but most of all for Wick. The innocent had paid the price for the mistakes of the incompetent. Lay-Vau was merciless but he had every right to be considering he existed solely by the heartless rules of voodoo.

Chapter 14

Fearful Suspicions

It had been a dark series of days for Magmalia. The cracks in their foundation were beginning to show and there wasn't anything the Paladins could do to fix it. Troyori Quait sat with her head down on a lonely bench, well away from the castle. She wore her normal clothing, hoping not to be noticed so she could keep to herself. The invasion of Slayers had forced the Kings and Queens to take a large amount of power from the Knights, restricting them only to external affairs. The civilian's admiration for them had bubbled down to near disrespect, for the easily-frightened population that feared for their lives no longer possessed the ability to put their trust in those who swore to keep them safe, therefore, the streets had become a lot less busy, and the Paladins had even minimized their informal appearances in public as well, all whilst everything calmed down. Quait and the others had been trained for every situation, all except the one they were currently in. If Paladin Soa's prediction of a traitor being among them was correct, the kingdom would crumble entirely, so time was of the essence. It made Troyori suddenly forget about all the good she had done over the years, and replace them with feelings of disgust and shame, as though it was her own fault the Knights were caught up in the dilemma. She just wished she was free of her shameful goggles, as they prevented her from blending in completely. She was trying her best to be alone and not to gain any attention, but the odd person would recognise her unique features and scowl as they passed. "If you're looking for seclusion, outside probably isn't your best choice," Captain Hockmunn said before taking a seat by her side, still wearing his suit of armour in an attempt to look confident and in control, regardless of the controversy. "I'd be less conspicuous if I didn't have you sat beside me in your armour, Captain," she sighed.

"I just came over to discuss some things with you in secret... regarding Soa's assumptions".

"You're trying to find out who the traitor is?"

"Yes, and what their plan is. They're trying to bring *my* city to disarray so that the Slayers can finally take over... but I won't let that happen".

"We've certainly underestimated the Slayer Kingdom".

"No, it's foul play... I won't stand for it".

"*Foul play*, Captain? This isn't a game, this is life and death... survival of the fittest, and they're doing whatever it takes to do so".

"You speak as though you're trying to defend them. Is there something you want to tell me?"

"No, I just wanted to see if you suspected me to be the imposter".

"It's my job to evaluate everybody. Don't take it so personally... it's not easy for me too".

"That's all you came to me for?"

"I want to know who *you* think it could be. I can't imagine it's Soa... he's been a Knight longer than anyone, and he shares the same passion to find out the truth as we do. I struggle to see how any of the other six could have orchestrated the attack... they're scattered all over the place fighting our battles as we speak. I know it isn't you, but being born outside of Magmalia, possessing those spectacles... you're going to get a lot of fingers pointing your way simply out of fear, I'm sure of it... so watch yourself," he warned. She ignored his helpful suggestion and turned to face him. "So that just leaves Vousa Falk? You can't possibly think *he's* the spy, he just joined our order only recently," she gasped.

"That's precisely why I suspect it's him. Don't you think it's coincidental that his first official day as a Paladin, we suffer our most painful blow?"

"It can't be, he seems so… genuine. He told me about his time in the Magmalian army. He fought against the Slayers dozens of times, he can't be one of them-".

"Troyori, I have numerous reports telling me of his services… but I can't find one person who knew him as a soldier. I don't know how, but the reports could have been forged. He conveniently failed to claim his sword from the armoury before his first day of duty, forcing his attacks towards his fellow Slayers to be minuscule. He's the only culprit on my list and I have more than enough compelling evidence to take action".

"If you've already reached a verdict, why come to me?"

"Because I wanted to see if I was thinking straight. I wanted to see if you agreed with me, or if I was turning nonsensical," he sighed. Quait turned away from him and reviewed his accusations in her head. Everything he said made sense, but she struggled to imagine the young newcomer to be capable of such secrecy and manipulation. "I don't want it to be true, but if he's the only possible suspect then what choice do I have but to agree?" she moaned.

"Thank you, Paladin Quait," he said before standing back up to salute her. He turned and began to walk back to his private base of operations to consult with himself. "What do you propose we do now?" she called over before he got too far away. The Captain continued to walk without turning around, but still answered her as he left. "We speak of this to no one. You keep an eye on him just as you were ordered to do, but this time you search for any signs of him being who we think he is. Sooner or later he'll slip up". Troyori's worries and concerns had only doubled since sitting down on the bench. She feared having to eventually stand up from it, knowing that the only destination awaiting her was the castle currently occupying a secret Slayer.

Later that night, Quait was forced to lay in the same room as the supposed imposter, but she refused to sleep in case he killed her whilst she slumbered. Hockmunn had fallen asleep in his private offices with his head against his desk, surrounded by notes. With the other Paladins absent, it was just her, Soa and Falk, but Soa was too old to stay up beyond the twenty-third hour and snored into his pillow. She could tell that Falk was awake as well because every now and then he would turn over or cough. Not even bed time could spare her from her spectacles – they were strapped firmly on her head, just as they had been for many years. The red, stained glass lenses enhanced her vision in the dark at least, so she could keep an eye on Falk in case he tried to creep out of bed. She laid on her back, tilting her head across to the other side of the room where he was, trying not to move so loudly in case it gained his attention. All of a sudden, he sat up and perched himself on the end of his bed whilst rubbing his eyes. Quait gripped her sword she'd hidden underneath her quilt and pretended to be asleep. After a daunting wait, he stood up and stretched. "What are you doing, Vousa?" she whispered across to him, unable to lay without feeling worried about what his next moves were. "I didn't wake you did I?" he asked, seeming genuinely concerned. "The Captain had me carrying sacks of coal for the miners, I'm afraid I did something to my back and now I can't sleep," he explained whilst prodding his muscles and bending his spine back and forth. Quait readied her sword the best she could without making it seem too obvious under the sheets, worried that he could have just leaped over to her and attacked if he wanted to. "Maybe you should lay back down, you wouldn't want to wake Soa. He gets angry if he doesn't get a good night's sleep," she suggested.

"Of course. Just wanted to stretch a little is all," Falk assured. He lowered himself back into bed and pulled the quilts over, making Troyori feel safe enough to let go of her weapon. "I'll be honest, I've been having trouble sleeping since I got here… and now we might have a spy in the castle. It's nerving. Just what have I joined exactly? I thought the Paladins were meant to be perfect in every way," he expressed.

"Well we all have a dark side we hide from others, don't we?" she replied.

"I suppose we have our personal secrets that we'd prefer not to share, yes. But being a traitor lurking in the shadows is more than just a personal matter, it's pure evil that affects the entire kingdom".

"That's right, Vousa. The Captain says he has a few ideas-".

"He doesn't suspect me does he? I haven't joined the Paladins to be labelled a Slayer in disguise. I know how he could think it was me… I'm the newest member. You had no problems until I arrived".

"Well you haven't made his shortlist," she lied, hoping that he wouldn't feel the need to be cautious around the Knights if the Captain didn't suspect him. It increased his chance of accidentally revealing himself if he didn't feel like he was being watched. "Who's on the list?" he asked.

"I don't know," she continued to fib.

"Oh, I just assumed you knew the names if you were aware that I wasn't on it".

"No, the Captain himself wanted to assure me that you wasn't one of the names, and that's all he said about it".

"That takes a great weight off my chest," he exhaled.

"I continue your training as normal and we leave matters in the hands of the Captain".

"Of course. Do you think he considers you to be a possibility? Because I don't think it's you for a second".

"Thank you, Vousa… but we don't discuss it anymore, understood?"

"It's just… I can't believe the Slayers actually managed to get into the castle. Whoever the spy is must be incredibly intelligent to conjure such a plan without the rest of us noticing".

"I said that's enough," Quait raised her voice. If Vousa *was* the spy, he didn't mind gloating about his schemes. It was all too much for her to get her head around. He was doing a good job at sounding uninformed and innocent, but the knowledge passed down from Captain Hockmunn was too convincing and made complete sense. For her to feel like he was telling the truth, she'd have to forget the obvious evidence that labelled him the traitor. She felt too clever to fall for any mind games he threw at her and stayed on top of them the best she could. "Can you two shut your mouths?" Soa croaked.

"I'm sorry we woke you, Paladin Soa," Quait said. She had deliberately spoken louder to wake him up because she knew it would force her and Falk to stop talking. The three of them shut their eyes and remained silent for the remainder of the night, dropping off into deep dreams one by one. There was only so long Troyori could stay awake for before her tiredness took over – even when there was a potential traitor several feet away from her.

The morning after brought with it their daily duties. Troyori was still tied with Vousa, but she at least had Soa with her on this occasion. He led the other two on the backs of horses, away from the city and towards a rumour regarding a small group of bandits, North of the land. Neither Quait nor Falk dared speak after waking Soa up during the night, so they travelled the numerous miles in silence, with nothing but the clopping of horse hooves and the splashing stream to the side of them which they followed, until reaching the Magmalian scout's treetop outpost. "Paladin Garjian Soa," one of them alerted whilst jumping out from the high branches. "What news do you have for me?" Soa asked.

"We spotted the bandits moving towards the ruins, just further down from here".

"How many did you count?"

"At least twelve".

"Thank you, scout," the old Knight said, before escorting the other two Paladins with him to find the bandits. It was nothing out of the ordinary. All the Knights were used to taking out small groups of enemies from time to time, but there was one thing that didn't add up this time around. "Tell me, you two, don't you think it's awfully strange that we're all sent away from the kingdom for a small task? Even Captain Hockmunn is away in the South to support our people down in Gu-Ram".

"What do you mean?" Vousa asked.

"None of us are in the city to protect it. It would be incredibly easy for us to be assassinated out here so the carnage could ensue within Magmalia," Quait answered for him.

"Precisely, but we can't ignore potential threats so we must continue with the mission, even if it *is* a trap. We don't want to act like we've figured it out," Soa responded. The three of them had made it to the ruins and proceeded with caution, where the air had been fittingly draped in fog, amplifying the tension further. Strangely, there were no sounds. Everything had fallen silent, accompanying the forbidding thick mist perfectly. Ancient stone walls and rubble from an age before littered the area. There could have been dozens of bandits hiding behind the heaps of old bricks, so the Knights got from their horses and split up with their swords at the ready. There could also have been archers in the trees for all they knew, so they crept around using what cover they could for themselves, but no matter how hard they looked, they couldn't find anyone, so after a careful few minutes, they reached the verdict that there was no one around. "The scouts made an error?" Quait suggested.

"The scouts did exactly what they were told to do," Soa groaned. Suddenly, an arrow hit him in the gaps between his armour, dropping him to his knees. "Soa!" Quait screamed. The scouts from before had followed them to the ruins with orders to kill. The Paladins were compatible with all sorts of situations, but the fact they had prepared for a different offence to the one that was occurring caught them by surprise, even if they *were* aware of a potential trap, they weren't able to transition their approach in the matter of seconds. They had to assume that the two scouts were Slayers, and judging from their efficiency in taking down Soa, it only solidified their identities. More arrows flung towards Quait, but she deflected them with her sword. Somehow, Soa managed to stand back up with an arrow stuck into a critical point in his chest, in an attempt to provide cover for the other two Paladins. "There's only two of them, come on!" he grunted, letting his anger and impending doom get the better of him. Quait charged at one of the scouts, forcing them to switch from bow to dagger, but it was a feeble attempt against her mighty blade. "Die!" she yelled, before recklessly slicing her foe to the floor. The other scout hit Soa with another arrow which ended his life instantly, knocking him down into a pile of rocks. Vousa ran over to check on him, not knowing that he was dead. "Paladin Soa is down!" he blabbered. Troyori's heart dropped to the deepest depths of the Earth and shuddered in shock. She looked at the old man's killer and glared at him. "Monsters!" she wailed, running at him and lobbing her sword as though it was a throwing knife. The large weapon span through the air until reaching the remaining scout, impaling him and sending his body flying backwards by sheer force of the projectile. She knelt down with Vousa to look at Soa's poor dead body. He was her closest friend and favourite Knight, gone in the blink of an eye. "What do we do?" Vousa panicked, but Quait didn't respond. Instead, she stood up and began dragging the old man's body towards their horses. Vousa helped carry and load him onto the back of his horse, to bring him back home for the proper send-off he deserved. "There's not much we can do until the Captain is back from Gu-Ram," she finally answered. They journeyed back home together, which forced Quait to keep her emotions to herself. She wanted to shout at Falk, rag him from his horse and ask him upright whether or not he was the Slayer spy, but she couldn't help but follow Hockmunn's orders of asking casual. The way back to Magmalia felt twice as long with a dead body as cargo, making the silence twice as excruciating as well.

Quait couldn't bring herself to attend Paladin Soa's funeral. Instead, she sat in the dormitory and watched the service from afar. All she could see from her distance was a fire and a small, pathetic crowd of people. He once had many supporters, but with the recent invasion, and the loss of respect, not even his own cremation was safe from faithlessness and ingratitude. If the Slayers hadn't have made the civilians lose hope in the Paladins, the number of people lining up to pay their respects would have been incredible. He deserved much more respect on his passing, but nothing could have been done to change things. Quait counted down the days for the Captain's return. Until that time came though, she sat on her own, thinking about her friend's unfair death and pondering on whether or not she should retire, remembering back to when Soa had hinted to his own retirement, stressing that it would have only been a matter of time before his luck was pushed. The Knights stationed within the city were out of action until Hockmunn's return, by order of the royals. It gave her time to think at least, but having time off from duties was a curse in itself. She was away from distractions, forcing her mind to fixate on Vousa. The two scouts only seemed to attack herself and Soa at the ruins. If Falk was the Slayer, it'd make sense for him not to be harmed during the assassination. She was entirely convinced that it was him at that point, but it was too much for her to think about rationally at that time. "Even if revealing the truth brings only death, I will die for you, Soa. I will restore our lost trust and if it kills me, it means that we can have the mighty funeral we both deserve," she said to herself, looking over at the old man's empty bed. Her city was changing, like an infection seeping within the bloodstream. Out of all the kingdoms in the world, Magmalia would have suffered from an enemy on the inside more than any other. The hidden Slayer evidently knew what they were doing right down to each and every footstep. The home of opportunity was slowly turning into a land of despair because of them, so the upcoming years were bound to be challenging for the true Paladins, but patience was their only option. All they could do was hope for a misstep by Vousa Falk. Until that point though, they had no choice but to include him and act as though he was one of them. The city balanced atop the brittle support of its Knights – all it would take to collapse was a small shift. With the tragic loss of Garjian Soa, it was up to Troyori Quait and Asieda Hockmunn to look out for the littlest piece of irregular movement in the grand but intricate scheme of things, unknowing the importance of both their futures.

Chapter 15

Dead Discipline

"You didn't sleep again last night?" Yewki asked Wick who was laying on the back of Moon. The three of them had journeyed through the Dewhills and climbed North-West across the Long Basin, which led to forest after forest. It was a two-day walk in total, all of which was endured without a minute of sleep. "How can I sleep when we only stopped for three hours rest twice?" Wick whinged, with his words spilling out of his mouth in a slurry. "This should be the last day of travel, don't worry," Yewki stressed.

"I can feel it itching inside of my skin".

"It's travelling through your veins, just try to ignore it".

"I'd like to see *you* try and ignore it! Do you think your friend will be able to fix it?" Wick nagged. Yewki stopped in a huff and turned around to the boy and the bear. "I don't know. I'm not the Wizard. It's best that you save your questions for him," he groaned.

"What's wrong?"

"It doesn't matter what's wrong with me. You're priority". Yewki continued walking through the spiny trees and sticky mud, leading the way in hopes that he was moving in the right direction. "What do you think he'll do to me?" Wick asked again.

"Stop! I don't know! We're going to get through this mud, we're going to find him and he's going to help you. Then you can stay with him and I can-".

"Go?"

"It's for the best-".

"You're going to leave me with a stranger?"

"I'm a stranger to you just as much as him. I'm no good for you".

"But you're my friend. I thought we were a team. I don't want you to leave me. I don't-". Wick suddenly flopped off of Moon's back, completely unmoving. Yewki was signalled by the thud of his body and the concerned grunt of the bear. Once he turned around, he saw the boy laying on the floor with his black blood streaming slowly out of his ears as Moon prodded him with his snout. His skin turned pale and his lips blue. The only thing moving was his chest due to his rapid panting. Yewki grabbed his small body and shook it slightly in a panic. The bear began growling and panicking himself until he pushed Yewki over in anger. "It's not my fault! It must have been the stress and exhaustion-". Before he could plea, Moon ragged him from side to side with his teeth until letting go and hurling him away. As soon as Yewki staggered back up he was towered over by the bear, plummeting down with both front paws crashing him back to the ground. "I'm sorry," he wheezed, showing no attempt to fight back. "We can fight later. We… we need to save the boy," he coughed. After a tense moment of hesitation, Moon agreed and plodded back over to Wick followed by an injured Yewki, but there were no signs of improvement. The two of them had no idea what to do and could only watch on as the boy panted faster, accompanied with cold shivers. "Someone help!" Yewki screamed, with his voice echoing through the empty environment. Out of nowhere, a strong wind carried leaves and fallen branches in a spiral. Stone and clumps of mud joined together to create a tornado of multiple materials, as if magic was at play. Strange whistling and humming noises came from all directions as the unnatural gust of wind let out sparks and debris. Rooted trees nearby were being pulled in gradually along with the entire horizon ahead of Yewki's eyes. After a stupendous flash of colours, a quirky-looking cottage house stood before them, letting off steam as if it was freshly baked. To break the magnificent spectacle, an elderly man clambered out of the front door, almost tripping over and falling flat on his face. "Seff! Please!" Yewki cried, overwhelmed with relief. The Wizard was old and balding with a puffy beard which reached the collar of his tatty gown. Strangely vibrant stains gave his robe some colour, but for the majority, he was draped in a fading black, as though it's the only thing he had worn for years. "What are you doing here?" Seff panicked whilst noticing the dying boy. "What on Earth has happened!" he gasped.

"It's voodoo. His blood... it's cursed! Do something, please!" Yewki begged.

"Inside, come on". Seff led the way whilst Yewki carried Wick over his shoulder, but before they could all get through the doorway Seff stopped. "Why is there a bear following you? It can't come in my house!"

"It can and it will. There's no time!" Yewki panted. Before Seff could argue back, Moon pushed by them and let himself inside in a hurry. "Clear the table," ordered Yewki.

"Not the table!" the Wizard gasped whilst protecting the intricate glass vials and tubing which littered the entire table. "The rug will do fine," he begged, pointing towards the fireplace. Wick was placed back onto the floor with an old pillow propping up his head slightly. Yewki explained the voodoo and the blood in a hurry, speaking far too fast, but Seff was too busy watching the bear as his large body bumped into stools and shelves. "Seff! Do something!" he yelled to the delirious old man. He pushed Yewki out of the way to get a closer look at the blood trickling out of his ears. "The purple one," he mumbled.

"What?"

"The purple one. The bottle over on *Shelf: Seventeen*. And for heaven's sake, make sure that bear doesn't knock anything over". Yewki fiddled his fingers around the many shelves, looking for the colour purple, but there was so many glass containers to choose from. "Which purple bottle?" he whined.

"There's only one purple bottle".

"This?"

"No, that's a vial... that's a tube... yes, that one!" Seff huffed as Yewki picked up an assortment of purple items until he grabbed the right one. "Good, now pour it into that coal bowl," he instructed.

"A bowl made of coal? What?"

"On the counter you can't miss- for goodness sake, I said keep an eye on that bear!" he cried as Moon backed up into a pile of strange contraptions. Whatever the device was that he broke, it let out a pop and a tiny blue gas cloud. Seff linked his hands together to create an obscure gesture with his fingers before pushing down gently on Wick's chest, mumbling a strange string of unknown words. Meanwhile, Yewki poured the liquid into the bowl and watched as the coal turned into a gold-like metal. "Now what?" he asked. Seff broke out of his chanting and pointed to an overgrowth of ivy that had invaded his house through the cracked roof. "Two leaves should do. Break them up and put it in the bowl," Seff ordered before going back to his peculiar mumbling. Yewki did what he was told and sprinkled the seemingly normal ivy into the mixture, causing the bowl to heat up until the liquid boiled and let off steam. "It's bubbling," he informed.

"Bring it to me," Seff ordered. Yewki grabbed a nearby cloth to help pick up the hot bowl and passed it over to the Wizard who was somehow able to hold it with his bare hands. He moved it around Wick's nose in a circular motion in hopes for the steam to be inhaled. "I won't ask how it works-".

"Good, because you never were good at listening," Seff jabbed.

"All I ask is if it *will* work". After a nervous few seconds which seemed like a lifetime, Wick coughed and sat up in shock as though he had just been brought back from the dead, only to fall back down to the pillow in a deep sleep.

After a strong slumber, Wick was finally woken up by the popping of bubbles and the clanging of wooden apparatus. His head was throbbing but his surroundings kept him entertained enough to ignore the pain. Spinning mechanisms and gears jiggled around on fragile frames, pushing and pulling around the bedroom, creaking and tapping as they moved. He had never seen anything so intricate before and had no idea how the majority of it was moving. Sitting up caused him to ache and realise how frail he was, but he decided to explore the house regardless, starting with the odd contraptions around the room. He poked the wooden pedals and gears, inspecting the machinery up close, but his curious hands resulted in parts of the frame snapping off, causing a domino effect across the room as more sticks and braces twanged everywhere. He left the bedroom in a hurry and closed the door behind him, too scared to see what would happen to the machine. The open space in front of him served as a kitchen *and* a living room, but that too was covered with strange devices. "Was that my Materialiser crumbling in the bedroom?" Seff asked, catching Wick by surprise. He turned to look across at the old man, trying to enjoy a cup of tea.

"Your what?" Wick asked.

"My Transfusion Materialiser. It helps me move the house around the forest in an instant".

"What language is that?"

"Sorry Yewki, the boy is as challenged as you," Seff sighed. Yewki popped up from behind the table with straw and feathers in his hands. "You shouldn't expect people to understand half of what comes out of your mouth," Yewki informed.

"Wait, am I... is this-".

"I'm Seffry the Wizard and yes, you've found my house. Well, I found *you* after you collapsed".

"Oh. I wasn't expecting you to look so…"

"So *what*, son? Old? Messy?"

"I don't know. I guess I didn't know what to expect," Wick muttered. Yewki rolled his eyes at Wick's words, knowing that Seff was a delicate flower that was easily damaged. He dropped the straw and feathers into a pan and wiped his hands only to find that the pan began jumping off of the stove slightly until one big hop onto the floor, spilling an indescribable ooze all over. "I told you, go easy on the straw!" Seff moaned whilst slurping his tea in anger. Yewki looked at him and scowled before cleaning up the mess, almost knocking over a small vial of turquoise liquid. "Watch out, oaf! That vial is more important than anything else in this house!" the old man growled.

"What's in it?" Yewki scoffed.

"Never you mind... just stay away from it". The boy was mesmerised by the strange items and colours. Substances and textures he never knew existed – all scattered before him. "What were you making? I've never seen anything like it," Wick wondered.

"Ask the Wizard," Yewki sighed.

"The question is, what *aren't* I making?" Seff gloated.

"Stop showing off," grumbled Yewki, sloshing a mop from side to side, not noticing that the spilt liquid was slowly eating away at it. "I make potions, spells. I discover and experiment with new and different things. I could explain in greater detail but I don't think you have the capacity to-".

"Wait, did you heal me?" Wick gasped.

"Yes... and no," Seff mumbled. His introduction of embellished grandeur had failed and Wick's hopeful face dropped. "He stopped you from dying," Yewki intervened.

"You collapsed from stress, and pure voodoo replacing your bloodstream. It was only a matter of time until the black curse would kill you, but I've made your heart compatible with the new blood," Seff explained.

"So it's still inside of me?" Wick exhaled. Seff and Yewki looked at each other, knowing that there was more bad news for Wick to hear. Seff placed his cup of tea on the stool by his side and sat up straight. "You need to realise something... and be prepared for what I'm about to tell you. This blood inside of you, this... curse... it's a part of you now. And that applies forever. Prepare for your life expectancy to... how do I put this?"

"I think he's heard enough," Yewki prompted.

"No, I need to know," Wick blubbered. Seff nodded and began informing him the best he could, using hand gestures to help with the explanation. "Sleeping is going to get harder, and your need for sustenance... food, water... will decrease. The only way I could save you was by reviving the soul – something I'm not experienced with. The will of your soul and the might of the curse are constantly pushing against one another, and I'm afraid there's no way for me to extract something outside of the realm of magic. To put things easier, you're half dead and always will be". Wick took in Seff's words the best he could whilst sitting down in the arm chair behind him. "It's a part of me forever?" Wick sighed.

"I'm afraid so," Yewki exhaled.

"I thought *you* were leaving?" Wick growled at him, completely changing the subject. Seff had continued to sip his tea but quickly spat it out in surprise after hearing what the boy said. "He's not staying here with me! I have enough on my plate!" he gagged.

"I just thought he would be safer here with you," Yewki exclaimed.

"He just wants to abandon me now that he's ruined my life," Wick jabbed.

"You brought this child into your world of danger, you should be responsible for him," Seff complained.

"Maybe your right, but he needs to stay here where you can take care of him," Yewki stressed. Before the argument could continue, Moon ran in from outside, knocking over all sorts of delicate items. Wick forgot the peril and stress for a minute upon connecting with his dear bear friend. He grabbed tightly on his fur as they hugged, sharing a long-awaited moment of relief. Moon licked his face and sniffed his ears with his wet nose in delight, shoving Seff and Yewki well out of the way with his rear end. "Does this house look fit for a bear?" Seff whined to himself, walking away in a hurry. Yewki stood watching the boy and the bear share their unique bond and remembered to when they first met, the journey they had, and the sense of fatherhood he felt whilst looking after them. Letting go of them would be too difficult for him, regardless of the dangerous life he led. He knew Seff was right. It was his fault Wick was cursed so he thought the least he could do was be there for him to fix his delicate soul, rather than leave it behind for someone else to mend. "One week. One week and we go together and leave the Wizard be," Yewki said.

"Are you sure?" Wick smiled.

"You're my responsibility". To Yewki's surprise, the boy ran to him for a tight hug. Moon was still angry and apprehensive, but refused to interject with the two of them. "Are you sure you want to wait here a whole week?" Wick said.

"It's okay, we've already been here a week, one more should be fine".

"What? I was asleep for a whole-". Yewki nodded at him as Wick's face jerked with surprise and confusion.

That evening, Wick found himself at the dining table – something that he'd never sat at before, especially surrounded by other people. Yewki hunched beside him and Seff sat opposite whilst the bear slumped alone, glaring out of the window to the moon. The table was empty except for plates, cutlery and a handful of vials in the centre, but the contents of the vials were about to be discovered by Wick. "Sorry in advance if you're wanting anything but vegetables," Seff apologised with a smile whilst handing the boy one of the potions. Wick studied the colours and density of the liquid by shaking the vial as Yewki and Seff waited for him to pour it. "Go ahead, put it on your plate," the giddy Wizard grinned. Wick yanked the cork off and slowly trickled it onto the old, wooden plate only to find that the liquid soaked into the cracks. Before he could show a sign of disappointment, a small carrot sprouted out of one of the cracks, followed by a cabbage the size of a pebble. He looked across the table to find the other plates growing varying vegetables until they all reached half of their natural sizes. Cauliflower the size of clenched fists, carrots the length of fingers and broccoli as small as white button mushrooms. The roots that the plants would usually require to live were nowhere to be found, but Wick was too mesmerised to question and too hungry to care. He wanted to enjoy meals whilst he could, before the voodoo said otherwise. "Not yet, we're waiting for one more to join us at the table," Seff explained before Wick could lunge forward for a carrot. "Lumni?" the Wizard called to Wick's surprise. After a puzzling few seconds, a sixteen year old girl wandered into the room and slouched into the fourth chair, uncaring that Wick had awoken. Her hair was long, blonde and covered her ears. Her outfit was a miniature version of Seff's with minor tweaks to get rid of the impractical cloak trails, as well as not being covered in messy stains. She constantly looked annoyed at something. Not even dinner time could alter her mood. He had no idea there was someone else living in the house, but felt too shy to ask about it at dinner. All the way through the feast they awkwardly stared. It would consist of Wick glaring in confusion and Lumni scowling back in annoyance. Seff caught wind of the eyeballs and chuckled. "Oh yes, this is Lumni. I've been taking care of her for about two years now. I found her crying near a pond," he smiled.

"Seff!" she gasped in embarrassment, prompting him to shut up, but he couldn't resist sniggering as a result. She grabbed a handful of food and stormed back into the room she came from. "And that's why I can't take care of Wick. One orphan is enough," Seff explained with a mouth full of cauliflower, shaking his head. The rest of dinner time was silent but it didn't take long for Wick to finish. After requesting to be excused from the table, he wandered outside to look at the houses exterior. The walls and beams seemed normal. He expected an odd building that made no sense, but he didn't give up and continued round the back. One thing he eventually noticed was a charred outline at the base of the house as though the ground had been scorched beneath it. As soon as he looked back up he was met with a deadly arrow inches from his face. "Move, boy," Lumni ordered. She sat in her room aiming a bow out of her open window. Wick moved and watched the arrow release and fly onto a carved bullseye on a distant tree. "You're an archer," he gawked with amazement. She tinkered with the bow string and readied another arrow. "I'm the best archer there is. I'm sure of it," she claimed. The next arrow flew and hit the mark perfectly again. "I didn't know you was living here," he said.

"And I didn't know you was going to be staying this long".

"Did you hear what happened to me?"

"Yes. It's pretty bad. It's a good job your Father knows Seff".

"He's not my Father".

"Okay. So you're an orphan too?"

"I suppose. Why are *you* an orphan?"

"That's none of your business," she hissed whilst firing another arrow by his head. "Why are you?"

"I don't know," Wick said.

"What does that mean?" she scowled.

"I don't remember anything. And then before I knew it, Yewki was looking after me".

"How do you know he's not a bad person then?"

"He's not. He's saved me".

"Saved you from what? Situations he put you in in the first place?"

"You don't know him".

"I know a threat when I see one".

"Really? How many threats do you see whilst you're sulking in your room, shooting arrows out of your window?" Wick growled. Lumni yanked him through the window and dropped him onto her bedroom floor. "You don't know what I've been through, so I suggest you stop," she warned, before going back to her archery practice with her back to him. "I'm sorry. I'm not used to talking to another child," he said

"I'm not a child," she hissed again. Wick looked around her room. Hand-carved bows and arrows hung on the walls and the floor was covered in wood chips and branches. "You made all this?" he gasped.

"You ask a lot of questions don't you?"

"So do you". Lumni let out an exaggerated exhale and turned around, placing her bow on her bed. She stood up and helped Wick back to his feet. "Your lost memories; Seff might be able to restore them," she suggested, showing a random sign of niceness. "He can do a lot with his magic. I'm sure he'd be happy to help if you ask".

"Do you think he could teach *me* magic?" Wick wondered. She snorted under her breath and shook her head as she ushered him out of her room. "He tried teaching me a few times. It's far too complex. He's the last person on Earth to master the discipline, and I'm pretty sure it's going to die with him," she explained whilst shutting the door on Wick.

A few days passed and Wick was slowly getting used to the pulsating feeling of the voodoo. The haunting night with Lay-Vau still loomed in his mind, but he tried his best not to think about it by helping Seff around the house. Yewki and Moon were getting along better, and Lumni was less aggressive to everyone. Wick had been gathering all sorts of items and ingredients for Seff in the kitchen whilst he fixed his complex machinery that was broken. "The Transfusion Materialiser should be working again now," Seff grumbled.

"And it's about time we moved," Lumni spoke up from the other side of the room. Yewki came through the front door with more unorthodox ingredients whilst Moon scratched his back outside on a tree he'd grown fond of. "Good timing, Yewki," Wick smiled.

"What?"

"We're moving the house," Seff elaborated.

"What?"

"How do you think I found you and Wick in the first place? I moved the whole house to your location, remember?"

"I thought it was a one-off emergency... trick, thing. Or that the house was there all along and you removed an invisibility cloak or something".

"Ah yes, my cloaking spell *was* my favourite back in the day wasn't it. But no, remember how I used to talk about moving an object through the Astral Vale? Making something that exists, stop existing and then reconstruct back into existence in another location?"

"I remember some of those words being said, yes".

"Well that's what my Transfusion Materialiser is for. I call it, *teleportation*".

"Why do you need to move the house? Surely turning it invisible was enough".

"Why not both? With the power of teleportation *and* invisibility, no one will ever stumble across my home".

"It just seems too much-".

"Every week or so, Lumni and I move the house to another corner of the forest which we've marked out," Seff explained whilst unrolling an in-depth map of the whole forest. The map showed black spots in various locations with thorough coordinates. "I would travel around the woods and summon Access Gates for the house to land on, which are those dots on the map".

"Don't you think this is rather excessive?"

"Safety can never be excessive!"

"And this... *teleportation*, it's completely safe?"

"Of course, it's been stable for us every time hasn't it, Lumni?" The girl didn't respond, not even with a nod or a shake. Instead, she remained seated in the armchair with just a slight hint of unsettlement. Seff instructed Wick and Yewki as they chopped, crumbled and mixed ingredients together, creating pastes and liquids in varying bottles. The Materialiser shook crazily as it span, making all kinds of obscure noises until Seff worked his magic around the house. After a frantic and noisy few minutes, the whole house filled with a thick glimmering smoke. To Wick and Yewki's surprise, the cottage began to float just above the ground, but the thicker the smoke, the higher it climbed. The amazement made them forget about Moon, but a nervous grunt from outside eventually reminded Wick. "Moon! He's not here!" he cried whilst running to the open front door. Looking down, he saw the bear standing on his hind legs concerned and confused. "There's not much time! Things are going to start collapsing!" Seff warned.

"Come on, Moon. You've got to jump!" Wick begged. Suddenly, the house started to crumble and bend in on itself, as well as their bodies folding and stretching towards the centre of the room. The whole process was harmless, but was still overwhelming for Yewki and Wick. Moon noticed the floating house collapsing and twisting and it was only a matter of time before the doorway would do the same. He ran towards the entrance as fast as he could where Wick stood waiting for him, but after a few seconds, the boy's body had been absorbed into nothingness with the majority of everything else. The bear leaped as high as he could, stabbing his front claws into the floorboards and dangling until the whole house sucked itself into a tiny yellow orb. The glowing wisp crackled like firewood before vanishing entirely, leaving only the charred Earth where the cottage once stood. Nineteen miles South, the same phenomenon Yewki had experienced started to unfold again. Just like before, the house materialised into existence in a sparkling wave of colours and objects inside of a tornado of debris. The charred, magical Access Gate soil was quickly crushed by the sudden arrival of the cottage. Inside of the house, their perception of reality was warped into shapes of all styles until the walls, roof, and windows all unfolded back into their vision. Yewki found himself looking up at the roof confused until he realised he was laying on the floor, whilst Wick had landed on top of the table, knocking over glasses and instruments. Thankfully, Moon was transported with them, half hanging out of the open doorway. Seff and Lumni on the other hand had maintained a graceful posture, both sharing tea between themselves in the living room. Once the smoke cleared, Wick and Yewki checked to see if Moon was okay and to look outside. The scenery had changed completely but there was still an element of disbelief in their hearts, solely by the sheer lack of comprehensiveness. "Now the invisibility cloak can be placed," Seff said, stepping outside to wave his arms around mystically. Wick observed his gestures closely, watching each movement of his joints and fingers before a cold breeze blew straight towards the house. Fizzing sparks crackled and whistling wind submerged the cottage, covering it with the image of the trees that stood behind it, making the house completely invisible. Lastly, Seff pointed his open hand in the direction of the house which revealed the home exclusively for their eyes only to avoid them bumping into it, for anyone else passing by though, they would definitely do so. "That was amazing!" Wick cheered.

"The cowardly Wizard who feels the need to move his home every week is amazing?" Yewki moaned.

"Don't be jealous that the boy shows an interest in magic," Seff giggled. The three of them and Moon swiftly re-entered the house to join Lumni for a much-needed sit down after the disorientating ride.

After the numerous magical spectacles, Wick watched Seff closely, what he thought was subtle, for the next two days, but it hadn't gone unnoticed. They stood together chopping mushrooms on the table, but after being glared at like prey, the Wizard finally decided to speak to him more deeply about his discipline. He put his knife down and slowly brushed his hand across his forearm, revealing an orangey glow underneath his flesh. Wick stared at Seff's arm as it shone bright like fire, running through his veins. "You find this interesting I see," the Wizard asked rhetorically.

"Ever since I joined with Yewki, I've never really felt like much help. His quests would be easier without me there making things harder. I just wish there was a way for me to look after myself... make sure Yewki isn't slowed down and so I can actually help," Wick explained.

"And you suggest that magic is your answer?"

"I suppose".

"Follow me," Seff smiled whilst escorting him outside. They walked a few paces away from the house and into the woods for peace and solitude. "Do you think you're ready?" he asked.

"I think so," Wick stammered.

"At last". To the boy's surprise, the ground seemed to be folding upwards, dragging the horizon with it until the floor reached his face, as though the world had flipped but he and Seff remained untouched by the movement. The Earth flipped over like the turning of a page, leaving the two of them in a gloomy realm of black. Random yellow wisps floated by their heads, travelling upwards infinitely as white glimmers trickled down to the floor wherever they looked. "What is this place?" Wick gasped.

"This is the Astral Vale. It took me thirty years to find it... and now I can access it as easily as I can chop mushrooms," Seff grinned. "This is where my powers come from. This is where Wizards as old as time journeyed to in hopes to harness the Empyrean Energy we can feel around us now".

"I can't feel anything," Wick shuddered.

"Focus your mind. Relax and let your soul breathe".

"I'm trying".

"Feel the power travelling through your heart". Wick fell to his knees but Seff helped him back up. He began to breathe heavily, suddenly feeling weary and weak. "I can feel the energy you said. It's too strong!" he gasped. He closed his eyes tight and tensed his body, reluctant to give up until he could fully relax and let the Empyrean forces fill his spirit. "That's it, boy!" Seff praised.

"I did it!"

"Well done. You're now imbued with the power of magic. Now comes the hard part". As soon as the words left Seff's mouth, he made all sorts of hand gestures, sending pure fire out of his wrists, gushes of powerful wind out of his knuckles and shapes made from compressed light, woven together to create solid objects. "Offence isn't my strong point, I'm more of an alchemist… but if you think it will help you on your adventures then I will teach you as much as I can".

Hours of training passed by inside of the Astral Vale. Seff discussed the importance of hand and finger placements, how to release power in controlled manners, all while focusing on the will of the soul. Once imbued, the Empyrean Energy was generated inside of the body, starting with the head which would then be passed down to the heart. The arms were the body's extractors – the hands symbolised the '*letting go*' of energy, relinquishing the power in varying forms, summoned differently by alternating finger placements. Since the dawn of Shamans, the power of Earth was held exclusively for them. Born chosen, they would later pass on their energies to their children, leaving behind the need to be imbued, thus allowing the Wizards to control the Astral Vale for themselves with the power of the remaining three elements, Fire, Air and Water. Through the years, Wizards learnt the different ways to release the elements at their full potential. "You bend your index and middle finger and push it down onto the beginning of your forearm. As I brush my hand down to my wrist, you notice the fiery glow inside of my arm? And then I just release!" Seff demonstrated, gushing out a trail of intense flames. "You make your little fingers crooked like so. Connect the wrists and push your clenched fists forwards like this". Out came a quick blast of wind. "After a while, you can push the air out of your feet but the last time I tried that, I shot up into a tree. Lastly is the altering of moisture. Water is the hardest because of its form, but I know a few tricks," he explained. Wick watched on as Seff twisted his wrists, making his fingers point to the ground. "You can extract moisture, turning anything into a solid or a gas," he said whilst gripping nothing but thin air. A cloud of vapour came out of nowhere, tampering with the air and creating a miniature cloud. Afterwards, he reached into his pocket and pulled out a small vial. "I want you to alter this liquid matter into something solid using the last gesture I showed you. Extract the moisture and you should be left with something quite amazing," he instructed whilst pouring the green juice onto the floor, creating a puddle for Wick to place his hands into. "I'm not sure I can do it. What if it goes wrong?" the boy said.

"Do you know why Yewki in unable to be taught? Because he is an adult, and adults are stubborn and lack belief. Don't let your childhood pass you by, Wick. Focus your mind and do as I did to the air," Seff assured. Wick looked at the back of his hands carefully and flipped them upside down. He dropped to his knees and leaned forward. "You can do it. Become one with your spirit and move the energy through your body". Wick loomed over at his reflection in the puddle, only to see a young, foolish boy – a child who had no identity, no family and no answers. He wanted to see the face of someone strong and bold, but only he could change what he saw in himself. Greenwick clenched his fists, scooping up some of the liquid in his hands before pulling backwards when he felt the energy being channelled through his arms. In an instant, vapour rose above him, leaving a singular emerald gem, unparalleled in beauty. Much like the spell he had summoned, his spirit was sculpting from an unknowing liquid to an unbreakable solid, shining and twinkling more and more with every boost of self-esteem. All he could do was smile, unable to cheer for himself as he stared at the magic he had accomplished. "I was right," Seff gasped.

"About what?" Wick asked.

"The voodoo is helping you progress quickly. I made sure not to tell you how long it took me to learn that one trick. The voodoo has technically already enlightened your spirit, allowing your body to wield the Empyrean Energy much easier. It took you moments to learn what took me a year. Then again, that *was* the easiest of the spells". Seff continued to show Wick the fire and air gestures as well as how to create what the Wizards called, *Hardlight* objects. In the ancient times where great battles were in abundance, Wizards were elected to help fight alongside soldiers. An experimental era of magic offence led to the discovery of solidified energy, created by extracting power all at once to compress into a weapon or a shield. For ambushing, large hardlight shields were cloaked with invisibility to allow soldiers to sneak up at close range. "Hardlight can be dangerous because if you don't weave the energy into a designated shape then there's a chance it will explode," Seff stressed.

"Oh," Wick exhaled.

"Not to worry, we shall learn that another day. I've worn my old bones dry," the old man moaned whilst raising his hands up into the air. For what happened to the Earth was happening again with the Astral Vale – everything began turning over to reveal the real world whilst Wick and Seff remained untouched. "It's still day time? But we've been gone for hours," Wick pondered.

"Time doesn't apply in the Astral Vale as well as reality. We technically didn't exist for a moment. It may have seemed like a long day for us, but it's still the same time we left. The only problem with that is that you're probably going to be ready for bed before dinner time," Seff laughed. The two of them walked back to the house to continue chopping mushrooms. "There's still much to learn so don't expect to be able to defend yourself just yet".

"I want to know everything. I want to make potions, I want to be able to harness the elements, I want be able to heal myself and others," Wick yammered.

"Don't forget, your voodoo has healing properties too. How else do you think it's killing you but keeping you alive at the same time?

If you could someday master both magic and voodoo, who knows… you could possibly combine the two which would create a whole new branch of Wizardry. I know it's a curse, but the best thing you can do is focus on its uses".

"You've taken him to that *Vale* haven't you?" Yewki interrupted out of nowhere, entering the room with animals he had caught on his hunt. "It was his choice," Seff sighed.

"Don't let him get your hopes up, Wick. He may have taught you dazzling tricks but you need to know that he's never fought in his life," Yewki laughed.

"That doesn't mean I can't teach the boy".

"A coward can teach anyone tricks, but a coward can't teach someone bravery… and bravery is what he needs, not magic".

"Leave Seff alone," Wick said.

"He's only teaching you magic so that it doesn't die with him. You should see his book of Wizardry – pages and pages of notes… and he'll want you to carry on his research once he's gone," Yewki hissed.

"You're wrong! I just wanted to help the boy," Seff whined.

"How about you help me? Where were you when I needed you?"

"What is this really about?"

"We could have stopped Yewnin together way before he obtained that accursed relic, but you told me you're not a fighter. Now he's using it to destroy the world".

"Oh no, what has he done now?" Seff gasped. Yewki pulled out a small note from his pocket as his chin began to wobble. "I received this message by hawk, it's from Lall. Yewnin has burnt the Dewhills to the ground. Piea is dead".

Chapter 16

Knowledge Avarice

Yewnin sat on the edge of a large cliff face, dangling his legs down with a spectacular view of the Dewhills. He had spent over a week possessing over the Day Relic, unable to let go of it since he first retrieved it. Long lost tombs and ancient cave scriptures led to the discovery of it. A dream once planted in his head by myths had come to fruition, and for something so powerful to actually be in hands made his theories all the more real. The tool glowed and reflected light as he tilted it in admiration. He had stared at every inch of it, but never grew dull of its beauty. Its orange and white patterns mirrored the dusk horizon ahead of him, as though the physical daylight was somehow connected to it. Yewnin felt that it was more than just a device to generate light, and his studies led him to believe that untapped potential still hid within it, but he needed more information. Years of research and countless Shaman interrogations wasn't enough for him. His need to know more stripped him of all patience, and a faster process of gaining information was required. The journey to the Dewhills offered him two prizes; the main goal was to test his new plan, which consisted of capturing the dense population of Shamans that lived there. No longer would knowledge come at a price for him. Secondly as a bonus, he had narrowed down the location of Yewki's hideout to the nearby forests, in hopes to rid the world of him and his posse of tampering parasites all at once. His only hope was that they were all still within the buried

Fellow temple, so that he could take out all important opposition at the same time, but unfortunately for him, only Lall and Piea remained, and they were travelling together on their way North. Tbrok was long gone too, and had gathered his Troll army and embarked far West towards Emmrin-Rashmada, expecting Yewnin to be there with the Slayers. Luckily, Yewnin didn't know of the Wizard's house sixty miles away where Yewki and Wick currently were. Besides the Slayers, Yewnin had gained an alliance with small clans of bandits and mercenaries, only in it for the anarchy, and a promise of future riches. "What is that thing?" the mercenary leader asked, who went by the name of Wolf. Yewnin shuddered out of his trance once the man spoke, then stood up with a moody face. "This... this is the tool I told you about," he replied.

"You actually got it? But you said it was underwater... that it was impossible!" Wolf recalled.

"Yes... but I've come to understand that nothing is quite impossible when you try hard enough". Yewnin grinned, showing Wolf the relic up close for him to admire. "It's so beautiful... so unnatural. But my boys only care for one shiny object, and that's money," Wolf hinted.

"Your money awaits you after you fulfil your duty. Take the Shamans to the Slayers for me and they will pay you what you want".

"Slayers? You never told me you were working with them. We don't mess with Slayers".

"You do know. Try not to mess it up". Wolf looked down at the floor in anger, but the notion of money kept him from revolting. He nodded and whistled for his men. Out of the nearby trees, one hundred men grouped together, all dressed in wolf fur and armed with nets and blow darts. "Catch as many as you can, then take the mountain pass West. Keep to the cover of trees until you reach the canyons," Yewnin ordered.

"You heard him boys! Let's catch us some Shaman!" Wolf howled, leading his squadron straight off the cliff edge, releasing their ingenious gliders made of thick parchment. From below, the sky became covered with flying silhouettes, swooping rapidly until dropping down into the trees. The small army spread across all reaches of the land, hunting the innocent Shamans quickly and effectively. Their darts were tipped with poison, causing their victims to fall to the floor, unable to move their muscles. Nets were flung over the bodies, elderly Shaman men and women beaten and dragged, all while Yewnin watched on from the top of the cliff, taking in their screams and cries. Now alone, his solo mission could begin. He gripped the relic tightly until it absorbed into his body, making his eyes glow and skin glimmer. He looked at the cliff edge, knowing that he was going to jump, but with no prior experience of flight, he became hesitant. With a deep breath calming him down, he ran and leaped straight off with a sudden surge of confidence. The relic allowed him to float like a feather, letting him soar through the air towards the buried hideout. Yewnin closed his eyes whilst feeling the wind on his face. He felt like a true angel, hovering over the land, leaving Wolf and his men to do their job. Old mossy bricks and pillars littered an open area in the forest, only noticeable from above. He swooped down to take a closer look before landing messily on the wet grass. After a brief look around, he found the access hole that Yewki, Wick and Moon had gone through themselves over a week ago. "Bear marks," he muttered to himself. "He's still working with the boy and the bear. That *is* surprising". Yewnin climbed through the hole and made his way into the secret hideout, prepared to kill without warning.

The library was empty with just clues to imply it was recently occupied. He found nothing but collapsed bookshelves after the incident with Lay-Vau, but the residue of the Iwa and his voodoo filled the air, only recognisable to someone as knowledgeable as Yewnin. "What happened here?" he pondered to himself, waving the relic around for light like a lantern. After a while, he soon stumbled upon the central room where the discussions had taken place. A dry puddle of black caught his eye, left behind from Wick's struggle with Lay-Vau. He brushed his hand across it for a thorough inspection and smiled. After more investigating, he eventually discovered the freshest of foot prints, belonging to Piea and Lall. Following them led him to another tunnel which spat him back outside several meters away from his original entrance. To his surprise, Piea and Lall themselves stood waiting for him to surface. They both aimed their swords, waiting for him to try and attack, but instead he laughed. "I came here prepared to find you, but I was still caught off guard. Where are the others of your circle? Thene is it? Tbrok? Batehong? My... brother?" he said.

"You don't get to ask anything. You give *us* answers. What are you doing with the Shamans?" Lall grunted.

"Ah, so that's how you knew I was here".

"We were miles from here actually but decided to come back once we discovered the innocent Shaman were in danger. We came back because we knew you'd be a part of this monstrosity," Piea spat.

"And your little secret order is all about stopping me isn't it? And now you have me," Yewnin grinned.

"Put down that relic, fool," Piea ordered.

"But it's a part of me now. I earned the right to wield it. Do you think I would ask you to relinquish *your* weapons?"

"Yes actually," Lall said.

"That wouldn't be a fun fight would it?" Yewnin laughed before pointing the relic towards them, sending an immense beam of light at them. Luckily the two of them jumped out of the way, but were met with more blasts to dodge. Lall's weapon was useless because she couldn't get close but Piea had a bag full of varying hand explosives. He threw a smoke bomb at Yewnin to give them a chance to hide behind the pillars and stone walls. "The Fellow family are always full of handy tricks. It's a shame that I hate tricks, or else I wouldn't have had to kill your sons... *and* your grandsons," Yewnin taunted. Piea grabbed another bomb in anger and threw it towards him, only for the explosion to be absorbed by the relic and then redirected towards one of the pillars, causing it to topple down and crush the old man's legs. All Lall could do was watch as Piea cried in agony, unable to free himself as Yewnin walked up to finish the job. "The Fellow family dies with you, old fool," he smirked whilst aiming the relic directly at Piea's head. A quick flash followed by silence told Lall everything she needed to know. She reached into a small satchel tied closely to her waist which was hidden under her trench coat, pulling out a small quill and a tiny ink pot followed by a small piece of paper. Yewnin knew Lall had nowhere to run so took the time to stroll around and ask more questions whilst he had her in his grasp. "I saw a puddle of black down there you know. At first I thought it might have been ink… or oil. It's not is it? It's blood," he chuckled.

"How do you know?" she questioned whilst writing a message quickly, hiding behind a wall. Unbeknown to Yewnin, a small hawk started circling the sky above the two of them, ready to carry Lall's impending note. "I thought Lay-Vau would be angry at me for taking the Day Relic from his maze, but I never expected one of you to be cursed by him!" he gasped with sarcasm. "He took his anger out on one of you didn't he? Who was it? I'm looking at Piea's blood now and his is still red. Batehong is made of fire, he doesn't have blood! And you… well, I doubt you'd be able to move about so quickly if there was voodoo inside of you. That leaves Thene, Tbrok and my brother. And since my brother was the one who failed to stop me I'm going to guess it's him!" he sniggered whilst shooting another blast at where he thought Lall was hiding, but she'd given him the slip whilst he flaunted his intelligence. Out of nowhere, she jumped onto his back to punch him in the face as well as attempt to choke him, but after a few jabs she was flipped off overhead. She hit the floor hard but slipped away down a steep hill, giving her more cover from the trees. As she slid, Yewnin fired dozens of beams down into the woods, but they all missed, forcing him to chase after her. He couldn't see her anywhere, but she eventually jumped out again, this time from behind a tree, wielding her sword. As she lunged, he moved to the side with supernatural reflexes, grabbing her by the arm and throwing her at a tree. Yewnin caught his breath after the chase whilst Lall struggled to her feet. "You act as though you're a god but you bleed just like us," she jabbed, taking notice of his burst nose and lip. He wiped his face and laughed, staring at his own blood he'd smeared onto his hands. "But I know there's *someone* in your group who doesn't bleed like you and

I. Tell me, which one is cursed?" he demanded, but she refused to give him what he wanted and changed the subject. "After a kidnapping of such great magnitude, don't expect it to go unnoticed! Prepare for rumours and stories to spread across lands, making your name and your actions well known to the whole world! Everyone will be against you after this".

"Yes, my reputation is important for future compliance. If everyday people know I've stolen Shamans well... no one's going to join my cause are they?" he laughed. "Thank you for your outlook. I know exactly how we can make sure no one escapes to tell the tale". All of a sudden, he span around with the relic, setting the nearby trees on fire. The ground became ash and slowly spread in all directions. "What have you done?" she screamed as she watched the huge fire eat away at everything around her. The relic glowed brightly as the intense power was released from inside. "I'm just practising. I want to see how powerful this is... and you gave me a great reason to try it out!" he smiled. Lall charged towards him and tackled him down whilst the fire engulfed their surroundings. They both rolled around the floor in a struggle with the occasional kick and punch, but he was eventually able to turn the fight in his favour. He kicked her away and began to float above the trees for an aerial attack, but when he looked down to blast, she'd made her escape. The huge forest flames made it impossible for him to look to the ground, allowing Lall to scurry as far as she could go, using the burning woods as cover. She quickly pulled the paper back out to finish the message and whistled for her bird, frantically coughing as the black smoke entered her lungs. She and the hawk had a special connection, as she came from a small clan of Bird Masters from the North that worshipped the winged beasts. They were able to communicate without words, which came in handy when telling the birds where to go. Her people believed that the gods of the wind and sky guided them to their destinations, allowing the creatures to find where and who they needed to go to no matter where in the world. Lall's hawk snagged the note from her hand after dodging the fiery trees and flew low to avoid detection. She knew the bird would deliver the message, so all she had to worry about was escaping the land before it was completely scorched. The Wolf mercenaries had finished their round up and set off towards the mountain pass, looking behind at the forests of flames. The ferocious power of the unnatural relic caused the Dewhills to burn to a crisp in the matter of hours, leaving only ruin and smoke. What was once a peaceful home for hundreds of Shaman became nothing but a graveyard of ash.

Chapter 17

Forwards

Yewki had dragged Seff and Lumni away from the comfort of their home in fear of Yewnin's journey of flaming wrath moving onwards to neighbouring lands. Moon had been equipped with an assortment of baggage, consisting of Seff's potions and ingredients whilst Wick ensured they didn't fall off. They made sure to move the house to the most distant location on the map, as well as giving it a cloaking of invisibility. Seff was nervous to leave for the wild, but at the same time, he knew it was for the best. He held the small turquoise vial that Yewki had almost knocked over, making sure no one noticed. Whatever was inside, he refused to tell anyone else – his only concern was to keep it with him at all times "Lumni, check the bags. I think I left my snail shells," he panicked.

"You packed them, I saw you do it," she sighed.

"Just check, please," he begged.

"No one's checking anything. If we stop again to sift through those bags I'm going to make you carry them all yourself," Yewki complained. Wick stayed to himself as they speed-walked, practising the magic hand gestures. The feeling of voodoo took getting used to, especially when it seemed to amplify whenever he focused on the Empyrean Energy inside of himself. "Where are you taking us?" Lumni asked, but Yewki ignored her. "I don't care where we go really, I'm just wondering. I'm enjoying being out of the house," she continued, causing Yewki to respond. "This isn't a fun family trip. This is the real world with real life and death consequences. Strength and bravery," he warned.

"I am brave!" she complained. "I'm not scared to fire an arrow at someone".

"Yes well we'll see when the time comes won't we".

"Don't you mean, *if*?" Seff stuttered.

"No. I mean, *when*. Especially the direction we're going," Yewki grumbled. Seff was too frightened to ask what they'd find ahead and started to look around with more vigilance. The five of them had been trekking for half a day in the opposite direction of the Dewhills to hopefully be in the clear. Unfortunately, they didn't know Yewnin's future plans and whereabouts, but staying relatively close to the destruction wasn't a risk worth taking. Yewki led them North-East towards a land plagued by monsters of the night. They had a better chance evading the creatures instead of potentially bumping into the Wolf mercenaries travelling North-West with the Shaman cargo. Whichever direction Yewki chose, there was danger waiting at each end. "So, Yewki, when do we sleep?" Lumni nagged.

"Preferably at night, I can't sleep with daylight," Seff whined.

"We don't sleep at all, definitely not at night," Yewki sighed.

"What?"

"Not until we find somewhere safe and secure to stay". Their walking speed slowed down upon hearing the unwelcome news, but quickly regained its speed remembering that the sooner they found refuge, the sooner they could rest. "Is it tedious travelling around so much like this? Never being able to stay somewhere and be safe?" Lumni asked.

"Why do you ask?" Yewki replied.

"I'm just wondering… because it's probably our lives too now isn't it? Now that your brother is destroying everything in his path".

"How do you know he's my brother?" he snapped.

"Your names start with the same letters and amount of syllables… besides, I heard you and Seff talking about him".

"What's a *syllable*?" Yewki asked, suddenly feeling rather uneducated. Lumni didn't answer and laughed instead. "You've had a good education it seems. Tell me, where are you from?" he wondered.

"It's none of your business," she barked.

"I'm sorry. I thought if you were able to make me uncomfortable, I was able to do the same. And to answer your question, no… this isn't your lives now. As soon as we find somewhere to stay, me, Wick and the bear are moving on," Yewki explained. Seff's face lit up with joy, knowing that he didn't have to take care of another child and a huge grizzly bear. "Wait, we're leaving them?" Wick gasped.

"Come on, Wick… I decided to keep you with me, I can't bring any more people. Seff would be dead in minutes and that girl is more stress to me than you are," Yewki explained as though the other two weren't stood listening. "You should let him go alone, Wick. He's only going to get you and your bear into trouble," Lumni suggested. Seff gulped and his eyes grew wide in nervousness, hoping that Lumni wouldn't convince Wick to stay with them. "He's strong and brave. He doesn't need companions. That's why he was unable to stop his evil brother. That's why Wick's cursed on the inside," she continued to taunt.

"And I suppose you're more equipped in this life than I am?" Yewki snapped.

"Let me help… I want danger, I want adventure. How can I have that if I'm stuck with Seff?" she confessed. Her words brought surprise to everyone. "That's funny, young lady. If you knew what dangers there were on this… *adventure*, you'd be begging for a safe place to live well away from it all," Yewki laughed. "You'd be thankful you have Seff to stay with".

"You don't know me".

"That might be true… but I know a lot more about this world than you ever will". Seff, Wick and Moon had grown tired of the petty arguing and walked ahead of them to escape the noise. They couldn't understand how anyone would actually want to be placed in danger. Lumni's quiet life in the cottage had made her deprived of the great outdoors. If Yewki hadn't come to their home and dragged them away, it would have only been a matter of time until she had ran away in search of a new, more adventurous life herself.

The chill of night eventually arrived, making their hike all the more trying. Lumni and Yewki had stopped arguing, but refused to speak to each other civilly. The clinks and clangs coming from Seff's bags seemed to amplify the darker and quieter their journey had become, making them uneasy about what may be out in the shadows possibly being attracted by the noises, but Moon couldn't help the bags swaying from side to side. With no signs to follow, Yewki had to assume they were going in the right direction. Across from him, Seff and Wick were keeping to themselves, staying occupied by discussing magic. The Wizard went through the stances and movements of various spells, but the boy found it difficult to copy them accurately. "The casts have to be perfect, or else all sorts of things could happen. The amount of times I've burnt my hands is incredible. Perhaps you should focus on air blasts for now," Seff said.

"I don't think I'm very good at that one," Wick replied.

"Remember, the wrists come together as you point your arms ahead, all whilst taking a deep breath. The jolt of your body will push the air outwards, so we raise our little fingers crookedly to send some of the air towards us, creating a channel for us to shift accurately. The slight straightening of the fingers will alter the strength of the wind". Wick practised the movement slowly to get used to the action, but when it came to actually casting the spell, he stopped himself. "What's wrong?" Seff asked.

"I'm a little scared".

"Come on, they're practically harmless. I wish I had the opportunity to do air blasts at your age". Wick composed himself then took the all-important deep breath and shoved his arms forward, forgetting to point the fingers. Without a second to react, the huge surge of wind hit the ground in front of him and propelled him several feet backwards. He flung through the air, flailing his arms and legs all over the place before landing on his back. "What on Earth was that?!" Yewki yelled. He and Seff ran over to Wick, prepared for the worst, but they found him rolling on the floor laughing at the surprisingly fun flight. "That's enough magic for today," Yewki grumbled whilst Seff tried his hardest not to laugh with Wick. The moment of joy was quickly eradicated though when a womanly screech echoed from ahead. Yewki pulled out his sword and looked around but couldn't see anything. Lumni joined his side, wielding her bow as though she was prepared to attack whilst Wick and Seff huddled together with the bear. "Stay here," Yewki said as he stealthily ran towards the noise, only to stop a few seconds after, hearing Lumni following behind. "I said, stay over there," he whispered.

"I can help," she stressed.

"No. It's too dangerous". He continued to run alone, leaving Lumni to sulk. After a quick search, he noticed a flour mill behind some bushes. There was no candle light coming from inside, but the front door was open and moving with the night breeze. He forced his way through the bushes and ran across the small wheat field nearby for cover. After a few minutes of surveillance, a creepy human-like figure staggered out of the doorway, followed by three more all exiting together. Yewki knew exactly what the creatures were, and expected them on their travels. Although it was a grim indicator, the monster's presence helped him figure out the town they were near. He wasted no more time and ran to the mill to check for victims. "He's gone! Father, no!" a middle aged woman wallowed as she ran outside, dropping to her knees in overwhelming sorrow. Yewki ran to her and tried to pick her up, but she screamed in surprise when he touched her, thinking it was another creature. "It's okay, it's okay. What happened?" he asked.

"Those Holhouettes! They ate my Father! There was nothing I could do, they just ate him in front of me, bones and all!" she wailed. It was just as Yewki thought. Before he could comfort anymore, a thud from the side of the building caught his ear. A wooden crate had accidentally been tipped over by a fifth Holhouette who was late to the feast. "They're still here! Kill it, please!" she cried. Yewki ran around the corner with his sword at the ready, but just a few seconds later, he was back, flying backwards in the air. The creature had thrown him away rather than attempting to attack or eat. Yewki didn't take the hint and ran at it again, leaving the Holhouette no choice but to defend itself. It swooped its long arms at him as he charged but missed, allowing Yewki to stab it in the stomach. The creature screeched and clambered backwards slightly, but seemed to quickly get over the fact it had a sword impaled in it and stormed straight for Yewki's head. Unarmed, all he could do was jump out of the way, but the beast's long hands grabbed him mid-air and slammed him into nearby barrels. The Holhouette walked up to end the fight, raising its pointy claws. Yewki was concussed and unable to get out of the mess of barrels and debris as the creature began swooping down at him. With just a second to spare, Lumni shot a precise arrow into its head, killing it instantly as it flopped down at Yewki's side. He looked over to the bushes to see Lumni's smug face before getting back to his feet to look at the damage. The creature's blood was a pale red, and its skin was old and rotting. The dead eyes were ghostly white and full of strained veins. "Thank you! Thank you so- look out! A bear!" the woman screamed, watching Seff, Wick and Moon run to the scene. Lumni caught up from the bushes, expecting an apology from Yewki. "What happened? What is that?" Wick gawked.

"Holhouettes! You knew these would be here, Yewki?" Seff panted.

"I knew you'd stay at home if I said we were going to be encountering Night Feeders," Yewki sighed, holding his wounded head. Amongst the horror, Moon's interest laid somewhere else – up to the sky for his nightly gaze at the shining crescent. "It's so ugly," Lumni scoffed. The woman started to cry again at the loss of her elderly Father, so Yewki went over to comfort her as an excuse to stay away from Lumni and her desire for an apology. "How was something like that still alive?" Wick pondered, looking at the creature's hideous dead skin. "Holhouettes are monsters of the undead, brought back to life against their will by their creator, known by many as the Remains – death itself. They didn't choose this life of eternal torment. The Remains makes them kill and eat humans," Seff explained with fear in his voice. He enjoyed feeling smart and knowing, giving the children knowledge in categories unknown to them, even if it *was* something terrible and haunting. Lumni pulled her arrow out of the beast's head and looked at the slimy residue left on it. "But why? Why does it want them to kill *and* eat people?" she asked.

"Eating the dead flesh keeps the Holhouettes alive, but it's unknown why the Remains wants this to happen. Some say it's to speed up the process of death – an unparalleled jealously for the living. Others say the spirits of the dead give the Remains strength and power, so the Holhouettes act as servants and provide fresh souls. But I suppose we'll never know because it lives in solitude within the Dead Forest far away from here… and anyone who enters there… is swiftly destroyed," Seff continued, entertaining them with answers as though it was all a made up story created to scare the young. "Then why are the Holhouettes all the way over here if that Dead Forest is nowhere near?" Wick asked.

"Legend has it, there's an underground hive full of complex tunnels where they take refuge from the burning day light. They live beneath an ancient burial ground which was once a battlefield, and the graves atop the soil belonged to soldiers that had died. Somehow the Remains was attracted by the large quantity of bodies and that's where his swarm of undead came from-".

"That's enough, Seff. They don't need to know anymore," Yewki said, listening to the story from a distance. "Even *I* didn't know that last part," he muttered to himself. He felt that the concept of death embodiment and undead man-eaters was a topic too heavy for Wick and Lumni. It was something he hoped they would never encounter so made sure not to make it a big deal. The odd horde of Holhouettes however, was very real and became the main discussion whilst they continued on their travels.

"There's probably one more day ahead of us before we reach shelter," Yewki alerted the group who had made it to early morning. "We could have just slept in the mill," Wick sighed.

"I said loud and clear, I am not staying where a man has just been eaten!" Seff moaned.

"It'll be daylight soon, Holhouettes can only come out at night," Yewki said.

"I say we get some rest whilst we can before the sun comes up," Lumni suggested.

"I said we're not stopping".

"If there's only a while left before day time, we won't have to worry about Holhouettes," she explained. Yewki looked around at everyone's tired eyes. Even Moon slouched his head and dragged his feet. "Very well. We'll get some rest," he exhaled. It only took a moment for them to roll out their woollen sheets and lay down. Moon laid across them all, blocking the cold wind like a shield with his thick body. Everyone managed to fall to sleep rather quickly except for Wick and Seff – both still awake for different reasons. Wick was kept awake by the voodoo even though he was beyond sleepy, and Seff was too scared to close his eyes in case of a Night Feeder ambush. There was still something Wick was dying to ask the Wizard, but hadn't had a moment to spare, so finally, he prodded Seff's shoulder, making him jump, then crawled closer towards him. "Why aren't you asleep?" the timid old man asked.

"It's the voodoo, just like you said," Wick answered.

"I wasn't expecting it to be this effective on your body so quickly. Perhaps I can make a remedy of some sort. Help you fall to sleep-".

"That's not why I wanted to talk to you. There's something else I was meaning to ask of you".

"I'm sorry Wick, I can't look after another child-".

"No, it's not that. Well you see, ever since I woke up alone with no one but Moon, I can't remember my past. I can't remember my parents or where I came from, or how I came to be friends with a bear. Lumni told me that you might be able to fix the holes in my memory".

"Hmm, there's a chance I can help, but it might be harder because of the voodoo".

"What do you mean?"

"When I search through your mind, I'm almost certain that the voodoo will fight back and prevent me. But I can try". Wick didn't care for Seff's warnings and focused on the possibility of finally discovering who he was. He laid down with his head facing up to the black sky, looking at the countless stars above before closing his eyes. He hoped that when he opened them again, he'd see memories of what was before. Seff searched through his bags quietly, looking for the right ingredients, then mashed together strangely-looking balls of mush and grime until a blue juice dripped out. The liquid trickled into a small vial until it was full to the brim. "Okay, the drink is ready," he whispered.

"How much do I drink?" Wick asked, confused with his eyes being closed, having no idea that Seff was guzzling it down himself. "It was for me," the Wizard explained as his face started to pout from the potion's bitterness. He shook in a cold shiver then placed his thumbs on the boy's eyelids and index fingers on both sides of his head, all whilst mumbling a string of unknown words. Wick could hear his heartbeat inside of his head, pounding like a big drum as Seff's hands began to glow white. "I'm now connecting my conciousness with yours, Wick. Don't be scared," the Wizard said as he closed his own eyes. "Okay... I'm now in your mind," he stuttered.

"What do you see?" Wick asked.

"Quiet, if you break from relaxation I could lose the connection". He continued to travel through the brain, retracing the boy's memories. "I see us at my cottage, chopping mushrooms. You, surrounded by people... and a Troll? I'm going the right way. Yes, I see you in the maze... my word, that looks terrifying. Sea-Theives. Yewki. You and Moon walking through a swamp. Here I am, I'm here. You awoke with the bear staring right at you! This is incredible. Ah, and now there's a black void... this is where the memories have been lost".

"Please," Wick muttered under his breath. Seff advanced through the nothingness in search of his memories, but the voodoo had come to evict the spell. Black, sharp spikes stabbed at Seff's projections, destroying his connection with Wick. "It's the voodoo. I'm losing the bond!" he panicked.

"Please try!" Wick pleaded.

"Ah, there, there! I've got one! It's your Father, Wick! Wick, it's your Father! You're in the woods." At this point, they had given up on being quiet and had woken Yewki and Lumni. Moon was still fast asleep. "What in world are you doing?" Yewki gasped.

"He's trying to get Wick's memory back!" Lumni smiled.

"Your Father... where's he going?" Seff asked himself as the projection in his mind continued. "He's... gone. He left you. He told you to *wait* and left in a hurry". The voodoo stopped Seff from getting any further and shattered his vision of Wick's mind, causing him to jump back and fall in pain. Wick sat up unharmed, trying to imagine Seff's description in his head, but there was no hope. "Are you okay?" Yewki asked Seff who was holding his head. "Yes, just a headache," he winced.

"He just left me," Wick sighed.

"Come on, Wick. It's okay," Yewki comforted.

"I had a feeling I was abandoned... but I thought Seff would be able to prove me wrong and show me what really happened, but it was true... he just left me, Seff saw it for himself". He started to cry but quickly stopped in shock – black liquid dropped from his eyes – not even his tears were safe from the curse. "Seff didn't see the whole picture, he was kicked out of your head before he saw any more," Yewki explained.

"Maybe the voodoo attacked Seff on purpose... to stop him seeing more. Maybe the voodoo wants me to feel mental pain as well as physical!"

"That's enough, Wick".

"You don't need a Father. You have Yewki now, and Seff... and me," Lumni said, taking everyone by surprise. Moon was woken up by all the talking and noticed his companion upset. He wandered over and sat next to him, letting him lean on his podgy body for comfort. "Besides, that bear has been with you since you woke up alone. He's taken care of you more than any of us," Seff chuckled, recovering from his head pain. "You don't remember anything but your name and the bear's name, that means he must have been important to you," he continued.

"You're all right," Wick exhaled. "Maybe I should stop looking behind me".

"If there's no way for you to remember your past, then all you can do is look ahead... and we'll all be here for you," Yewki smiled.

"Thank you Seff, for trying... I should focus on more important things, like helping you stop Yewnin," Wick said to Yewki. "But that doesn't mean I don't hate my Father. I hope he regrets what he did".

"You're in more capable hands now... I think," Yewki laughed to lighten the mood, followed by the sun's dawn to lighten the day ahead.

Chapter 18

The Holhouettes of Favarly

At long last, the five wanderers had reached a place of refuge far away enough for Yewki to feel comfortable, but safety was still a concern with a new danger they'd soon be in the thick of. The large town of Favarly was full of dark wood and clay. Gloomy houses and unwelcoming taverns filled the majority of streets, but what stood out the most was the large number of churches, all pointing upwards with crooked spires. The people were in the few, uncaring for the new arrivals. They seemed to rush around as though they didn't like being outside. Not even the bear attracted their curiosity, only the odd look of surprise and disgust. The paths and roads were gravel, indicating that the town didn't have time for renovations. Their primary focus was keeping their families close and their doors shut. "Excuse me, can you-," Yewki said to a passer-by, but they didn't stop to listen. "Hello, could you- ah, this is hopeless!" he moaned after being ignored again. The group continued roaming the town in search of a place to stay, but every building looked the same. There were no signs highlighting anything of interest, making it even harder to depict what was what. Wick ran ahead towards an old woman who was hobbling around an unused market square. "Excuse me, I have no place to stay. Is there anywhere with beds for a night?" he whimpered, pretending to be alone and incapable, in hopes to win a response through sympathy.

The old woman looked down at him with sad eyes. "Yes," she said. "There's the Duckbill Inn further down the road".

"And how many beds are there?" he asked.

"You're not by yourself?" she huffed then looked around and noticed the other four loitering. She scoffed at the sight of them and carried on walking. "There's a place to stay, further down the road," he notified the group as he ran back to them. "Cunning work, boy," Yewki smiled. They wasted no time to hunt down The Duckbill, making itself known by the tiny, easiy-to-miss duck carvings on the front door. All were apprehensive to knock but Seff, desperate to lay down. After banging on the door, they waited for a moment then heard the jingling of keys and the scraping of five locks being pulled out until the door creaked open slowly. A stumpy, middle-aged man stood peeking out from behind the door. "What d'ya want?" he croaked.

"We're looking for four beds and a place to keep… a bear," Yewki informed.

"Oh yeah? Well I got plenty of beds… but I ain't havin' a bear in 'ere".

"Please, this might sound strange, but he's completely safe… he's a pet," Yewki said with cringe. He knew that Moon would be looking at him with disgust after being labelled a *pet*, so he didn't dare turn his head. "Oh no it's not that. I can't have any other animals in 'ere… they'd scare the ducks," the man explained. Yewki was beyond the point of surprise, nor did he choose to care that the man was housing ducks indoors. He closed his eyes to calm himself, sighed, then continued to beg. "How much money do you want?" he asked.

"Money? But we don't have any," Wick whispered. Yewki placed his finger over his mouth, prompting Wick to keep quiet. He then looked over to Seff and started mouthing the word, *'Money'*, whilst twiddling his fingers and raising his eyebrows. The Wizard caught on with the ploy and started rummaging through his bags. "This isn't about money… it's about the well-being of my ducks," the man spat. Seff was working quickly on making gold coins, but the inn owner stepped from behind the door to look at the group closer. Moon shoved himself in front of the Wizard to hide his dirty tricks whilst the man observed him. "I don't even think it would fit through the door," he sighed. "Look, I know you need the rooms but I can't have that bear-".

"Lots of money!" Seff shouted nervously whilst jumping from behind Moon. He held a large sack full of freshly made fake coins, ready to burst out the seams. He chuckled anxiously as he passed the bag over to the small man. "I'll help you get him through the door," the inn owner stammered with shock and delight at the sight of such a great handful of money. The five of them clambered through the doorway to behold the horde of ducks and ducklings waddling around on the floor, atop tables and chairs, sat on the stairs and window ledges. They all flapped and quacked as Moon entered, making sure to stay well out of his way. "Thank you for your change of heart. What's your name?" Yewki asked.

"Areick. My family have owned this inn for quite a few generations," he answered.

"Why the ducks?" Lumni scowled.

"Well I *did* have them in the garden out back but y'see, since those Night Feeders started coming, I decided to breed 'em and farm their eggs in 'ere. That was a long time ago... we only had six of 'em at the time," he said whilst looking around at the escalated population.

"Holhouettes only eat people," Yewki interjected.

"Well how do you know?"

"I've had experience with them before. I know more about them than most, let's put it that way".

"Oh, so you're a monster hunter are ya? Well believe me, we've had loads of people like you coming here, gloating, saying they can get rid of the infestation, but they always die".

"I'm not here to fix your town's problems".

"That's probably for the best... if you value your life," Areick laughed and coughed. The town had grown so used to Holhouettes invading the land and eating people that they gave up on trying to fight back long ago, but they still feared them greatly. "So what brings you lot to Favarly? It's not somewhere many people come to visit," he asked.

"None of your business," Lumni snapped.

"Well you lot better not be on the run from someone... we don't want any more trouble here".

"We won't be a problem," Seff expressed.

"Right then... here you go. I'll give you a downstairs room so the bear doesn't have to climb the stairs. I think he'd fall through them". Areick passed the keys to Yewki and let them be. "And just a warning... I know how many ducks there is so if that bear has any, I'll know it!" he chuckled as they walked down the hallway.

Lumni and Wick laid down with Moon slotted in the gap between their beds, receiving strokes and scratches from both of them. Seff snored like a beast at the other side of the room, curled up tight with the quilts smothering his face. Yewki on the other hand was busy holding a dagger he had strapped to his side. "Wick? Are you awake?" he whispered.

"Yes. I still can't sleep".

"Come over here for a moment". Wick walked across to Yewki's bed and sat at the end of it with him. They both had a view of the sun setting through the window. "It's going to be dark soon. You know what that means don't you?" he said to the boy.

"Why don't we help rid these people of the Night Feeders?"

"Because it is not our problem... and I'd say we have a bigger one ourselves".

"It's not fair for them to live in fear like this".

"Well at least they're used to it... because the whole world is going to be in the same state after Yewnin". Yewki sighed and passed him the dagger carefully. "You need to be able to protect yourself tonight, just in case," he stressed, changing the conversation back to the Holhouettes. Wick stood up and started walking back to his bed. "You and Lumni killed one so why can't we stop the rest?" the boy asked.

"Because Lumni was being foolish, we were lucky… and we don't know how many of them there are!" Yewki tried his hardest to whisper aggressively then swooped down into his bed in anger, hoping for a good night's rest. A few hours of slumber led to midnight. Wick had managed to sleep lightly so the slightest noise would shudder him awake again and again. He rolled over from left to right, then back over in a constant battle between his reluctance and need to sleep. The thought of his Father leaving him to fend for himself played on his mind, and the fact there was no word of memory of his Mother made things worse, but there was nothing he could do about it. His thoughts and dreams drifted between each other, making his consciousness delirious and unsettling. The absolute silence prevented him from focusing on anything else but his mind, until a scraping noise from outside grabbed his attention. The window was located on the other side of the room next to Yewki so he couldn't look outside in fear of waking him up. What sounded like heavy footsteps on the gravel paths became fast, running stomps. Wick wanted to help, but he knew he couldn't do it alone. Yewki and Seff wouldn't help and Moon would stop him from leaving, so he shook Lumni awake. She turned around in confusion to see Wick gesturing her to stay quiet. "What's a matter with you?" she whispered.

"Those monsters are running around outside".

"How many?"

"I don't know, I didn't look". Lumni didn't even need to be asked to help. She yanked her bow from under the bed and grabbed a hand full of arrows whilst Wick helped attach her quiver to her back. They crept out of the room and tiptoed down the hallway, only to remember that there was a flock of easily-scared ducks waiting for them at the end. Instead of trying to get by the birds, they unclasped a small window and squeezed out into some long grass at the side of the inn. Dozens of Holhouettes scurried past them sniffling and gargling, but they didn't seem to be entering any houses nearby. Lumni pulled Wick by the hand and escorted him forwards into the streets when suddenly, another group of Night Feeders ran by, almost knocking into them.

They stopped to look at one another before running and catching up with the rest. Wick thought it was the end – that they were going to be killed there and then. He wasn't expecting the beasts to carry on going. With no time to wonder why, they followed the pack from a distance down numerous roads and alleys until they reached a seemingly normal house among the rest, which the Holhouettes seemed to have taken a liking to. At least thirty of them were climbing up the outside of the building whilst more began smashing through the door and windows, followed by a manly cry. "Come on!" Lumni panted, dragging Wick closer. He was having second thoughts about attacking now that he'd seen the sheer number of them, but Lumni didn't seem to care. She ran through the open door with Wick traipsing behind. "No!" the man upstairs yelled. Thuds and scratches from the above floor boards dropped dust onto their heads. Lumni ran to the stairs but was stopped by a Holhouette making its way down, causing her to fall backwards, and roll to the floor. Wick ragged out the dagger and held it with both hands, pointing it to the creature as it made its way down and past Lumni, unable to stop his hands from shaking. It shrieked and hissed in his face which hurt Lumni's ears, but Wick didn't hear it. Instead he heard a voice in pain, struggling to make itself heard, trapped inside of a monster. "I don't want to have to hurt a child," it said.

"You can speak?" Wick gasped.

"You can understand us?" it replied, more shocked than the boy. To everyone else, the monsters only let out horrid death cries and growls, but somehow, Wick was able to hear the true voice within. "Come on men, the feast is done, let's move," another one ordered as it staggered downstairs, acting like their fleet commander. "Why aren't you moving, soldier?" it asked the other one who was amazed by Wick. Lumni sat up stunned at what she was seeing. "Are you going to eat me?" the boy cowered.

"Why are you listening to him? He won't understand you," the commander grunted as he led his group out of the windows. "No, child. We don't want to eat anybody," the curious Holhouette explained.

"Then why have you just killed somebody?" he shouted.

"We must, we have to… we try to choose the sick ones… the old and the dying ones. We don't want to but we have to!" it begged.

"Get out! Leave! You've taken my wife now leave you monsters!" the owner of the house cried out as he ran down the stairs with a pitchfork. Lumni fired her bow, hitting the monster in the back. The Holhouette wailed and ran away to catch up with the rest of them. "They ate my wife! My darling Deordrai," he continued to sob. He was too distraught to question why there was two children in his house, and Wick was too dumbfounded by the fact he was able to understand the creatures. Suddenly, Yewki barged in with his sword about to swing. "They're gone! They killed my wife!" the man explained to him whilst rolling on the floor in emotional agony. "What are you two doing here?!" Yewki roared at Wick and Lumni.

"We only came to help!" she moaned.

"You could have died!"

"I spoke to them. I can hear their voices," Wick exhaled.

"What?" Yewki and Lumni said together.

"It told me-".

"They don't speak! We've all heard them, their screams are deafening!" Lumni scoffed.

"You must have imagined it," Yewki huffed as he dragged him out of the man's house, leaving him to cry and whimper. "I didn't imagine it! It told me they don't want to kill but they have to, they can't help it!"

"That's enough, boy!"

"They try to go for the old and the dying, it's against their will!"

"I said stop it!" he shouted. "Don't be foolish. You and Lumni almost died, what were you thinking? Is it because I gave you that dagger, you suddenly thought you could take on the world? You're just a child, and you need to start focusing on what I tell you!" Yewki's blood was boiling with rage, but deep down, it was fuelled by the fear of the two of them being killed. He snatched the dagger back off of Wick and dragged him and Lumni to towards the inn. As they turned the corner, a mob of citizens stood waiting for Yewki. It was unusual for the people to be socialising, especially in the middle of the night, but they all had the same desire. "You, creature killer!" one of them said at the sight of Yewki, causing everyone else to bombard him from all sides. "What did you call me?" he gasped.

"Areick told us you're one of those monster hunters!"

"What? No... I said I *wasn't*. Does it look like I killed any?"

"Well it looks like you could have," a woman said, looking him up and down. The crowd surrounded him, begging for his help. "We've finally had enough. We're tired of hiding. We've never seen so many attack at once... it's getting out of hand!" one of them shouted.

"Yeah! We saw those children chasing after them and thought, why aren't we?" another one agreed.

"By all means, be my guest. You know where the Holhouettes are coming from," Yewki hissed, curling up a false smile. "No, *you're* the monster hunter!" they argued.

"I'm not here to fix your issues!" he whined.

"Don't listen to him, he's strong and brave. He could take them all on if he wanted!" Lumni cheered, purposely winding him up in front of the crowd. "I don't have time for this!" he scoffed to the crowd whilst scowling down at Lumni. He continued to drag her and Wick but the mob followed them. "We need your help!" they shouted.

"Believe me, I'm trying to help on a larger scale... you just don't know it yet, and you should be thankful for that," he grumbled to himself whilst entering the Duckbill Inn.

The bedroom was quiet, but no one was sleeping. Seff had been hiding with Moon whilst Yewki ran out to find Wick and Lumni. He was interested in what the boy had to say about the Holhouettes, as Wick told them about being able to talk to the Night Feeder, and the fact they were trying to eat the old and dying, all whilst Lumni argued away with Yewki about doing what the people asked of him. The only thing left afterwards was awkward silence as the morning light lifted from behind the houses. Areick knocked on the door knowing that he could potentially be torn apart by Yewki, so he brought eggs and milk to apologise for his loud mouth. "Complimentary breakfast. Enjoy," he chuckled apprehensively.

"Stop right there," Yewki barked as Areick tried to quickly leave the room. "You told everyone I was a monster killer... when I made it abundantly clear-".

"It's not his fault, Yewki. I speak as a man who knows a lot about fear... maybe he just hoped you would try and help the town. They have no one else to turn to," Seff interrupted.

"I don't want to hear what you have to say too. I've already had a mouthful from the other two".

"They're scared, Yewki! If Yewnin was behind all of this you wouldn't hesitate to put an end to it".

"But he's not behind it is he... it's the Remains, and no one can tamper with death... you of all people should know that".

"No one has to kill anything, if I can hear what they have to say then maybe we can-," Wick began to suggest, but was cut off by Yewki angrily standing up from his bed. Areick left quietly without any one noticing as they argued. "Things were a lot easier when I was alone".

"Well you're not anymore. You made a promise to Wick," Seff said.

"Do you want to help me fight an army of Holhouettes, Seff? I didn't think so".

"We don't have to fight them!" Wick cried.

"They're undead monsters! They have no purpose but to die. It's probably what they want".

"Wick is right. We need to help these people. We need to try," Lumni moaned.

"No, you just want to run into the midst of battle, firing arrows everywhere. But you'll die," Yewki sighed.

"I believe Wick... he can speak with them," she confessed.

"Surely you don't think-".

"I agree too!" Seff said. Yewki turned round to him, looking confused whilst folding his arms, awaiting an explanation. "I've been thinking about it for a few hours now. If he *can* speak to them, then what element of Wick is it that allows him to talk to the living dead? The voodoo might be letting him understand them just as the Holhouettes communicate between themselves. The curse is killing him from the inside whilst his soul fights back... technically, Wick is living dead too". Yewki took time to think about Seff's theory. The Wizard was the smartest person in the room, but he still didn't want to believe it. "If that's true then we're still left with another question. If they're aiming for dying people and the elderly, how are they able to know and differentiate?" he asked.

"My only explanation is their connection to the Remains. Perhaps they can sense impending death and focus on killing those in an attempt to steer away from the young and fruitful. They seem to still be humane at heart, but the impulsive instinct inside of them forces them to hunt," Seff explained.

"Okay, so if the boy is in a way, *dying*, why didn't they have a greater urge to attack him?"

"That I don't know."

"Exactly, so it's too dangerous".

"But we can find out!" Wick stressed. Yewki flipped the small table at his side, sending it crashing into the wall. He was tired of letting the others walk all over him and ask things of him. Whilst alone, he had time to focus on himself and complete his missions, but with three more people and a bear, his direction was pulled and tugged all over the place. In a way, he regretted promising Wick that he would look after him. Leaving him with Seff was the logical option, but the boy's emotions got the better of him. Then before he knew it, he found himself having to look after even more people, thanks to Yewnin forcing them all to leave the cottage. His lone wolf style of working had been compromised and he found it difficult to adjust. Even if he could, their ideas and opinions were impossible to put to rest unless acted upon, making him feel like less of a leader with a final say, and more of a slave to whatever they demanded. The worst part was that he knew they were right about the Holhouettes, but not knowing Yewnin's plans, he was scared to waste time on any other agenda. He turned to look at

Wick. "If Seff was able to save you from the verge of death, could there be a way of replicating the remedy on a larger scale?" he wondered.

"What do you propose?" Seff asked.

"Maybe you could retract the death inside of the Holhouettes the same way you did for Wick... letting them live above their unwilling urges just like you made Wick unable to fully succumb to the voodoo".

"Yewki, it was rushed... and experimental. I don't know if it would work on them. Necromancy and voodoo are completely different".

"I've changed my mind, I'm trying to help Favarly, so you need to help me," he said with remorse in his voice. Wick and Lumni grinned, knowing that they had won over the stubborn man, whilst Seff realised convincing Yewki was a bad idea, now that he had to help with the monsters as well.

Chapter 19

Troll Crusade and the Crystal Messenger

The Slayers of Emmrin-Rashmada were above all other global threats. Nothing ever managed to scare them or take them by surprise, except for an army of dragon-riding Trolls attacking their kingdom without warning – a race of people so malicious didn't deserve to be notified. The Trolls had an outgoing mind-set of just getting things done, which was why they were attacking at full force, regardless of whether or not Yewnin was present. If they were to be successful, they would lay waste to Yewnin's largest and most valuable ally. Tbrok fulfilled his duty and led the huge fleet across the Slayer borders on a thousand Jevetin dragons. The fat, winged beasts drooled molten lava from their mouths, splashing and scarring Emmrin-Rashmada's fields of dry land, finally gaining the attention of watchmen. Horns blew, bell towers rang, soldiers readied and catapults were armed, all in a frantic scurry. The Slayers had no evacuation technique for their civilians because they simply didn't care, nor was there a defence strategy. They welcomed challenge with open arms, even if they weren't previously prepared. The daunting mile left between the two sides became shorter and shorter by the second, but both Troll and Slayer were ready for anything. The flapping of Jevetin wings crashed the air like thunder and roars from both dragon and Troll vibrated the Slayers' metal armour. "We were born to fight!" bellowed Tbrok. "We were born to dominate! We were born to win!" he cheered whilst waving his fists in the air. At the same time, Rowdun the Woundless stood with his older brother, Hundo the Wise and commanded the East and West sides of the walls together. "We were born to slay!" Hundo yelled. "We were born to rule! We were born victorious!" he screamed. The two armies shared the same confidence but only one of them would prevail. The Trolls had reached the walls and were met with a volley of arrows, sending a moderate portion of the dragons to their early graves, but the survivors poured lava as they flew low over the city. The Jevetins dropped a molten barrage directly at the volley archers, dowsing the majority of them successfully. Rowdun commanded the catapults to fire towards the front of the flock in hopes of hitting Tbrok, but the large clumps of stone missed all of them thanks to the clever coordination of the Trolls.

    It didn't take long for them to reach the other end of the walls. They wasted no time turning back round, but this time they split into two squadrons to attack the left and right sides simultaneously. King Zamanite watched the battle ensue from his castle tower, uncaring for the fact that a dragon could crash into the building at any moment. The entire building was coated with metal sheets, ending with ragged spikes and points so the Trolls made sure not to fly too close. Ecklethorpe observed from his bedroom, angry that he couldn't be a part of the fight. His age meant that there was no respect wasted on him. At seventeen years old, his skills were being overlooked but he knew how capable he was. Unfortunately for him, admiration was something he had to earn, so he opened his window and started to climb out of it. Breaking the rules would gain people's attention by force and prove to his Father that he's more capable than he thought. He began his descent down the steep walls with only a few cracks and slits to place his hands and feet. Slow and steady was key, but the longer he took, the less fight there was left. His only hope was to reach the bottom before the Slayers won. By this point, the Troll fleets had been thinned out greatly, with only a few hundred left, but the survivors consisted of the strongest and deadliest troops. Jevetins began to land within the walls, allowing foot soldiers to attack the city. The Trolls were tall and towered over the Slayers with ease. They used stone clubs and hammers to whack whole groups of men at a time. Arrows hit their rough skin, but the majority of them bounced off on contact. Slayers started to throw large harpoons to penetrate the thick hide and pull them down to the ground with ropes and nets. The streets were full of man and Troll, both knocking one another down, bursting through nearby buildings, all whilst dodging the rain of lava from above. "This is chaos! I love it!" Rowdun cackled whilst equipping his infamous twin blades. He jumped down to the thick of it all, slicing away at the Troll's weak areas whilst jumping and flipping over obstacles. "The Woundless!" a Troll sergeant cried. The alert brought six large Trolls to the scene, making a circle around Rowdun. He smiled as his enemies got closer, but he ducked and weaved through their attacks, causing them to stagger in confusion. Before they knew it, their bodies were covered in deep cuts. The sergeant charged towards the Prince as his comrades slammed to the ground all at once. It didn't take more than two seconds for the Woundless to jump in the air and push both of his swords through the Troll's skull. He flung a handful of throwing knifes from his belt, knowing that there were three more enemies creeping up behind him. They all fell each with a knife in their foreheads. Meanwhile, Hundo had used all remaining catapults, and the number of volley archers still standing was down to a dozen. He decided to lead a small group of soldiers towards the Dragon Port in hopes that they had time to prepare an aerial offence of their own. Tbrok himself had landed, dropping from two stories up and landing with a roll, running over and crushing a group of men with his bouldering body. He left his Jevetin above him to provide air support as he advanced towards the castle, set on pulling the Slayer King's head of with his bare hands. His old, stumpy feet prevented him from manoeuvring fast, but he made up for it with strength. He span his stone mace around, snapping pillars and crumbling walls in his way as he advanced. Two bodyguards ran to assist and cover his sides but Eck dropped from above, slicing the throat of one of them and riding the other one like a wild horse. The Troll span and swung around in a panic, but the Prince quickly ended him, leaving only Tbrok in his way. "Look at you!" the Troll Lord scoffed. "You're too young to be fighting in a war!"

"And you're too old to be standing!" Eck taunted.

"Do you even know what this war is about, child?"

"I don't care... war is war and there can only be one victor". Eck ran towards him with twin blades of his own, but the Troll had a hundred years more fighting experience than he did. He swung his mace diagonally, just missing the Prince's head. Eck was fast and nimble which was the opposite of Tbrok. The only advantage he had now was his rock-like skin, even harder than the usual Trolls because of his old age. Eck sliced and lunged at Tbrok's legs, but his blades did nothing. The Troll Lord kicked him away during his moment of confusion, sending him several meters back and through a window. He crashed into a house and barrel-rolled through all the glass, taking a moment before standing back up. Tbrok ripped off the whole front of the building and reached in to grab Eck but he dived out the way, allowing him to run up the giant's arm and stab him in the neck. At last, blood poured out of his enemy, but victory was still far away. The raging Troll smacked Eck off of his shoulder and pulled out the sword without a single sign of pain. He placed the Slayer's weapon in his mouth and chewed it up as though it was made of glass. With only one blade left, Eck took a step back to recalculate a plan of attack. "You should run, child," Tbrok grunted.

"A Slayer always faces a challenge head on," the proud Prince spat.

"Do yourself a favour and leave this kingdom while you're still young, before it's too late". To their surprise, Rowdun entered the fight, ending the conversation before it could even begin. He fought with the Troll Lord one on one. "They're storming the castle!" a soldier screamed. Eck left his brother to fight and helped defend the castle entrance.

"My Prince, Hundo has prepared the Clawkings for flight at the Dragon Port," Rowdun's lieutenant informed. The Woundless was in the midst of fighting but he still had time to respond. "No, tell him to wait. We still have one more thing to try," he panted. The lieutenant ran back across the battlefield to let Hundo know, but the Wise mounted his personal dragon anyway and used it to breathe fire from a static position. The Clawkings were one of the largest winged beast species, with the greatest wing span of them all. Its wide-radius fire blast was unmatched and burnt everything it touched just as quickly as the Day Relic. Hundo started to steer it through the streets, but its huge grey body was seen from a mile away. He blew bursts of flame through the narrow paths and alleyways, sending it gushing around corners and catching everyone off guard. He knew what Rowdun wanted to try before releasing the dragons and was on his way towards it. The Slayers were gaining the upper hand quickly as the Trolls diminished. King Zamanite stood at the entrance with his elite guards, pushing the invaders back faster than they could advance. Eck made sure to be battling in the middle of the skirmish so that his Father could see, but the roar of Hundo's Clawking caught his attention instead. The two older Princes stood together on top of the city walls, readying their men with scolding swords. The blades were freshly placed within the Clawking's fire, superheated and ready to melt through anything. "Now!" Hundo yelled, ordering the soldiers to cut through dozens of chains around the wall. Their glowing hot swords sliced through the metal like knife through butter, releasing parts of the wall's restraints. Down came crashing sheets of metal like falling trees, landing inside of the city without a care for collateral damage. The inside layers of the wall had plenty of metal reinforcing it so releasing some didn't compromise the structural integrity. The trap was designed by Hundo himself and now he was able to put it into action in front of the King. The huge pieces of metal boomed onto the floor, killing most of Tbrok's remaining soldiers as well as destroying a large percentage of houses and other buildings, but the Slayers still didn't care. Instead they cheered, watching the remaining Trolls start to retreat on their Jevetins. Rowdun joined Hundo on the Clawking to catch the escapees. Unexpectedly, Eck jumped on board last minute with a bow. "What are you doing here?" Hundo asked.

"Never mind that. Get me close to those Trolls," he shouted.

"You think you're going to kill Tbrok and take all the credit? You're not the only one with a bow," Rowdun snarled, grabbing another bow from the side of the saddle. There were six Jevetins left ahead of them flying in a row, but Eck only had two arrows and Rowdun had three. The Woundless shot his first and hit one of the Trolls on the end of the row, sending it soaring to the ground. Eck shot one and hit a Jevetin near the wing, causing it and its rider to plummet to their death. In the space of him getting his last arrow ready, Rowdun had shot his remaining two; one missing and one hitting. "Give me your arrow!" The Woundless barked, but Eck refused. Three Trolls were left and one of them was Tbrok. If he could pick the right one, his Father would praise him for a lifetime. "What are you waiting for? It's the one of the left," Hundo said.

"No it's not, it's the one in the middle!" Rowdun whined. Eck chose the Troll on the right hand side, refusing to be swayed by his mischievous brothers. He let go of the bow string and watched as the arrow whizzed through the sky. It hit the beast perfectly in the back of the head, but it wasn't Tbrok. All he could do was watch the wrong one fall to the floor. "Quick, we can catch up! Let the dragon get them!" he begged, but they chose to turn around and fly back to the kingdom. "What are you doing?" he screamed.

"Don't worry, we'll tell Father you tried… but we'll also tell him *you* brought us back home," Hundo smirked.

"Stop it!"

"You should have given the last arrow to me!" Rowdun growled. They landed at the Dragon Port and made their way to the castle, passing all the death and destruction they had a heavy hand in creating. "That Troll won't do us any more harm now that he has no army left. But Father won't see it that way," Hundo explained. "Why waste our time killing him when we don't need to? It's perfect… now we can blame you for it too". Eck always tried his hardest, but was forever foiled by his brothers who made it their life's mission to keep him well away from the good books, like pushed to the dirt before he'd even had chance to stand.

The three brothers discussed the battle with King Zamanite, lying at every possibility to make them sound better than what they were. Eck on the other hand kept his mouth shut, knowing that his Father wouldn't listen to him and his brothers would do everything they could to deny him. Rowdun told Zamanite that Eck refused to share the scarce arrows and then deemed it pointless to keep chasing Tbrok. "You're a Slayer, Ecklethorpe... a Prince! We do not allow our enemies to live!" the King exploded with rage. "You let him escape. The on thing worse than a coward is an even bigger coward who doesn't dare finish the job!"

"Eck snatched the ropes from me and turned the Clawking around, Father. He wouldn't give them back. He said that Tbrok has no army left so we shouldn't have to kill him," Hundo lied.

"You know he's young and stupid. You two should have taken the ropes back by force!"

"But he seemed so dead set. He said he was following your orders, so we didn't question him... until we landed and he confessed to lying," Rowdun stuttered.

"Is this true, Hundo?" Zamanite grunted.

"Yes, all of it. I can't believe it myself, Father," he falsely gasped. The King unsheathed his sword and pointed it at Eck with a deathly stare, prompting him to arm himself. He did as his Father wanted and took out his remaining blade, not even remotely prepared to take on the King in a fight. "Where's your other blade?" Zamanite asked.

"What?"

"Your sword has a twin, does it not?"

"The Troll Lord chewed it to pieces, I saw it," Rowdun pointed out to help humiliate his brother. The three of them laughed at him. "Why does it matter? I can still fight with one".

"It matters because you were clearly able to be disarmed. Besides, you had no place in that fight. I told you to stay in your room. I told you, you were incapable but you joined in anyway... and all you did was prove me right. So now you have one last chance to prove me wrong. Show me that you can still fight with just one... or get out of my sight!" the King yelled whilst swinging his sword towards Eck, knocking his son's blade out of his hand and cutting his cheek. Rowdun and Hundo leaned forward, eager to be entertained, but Eck ran away to his room. "I may as well rule him out as a throne contender right now. Or maybe this will make him try even harder," Zamanite pondered. He left his other two sons to go about their day of celebration and made his way to the dungeons deep underneath the castle. The spiral staircase travelled downwards, sending up screams of pain from below. It was music to his ears as he strolled down the dark, narrow corridors in search of a certain cell. "Your Majesty," a dungeon keeper smiled and bowed. "Congratulations on your victory today. Another species extinct," the man praised, not knowing that Tbrok wasn't killed. Zamanite clenched his fists and held in his anger. "I'm looking for the one-eyed Shaman. Which cell?" the King asked.

"She's got no eyes now, m'Lord... we took the other one out too!" The keeper escorted him to the right room and left him alone with the Shaman. She was old and shivering, slouched against the cold wall slowly losing the will to live. "Baba, we told you – we'd take your eyes out if you didn't comply, now look at you. You're hideous!" he pestered. "You see, if you'd worked with us then you wouldn't be in this mess. We would have killed you quick and clean... but you refused to help, so I'm afraid we'll have to keep you alive. You won't like it though. Your only wish will be to die, just to rid yourself of the pain, but you won't have the strength to move a muscle. Now, you better listen carefully because you have one chance left. My accomplice, Yewnin... he's giving me all the Shamans I could ever want all the way from the Dewhills... you probably know a few of them. I'm going to do to them what I've done to you if you don't give me something right now! Please, for their sakes". Baba shuddered in fear, but eventually nodded her head slightly. "Good," he smiled sinisterly. He reached into his pocket and pulled out a small, bright blue gem which pulsed with a glowing light. "Yewnin gave me this stone when we first met as a symbol of trust. Do you know what it is? Go on, you can hold it". He placed the gem in her hands causing it to pulse more frequently like a panicked heartbeat. She felt it delicately, relying only on the sense of touch, but it didn't take long for her to figure it out. "The Stone of Voices," she crackled.

"That's right. And it allows you to convey a message through the Astral Vale, correct?"

"Yes".

"Excellent". He ragged her by the hair and pinned her against the wall. "Whatever premonitions you tell me, you tell it to him. He'll be waiting". She no longer valued her life and begged to be set free to the afterlife so wasted no more time. Her chest started to glow white as her breathing got heavier. The evident usage of Earth energy when soothsaying helped the Slayers know when they were telling the truth. If they pretended to give them information they would know about it and there'd be consequences. Zamanite pointed the stone closely at her mouth as she started to talk. "The consequence of battle leaves behind an undying reminder. Slaves of the Remains are taken from him and causality creates a new age when their illness is purged," she groaned. Zamanite had no idea what she meant but knew Yewnin would fare better with her cryptic words. "Thank you for your cooperation. I just need the blood of a Shaman for the message to be transported through the Vale. If you'd be so kind". He sliced her throat with a dagger before she had time to react, then held the gem near her neck so that her mystical blood would pour all over it. Meanwhile a hundred miles away, Yewnin sat alone, surrounded by candles and a ring of Shaman blood belonging to the body behind him. It was a practice he'd do most nights on the off chance that King Zamanite had information to disclose. Like Seff, he was able to use the Astral Vale, just not in the same sense. Seff had the ability to shift his entire existence into the Vale, but Yewnin could only send his mind, though he hoped in time, he'd be able to master the technique. Luckily for him, it was enough for an oral message to be received. He sat waiting, meditating, getting his head in the right state of mind, sensing that the Stone of Voices had something to say. His head twitched back as Baba's voice entered his brain, as though she was speaking directly from inside of his skull. *"The consequence of battle leaves behind an undying reminder. Slaves of The Remains are taken from him and causality creates a new age when their illness is purged,"* the stone repeated. He shook his head, opened his eyes and thought for a moment, then stood up and grabbed the Day Relic. He glared at its shape and its mesmerising aura of energy then absorbed it again. Unlike Zamanite, he knew exactly what needed to be done.

Chapter 20

Free Life if Only for a Second

It wasn't every day that the people of Favarly had reason to come together and applaud. Whether Yewki liked it or not, conventions were always altered and affected wherever and whenever he intruded. With much reluctance, he led Greenwick, Moon, Lumni and Seff out of Favarly, on the dangerous trail towards the Hive of Holhouettes. Yewki's shell was evidently softening the more he let others get their own way, but he knew they were off to do the right thing. However, the undead catastrophe still seemed slightly pointless to him, as his mind only wanted to care for Yewnin-related dilemmas. There wasn't much space for compassion left in his head, to the point that he began questioning the need to take care of the boy again, let alone escort him to great danger. It was a constant back and forth inside of himself – too afraid to offend but too tired to settle for something he didn't ask for. It was too late for him to back out of the Holhouette issue though, so he kept mostly to himself the whole trip with an empty mind, too scared to think about the ways he could leave the group and continue alone afterwards, wanting an answer, a plan, but unable to find the will power to do so, knowing the sort of uproar it would cause. His thoughts remained numb yet countless, similar to his footsteps as they trudged along forwards to their destination. The ancient battleground they ventured towards wasn't hard to miss, as no vegetation was able to regrow ever since the blood pour and carnage that violated the soil. Not even time itself could fix the heavily damaged land. The living carcasses nestled far beneath their shallow graves of old to avoid the sun's harmful rays in a giant underground city exclusive to them. Both tunnels and open spaces were filled with nothing but Holhouettes and the cold darkness, keeping one another company as though they were somehow connected. The infamous Remains had well and truly created an accursed hell on Earth, but a potential fix was on its way. For Wick personally, it was his longest journey by foot yet, but his desire to help the Holhouettes stopped him from complaining. He and the others endured a week's worth of freezing nights, muddy trails and Moon's compulsory night gazes, but thankfully, all journeys reach an end eventually. Before them stood wooden signs, differing in age. Some were placed centuries ago whilst others were only a few decades old, but all shared the same warning. "*The Land of Death's curse, beware.* That's appealing," Seff recalled sarcastically whilst rolling his eyes. They split up and looked around at the incredible number of signs either sticking out of the ground or nailed onto dead trees. "They all say the same thing," Lumni murmured.

"What about that one? That one says, *Dedwi ara lu'ou Kur*," Wick blabbered allowed terribly.

"That's Olash for, *Only Death ahead*," Seff explained.

"Yes well what else would you expect here?" Yewki scoffed, confused as to why everyone was so shocked at the scary warnings seeing as though they knew where they were going. After all the signs, there was a clear cut off point from nature. Only a few weary trees and bushes remained standing until a huge open land of nothing. "How can somewhere be so empty yet full of foul emotion at the same time?" Yewki gulped.

"It's the notion of what lies beneath," Seff shuddered.

"How many do you think there is down there?" Lumni wondered.

"All that matters is how many we save," Wick answered, sounding too concerned for someone his age. Moon walked behind slowly with much apprehension, knocking over the old signs by accident. The sentient maze tunnels and the underground temple were enough below-the-surface experiences for him, but the scariest was yet to come. Wick tugged the bear's fur to make sure he kept walking whilst they scanned for some sort of entrance. "I can't believe we're doing this," Yewki said.

"There's still time to reconsider," Seff whimpered, clenching tightly on his satchel of vials and ingredients. The rest of his belongings that Moon had been carrying to Favarly had been left at the Duck Bill Inn, as their intention was to travel back to the town to announce the outcome of their adventure. They only hoped that they would return with good news, but it was too early to think about the way back in case the worst were to happen. Although fear was the dominant feeling, the daylight helped them feel somewhat safer, knowing that there wouldn't be any Holhouettes above ground to spook them, but the longer it took for them to find a hole, the dimmer the day got.

"What's that smell?" Lumni gagged. Everyone looked to the bear in hopes that he would be able to lead to the source. "Come on, Moon, we know you can smell it. Your nose is better than ours," Wick nagged. Moon laid down on the floor, not wanting to move, but all four of them pushed and pulled him back to his feet. "Come on!" Yewki growled whilst using all of his strength to heave the beast. After a moody grunt, the bear slowly followed the rotten stench that was seeping out of the hive entrance. Before long, he found the hole but then laid down again. He looked at the width of the tunnel and knew he'd be able to fit down it, but the others would have to push him down it for him to move. The smell was beyond ghastly and they weren't even underground yet. It was like a thick wave of rotten flesh and bile constantly wafting in their faces. "Are you sure you want to do this, Wick?" Seff asked, but there was no answer. Now that Wick was faced with impending horrors, his urge to assist the creatures had diminished, as though the stinking tunnel blew away his confidence downwind along with its own odour, leaving only the smell of fear. "After you, Wick," Yewki prompted in an attempt to scare the boy further, but he was too busy avoiding eye contact. "I had a feeling this would happen. Now that you've experienced true danger you can fully understand why we shouldn't be doing this," he continued.

"I'm behind you, Wick," Lumni smiled. Seff stayed quiet next to Moon, both competing to be the most cowardly. Wick knew he had to prove himself. Going first through a deathly hole was somehow more bearable than Yewki bragging about how right he was, so he began to clamber down. "Whoa, no. You didn't actually think I'd let you go down first did you?" Yewki stammered, pushing the boy out of the way to look somewhat still in charge. He climbed down first as the others looked on. "This tunnel is fairly deep so make sure you hold on tight to the sides… you wouldn't want to fall," he explained whilst catching his breath during the slow and strenuous descent. "We shouldn't be doing this. What's happening? What happened for me to be here?" Seff panicked.

"Quiet, Seff… I'm trying to focus on-". Suddenly, Yewki was dragged downwards into the darkness before he could even yelp. The others jumped and stuck their heads in the tunnel but it was pure black. "They've took him!" Seff gasped.

"We need to help him!" Wick begged, but Moon pulled him away from the hole. Lumni pointed her bow down it, just in case a Holhouette popped up out of nowhere whilst Seff walked around in a scurry, babbling to himself. Scratches and crumbling could be heard beneath their feet, but they had no time to react as large chunks of the ground collapsed, creating pitfalls which revealed fresh tunnels made by hungry Holhouettes. The creatures each dragged a victim downwards in individual chasms. Moon on the other hand required a whole team to pull him. Their visions were compromised. All that could be seen was darkness and the hole they had fell through getting smaller the deeper they travelled. Other than the hideous smells corrupting their nostrils, the only senses they could rely on whilst being dragged were sound and touch. The frantic gargles of monsters and scuttling claws echoed through the tunnels, making it difficult to focus on the screams from other group members, and their bodies scrapped across the cold, damp and squishy dirt whilst rough hands yanked on their legs, causing them to roll around and slide uncontrollably. All five of them struggled and screamed but there was no one above to hear their cries, as they clambered lower and lower towards the heart of the complex.

After crazy landslides of soil, all but Seff were reunited by being plopped into a large, open area. A ring of screeching Holhouettes created an arena with the four of them nervously placed in the centre, huddled up together with Moon stood on his back legs to intimidate. They helped each other up and awaited Seff's arrival. It was made apparent that the Holhouette responsible for transporting the Wizard had lost its patience with him, as they finally rolled into the ring together. Seff kicked his legs and waved his arms around, making the monsters job all the more difficult. It ripped the old man's satchel off of his shoulder and threw it towards the crowd in anger. The hungry spectators started to rip and shake the bag, all trying to grab it for themselves. "Don't damage the bag! Don't let them!" Seff wailed. Wick tried to focus his mind so he could hear the monsters speak, but it was too hard to listen in to one voice as hundreds of them shouted and roared at the same time. Seff finally calmed down and the Holhouette left him alone to join the rest of the crowd. "If those potions smash and mix together, it could tear everything in here to pieces, including our bodies," Seff panicked, looking over at the curious creatures fighting over the satchel. One potion fell out onto the floor and smashed, making a splash of purple liquid and a small popping sound. The monsters looked down at the spillage confused and annoyed, sending them into a panicked outrage. "Tell them to leave the bag alone before something explodes!" Lumni gasped at Wick.

"Do it, boy!" Yewki shouted.

"They can understand all of us. It's just only I can hear their words," Wick stuttered, suddenly scared to speak up. Seff covered his face with his hands, too anxious to watch his precious concoctions being damaged. "Drop the bag! It could kill us all, you vile creatures!" Yewki stepped forwards and demanded, but they continued to rummage. "The man begs as though we will answer to him," one voice joked amongst the crowd that Wick picked up. "But you can answer to me!" the nervous boy shouted in response. The nearby Holhouettes stopped and gasped which caught on and travelled across the entire circle until all were aware that Wick could hear them. "Now put the bag down because the… the things inside of it can be dangerous if they're mixed," he continued. They wasted no time to comply and gazed on in disbelief. "They can hear us. That's not right," members of the crowd whispered and discussed.

"Just me. I can hear all of your voices," Wick answered. Lumni, Moon, Seff and Yewki could do nothing but watch on, only able to understand half of the conversation. It was jarring from their perspective but they were just happy everything had calmed down. Suddenly, an angry-looking Holhouette marched through the wall of undead bodies and towards Wick, causing the group to arm themselves in case it attacked. It seemed unconcerned about Lumni's bow aimed at its head and loomed over the boy's body. "Explain now, child!" it grunted. To the group, it just sounded like a croaky hiss. All they could do was guess what the monster was saying, using Wick's responses as clues. "You dare roam the ancient battleground? Do you want to be eaten?" it continued.

"No, no! We want to help you," Wick enlightened.

"You come in here with weapons… with a bag full of dangers".

"Please believe me". Yewki gripped his sword tighter, feeling as though the Holhouette wouldn't tolerate the conversation for much longer. "Are you the leader?" Lumni asked it. The creature chortled and groaned, but Wick provided the translation. "He says he was Chieftain of his men… he took it upon himself to lead. He says even though their hunger is against their will, there still needs to be someone in charge for order and structure," Wick recited slowly.

"Why can't your friends hear me? Why you?" it asked the boy.

"There's something wrong inside of me. My friend, Seffry is a Wizard so we figured-".

"A Wizard? There are no Wizards anymore".

"How do you know?"

"Because the last of them died! A large portion of this crowd were once Wizards of war!" it exclaimed, causing the masses to talk mysteriously between themselves. Wick was taken back, almost forgetting the fact that the Holhouettes were once men and women, all disfigured and mutated. Yewki didn't like the escalating whispers around them and began to worry. "What did it say?" he asked Wick.

"The last of the Wizards... they're all around us," he replied.

"Well I'm a Wizard! So whether he likes it or not, magic is still alive!" Seff complained.

"Magic is dangerous! Magic is what caused our war of old. Magic is what cursed us!" it growled.

"No. What cursed you was the Remains," Wick scowled in an attempt to defend Seff's discipline. All at once, the ring of undead scuttled in closer. "And how do you think that necromancer cursed us? The irony is that the existence of magic is a curse in itself," it sighed.

"Death uses magic?" Wick pondered.

"Ah-ah-ah! Death uses *dark* magic, there's a difference," Seff began to reassure.

"Tell your friend to stay quiet. I have the right mind to kill such a person. No one should be prolonging the art of Wizardry... it should have died with us!"

"Please don't kill him," Wick begged.

"*Kill*? Wick, what is he saying?" Yewki panicked.

"We just want to help you!" Wick stressed to it, but the Holhouette had grew tired of confusion and the translation interludes began to test his patience. Instead, it decided to take matters into its own hands in search of a quicker access to explanations. It sniffed Wick up and down like a dog, twitching its body in disgust with every breath. "Voodoo?" it exhaled whilst stepping back. "You trespass here and bring a bag of magic *and* a body full of voodoo?!" The swarm clambered in even closer and wailed in unison, jerking their bodies in fear and overwhelming sickness. "Please! We don't want to hurt any of you!" Wick shouted.

"No one comes to help the Holhouettes! We feed on people against our will! We're monsters of the night! No one feels what we feel! People come to eradicate us... not to fix us! Why should we trust you?!" it roared.

"Because you and I are not that much different!" Wick bellowed. The crowed fell silent with sudden respect and empathy. Yewki prompted Lumni to lower her bow as he placed his own weapon on the ground. "An Iwa did this to me... and now I'm cursed from the inside out. It's hard to sleep, I-I'm rarely hungry and when I *do* eat I feel even worse. My own blood is turning against me... I was going to die if it wasn't for Seff making things more stable! I've not been cursed for long, but I know if there were people who could save me I would at least be happy for it! I'm dead inside... just like you," Wick argued in a strop, suddenly uncaring towards who he was talking to. It did the trick at least. The thousand year old Holhouette was given a revelation from the thirteen year old boy. "If you truly *have* come here to end our suffering, I suppose it doesn't matter how you do it. Whether you kill us or mend us, it will save our souls," it sighed.

"Please trust me. We're here to mend," Wick said with a slow smile. Seff was ushered by Wick to explain the plan. Even though there was an evident truce, the old man still spoke nervous and weary. He explained to the Holhouettes that the fumes he made Wick inhale had a chance of reverting them all if there was a way to disperse the gas on a larger scale. The tunnels would help transport the steam around the hive, fully reaching every area of the complex at once. The definite outcome was unknown, but they hadn't travelled all the way there to be precarious. Seff dug through his tattered bag for the same things he used when operating on Wick. His coal bowl was damaged but it was still able to function, and all the important vials and bottles were still in one piece thankfully. New ingredients made an appearance this time though, with the purpose of amplifying the spell and its fumes. Yewki helped the Wizard tinker whilst Wick tried to get a little friendlier with the Chieftain. He explained his situation and his business with the bear to help pass the time, unbeknown to him that the Holhouettes were trying their hardest to resist eating anyone.

A few hours later, the sun had finally fallen below the horizon. A couple of miles away from the hive, Yewnin was wandering around empty fields, completely alone and surprisingly peaceful. Heavy rain fell all around him, covering his sight with a sheet of manic downpour, but strangely, the rain avoided him thanks to the powers he obtained, allowing him to stay completely dry. A family of wild horses fled upon sight of the man as he marched forwards with the Day Relic in-hand. Soaking birds taking shelter under the branches of trees had no choice but to fly away. Yewnin's aura was coated in dread and dismay which the wildlife could somehow sense, as though it was instinct for them to keep out of his way. After hearing the message from King Zamanite's Stone of Voices, he had been making his own way towards the hive, putting aside all other plans he had. The voice of Baba, the dead Shaman, echoed inside of him. *"The consequence of battle leaves behind an undying reminder,"* he heard in his mind. His extensive knowledge made the riddle-like statement far too easy to figure out. It was obvious that it meant the Holhouettes, but the second part of the premonition was a little more baffling. *"Slaves of The Remains are taken from him and causality creates a new age when their illness is purged,"* chimed around his head. He had no idea that anyone would be able to revert the Remains' curse, let alone the fact that Seff and friends were deep in the hive doing that very thing at that very moment. The night brought with it several stray Holhouettes on their way home from an evening of human consumption, but they were blocked by Yewnin and his disturbing grin. The creatures were scared out of their minds once they noticed him and tried to get around to refuge, but one gush of light and fire prevented them from progressing. Yewnin killed a handful of them without warning and let the rest run away in fear. He levitated and chased after them slowly on purpose. One after another, the Holhouettes were disintegrated in an instant, until just two remained. "Faster, you monsters! Run!" he taunted whilst killing one more. The last creature made its way towards the hive for safety, unintentionally leading Yewnin there with it. The false pursuit would soon land him at the ancient battleground where he planned to unleash the full force of the relic and prevent a '*new age*'. Only he wanted to be responsible and orchestrate what happens to the world, so any premonition, big or small, was met with a thorough counter-offence.

Back within the Holhouettes home, Seff had set up his apparatus and began to brew the magical liquids. Lumni held a flaming torch close by to help him see. The creatures had huddled around their visitors closely and impatiently, making the Wizard's job all the more difficult. "Wick, my boy, come here and give me your hand," Seff asked.

"Why?" Wick hesitated.

"I don't expect you to conjure this spell with me, but I can at least channel your Empyrean Energy to help expand my effect radius," he explained whilst grabbing the boy's hand. He closed his eyes and placed his free hand above the small coal bowl on the floor as it turned into the gold material, but this time he clenched his fist whilst moving around in a circular motion. Everyone watched on in amazement whilst the golden bowl thinned out and grew wider and larger whilst maintaining perfect symmetry and circumference. It eventually reached the size of fat cauldron and began to boil and bubble. "This is it?" the Chieftain asked Wick with surprise and delight. The creatures started to step back to observe the giant bowl from a distance. "What now?" Wick asked Seff to provide clarification for the Chieftain. The Wizard was too busy whispering and chanting quietly to himself with his eyes closed. "I think the fumes will rise any second now," Lumni answered for him with a smile. All of a sudden, the Holhouettes lowered themselves down to their knees to bow. Yewki was amazed. His view of the creatures had changed entirely and he actually felt happy to help them get their lives back. "To all of you, I'm sorry. I was actually against Wick's idea of helping you all… but now I see that all lives carry the same importance. All affairs are important… not just those that regard my brother," Yewki said. Wick smirked over to him and giggled with joy. At long last, the smoke rose from the bubbles. The Holhouettes kept their heads down and awaited whatever outcome. "This abrupt act of kindness, especially on such a scale as this… it's unheard of my child," the Chieftain explained.

"I just wanted to help," Wick replied.

"That urge to assist… your passion to come all this way for something that doesn't concern you is hard to comprehend. It's a special heart you have… and no matter what that voodoo does to your soul, your heart will always be yours. This world is cruel and full of hardship as you will have already discovered… all I ask is that you keep hold that heart of yours because the world needs more of it. Bless you". After a daunting wait, a thick smoke consumed everything around them. Moon brushed closely against Wick in fear of a bad result, but the boy welcomed the comfort. Fizzing and crackling filled the air as well as sudden gusts of ghostly wind, which flew upwards to escape the underground. It was hard to see if anything was happening, but a few groans and sighs popped up from the crowds. "My hunger is gone!" a voice gasped. One audible voice turned to a dozen, and a dozen quickly turned to hundreds. "They can speak! We can understand them!" Lumni cheered. Conversations turned into applause for the group of saviours as the smoke cleared, revealing creatures of paler skin and tamer mutations. Their bodies shrank down and had slightly reconstructed into a better human form, eroding away their claws for more of a hand shape. "I can feel once more," the Chieftain exhaled in amazement. Their urge to feast was gone and the Remains' hold on them had vanished. Even though their bodies were unable to fully revert, they were still happy and appreciative of Seff's efforts. "The Remains no longer controls us!" they all cheered.

"How can you be sure?" Yewki asked the Chieftain.

"I can't explain it… our souls feel… free," he replied, overwhelmed with everything. Wick cuddled with Moon whilst Lumni was across from them hugging Seff. They felt humbled at the fact that they had gone out of their way to help. The notion of more people in need around the world made them want to do more before they had even finished with the Holhouettes. Yewki looked at the four of them finally happy and full of faith. "Good call, Wick," he smiled.

"Thank you," the boy grinned back. Yewki pulled him away from Moon for a moment and knelt down to talk to him on a more personal level. "Look, perhaps it's a little early to discuss this but... my friends have disbanded. I don't know what happened with Tbrok's crusade, I have no word from Thene, Lall is far South and Piea and Batehong have been taken from me. My group is no more... and I need new warriors by my side," he eluded.

"You mean?"

"I can teach you how to use a sword, Seff can continue his training with you, and it'll be nice for you to have someone around your own age like Lumni... just don't surpass her at archery because she'll kill you". Wick hugged him tightly, and for the first time, Yewki hugged him back the same way, accompanied with a pat on the head. Unfortunately, good moments didn't last long when Yewnin was nearby.

To everyone's surprise, a huge bang ruptured and vibrated across the hive, dropping dirt and rocks from the cave roofs. The floor shook and sent everyone into a frenzy, all whilst smaller explosions struck from nearby areas. Only Yewki knew who and what was responsible. The idea of his brother being above ground, slowly burying them made his body pulse with a cold shooting pain in the form of adrenaline. Former Holhouettes ran around to avoid the collapsing roofs and crumbling tunnels, but the Chieftain stood his ground and awaited the worst. "We need to move!" Yewki shouted. After a few steps, Seff stopped and patted his robes in a panic. "I said move! Come on!" Yewki yelled.

"Wait, it's not here... it's fallen out!" the old man stammered.

"What are you talking about?" The Wizard looked around quickly, even getting on his hands and knees, until he found his mysterious vial sat in a pile of dirt. It was clear that whatever was contained in the turquoise liquid was important to him, but there was no time for the others to ask. After wasting time potion hunting, he shoved it back where it belonged then led the way through a steep passageway with Lumni, in hopes that they'd make it back to the surface with the others close behind. Wick looked across to the Chieftain. He had knelt back down, this time in despair. Wick wobbled around the uneven floor and screamed over to him, "Come on! We can't stay here! Your people need to get out-".

"No, child. Perhaps this is what we deserve – thinking we of all people would be allowed to be saved," he moaned. His body had been taken over by pain and anguish and there was nothing Wick could do to convince him to move. Yewki looked behind and shouted to them, but neither the boy nor the Chieftain responded. "But we've just saved you!" Wick cried.

"And I thank you for that. There is no effective way for me to fully convey the amount of gratitude I have towards you and your friends… perhaps we need to fulfil our death sentence, as that's what was seemingly in store for us the day we went to war… many, many centuries ago. We've overstayed our welcome on this Earth and in the process, we've created nothing but hate, fear and turmoil".

"But not anymore! You have another chance!"

"And we have you to thank for that… and even if it is just a moment of bliss, I'd rather die with my soul and consciousness prepared and at peace. Go, before it's too late, Wick".

"No! Come on, please!" Before Wick could stay and beg, Moon and Yewki dragged him away towards the escape tunnel against his will. He screamed and revolted whilst looking back at the unmoving Chieftain, ready to die. More and more tunnels collapsed around them until there was just a single narrow climb upwards. More shakes and explosions ploughed their way underground, trapping and crushing Holhouettes around the group as they ascended. Flashes of light from above disturbed the night sky similar to lightning, indicating that the threat was coming from above, meaning that their climb to safety would only result in more danger.

The near-vertical push to the surface came to an end with Lumni and Seff climbing out first, followed by Moon who was being shoved from behind by Yewki and Wick. When all five of them had squeezed their bodies out of the mud, they quickly ran in the opposite direction to the noises and lights. They had no time to appreciate the fresh, clear air as the only thing on their minds was the culprit fifty feet away from them, floating slightly and sending beams of scorching energy down into self-made holes. "Who *is* that? Is-is that your brother?" Lumni panted. Seff looked at Yewki and gulped. "That's Yewnin?" she continued, finally able to put a face to the mysterious man she'd heard so much about. They hid behind a large mound of rubble for the time being to inspect. It was too close of a shave that could have ended in catastrophe. "How did he know about this? Do you think he knew we were down there too?" Seff asked.

"This can't be a coincidence," Yewki stammered, struggling to figure out the reason for such perfect timing. Wick stayed dead silent, scowling and fixating his eyes towards the distant figure. "We can't stay any longer, we need to head back to Favarly right now," Yewki stressed.

"What's a matter? Scared to take on your brother?" Lumni chirped.

"Not now, girl". The group retreated another fifty feet back and crept behind another heap of soil. Yewnin had ended his barrage abruptly and took a moment to tamper with the relic. There was only so much they could see from the distance they were at, but it was certainly clear that he was preparing for something big. "We're getting out of here," Yewki ordered. He flung Lumni onto his back whilst Wick climbed onto Moon's. The bear, Seff and Yewki ran at full speed. "Come on, Moon!" Yewki screamed. None of them wanted to look back and rightfully focused on getting as far away as possible. Promptly after their escape, Yewnin aimed the Day Relic down a large hole he had made into the hive. He floated higher whilst his eyes glimmered white light like distant stars. An entire mile radius had been absorbed in a strange, deep humming sound, as though all noises were being sucked towards the relic, until one giant gush blew all noise and light into the hive in the form of a controlled stream of sunshine, so immensely bright that one would be instantly blinded upon looking at it. The deep humming turned into a high pitched squeal and then absolute silence. For a fraction of a second, all that could be seen was white, then the beginning of the giant explosion. Cracks weaved through the ground at the blink of an eye, causing light to seep through them from below. The surrounding area itself had been well and truly demolished. Giant chunks of Earth were flung into the air like a volcano had just erupted. The rippling waves of rock and dirt was difficult to comprehend. It towered higher than imaginable and seemed to be hurtling through the air in slow motion. There was no ancient battle ground *or* underground hive left, only a smoking crater the size of a city. The pure, explosive power of solar energy was unmatched and unforgiving. Speeding tremors had reached the fleeing five which only caused them to run faster. Wick gripped onto Moon's fur tightly and looked back at the damage. His eyes were scarred from the sheer destruction at play, but he couldn't help but morbidly gaze at its stupendous scale, mainly due to disbelief. The Holhouettes were eradicated in a quick flash as though exterminating an entire race was as simple as crushing a single insect. Yewnin's powers and capabilities had truly sunk in and made themselves known without warning. After a few miles of sprinting, their bodies couldn't take anymore. The tremors had calmed down and they were well away from the open wastelands. They hid in the trees, surrounded by the old warning signs, waiting to see which direction Yewnin would leave, but he just seemed to stay floating among the debris. Large rocks were still dropping from the air, enclosed in clouds of dust, but the only thing on his mind was the chaos he had just caused. He looked down at the relic and closed his eyes, entrapped in pure euphoria for a moment. "The only *new age* is the one *I* create. This is the start of *my* age –an era free of Holhouette scum," he panted to himself. Finally, he put his levitation powers to good use and flew away, but not in the direction Yewki was hoping. "Get down!" Seff gagged as the menace whizzed overhead in the direction they were planning to go. They stayed low until he was nowhere in sight. "Why is he going that way?" Yewki pondered to himself in anger. "He's going to Favarly, I know it". He kicked the dirt. "How can you be so sure?" Lumni asked.

"I just know. There's nothing that way for miles and miles... and if he knows about the Holhouettes then there's a chance he's going to Favarly to spread the word".

"What if he finds out we were there?" Wick worried.

"There's something bigger at play... we've been left in the dark severely. Something's brooding... something big is going to happen, I can feel it. The only thing I know for certain is that we should move in the opposite direction. No towns, no hospitality... we no longer leave a trail of existence. The forests are our only safety now," Yewki alerted whilst scratching his head. For once, no one challenged him. At last, he achieved the final say, but it was only because they knew the dangers as well as him by looking into his honest, unsettled eyes. If it wasn't his words that convinced them, it was his dreaded expression.

A few days later, Yewnin reached Favarly, just as his brother predicted. His arrival was loud and obnoxious, forcing the civilians to peek through their windows. He walked around the same stony paths with absolutely no idea that Yewki and the others had done the same just over a week before. He had the same disgust for the town as they did, except he wasn't scared to make it clear in his facial expression. "Strange... I've never actually visited this place," he shouted to himself in an attempt to acquire an audience. "But it's just as I imagined in my head". Onlookers watched the rude man raise his arms and spin around slowly. "It's horrid! It's filthy!" he emphasised, pointing at every aspect of their homeland. "Why is that?" he asked the town.

"It's not our fault y'know!" one woman barked out of her window. Other people started to creep out of alleyways and from around street corners to get a better look at him. "Then who's fault is it?" he replied.

"It's those damned Holhou-".

"Holhouettes you say?" he interrupted then pretended to look dumbfounded and chuckled to himself, making the growing crowd feel stupid. "But there are no Holhouettes anymore. I destroyed them all!"

"Impossible! You can't kill an entire race!" one civilian erupted. More people came forward out of their homes and into the town square where he stood. "You can when you have the powers I have".

"What are you really doing here?"

"I simply came to tell you your troubles are over! The Holhouettes are gone, I assure you". A few people started to burst into joyful tears whilst others still needed convincing. It was too good for them to believe. "Favarly has fell victim to those hideous monsters for too long. If you're lying to us-".

"There wasn't anything left for me to scavenge as proof, I'll admit, but it's because I vaporised them all instantaneously".

"Ha! And how exactly did you do that then?" one cocky bystander chortled. Yewnin raised the Day Relic into the air and released a spiral of sparkles, circling a thick beam of light until the clouds above them broke apart to make way for the energy. The spectacle was short lived though, as the beam pulled itself back into the relic intentionally, just to give the audience a quick and frightening taste of its abilities. Yewnin looked around and saw rows of people either speechless or cheerful. "The Holhouettes are no more! They're history! Rejoice, people of Favarly... you deserve to be happy! Spread the word of my accomplishments... spread them wherever you travel because this is merely the beginning of my heroic deeds!" he shouted to the crowd. It was his first experience of worship and he loved every second of it. People crawled up to him just to touch his robes and bless him for his efforts. None of them had any sympathy towards the slaved beasts as they lacked the knowledge to do so. When Yewki, Wick, Moon, Lumni and Seff told Favarly they'd stop the Holhouettes, they assumed it meant destroying them, not reverting a curse they had no idea existed. To the townsfolk, they were monsters and nothing more, and monsters were slain, not mended. "What's your name, saviour?" one woman cried.

"My name is Yewnin! Let it be known around the world – I'm the one who vanquished the creatures of the night!" he demanded.

"Where are the others?" someone asked. Suddenly, Yewnin raised his hand and the crowd instantly silenced. "There are no others... It's just me. You confuse *me*... me of all people with... someone else? A group of people?" he jabbed.

"Oh, no, it's just we had some visitors last week who went out to do what you did".

"There are no others that can do what I do!" he raised his voice.

"I'm sorry! Please-".

"Who were they?"

"I-I don't know. They stayed over at the Duck Bill Inn". Everyone turned their heads to the inn owner, Areick, who had merged into the crowd. They peered over to him to push the interrogation onto him. The short man stumbled backwards as Yewnin walked closer. "Where's your inn, my good man? We have matters to discuss," he grinned forcefully. Areick moved his little legs as fast as he could through the clumps of people and down the road towards the Duck Bill. Yewnin walked behind him, leaving the crowd to go about their business. "Here we are," Areick announced nervously with sweat dribbling from his forehead, somehow out of breath just by walking quickly. He fumbled with his ring of keys and giggled anxiously. The front door creaked open slowly. "Make yourself at home. So, h-how long are you wanting to stay? I have all sorts of rooms," the small man asked.

"Be quiet, you scum," Yewnin hissed whilst dragging Areick by the ear into the inn. He flipped him over onto one of the tables, sending the horde of ducks flapping crazily. With no actual escape route, they either flew upstairs or smashed their way through the windows without concern. "Who stayed here? Their names?!" he heckled.

"I can't remember, I swear!" Areick was dragged again and thrown across the reception desk. His face was covered in cuts and scrapes but he still managed to get up and run. Yewnin pulled out his sword and tackled him against a wall, pinning him against it in the process. "I don't remember, I don't remember, I promise! There was three or four of them and a bear. The bear I know for certain," the man wept. Yewnin released the hold he had on him and went around the room to kick and throw furniture, screaming and growling with every bodily movement. Areick covered his face and cried. "Was there a man... around the same age as I? Yewki?" Yewnin panted.

"Yes, yes... that was him. There was two children and an older man too".

"I need more information! Who's the elder?

"I don't know... but when they left I realised he'd paid me with counterfeit gold. It looked so real at first glance. I don't know how he did it... it was like some sort of alchemy".

"You're insinuating the old man was a magic user? A Wizard?"

"Yes... but n-no, he can't have been because there are no Wizards anymore, I'm sorry". Yewnin pondered to himself. *He* could access the Astral Vale so the chances of an actual magic user being alive somewhere with Yewki wasn't an impossible idea. "And the children? I assume at least one of them was a boy," he asked, knowing that if the bear was present, Wick would have been too. "Yes, and a girl but she was a little older than him". From Yewnin's perspective, he had no idea what was going on. He felt annoyed, knowing that he would have been close to them if they were travelling to the Hive of Holhouettes. "Anything else?" Yewnin sighed whilst clenching his fists and tensing his body. "Well, I-I don't know. I suppose that boy and his bear had a strange friendship now that I think about it. But I do remember eavesdropping the night before they left".

"Anything unusual?"

"I heard them talking about something called, *voodoo?*"

"Yewki?!"

"No, no... I think it was about the boy". Yewnin leant against the reception desk to compose himself. He only came to Favarly to boast and spread the word, but he was blessed with a lucky dose of information that would alter his next move in the grand scheme of things. Wick had suddenly became more of an interest to him. "Of course, it's the boy that bares the black blood. This is perfect," he muttered to himself.

"What?" Areick stuttered. Yewnin didn't answer and walked towards the front door, but first he wanted to finish his business with him. "I'm sorry for damaging your lovely building… and your body. But those people you let stay here are villains. You're responsible for giving them an undeserved night's stay".

"I'm sorry, I didn't know! I didn't like them, I just wanted the money".

"I'm going to leave now… and you're going to tell everyone about the people that stayed here. If you don't then I'll know about it".

"You have my word," Areick blubbered.

"Tell them how many there were, what they looked like, what they did to your poor inn".

"What did they do to my inn?" he asked. Yewnin slammed the door behind him and made sure no one was looking, then quickly pointed the relic towards the roof of the building, sending wooden chips flying into the air and leaving a huge hole. He made his way back to the town square where the crowd awaited his return. They ran over to with questions and pleas but he couldn't have cared less. "Spread my story, that's what you owe me," he reminded them before shooting off into the sky like a bird of prey. They watched and cheered as he flew away, never to be seen again. Wick was the only thing on his mind. Yewnin had no personal experience with voodoo, but he knew a lot about it. He planned to use the knowledge to his advantage. Wick would soon be forced to face Yewnin, all thanks to the curse inside of him.

Chapter 21

Lay-Vau's Tomb

Yewnin's mind and heart was taken over whenever he used the Day Relic for his own personal gain. Each second bound with it corrupted him greatly. He didn't have much time, or will power left to resist its urges, like a painful addiction creating a feeling of momentary pleasure that came at a price. It felt more like a conformity rather than a sacrifice. His soul and the relic were soon becoming one of the same, causing his senses to be heightened and his emotions scarred. Simple touches of life around him had started to give him all the serenity he could desire. The breeze brushing across his face as he soared through the sky made him feel weightless and free from everything. He navigated the winds with his eyes closed, as though his mind was guiding him to his destination. A rugged mountain range North-East, far from civilisation was where he'd been flying to for the past four days, all without food or water. The only sustenance he needed came from the energy he held onto. He was on his way towards Groo'ma-du Mountain – one of the highest peaks in the world, used as an undisturbed access point to the sun. The air was dangerously thin at Yewnin's altitude, but he was too happy to care. His face lit up upon finally reaching the mountain top. A crumbling, thin castle poked up from the peak for optimal height. Its spires pointing up like flowers fighting for the most sunlight, held together impossibly as though it disobeyed all laws of gravity. Stone bricks and slabs floated and orbited the structure in a graceful dance, whilst small chunks of reflective metals glimmered and bounced around as the sun hit them. Yewnin landed just outside of the entrance to stop and admire it for a moment. He was taken back by the unorthodox architecture and sheer beauty. Even though the structure was old and worn, it was still occupied by a few people. They were voodoo guardsmen, covered in dangling bones and red body paint. Their spears had jagged ends, designed to kill intruders instantly. Four of them steadily marched out of the gaping doorway, all pointing their weapons at Yewnin's head. "Ah, Yes. Gentlemen!" the mad man cheered.

"We're not gentlemen," one of the guards muttered with a strange accent.

"You mean you are not men? Or that you are simply not *gentle men*? Or maybe you mean-".

"Quiet, now!"

"Oh, it's because you're not human isn't it? Spirit servants of the Iwa-".

"You know nothing".

"I know enough obviously, why else would I be here? I've always wanted to visit this spectacular place... but I've never been a great climber. Now here I am, years later, evolved... and able to fly," he sniggered. All four of them ran towards him and attacked. Yewnin swung his sword around and cut their weapons in half one by one. They switched to daggers and struck again, but the closer they got to him, the harder the fight became for them. He stabbed one and sliced another, making them disappear, leaving behind only the bones they hung from their bodies. The remaining two jumped back to calculate. "How can you deflect the Spirits of Day?" one shouted in confusion. Yewnin laughed and revealed the relic – the one thing they lived to protect and worship. "Impossible!"

"Evidently not," he cackled.

"Thief! Lay-Vau will end you!"

"I doubt that. Now hold still... let me kill you with the instrument that gave you life, how embarrassing". He swooped the relic from left to right, engulfing the two guards in white flame which decomposed their bodies. Yewnin smiled at the sight of their deaths then looked around in case there were more hiding, but the castle was ancient, and Lay-Vau's servants were scarce. Without obsession of the Day Relic, the Iwa was unable to create more spirit soldiers. Yewnin was dominant, even if Lay-Vau didn't know it.

He strolled into the castle and looked around with great interest, as though he was walking around leisurely in an antique gallery. Marble pedestals held up delicate pottery and bone-coated instruments which littered an endless corridor. There was no interior colour other than the dull, grey stones and bricks. Any life the structure once contained was long gone, but luckily, Yewnin didn't travel just to appreciate the cosmetics and decoration. He had access to the highest points of the building yet his attention was fixed on the underground, for deep within the mountain, the Tomb of Lay-Vau nestled in secrecy from the world – except for the likes of Yewnin who seemed to be becoming famous for discovering hidden areas of importance. The power of the sun would be absorbed from the spires which then travelled down the castle and into the tomb to keep the Iwa's entity alive, without the need for the Day Relic. Large staircases were placed all over, all going up, but Yewnin found a small, inconspicuous shaft that travelled downwards, no wider than a barrel. It wasn't intended to be an access point to the tomb, as the only thing that ever passed through the tunnel was sunlight. "I'm sure I can fit," he assured himself before getting down on his hands and knees. A cold draft blew out of it and into his face. "You don't scare me," he muttered, crawling forwards into the hole. Once his full body was inside, he was able to slide down the slanted shaft, but he quickly gained too much speed to steady himself, making him lose control of the descent. His body flipped and rolled down for a disorientating few seconds until the shoot spat him out into a giant, square room. Just before his body splatted onto the floor, he levitated to break the fall, then landed gracefully on both feet as though his troublesome clambering never happened. He brushed off his robes even though no one was watching. "My, my, it's cold down here. I thought being orientated around the sun, it'd be warmer," he chuckled. The tomb was so big, there was a need for dozens of thick, tall pillars to support the roof. It was fairly empty other than the odd pile of bones and unlit torches, but the focus of the room laid in the centre. A rectangular stone slab sat in the middle of everything, with Lay-Vau's infamous drum placed ominously atop. He walked up to it, making sure the Day Relic was tightly clenched in his hand to taunt the Iwa. "I raided your maze, now I trample in your tomb. How does that feel, Lay-Vau?" he jabbed. After brushing the dust and grit off of the slab, he playfully jumped up and walked around on top of it like a foolish drunkard dancing on pub tables. Yewnin was audacious enough to violate the tomb without being inebriated though, even so, the sight of the drum was incredibly sobering. "I want to kick that silly instrument off, but I don't know if it smacking onto the floor would count as, *banging the drum*, so I'm not going to chance it. I bet you would've liked that wouldn't you? A big, harsh bang of the drum and then those torches light themselves, you sprout out of nowhere and you try to kill me," he laughed and picked up the morbid instrument, hoping Lay-Vau was inside listening reluctantly. "Is there a way for me to destroy it? No, luckily for you, it's too much of a risk for my liking". He raised his hand and swooshed it down before grinding to a halt inches away from the skin of the drum. "That was close. I bet you were seconds away from leaping out and destroying me weren't you?" he laughed. "What must it be like? Trapped, unable to take this relic from me". A strong blast of wind ran laps around the room, groaning and wailing as it went by. "Are you trying to scare me? Because you're failing. I don't care for your voodoo… but I *do* need it for one small thing". He put the drum down and hopped off the tomb to take another look around. "I can't believe you punished that boy because of what *I* stole. That's so malicious! Although, I'm slightly offended that you didn't come to seek revenge on me. Is it because I'm stronger than you?" He scraped away the dirt on the floor to find strange, differing symbols scattered around. "The sad thing is, I'm not here for you, Iwa.

I want the boy. I don't know anything about him, but if he's accompanied by a Wizard there's a chance he has a connection to the Astral Vale". He sat down on the cold floor in the middle of all the chiselled symbols he'd unearthed, which came together to make one big, circular pattern. Because the tomb was the heart of all voodoo, it acted as a secondary access gate within the Astral Vale, like a temporary fork in a road, allowing Yewnin to travel through and connect specifically to Wick's curse with great precision. His body entered a dream state as his spirit transferred through the gateway. The hunt for the boy had begun.

Chapter 22

The Lone Olash

The Troll crusade on Emmrin-Rashmada had taken its toll on Tbrok's people. The majority of his brothers were lost to the tenacious Slayer backlash none of them were truly prepared for. Not even their size and number was able to help them. The master of Trolls underestimated the enemy greatly thanks to the stubbornness and pride of his nature. Nonetheless, he returned home with his two remaining soldiers, to the private and uncharted regions of N'tur Grung, which loosely translated to Caverns-Colossal. No human ever set foot there, unless they wanted to die. Their only exception was Tbrok's close friend, Thene who was absent during the crusade. Although her initial plan was to follow her large associate into battle, she was burdened with staying at the Caverns to lead a defence. The Troll's homeland had been cleared of the majority of its warriors to fight the Slayers, so it was logical to leave Thene behind and take charge, in case someone took the chance to pounce whilst the herds were thinner. Thankfully, no said challengers came forward during the span of Tbrok's absence. It may have made her job easier, but being a deadly warrior, she was bored out of her wits. Whether she had to fight or not, Tbrok was grateful for her services. After a droning week of looking after the Troll colony, she was set free to get on with whatever things she needed doing. It was a long walk home to the Olash villages, seventy miles South beyond the many mountain ranges. The Trolls couldn't even spare a Jevetin for her to fly home on, but she preferred to walk anyway. Even though the Olash were fierce combatants, they balanced their aggression with an eagerness to relax and meditate in hopes of connecting to the world on a more spiritual level. There was no better way for her to feel tranquillity than being alone for a very long time. However, she still hoped in the back of her mind that Lall's bird messengers would swoop down and provide her with an adventurous mission to embark on, to outweigh the tedious week she'd just endured. Her rough, bare feet were used to being exposed to the hardness of the Earth, but there was no other place that was so heavily littered with sharp, rocky lands than on her way home. The idea of a forest, or even a tree being nearby was ludicrous. Anyone expecting to sleep or take refuge in the surrounding harshness was bound to be new to the area and ill-informed of it. Only the most cruel and cold kind of people could relate to the barren region and use it for shelter. Even then, they'd have to be desperate. So when Thene saw a curled up person sitting underneath a large rock, she had to look twice in case her eyes deceived her. She slowly walked forwards to get a better look. The person was the size of an adolescent and shivered uncontrollably, covering themselves up in a long, hooded cloak for warmth. "Are you lost, little wanderer?" she asked soothingly. She wasn't expecting the youngling to jump out of their skin and turn around with a sleek blade in-hand. It was Ecklethorpe on a covert solo mission. He had left the Slayer Kingdom alone without telling anyone and travelled for a number of days with his head down and weapon hidden, she had no idea it was one of the Slayer Princes. "Stay away," he ordered.

"Calm down. I'm not here to mug you. I want to help," she explained.

"I do not seek charity or hospitality. Be on your way".

"Why are you out here on your own?"

"That's my business". She scoffed at his stern attitude and looked down at the sword, noticing the unmistakable Slayer emblem, refusing to believe that the teenager was all the way from Emmrin-Rashmada. "How did you come by that weapon, child?"

"I'm not a child and this sword belongs to me," he barked whilst pointing his arm out further, which inadvertently pulled his long sleeves back, uncovering the Slayer branding on the back of his hand. She rightfully gasped and took a step back. "So which one are you?" she wondered.

"I am Ecklethorpe, youngest son of Zamanite the Relentless," he announced with pride.

"So what's *your* subtitle?".

"I-I beg your pardon?"

"Your subtitle... I want to know what makes you infamous, so I know what I'm in store for when you try to kill me".

"How do you know I'm going to kill you?"

"I can see it in your face. You gave me the courtesy to let me go on my way, but when I discovered who you were, your eyes changed and you've been contemplating how to cut me up for the past thirty seconds".

"Smart. The Olash people are said to be vigilant warriors but I've never had the privilege of fighting one myself".

"Maybe that can be your title – *the Olash Killer*".

"How did you know I didn't have a title?!" he squawked.

"You just told me," she teased. Eck had enough of being made a fool of and threw the cloak over her face and attacked. Even though she couldn't see, she sidestepped the sword and tripped him over with his own momentum. He rolled out of the tumble with lightning reflexes and charged again. Thene pulled the cloak off of his head and held onto it for evaluation. "This doesn't look like Slayer uniform," she said whilst blocking Eck's swings with her other hand effortlessly. "You don't want to look like a Slayer for this mission do you? You're young and rebellious. You're here in secret aren't you?"

"Stop talking and fight me!" he shouted.

"I am," she sniggered, then brought the clothing close to her nose for a sniff. "You rode here on a dragon," she sniffed again, "a Chuck dragon I think".

"Fight me properly!" he screamed. His unusual plea for a fully focused fight made her drop the cloak and look at him. "Do you really think it's wise to face me when you have my undivided attention?"

"I'm ready for any battle!"

"You haven't even noticed that I took your dagger from your belt," she huffed. He looked down to his waist in a panic, allowing Thene to backhand slap him on the ear. "You weren't even carrying a dagger!" she laughed. Eck jumped back to ready himself for a more calculated fight. He and his brothers were used to aimlessly slaughtering people that derived their talents from brawn. It was refreshing to meet an adversary that used an unparalleled intelligence and attentiveness. She stood ready with her legs wide apart and her arms raised in-line with her shoulders. He stormed towards her again and doubled the speed of his attacks. To his surprise, she was still able to duck under swoops and move her body out the way of deadly lunges. All she used was her hands and feet to chop, punch and kick back, but she was being gentle so she didn't accidentally kill him. She still had questions that needed answering, so she just played with him until he tired out. However, his fury and good stamina kept him trying for a good while as they jumped and ran around the terrain, across boulders and atop heaps of rock. There was no sign of sweat on either of their faces, so to speed things up, Thene kicked him in the chest and pulled his sword from his hurtling body as he flew backwards onto the painfully hard ground. She flung the blade away with no interest of using it for herself. The Olash were trained with just their bodies and looked down at anyone that required an extension or accessory for their hands. "You let your rage fight for you. How do you expect to move around with an open mind?" she expressed. Eck got up and caught his breath, still encumbered with the urge to run at her again, but intrigued with her advice at the same time. "Why do I need an open mind?" he growled.

"Because you're from the Slayer Kingdom… and everyone there sees things narrowly. You all *want* the kill, but don't take the time to study your opponent. That's your downfall".

"How dare you!"

"Attack me again if you still need convincing".
"No, I'm done," he muttered.
"Why?"
"I just don't want to".
"Oh I see," she smirked.
"Silence! I could beat you if I wanted to! I'm saving my strength for something more important than a passing traveller".
"Really? And what would that be exactly?" she asked, gradually taking steps closer to him for more of a personal conversation. "I already told you, that's *my* business," he grumbled whilst starting to pace side to side. He was trapped in an awkward interrogation, knowing full well he wouldn't be able to resolve it by fighting. His enemy was far too skilled for him, even if he refused to admit it. All the Slayer could do was stand around and be made a fool of. "You keep your business to yourself because it's important that you do so. I know what Slayers are like… they'll gloat at any given opportunity so if you don't want to tell me, it's because I could hinder your plans if I knew. Your kingdom was recently visited by the Trolls of N'tur Grung and given the fact that they're only several miles behind me, I'd say you're on your way to finish them off. You knew I came from that direction, plus, now you know that I'd beat you in a fight, so you're keeping your mouth shut in case I stopped you in your tracks… but I seemed to have done that anyway".
"Stop it!" he moaned.
"But why would you come on your own and in secret? Why wouldn't King Zamanite order you to kill the invaders of his land? You're young, he thinks you're too incompetent. When it comes to his sons, you're his least favoured. This is a redemption mission, is it not?"
"There's more to it than that," Eck sighed, finally giving in to her deductive capabilities. "Just give me back my sword," he nagged.
"You know I can't let you go to N'tur Grung. Or maybe I should. There's hundreds of Trolls in those caverns. Plus, this is their territory. Do you know how frequent this place succumbs to heavy fog? How are

Way of the Moon Bear

you going to traverse deadly rocks whilst fighting giant beasts? Why else do you think their homeland remains untouched by Slayers?"

"You may be clever but you can't predict how I'll fare against my enemies".

"If I didn't think it was suicide for you to go, I would have stopped you going already". Eck kicked the ground and whined. "This is what this is, isn't it? A suicide mission... a cry for attention," she stated.

"You don't know me!" he yelled whilst running right at her. The young Slayer jumped off a nearby boulder to gain some additional height then activated a concealed blade from the tips of his boots. He swung a heavy kick at Thene's face but she covered her head with her forearms quickly, taking the impact of the mini blade. Her arm was given a long, unexpected line of gushing blood, taking her by surprise. Whilst he was still falling, Eck kicked his other leg out and jabbed her in the abdomen. She pushed him away but the damage was already done. "You're lucky that wasn't my sword, or else you'd be dead on the floor!" he cackled. Just like when he'd snapped in front of his brothers and father in his bedroom with the man he was forced to kill – his rage and annoyance transformed him into a killing machine. Thene's invasive vigilance had backfired and now she paid the price. Her belly stung, leaving her with no choice but to hold it to stop the bleeding. She had already fought him with one hand before but he was no way near as vigorous last time. "I hope you're friends with those stone monsters... because after I kill you, I'm going to make them extinct!" Eck grunted. Thene had no more denigrating responses up her sleeve and focused on keeping him from killing her. Slayers were well-trained in hand-to-hand combat too in case the situation arose that their weapons were out of reach. They both flowed in their own ways, trying to deal a blow whilst dodging their opponent at the same time, like two powerful rivers pushing their currents against each other. After a frantic few minutes, Eck finally managed to make her stumble. Whilst she staggered, he jumped up for a mighty spinning kick, sending his foot across her face and dropping her to the floor. Whilst she was down, he ran over to grab his sword. Thene was shocked that someone so young could brawl with such sudden competence, let alone beat her. As she turned and got to her knees, Eck stood in front of her with his sword back in his hand, prepared to finish her for good. "Anything else you want to depict about me?" he scoffed.

"You're too young to be acting so cruelly," she coughed.

"Those creatures came to *our* kingdom. They deserve my wrath!"

"Now you know what it feels like to be invaded by foreign monsters".

"Anything outside of Emmrin-Rashmada was put on this Earth for us to kill".

"You can't justify your nonsensical behaviour. Yewnin's not one of you... but him and your father are well-acquainted. Why doesn't your rule apply to him?".

"My Father's allegiance is none of your concern".

"So you're just going to let him worm himself into your people's land like he's one of you?"

"That's not what's happening! The Slayers wouldn't let that happen".

"Oh really? Then please tell me what *is* happening?

"Yewnin has an all-powerful artefact, capable of destruction on such an amazing level. Father is going to kill him and take it for himself, I just know it, I can tell by the way he talks about it".

"I doubt it. If he so badly wants the artefact for himself, why hasn't he already killed Yewnin for it?"

"Fool. Because Yewnin is away fulfilling his own schemes". Eck was unintentionally giving Thene a large amount of information. Her use of questions and manipulation was slowly driving her towards the truth. "I've heard a lot about this Yewnin. Some say he's a made up nightmare, conjured up by you Slayers".

"I wish that was true. I can't stand outsiders tampering with the affairs of our kingdom," he snarled.

"I don't believe you".

"I'm about stab you through the heart... why would I lie?" he huffed.

"If Yewnin *is* away fulfilling his own schemes, whereabouts is he then?"

"I don't know".

"That sounds awfully convenient".

"Shut it! I overheard my Father communicating with a talking stone he'd given him. Something about a mountain… and a tomb". Thene tried her hardest to put the clues together with the little time she had. There weren't any tombs coming to mind that were set on something as impractical as a mountain which meant that the height held significance. Whilst Lay-Vau was a member of Piea's secret order, the group's knowledge about the world of voodoo was expanded upon. It would have been too coincidental if Yewnin was visiting mountainous tombs when Greenwick had recently been cursed by the only Iwa she knew that resided high above the clouds. All thoughts led to the secluded Groo'ma-du Mountain, original home of Lay-Vau and the Day Relic, sitting in the middle of the Eastern side of the mountain range. The only thing she was uncertain about was Yewnin's motives, but anything regarding both him and the menacing Iwa was bound to be trouble in her eyes. She was struck with a sudden sense of urgency to get up and go, but before she could gasp in shock, Eck shoved his sword through her chest and left it there. "I've spent too long toying with my prey. Why should I be convincing you of what's real and what's not?" he elaborated. Thene's already pale skin somehow whitened even more due to the pain. Her body shivered as the cold blade froze her from the inside out. Somehow, she was able to put everything aside and open her mouth. "Thank you for the information… *Ecklethorpe the Inexperienced*," she spluttered.

"What?" he spat.

"I'm glad you weren't one of the older brothers. A young mind is easier to manipulate and exploit".

"I told you nothing!"

"So reluctant to think properly. You told me where to find Yewnin and now I'm leaving to go after him and separate him from that dreaded Day Relic".

"You know about the Day Relic? Just who exactly are you?!"

"I am Thene, member of Piea Fellow's secret order, bound together to rid the world of the evil that man creates. I know exactly what he possesses".

"Wretched sneak!"

"I warned you to be more perceptive, child... but there's still one more important thing you failed to know". To Eck's surprise, Thene slowly pulled the sword out of her chest with her blood still pumping. "Olash carry their hearts on the *right* side of their bodies, and we heal... very... very... fast," she explained as the cuts on her body began to seal themselves shut and her face returned to its normal colour.

"No!" Eck panicked, but before he could claim is sword back from her, she threw it as far as she could into the rolling mist ahead of them. "I'm taking your Chuck dragon and you're not going to stop me".

"I'd like to see you try. You don't know where I chained it". Thene stared at him and grinned, ready to wind him up on an even higher level. "When I first saw you, you were cowering behind a large rock to shield you from the cold air. If the wind was giving you so much grief and you needed to take shelter from it, that means you were travelling against it, which is Westerly". Eck paused for a moment to confirm her conclusion in his own head, then sprinted straight for her before she could find the Chuck. Thene ran West, down steep mounds of rock, being careful not to trip as the furious Prince struggling to keep up. It didn't take her long to find the armoured dragon sitting calmly in a sea of fog. She had managed to gain an adequate distance from Eck, but there was still the matter of untying the thick chains. The dragon was startled when it noticed Thene scurrying over to it, but she took the time to calm it down with her soothing voice whilst tugging at the restraints. "I'm going to kill you!" a distant Eck screamed. After pulling and loosening the chains crazily, she was able to climb on the creature's back and get it to flap its wings. The young Slayer was getting close but the dragon was already elevating. All he could see was the end of the chain as the rest of it disappeared in the mist. He dived across and reached out to grab hold, but Thene had steered the dragon upwards to keep the dangling restraints well away from the ground. "No!" Eck cried, looking up at the devious fog. Thene's cunning wit had worked wonders, all for the safety of the world. The long, peaceful walk she'd set her soul on had quickly changed to capturing the most dangerous person known to man. There was no way of knowing what to truly expect, but she still journeyed onwards to Groo'ma-du Mountain, hoping that there was some evil to prevent, or at least some good to save.

Eck spent the next couple of hours searching for his lost sword on his hands and knees, but the thick mist kept it well hidden. He didn't know if he was even in the right vicinity either. There was no advancement to the mission until he retrieved the weapon. However, the longer he wasted time searching, the more idiotic his plan felt, and the more he began to reconsider to just go back home. For that though, he'd need a dragon. The sword was the advancement and the dragon was the escape, but both had been taken away from him, leaving him with no options. He felt trapped and foolish. Completely defeated, the young Slayer decided to just lay down and look up at the white, cloudy sheets of nothing. He reflected on the fight with Thene and what she had told him about being alert and knowledgeable. After pondering for a while, her advice was subconsciously taken on board which affected his fighting style from that point on for the better. In the midst of day dreaming, a shadow of a dragon swooshed by above him. The Prince panicked and sat up. His first thought was that it was Thene again, flying around the region absolutely lost. The unknown dragon made a thud nearby, indicating that it had landed. Eck was prepared to take the Chuck back by force, but when he finally crept to it, no one was there, and it was a different dragon. "I've been tracking you for days," Hundo the Wise said from behind. Eck wanted to say his many thanks for finding him but his rebellious attitude dominated over his gratitude. "I didn't ask to be followed," he moaned, trying not to be caught by surprise.

"Were you honestly set on killing a whole race of Troll? Such a feat would have made anyone Slayer King, but we all know how ridiculous that would be," his brother chuckled.

"I could have tried".

"Then there'd just be Rowdun and I left to take the throne... because you wouldn't have came close to succeeding". Eck finally admitted to himself that he would have failed miserably. His life of stress and torment had prevented him from thinking properly up until that point. He kept his revelation to himself, not prepared to express his feelings too much to Hundo. "So, why did you come after me? Did Father ask? He's going to kill me for sure," he pondered.

"He doesn't even know you're gone. For all he knows, you're somewhere in the castle".

"Why am I not surprised?" Eck asked rhetorically.

"I came looking for you, thinking I'd be picking up your body... but you're still alive which is unexpected".

"I can leave the kingdom without you or Rowdun. I'm ready to lead soldiers just like you and him".

"Ha! Just get on the dragon".

"You know, you could just kill me now... then lie to everyone and say you found me dead. What's stopping you?"

"Being rivals and companions at the same time can flip relationships in the blink of an eye. We could help each other for a greater prize one day, then betray each other the next. The life of shared royalty is conflicting, and it's made worse that we travel towards the same throne. The closer we get, the narrower the path becomes. Only one of us will become Slayer King and we'll battle between ourselves up until that point... but you are my little brother and perhaps being the wise one makes me the slightest big empathetic. I show that trait in front of anyone else and I'll be chewed up and spat out for certain. So you keep this to yourself. You owe me that much for rescuing you".

"I guess," Eck muttered, surprised by his brother's words. Hundo felt a tiny speck of guilt after shaming him in front of Zamanite after the Troll crusade. The two of them jumped on board and made their way back to Emmrin-Rashmada. Eck kept quiet about crossing paths with Thene and the fact he'd accidentally told her a great deal about Yewnin. He hated the man's inclusion in the Slayer Kingdom, so in a way, he hoped that bad things would reach him. "Rowdun would have done it," Hundo said out of nowhere.

"Done what?" Eck asked.

"When you asked me why I don't just kill you now whilst we're alone, if Rowdun was the one to come after you, it would have been to kill you".

"I wouldn't give him the chance".

"That's the spirit, brother," Hundo chuckled.

"He's not going to like the fact that you've helped me".

"Rowdun doesn't scare me. He already hates us all, what difference does it make? I'm going to enjoy seeing his face when I get the throne". Eck's selfish journey towards the Troll's caverns was destined to be meaningless no matter what outcome arose. The only beneficial factors he took from running away was the unintentional battle tips from Thene, and the notion of having a brother that carried a small piece of compassion towards him. Although it was a humbling feeling for Eck's fractured spirit, Hundo's brooding morality and emotions were bound to get him killed just as his Father had said to Rowdun – he was too wise for his own good.

Chapter 23

One More Fellow

Since Yewnin destroyed the Dewhills, the bandits he'd instructed, led by Wolf the mercenary, were slowly making their way through various lands with hundreds of Shamans bound in chains inside of cages. Large bulls pulled them atop wagons whilst the bandits led the way, keeping their eyes out for ambushes. Fortunately for them though, they were accompanied by all three Slayer Princes, by order of King Zamanite. Hundo and Eck had only been back home for a day and were already sent out on a mission with Rowdun. Thankfully, Hundo had kept his word and hadn't told Rowdun about Eck running away foolishly. The young Slayer felt uncomfortable enough whenever he worked with the Woundless, but he couldn't go against his Father's commands. Neither one them wanted to be there to help Wolf, but the Shamans were important to Yewnin's plans, so it was imperative that there were no setbacks, and the Slayers were present just in case. However, Wolf took offence to the Princes being made a part of the trip – he knew he didn't need their help. The bandits had took the Shamans from the Dewhills and North-West towards Slayer territory. It wasn't a part of Emmrin-Rashmada, but the Slayers had claimed the seemingly desolate regions as their own. There was a fortress nearing the end of its construction, just ahead in a secret location that would be used to imprison the soothsayers. They had been travelling for almost two weeks with their heavy cargo, praying that they wouldn't encounter any problems nearing the final stretch. The roads they followed were barely visible, but the Princes kept the incompetent bandits on the right track. Hundo paved the way ahead, Rowdun walked on the left, and Eck to the right. There wasn't much desire for conversation amongst the men and women, and the prisoners had given up crying for help. It wasn't until one of the bulls collapsed that they had to communicate. The beast let out a deep groan and crashed to the muddy floor, almost tipping its wagon over on its side. "What now?" Rowdun growled. Hundo raised his hand at the other fleets to grind the journey to a halt, whilst Eck jogged over to the fallen bull. "Boosie needs to rest," Wolf said.

"You name your bulls?" Rowdun scoffed.

"Don't patronise me, Slayer. I work for Yewnin, not you".

"Say that again".

"Rowdun, it's not worth it," Eck begged whilst tending to the large animal. Hundo walked to them and placed his finger on his lips, prompting them to be quiet. Wolf looked at him puzzled, demanding an explanation, but Hundo turned away and readied his sword, causing his brothers to follow suit. The bandit leader refused to be left in the dark and started to look around for answers. He walked around the fallen bull, noticing a deep cut on one of its back legs. "Where did this come from?" he gasped. Hundo turned back around to see what Wolf was talking about, as well as to shut him up. "We're being followed. They've been waiting for us to stop," the Prince explained after observing the mysterious cut. Suddenly, smoke bombs surrounded them from all directions, popping open one after the other to release their thick walls of mist. Before the Slayers could enact a plan of action, a second wave of bombs were thrown through the smoke, erupting in huge explosive blasts. The majority of bandits were flung into the air, but the Princes' quick reactions allowed them to take cover and evade what they could. The several bulls started to gallop around in fear, swinging their Shaman-filled wagons left and right. "Control your damn *Boosies*, Wolf," Rowdun shouted over to the bandit leader, but he'd been thrown upwards by a bomb and was laying on the floor seemingly lifeless.

"Eck, round up those animals… get them out of here!" Hundo said. He didn't hesitate to comply, as the Wise had earned his respect. If Rowdun had ordered him about, he would've been more reluctant to listen. Just then, a third wave of bombs entered the ring, eradicating the remaining bandits, leaving the Hundo and Rowdun alive, standing back to back with their twin blades at the ready. "They obviously don't know who they're messing with," Rowdun laughed.

"Or they do, and they're stupid enough to try," Hundo replied, ready for a fight.

Eck ran ahead to nudge the crazy animals in the right direction, but he quickly noticed he was being apprehended by five men on horseback. The bottom half of their faces were covered by scarves and masks, showing only their dead-set eyes, focused on the Slayer. They caught up to him with ease and began throwing an assortment of explosives, differing in colour, size and effectiveness. The ambushers laughed and mocked Eck as he ran away clumsily with his ears ringing after numerous loud bangs. For some reason though, they weren't interested in either killing or taking the bulls and their cargo. It seemed like a revenge mission, but Eck had no idea why, other than the fact he was a Slayer of course. The Shamans inside the cages were being thrown about into one another and against the bars, but there was nothing they could do to stop the fiasco. Out of nowhere, a sixth horseman jumped in front of Eck with a lasso spinning around above him. One of the front hooves hit him in the head and almost knocked him to the ground. Unfortunately, he couldn't help but stagger, allowing the enemy to catch him with the rope, flinging him to the floor with no means of escape. The other horsemen trotted around their prize, shouting and wailing in an unknown language. Eck wriggled about, but there was no hope. He was always too ashamed to cry for help, so he laid on the dirt accepting his fate. Thankfully, he'd managed to lead the bulls the right way towards a narrow canyon crevice ahead, ensuring there was no chance or opportunity for them to break off in unwanted directions. Slayer soldiers would be waiting for the cargo to

Way of the Moon Bear

arrive on the other end, so if Eck was to survive the conflict, his Father and Yewnin would have no reason to be disappointed. The sixth horseman slowed down to an eventual standstill, then hopped off the saddle with a spring in his step. He wore a rather large and wide hat with a feather attached to it, titled to one side. He walked over to the Slayer Prince slowly as his merry men giggled and sniggered. His boots were surprisingly clean, along with the rest of his outfit, which consisted of tight-fitted trousers made of hide, and a top half made up of dull, baggy drapes, with no sign of actual armour anywhere. He stopped right in front of Eck's head and bent down to take a closer look, pulling his scarf away from his mouth in the process, revealing that he wasn't much older than himself. The young man had a somewhat cheeky look to him, as though he wasn't taking his own attack that seriously, but either way, anyone would seem delighted by successfully catching a Slayer Prince. "Hello there, Slayer. How goes you?" the young man said.

"I don't care what you have to say," Eck hissed.

"Oh, I don't *have* to say anything, but last I checked, I'm in charge here... unless you plan on breaking free and catching me with my own rope," he laughed.

"Let me go – see how quickly I kill you".

"Calm down, I'm not after you. Imagine if I killed King Zamanite's youngest son in an unjust manner. I'd rather not have your entire kingdom after me".

"Who are you after then?"

"That chap named, *Yewnin*... sound familiar?"

"I'd usually not tell people information, but a part of me wants to tell you all I can so that you can go to him and die in the matter of seconds".

"Don't worry, lad, I know enough about him. He scorched those Dewhills to the ground, he has a relic of immense power, but most importantly... he killed my Grandfather... Piea Fellow," the man said, strangely with a cheery smile. Piea was said to have been the last of the Fellow line, after all his remaining family being eradicated during a number of Slayer conflicts. All but one however, unbeknown to anyone – Piea's last remaining Grandson, carrying the last of his blood.

"The Fellows are all gone, liar," Eck grumbled.

"Pleased to meet you, my name is Wayhal Fellow, but people just call me, *Fellow*, for short seeing as though I'm the last on left. According to you and most of the world, I don't exist," the man chortled.

"I don't believe you".

"I suppose you don't have to if you don't want to. I don't care. What I *do* care for however is the whereabouts of one, *Yewnin*, please".

"Let me go and I'll show you".

"Yes, of course," he chuckled as he unexpectedly cut Eck free. It took the Prince a while to wrap his head around what had just happened, but he soon charged at the enemy without question. However, Fellow threw a handful of explosive pellets at Eck's chest as he ran towards him, letting out a strange gas for him to unintentionally inhale. After just a small intake of the smoke, Eck's body seized up and slammed to the floor like a falling tree, causing Fellow's men to laugh uncontrollably. "We Fellows are masters of chemicals... explosive perfectionists. You see, if you believed me to be a Fellow then you would have expected a bomb-orientated defence, so you only have yourself to blame". Eck was unable to move his mouth, otherwise he'd have been screaming. "Not to worry, child, I'll ask your brothers... they seem more competent than you," Fellow said whilst walking back to his horse, but before he could mount, Hundo and Rowdun knocked him over. "What is it you wanted to ask?" Hundo said as Rowdun stepped on his chest with a sword pressed against his neck. The other horsemen stormed at them, but Hundo took them all down one by one with little effort. Their horses galloped away, abandoning the cause and leaving Wayhal alone with the Slayers.

Fellow held his hands up to surrender, but Rowdun couldn't care less and pushed his blade closer against his throat. "How long's my brother going to stay like that?" Hundo asked.

"Not much longer," he assured. Eck started to relax his muscles and move his limbs slightly, as Rowdun looked across at him in disgust. "You look like such a fool, Eck," he complained.

"I concur," Fellow sniggered.

"Quiet. Tell us what this is about. You let the Shamans go, but you killed all the bandits, what is it you want?" Hundo asked. Fellow rolled his eyes and tried not to laugh, but he couldn't help but chuckle, even when in the midst of life and death situations. "Sorry, I laugh under pressure," he confessed.

"Answer me".

"I'm after your friend. *Yewnin* is it?"

"Why?" Rowdun snarled.

"He killed my Grandfather... now I'm the last one that carries the *Fellow* name".

"Well that *is* surprising".

"Indeed... your little brother didn't believe me".

"Shut up!" Eck shouted, finally able to talk and move. He slowly turned over to his front and picked himself up. "Let me kill him, for the love of Emmrin-Rashmada, let me stab him in the face," he begged his brothers.

"No, Eck... he probably has more rebels somewhere for us to sniff out," Hundo explained. Before they could agree on a plan of action, Rowdun heard rustling in the distance. "There's someone else among us!" he shouted, forcing a Magmalian Knight to burst through the nearby treeline, after watching the conflict from the shadows. She charged on her horse, with no choice but to take on all four of them. It was unusual to see a Paladin so far and so close to Slayer regions, but she'd been tailing the bandits for a few days to gain more information. With her cover blown, she rode into battle in hopes to kill who she could before having to flee. The Princes grouped together, leaving Fellow to get up from the ground. "She's not with me, I swear!" he chuckled before leaping onto his horse. The Slayers no longer cared for the foolish rebel and let him ride away for them to fight with another day – they had more pressing matters to attend to. The skilled knight ran circles around them, occasionally lunging in with her longsword. Unfortunately for her, the three brothers had developed a number of teamwork attacks through the years. Eck placed one foot in Hundo's hands and the other in Rowdun's for them to hurl him up into the air with his sword aiming down at the Paladin. The Knight deflected the heavy attack but had to move back before the other two tried to pounce. "My name is Paladin Shayl. Whatever you're planning, Magmalia will stop it!" the Knight announced in an attempt to scare them, but they didn't seem to care. "Come closer," Rowdun taunted, hungry for blood. Unexpectedly, a handful of Slayer soldiers had travelled through the canyon crevice to offer help in the fight, after receiving the Shamans without anyone to accompany them. They fired arrows at the Knight, making her horse panic and causing her to lose control. One arrow landed in Shayl's shoulder, just missing her neck. "Hold your fire!" Hundo shouted to the soldiers, wanting to kill the Paladin themselves, but the Knight made the decision to retreat, no longer feeling in control of the situation. The whole conflict was strangely abrupt and out of nowhere, but it proved that it was a wise choice by Zamanite to include his sons on the mission, otherwise the mysterious Fellow rebel would have prevented the Shamans from reaching their destination. "I have the right mind to slaughter you, fools! That was *our* kill," Rowdun hissed.

"We're sorry, your majesties... we only sought to provide assistance," one of the soldiers blubbered.

"Does it look like we need help?" Hundo growled.

"Maybe Eck needs help, but not us," Rowdun jabbed, but Eck was too tired to respond – he felt a rage-fuelled urge to pursue the Knight – not because it would've been the right thing to do, but because he wanted to prove that he wasn't as useless as what his brothers thought he was. It hadn't been long since Hundo had fished him out from the middle of N'tur Grung after running away to fight the Trolls though – there was no need to go through a similar scenario. "Who were they?" the soldiers muttered to themselves.

"A Paladin who pushed her luck, and a group of pathetic rebels that won't last long," Rowdun responded.

"More importantly, did the Shamans make it through the crevice?" Hundo asked. Eck's heart started beating fast, hoping that he'd done an adequate job in the middle of the ambush. If the bulls hadn't made it through, then he'd be killed somehow – if the Princes wouldn't kill him, the King certainly would've. "We have the Shamans. We're moving them over to the fortress," one of the soldiers answered. The Princes let out their own subtle sighs of relief, but Eck's was significantly louder. Together, they barged past the insignificant soldiers and strolled through the narrow crevices of the canyon. Another successful mission, and it couldn't have been a more important victory. King Zamanite would soon become more inclined to choose the heir to the throne, once he received word of the Prince's efforts. For the time being though, the brothers had to watch over the secret fortress that was built in the cracks of Foulfell Canyon, intended to imprison the kidnapped Shamans to abuse their soothsaying abilities – something both Yewnin and the Slayers were used to doing, but never on such a large scale. The lack of Shamans in the wild also meant that their enemies would struggle to seek them for guidance, ensuring no one could gain any upper-hands. It was a vile method to extract knowledge and intelligence, but the Slayers knew nothing of morals or ethics. Hundo, Rowdun and Ecklethorpe would reside within the walls of Foulfell Fortress for as long as their Father ordered.

Chapter 24

Dreams for Spirits

Far away from Groo'ma-du Mountain, across an ocean of water and miles of land, Wick sat alone with Moon. Lumni and Seff sat together by a fire, talking between themselves whilst Yewki hunted nearby for some form of food. Their home for the night consisted of a fairly open space in a forest, with a large cliff face wrapping around one side of them, technically trapping them against a wall if enemies appeared, but their energies were low and the darkness of night left them no choice but to stop and camp. "I wonder if this is what are lives are going to be like now," Lumni whispered to Seff. He was poking and prodding the fire with a stick, keeping it alive with not much to say, but she continued to pester him. "We should just find out where Yewnin is and fight-".

"No," Seff finally answered.

"But then we won't have to live in hiding. You could go back to your home".

"You mean, *we*?"

"Well once this is all over I'm staying with Wick and Yewki".

"This is never going to be over, Lumni".

"You're such a pessimist," she hissed and walked to the other side of the fire to be alone. Wick overheard the argument but didn't want to get involved. He was too tired to care and all he could think about was failing the Holhouettes. His anger and hatred towards Yewnin was personal since he saw the man's unforgiving nature in action. The importance and severity of Yewki's brother had finally sank in. It wasn't a fun adventure for him anymore, but he was warned countless times so he could only blame himself. Although the bear couldn't talk, he was the boy's biggest support, and looking back at all the times Moon had helped him through near-death experiences, he was grateful to call him a friend. The days of fear and confusion towards the beast had left his head entirely. It felt as though they had been friends all their lives, and Wick's necklace was worn more with pride than necessity. Moon was in the middle of his fixated night gaze, but Wick still spoke to him as if he wasn't because all their conversations were one-sided anyway. "I wish we could have saved them. They were finally given a chance to live free, but Yewnin just killed them all. It's not fair". His anger made him tense up, giving him a headache from the black blood pulsating forcefully around his skull. The pain started to grow stronger on its own, as though the voodoo had awoken from the stress. His body relaxed against Moon's, and shut down completely whilst his brain fought itself. Yewnin the intruder was passing through using the voodoo. His spirit self pulled Wick's into the exclusive cursed dimension within the Astral Vale – a temporary channel for them to see one another as though they were interacting in person. Their existences both stretched between Wick's location and Groo'ma-du Mountain at the same time, creating a bridge of visual communication.

Wick's spirit body shuddered around on the invisible floor of the Vale. It didn't look like the same beautiful, wondrous place Seff had transported him to. Everything had a rotten, green hue and big blobs of oozing black slopped and dripped as they floated by. Because they were both connected in a shared dream state, Yewnin was quickly able to imagine a more tranquil environment for them to traverse. He pictured a warm summer's day in a peaceful garden of flowers and small trees, with a trickling stream cutting the ground in half, healthy grass full of bees and butterflies, all topped off with the soothing sound of songbirds. Luckily for Yewnin, he constructed everything before the boy joined him so he wasn't repulsed by the true atmosphere. Wick finally opened his eyes and gasped for air. He looked around at the garden and instantly knew it was too good to be true. "Am I dreaming?" he asked himself, not expecting Yewnin to be behind him, sat on a newly imagined bench. "Technically yes, this is just a dream," he replied. Wick jumped back in surprise to see his enemy calmly sat with his legs crossed. "Don't touch me!" Wick huffed.

"I said it's a dream. I couldn't hurt you even if I wanted to".

"Then why does everything feel so real? Why do I feel so-".

"Aware?"

"Stop talking to me. Get out of my head".

"We're actually in both of our heads at the same time". Wick had no interest in listening and tried to run away, but once he reached the end of Yewnin's imagined world, his feet unwillingly ran on the spot, stopping him from getting any further. "Why can't I leave?" the boy panicked.

"Because right now, this garden is all what exists. So you can either stop and take a seat, or you can keep running towards nothing".

"If I could hurt you right now, I would".

"What with? That dagger Yewki gave you? Wow, he was foolish to make you think you could handle yourself".

"How did you know-".

"Like I said, we're in each other's heads… but this came about by me invading your *mind*. My, my, Yewki really has been dragging you through hell hasn't he?"

"Yewki is my friend!"

"Yes, well he's my brother… and that's a bond stronger than what a friend could ever be".

"He's going to stop you".

"Please, he doesn't even know what I'm trying to achieve. He doesn't even know where to find me," he chuckled. "Now come, sit next to me so I can tell you the truth". Wick looked over to the man shimmying across the bench to make space, but he stayed put. "You're far too stubborn. Yewki has well and truly brainwashed you to despise me".

"You did that yourself when you killed the Holhouettes". Yewnin scoffed at Wick then shook his head and laughed. "I received a premonition. You and your Wizard's tampering with the Holhouettes would have created a new age… and the prelude to new ages can be mysterious and dangerous".

"You're the one who made it dangerous".

"Could you have predicted the outcome? What would have happened once you treated them? Were they planning to live amongst men once more? They wouldn't have been welcome anywhere. People would still want them dead. People are cruel. They see something new and unknown and they blow things out of proportion. People just want to kill things they don't agree with… it's sad but true. You and my brother are living proof of just that".

"Why are we?"

"Because you're trying to kill me! Just like what would have happened to those poor creatures. Maybe you'll understand when you're older… life is full of difficult and compromising decisions. Trust me, I was doing those monsters a favour".

"They weren't monsters!"

"Oh yes, of course… *I'm* the monster to you, aren't I?"

"Because you're evil".

"You see, I think I'm just about tired of that. Why don't you sit down and let me explain from my point of view!" Yewnin smirked. He constructed a wooden chair that crept up from behind Wick, causing him to trip back into it. The arm rests spawned metal restraints that wrapped around his arms to keep him still. He didn't react because he didn't want to look scared, so sat calmly and scowled over to Yewnin. "I'm sorry for that, hand on heart," he stressed.

"What heart?" Wick murmured.

"The same heart that you have inside of yourself! The Holhouette which called itself a Chieftain, he told you to use your kind morals for good, yes? He made you feel important… like you were doing the right thing and you should keep doing it. Well that's exactly how I feel! I've been chosen by entities a little more important than foolish undead creatures. The gods themselves chose me".

"To destroy the world?"

"To save it! I don't want to destroy anything, but sometimes destruction becomes a collateral".

"You think people want *you* to save them?" Wick hissed. Yewnin got up from his bench and leaned over the boy. "And you insinuate that they deserve my help in the first place!" the crazed man panted. His mind focused on chaos and all that was wrong with the world. Screams of men, women and children gargled from all directions, as the majestic garden environment decayed and transformed into fire and ruin, showing Wick everything Yewnin was thinking about as he spoke. "You truly think these people are worth saving? People so ungrateful for their own being? I've travelled this world far and wide, and all I've seen within people are dark clouds of malice. Brooding storms within their minds and rolling thunder orchestrating their thoughts. Pure hatred and a blood-red vision, bleeding from their eyes, disguised as tears. Empty shells make play they're still bodies, long lost at the bottom of an ocean of desperation with nothing left inside them but a beating heart – an organ solely fulfilling its purpose, no longer holding any symbolism for love and compassion. Humans are useless creatures who look down at everything else as though they have the right to be demeaning... but they have no rights at all! All of the anger, all of the rage, chewing through this Earth like it's nothing! Everything they do brings them closer to turmoil. Yet here I am... still headstrong... still fixated on not only saving humanity, but saving the place they call home. We are not blessed with life just for us to throw it away". There was evident emotion behind Yewnin's speech. His voice cracked and chin wobbled, so he took a moment to compose himself and for Wick to take in his words. The boy was blown away by the unexpected passion. The longer he thought about it, the more valid the statement became. If Wick was able to translate his feelings into meaningful words, it wouldn't have been far off what Yewnin had said, and that's what scared him the most. He started to question everything, even Yewki's motives. Both sides of good and evil seemed to have been torn apart and woven together. Thankfully, the dramatic atmosphere had calmed down and reverted back into the garden as Yewnin stepped back to catch his breath. He sat back down and apologised whilst sniffling his nose and wiping a single tear. "I wish I could explain better," he sighed.

"What if you're wrong... about everything? What if this isn't your purpose?" Wick stuttered.

"I have been wrong before... but what's important is what I get right. My purpose is to discover what everything means and whatever that entails, even if it means my own death. You ask me about purpose and you don't even know your own. Perhaps this is all too deep for you, child. I'm on a journey to discover every aspect of this Earth. Why things are the way they are and what can be done to fix-".

"So, you think you've discovered the meaning of life or something?" Wick interrupted.

"Oh no. You see, there *is* no meaning of life. No meaning for anything. Your purpose in life is to give it meaning... and that's exactly what I'm doing".

"But you're still wrong, I just know it".

"You still see me as the villain? Me of all people who's sitting here with you, trying to guide you proper? Have you ever stopped to think that perhaps your little child mind has been twisted by my brother's words? After all, he's the one you met first so of course you're going to favour his opinions. What would have happened if I was the one who found you and your bear?"

"You probably would have killed us".

"Come now," he scoffed. "Let's be frank, our meeting in the maze was hardly a great first impression was it? So in a way, I don't blame you for sticking by Yewki's side. You saw things out of context. You've been shoehorned into his life of danger, lacking equal knowledge of both parties. All I ask is that you give me a chance... then perhaps you won't be so quick to judge".

"You've gone to all this effort to talk to me... so why? You don't know anything about me," Wick said. Yewnin made the shackles disappear to make the boy feel more comfortable. "I invaded your mind, remember? I know your name now. It's Greenwick isn't it? My brother is taking care of you, a Wizard named Seffry and a girl called Lumni. You're accompanied by your pet bear, Moon, which is a great choice of name seeing as though he loves to watch the actual Moon... but the most important thing about you, the part that I'm intrigued by, is the voodoo".

"What about it?"

"It's taken over your bloodstream, yet you're still alive".

"It's a lot more complicated than-".

"I know. But that's not what I want to talk about. What excites me is the untapped potential of your curse".

"There are no benefits. It's called a curse for a reason".

"To the untrained, yes. I know for a fact if I was lucky enough to survive such a severe punishment, I would want to learn what I could do with it, so in the future I could maybe use it to my advantage".

"If you were *lucky* enough?!"

"Greenwick, Iwas have incredible powers. They can heal the sick, they can bleed between Earth and the realm of spirits and exist in both at the same time. Apply that with the Astral Vale we're in right now and-".

"We're in the Astral Vale? So that's how you're doing all of this".

"Trust me, I'm no Wizard, but I learned the basics of magic so I can access this wonderful place. That's something else I'd like to talk about – your friend, Seffry could teach me the things I'm missing-".

"No, that's enough! How did you find me through the Vale?"

"I fed my consciousness straight through to your voodoo if you must know. It stood out like a wolf among sheep".

"Are... are you an Iwa?"

"Of course not, you fool!" Yewnin laughed.

"Then how did you use voodoo to find me?"

"The Tomb of Lay-Vau is a great source of Voodoo Energy. Attaching that with my limited Empyrean Energy allowed me to track you down".

"You couldn't have! He's a monster! He would've killed you the moment you got there and taken his relic back".

"Believe me, he was fast asleep in his idiotic drum".

"You're lucky".

"I could have woken him up if I wanted, but I was too scared. I've never fought an Iwa before. You've faced him... what's he like?"

"Dangerous. More than what you could ever be".

"Ha, I find that hard to believe," Yewnin snorted.

"Bang the drum and find out".

"If he *was* so powerful, then why does he need to be manually unleashed?"

"Well I know if he wanted to have been freed, he'd have found a way for the drum to be hit. So maybe he had no business with you".

"But I have the Day Relic with me... inside of his own tomb! What better excuse to jump out and strike me down?!".

"Maybe he's waiting for the right moment".

"You're a funny child. I'm glad we've had this time to talk".

"Me too".

"That's good to hear. I'm glad I've opened your eyes a little".

"That's not what's happening".

"I'm sorry?"

"You invade my mind, I invade yours. You needed a source of voodoo to do so, but forgot I was a source of my own". Yewnin stood up and began to panic. The strain he had on the dream state had started to crumble. Wick had been secretly digging through Yewnin's mind to uncover his mysterious plans, but his inexperience allowed access to only fragmented portions of information. The thoughts and experiences of his enemy were flooding into his brain at a dangerous speed, causing him to fluster and loose the connection. "No, no, no!" Yewnin shouted. He tried to grab the troublesome child but his hands went straight through Wick's body. The bond was inadvertently broken due to the two of them unsettling at the same time. Yewnin's consciousness returned to his body at Groo'ma-du Mountain and Wick's jumped back at Moon's side. Both of them woke up with no actual time passing in real life. Yewnin got to his feet and screamed at the top of his voice. His location was known, and so were the outlines of his plans. Before he could leave the tomb though, a fresh pile of bricks and rubble came out of nowhere and linked together to make a fortified wall, blocking the hole he had entered through. He flung the relic around in anger, but the beams of light were somehow absorbed by the tomb walls, as though Lay-Vau was able to negate its power. "You're trapped underground with my drum, they know where to find you, they know your plans. They're coming for you," the Iwa's voice bellowed around the room. "Show yourself!" Yewnin yelled.

"Bang my drum and I'm all yours," Lay-Vau taunted, knowing that he wouldn't dare do such a thing. The two of them awkwardly shared the same room with no escape. Yewnin wasn't used to being trapped with no way out of a situation, so he just paced back and forth, getting annoyed at himself for being fooled by a boy. There were no contingency plans he could put into effect, making him feel weak and powerless, just like the human he was that he'd tried to transcend from.

Wick had got to his feet also upon waking up. He ran to the camp fire and shouted for Yewki. Seff and Lumni stood up in confusion, trying to calm him down. "What's wrong?" Lumni panicked.

"Is it the voodoo?" Seff asked.

"No... it's Yewnin. I know where he is, I know what he's doing, he spoke to me in the Astral Vale but it wasn't just the Astral Vale, it was a dream land," Wick blabbered. Yewki followed the sound of the yammering and made it back to camp in a hurry. Moon had finished his gaze and lumbered over to the gang, frightened by the speed of which Wick was talking at. He explained everything that had happened, including how it was managed and how it all felt. Seff trembled upon hearing the words, *Groo'ma-du Mountain*, and Yewki had to sit down after Wick told them he knew the purpose of Yewnin's schemes. "Just try to breathe. Calm down and focus," Lumni stressed.

"I couldn't take in everything. It was so intense," Wick wheezed.

"Just tell us what you know," Yewki begged.

"Now, I don't think he's in the right condition for interrogation," Seff suggested.

"Enough, Seff! Tell us, Wick," Yewki snapped, demanding answers regardless of Wick's physical and mental state. "He thinks he's been chosen by the gods," the boy answered.

"What gods? He's gone mad! Only the Slayers are foolish enough to believe in such folly," Lumni scorned.

"Although there isn't proof, that Relic of Day seems to predate pretty much everything," Seff exclaimed.

"What do you mean, *everything*?" Yewki said.

"Everything! All recorded eras, Wizardry... even something as ancient as the Remains has an estimated date of existence".

"So we're talking about something beyond a bygone age? But how does this prove that these gods are real?"

"If something predates all knowledge, then surely it must be some sort of universal arranger that existed before... *our* existence. Either that or it's something that's pretending to be said entity," Seff muttered.

"Continue, Wick".

"He's trying to become a saviour in the eyes of the world... get everyone on his side. That must be why he destroyed the Holhouettes. The Day Relic has the ability to connect him with its creator, granting him with complete control of the sun... but he hasn't discovered how yet".

"Because knowledge alone isn't enough, he wants inhuman power," Seff sighed.

"No one can control the actual sun. What would he achieve by doing so?" Yewki wondered.

"The sun is what gave the world life!" Seff explained.

"He just wants to be in control of the Earth's fate. He's just trying to see how far he can push human capability," Lumni growled.

"If he has that kind of power... even if he *did* have good intentions... outside of this world is out of our control! Grasping the ability to tamper with the natural code of reality is simply unethical. Wizards of old tried to achieve the same kind of power and that caused disastrous fallouts, countless wars and the near-extinction of the discipline".

"We need to stop him before it's too late!" Wick begged. Yewki stood back up and walked around, trying to process all of the heavy and dramatic accusations. "He's right," Seff confirmed. Even the cowardly old man knew how important beating Yewnin was. "I know, I know! The power you described is... is just inconceivable," Yewki sighed. Wick grabbed Yewki's hand for comfort and looked up to his troubled face. "We can face him together... but he's your brother, so you need to lead the way and not be afraid to do what must be done," Wick said to him, sounding far too grown up. The group fell silent for a moment, leaving the fire to crackle and pop. Yewki sighed again, then looked over to the four of them, "I can't ask this of any of you-".

"Stop right there. We want to help. We *need* to help... don't we, Seff?" Lumni interjected.

"Oh, well yes, of course we do, but I don't know what use I'd be in a fight," the Wizard stammered.

"Don't be silly, Seff! You're the most powerful of us all!" Wick expressed.

"If Lay-Vau is there, we'll somehow have to make him talk about who or what put him in charge of protecting the relic. Then we'll know what sort of being we're dealing with," Lumni suggested. Yewki sniggered to himself, looking at them and feeling their confidence resonating. "There's just one more member of the team you have to convince," he hinted to Wick, looking over at the confused bear. The boy walked to Moon's side and stroked his fluffy head slowly. Their quest was no place for a bear, but he had followed valiantly up until that point. All four of them had affection and respect towards him, but no one came close to the compassion Wick had for him. "Moon, you're my best friend. You were there when I woke up and you've been by my side ever since. I've never known an animal show so much love. You've travelled so far with me. Most of what's happened you probably don't understand, but you've stuck with me no matter what, even when we could have died. This trip is going to be the most dangerous, so I don't blame you if you don't want to follow us this time. I love you," he blubbered, tearing up in the process. Moon wasted no time to lick the boy's sobbing face and rub his head on his shoulder, nudging him back slightly. "You don't have to stay by my side anymore if you don't want, not this time," he exhaled. To his surprise, the bear moved and stood in the middle of the whole group, indicating that his place was with the team. "We'll take that as a yes then, bear," Lumni chuckled. Wick wiped his tears and looked over at Moon in admiration. He was more than a companion. "I don't know what to expect when we get there. It'll take a few weeks too, then we'll have a mountain to ascend," Yewki warned, quickly dampening the mood. Everyone huffed and sighed at the same time, but Wick eventually came up with an idea. It was risky but to get their almost instantly, it was their only option. Seff was taken back by the plan with sheer amazement. His desire to try new things and experiment was the reason he studied the art of magic in the first place. "I don't believe it... that could just work, Wick! *Now you're thinking like a Wizard!*" he cheered.

Chapter 25

Fighting for the Sun

Seff brewed what potions he could whilst Lumni sharpened her arrowheads, cramming her quiver with as many arrows as possible. Yewki adjusted his belts and straps, making sure his weapons were easily accessible. Wick and Moon watched on, not having anything to prepare other than their bravery. This was it. Just like Yewnin transported his consciousness, Wick planned to do the same, but this time with his actual body, as well as everyone else's. If it was possible to travel through the Astral Vale using two strong sources of voodoo as gateways, it would enable them to teleport inside of Lay-Vau's tomb. The key was to focus on finding the access point in the cursed dimension, but first, they had to get there. Seff created a hardlight dome which surrounded the five of them. It meant that the transportation would be applied to everything inside of it, not just Wick, allowing them all to travel together at once. With help from the Wizard, Wick pulled everyone into the Vale, but instead of letting the Empyrean Energy flow harmoniously, he deliberately let his voodoo take over, forcing the two power sources to combine into one. Thus, the cursed dimension folded into existence. It made it all the more easier to pinpoint Lay-Vau's energy seeing as though Wick's black blood came from the Iwa. "Good! Now focus in. You're body is the source. Branch out your consciousness and your body will follow," Seff informed.

"You can do it, Wick," Lumni praised. The boy honed in on Groo'madu Mountain. He could see the underground tomb as plain as day, pulling everything within the hardlight bubble to its location in real time. Visions were warped and bodies bent harmlessly. The instant shift from one place to another caused the Vale to flash and wobble, before dropping the five of them back into reality. They looked around the large room and quickly caught their breaths. "It worked!" Seff cheered.

"But where's my brother?" Yewki scowled.

"You're going to have to teach me how you did that," Yewnin's distant voice echoed, intrigued by their arrival. He was still trapped with them inside the tomb but he was well hidden, so the group had no more time to applaud their successful teleportation. The mad menace lurked around them in the shadows. It was time for a long-awaited conflict between opposing beliefs. Even though Wick, Moon, Lumni and Seff were fairly new to the world of danger, they had seen and experienced enough to side with Yewki. They looked on and listened carefully, but Yewnin was nowhere in sight. "It's over, you freak," Lumni grunted.

"Respect your elders, girl".

"Not when they have no respect for life!"

"That's a rude accusation. Did Wick not tell you what I told him? He saw into my mind after all".

"He wasn't convinced," Yewki interrupted. The five of them kept together and walked around slowly, each facing a different way. The large pillars were scattered around the room but only one was keeping their enemy hidden. There were too many to choose from, and one false move would have easily exposed them to the power he possessed. "Oh, brother of mine," Yewnin sang.

"Stop it. You no longer have the right to call me that! Show yourself, coward," Yewki demanded. A sudden rumble arose from ahead. One of the pillars had begun to shift and break. "Move!" Seff cried, as the five of them scurried out the way of the collapsing stone tower. It fell down effortlessly like a chopped tree, until its connection with the hard ground created a tremendous crash, shaking the whole room. "Enough of your cheap traps!" Yewki roared.

"You're right, yes," he answered, walking calmly from behind another pillar. He just stood in front of them and raised his arms as though he welcomed them. It was the first time Yewki had seen his brother's face for a while. It was so polluted with rage and exhaustion, not even his troubling grin was enough to hide the pain. His eyes had darkened and sweat dripped down the sides of his face. He walked towards the group, not even feeling the slightest bit threatened by their number. "You brought the bear. That's incredible," he panted.

"We're all here. Why would that be different?" Yewki replied.

"I see. So this is your little band of warriors is it? An ageing Wizard, trembling in his boots. It's a good thing I can't smell fear or else I'd be chocking on it. A girl who doesn't belong, trying too hard to be brave and noble. A boy and his pet bear, once roamers of the lonely road, now forced into this life of ruin. They will all die, Yewki... and their blood will be on your hands. Can you handle that much death?" Lumni had enough of his intimidation and shot an arrow at his eye with no warning. Yewnin stepped to the side and watched it fly by to the back of the room. The relic had given him inhuman reflexes without him knowing it, but he accepted them with open arms. "Oh my, that was close. Is that your go-to action? Just point and shoot? Do you not think further towards the repercussions?" he laughed.

"Leave her alone!" Wick shouted whilst stepping forwards slightly, triggering Moon to do the same. Yewnin's eyes opened, but then soon dimmed again. "Greenwick. You're just full of surprises aren't you? The most surprising is the fact you follow my brother around like he owns you".

"Don't talk to the boy," Yewki snarled.

"Look at you, brother! Protecting the boy as though he's your own... but the only thing he needs protection from is you. Why would you invite him into this? Why would you then invite more? Are you truly that desperate?"

"If the innocent feel the need to step in and stop you then what does that tell you?" Yewki stuttered.

"Innocent? Or just uneducated?" Yewnin pointed the Day Relic at them and smiled. Seff shuddered in fear but the others stood their ground. "That relic doesn't belong to you," the Wizard blubbered.

"I'm sorry? Did the old man say something?" Yewnin sniggered.

"No one should tamper with the nature of reality. It's beyond our comprehension".

"But I comprehend everything! This relic is mine... it's me just as much as I am it".

"Listen to yourself! This has gotten out of hand. It needs to stop." Yewki begged.

"There's no point," Yewnin muttered.

"If there *is* no point to any of this then why do you persist?" Wick asked, remembering back to the things he told him about the supposed meaning of life. The man paused for a moment, struggling to think of a response, but quickly returned to his talkative self. "I have a great story. Well, it's not a story as such... if you could all just bear with me a moment-".

"Enough!" Yewki shouted. His brother stormed forwards with the relic aiming at them one by one. His face became pure anger and his body started to tense and shake. "I said bear with me a moment!" he roared. The five of them complied to reduce the chances of being disintegrated. He took a deep breath and closed his eyes for a quick second, then proceeded to belittle them with his story. "Do any of you know much about the river salmon?" he asked rhetorically. "Their lives begin in the basin down near Gu-Ram. They grow and follow the river into the ocean. There they swim and feed for the majority of their life span. Day in, day out, that's all they do – swim from one place to another. But then, all of a sudden, they all make the journey back into the river as though it calls them. They're much larger fish now compared to what they once were, so the water is far too shallow... but they all endure it for the sole purpose of finding a mate. After battling it out and reproducing, the salmon lay their eggs in the same place they were born. Their purpose is now fulfilled. They've continued their legacy through their off spring, so now they just wait to die. Then of course, the new wave of salmon are born... and they do the exact same thing. They swim to the ocean, live their lives, just to eventually return to the basin and die. You can't deny the fact that it all sounds rather pointless, correct?"

"What has this got to do with anything?" Wick pondered.

"It doesn't seem pointless to the salmon does it? But it seems pointless to us. Imagine another creature peering into *our* lives – watching us running around headless, killing the innocent and sparing the guilty. Our lives have just as much value as those salmon, and if you see their purpose as pointless then why should our squabbles be deemed important? Life – it's all nonsense!"

"Then why fight so hard to destroy it?" Lumni said.

"I could ask you and my brother the same question. Believe me... this is so hard," he wheezed, clenching his eyes shut in internal pain. "One minute I'm wondering what's stopping me ruining everything. The other I'm asking myself, is there any point to this... or anything for that matter?" he continued.

"Do you not notice that searching for answers too thoroughly has narrowed your attitude and outlook rather than broadening it?" Yewki stressed. What the group hadn't noticed during the conversation is that Yewnin had aimed the relic upwards. The daylight energy was still negated by the walls, roof and floor, but the pillars were still able to be broken. Doing just that, he caused two to topple over, which rushed down towards them all. The group split in half to evade them both. Wick, Moon and Lumni stood apart from Yewki and Seff, with the rubble between them preventing a reunion. Yewnin didn't know whether to point to his left or his right. "Who wants to go first? I can only aim at you three or those two. If only I had the other-".

"Aim at me, Yewnin... and watch how quickly I stop you," Yewki screamed, cutting his brother off mid-sentence. "This won't bring me any satisfaction, I hope you're aware," Yewnin chuckled, swishing the relic over his head as though he was casting a fishing line. The time for civil talk had ended. Hearts flowed as quickly as they could pump and bodies transitioned into battle mode.

Yewnin let out controlled beams towards Yewki, but Seff jumped in front and formed a shield of hardlight at the last the second. Wick, Lumni and Moon ran in the opposite direction whilst they could. The Wizard's compressed sheet of light was no match for the pure light and quickly shattered, forcing them to dive to the side. Yewnin tilted and twisted the relic which made it shine brightly as though Yewki and Seff were staring directly at the sun. The only thing they could do was slam their eyes shut and bob down to the floor in hopes of being avoided, but he had a direct shot. All would have been ended at that moment if Lumni hadn't fired an arrow from behind. Yewnin's body reacted against its will again, making him slide out of the way and turn to face her and Wick. "Absorption, boy! Absorption!" Seff screamed, reminding Wick about the magic he'd been taught. A rapid surge of shining fury whizzed towards the boy, but Moon jumped across and knocked him to the ground with Lumni. Wick quickly remembered the right gestures for the extraction spell and retracted the moisture from the surrounding air, creating a large cloud of steam and mist for them to hide inside of. Seff did the same for him and Yewki and made their way to the children. Yewnin was furious and full of wrath. He didn't hesitate to aim the relic in every direction in hopes to hit at least one of them, but all remaining pillars were knocked down in the process. An intense minute of evading debris broke the group apart again. This time Wick and Moon were alone whilst Lumni and Seff ran to keep up with Yewki, but falling stone stopped them in their tracks which meant that Yewki was on his own. At this point, chunks of stone began dripping from the roof just to add to the list of things to dodge. Once the quakes had stopped, Lumni was able to shoot more arrows precisely. As they left her bow, Seff flicked fire onto them from his wrists, giving the arrowheads more of a deadly effect. Yewnin moved through the incoming volley of flames and advanced towards the two of them. He was so unstoppable they began to reconsider even trying. Seemingly from nowhere, Wick rode on Moon's back and charged right at him with a sudden gush of courage. He was unable to dodge the width of the bear and fell to the side and banged his head on the piles of rock. The team had the chance to quickly regroup, then waited to see if Yewnin would get back up. After a groan, he lifted his bloody head. "You still bleed, you fool! Don't forget you're just as human as us!" Yewki begged, hoping that the fighting could stop. Unfortunately, after a few seconds of double vision, Yewnin climbed back to his feet with the relic still clasped tightly in his hand. "You can't win," Lumni said, looking on at the weary state of him. He'd let them get the better of him once too many. "There may have been a little underestimation on my behalf. Obviously your unexplained vendettas gave you the upper hand... but I think I'm going to end that now," he panted.

"No don't!" Yewki bellowed. The relic absorbed into Yewnin's skin, turning his entire body into a weapon. He was able to blast thinner beams of light out of the palms of his hand at a rapid pace, as well as small, glowing orbs. The projectiles quickly filled the room but the team stuck together and veered around the tomb as a unit. Their opposition had taken flight and shot from above, but Seff conjured as many hardlight shields as he could above their heads as they ran. Yewnin's offence had changed for the worse, so it was time for a different approach. "Lumni, fire as many arrows as you can. Keep his attention on your attacks. Seff, is there a way you can get me into the air?"

"I can release a gust of wind but it's too dangerous," Seff began to explain.

"Do it on my mark!"

"What about me and Moon?" Wick asked.

"Just stay out of the way".

"But-".

"Do as I say!" Just as Yewki requested, Lumni twanged an array of projectiles towards Yewnin, knowing he'd be able to dodge the lot. "Now!" Yewki ordered, making Seff whip out a strong air blast beneath his feet which flung him into the air. Yewnin noticed his brother flying towards him head first but it was too late to react. Yewki grabbed hold of him and dragged him back down to the ground, but his body was glowing and hot which made the struggle all the more painful. Now that they were back on the floor and in close proximity, the light beams would be more difficult to ignite due to Yewnin's hands being too busy with blocks. As a result, the two of them unsheathed their swords and clashed. Yewki had always been the better fighter out of the two back when they were children fighting over nonsense, but their lives of innocence and tranquillity was lost. Real stakes were face up on the table for all to endure. They fought as the others watched on, not knowing what use they'd be if they intervened. It gave them a moment to look around at the destruction which seemed to have escalated in the matter of minutes, even though the whole battle felt like they were trapped in slow-motion. Chips of rock were still falling from the roof and the number of things holding the tomb together had fell to none. Somehow the room failed to collapse in on itself as though Lay-Vau was preventing it from inside the drum. The brothers' swords clanged together just like their views, sending a painful scraping sound into the ears of all. Yewnin's unstoppable will and might allowed him to deliver a deep cut across Yewki's chest and shoulder, knocking him back slightly. The others felt the need to finally try and jump in, but the fight was overpopulated and difficult to traverse without hurting a fellow team member. Swords, daggers, claws and spells cluttered and juggled around, causing more harm than good at first, but after a few moments of awkwardness, they took one another into account and attacked him efficiently and as a team. They surrounded and struck him at alternate times, but the force of the relic kept Yewnin from harm's way. He still fought back as he swooped and weaved. Yewki blocked what attacks he could whilst Seff blew unavoidable strikes out of the way with blasts of air. Lumni used her actual bow as a weapon until she was finally able to hook the string around his neck. With one hand on the bowstring around his neck and the other holding tight to his sword, Yewnin still had the strength to attack his brother. Wick held on tight to Moon's back whilst he stood on his back legs as he flailed his paws around. At last, three of his claws struck the right side of his face, slamming him straight down with an excruciating cry. He dropped his sword and covered his head with his hands. Wick jumped off the back of the bear and clambered over to Yewnin with his arms ready to absorb his body heat. "Do it!" Yewki yelled. Wick looked at the bleeding man and started to reconsider. "This is no time for pity!" Lumni huffed. With a slight reluctance, Wick extracted the warmth inside of Yewnin, which removed the internal energy from the relic, causing it to reconstruct outside of his body. His connection with it was temporarily cut until he had the opportunity to grasp it again. For once in a long time, Yewnin was just as powerless as every other human, but his urge to be with the relic made him forget of the pain in his face. He crawled across the floor to grab it, but Wick kicked it over to Yewki. "That's mine!" the bleeding man whined.

"It's no ones. Just how it should be," Seff jabbed.

"Actually, it's mine," Lay-Vau's voice erupted.

The six of them turned their heads over to the drum which rested atop the central stone slab. Wick was the only one who felt intimidated by the hallowing voice. The others couldn't imagine how the Iwa would be able to take the relic back for itself trapped inside of a musical instrument, but Wick recalled what he had told Yewnin during their spirit dream; about how Lay-Vau would find a way to release himself if he wanted to. The roof had begun to crack from the lack of support which only increased the amount of falling rock even more. "He's coming," Wick panicked. All the others could do was look on as a convenient little stone fell from directly above the drum. It seemed to drop for a lifetime, but the haunting bang of the drum soon snapped them back to reality. The stone had hit the skin perfectly, sending out a vibration across the room. Other drums that didn't exist began to play rapidly as scattered torches ignited themselves. "No, no, no! Don't let him take it! He doesn't deserve it!" Yewnin blubbered. Out of the mysterious void of voodoo, Lay-Vau materialised atop the stone slab, looking just as round and threatening as last time. He took a deep breath out and stretched his limbs with delight as though he'd been sleeping for weeks. Yewnin whined to himself on the floor as the others stood and watched the Iwa float towards them. "Well this has just been one underground excavation after another for you all, hasn't it?" he laughed. His bone jewellery clattered and clinked as he moved in a surprisingly cheerful manner. Seff and Lumni hadn't seen anything as spectral before, but his ghostly body quickly turned more physical the closer he got. "You all seem scared. Rejoice! For this is your redemption!" he chortled.

"I'm sorry?" Yewki muttered.

"The Day Relic was entrusted to you, Yewki... but you let your brother take it. You were supposed to be its next protector, don't you see?! But you failed miserably," he laughed. "Regardless, you've returned the relic to me and I thank you for that," he continued.

"I was told to take the relic simply for relocation," Yewki stuttered.

"Yes, from the maze to your hand".

"I've seen what it's done to my brother. I don't want any part of it".

"But aren't you the slightest bit curious to see how you would cope with its tremendous power? You could have stopped your brother with it... *all* evil in fact!"

"Even you?" Wick interjected.

"Oh, hello again, Greenwick. How's the voodoo? No hard feelings," Lay-Vau sniggered.

"Can't you relieve the boy of his curse?" Seff asked.

"Where's the fun in that?"

"Piea and I were fools to think we could have you on our side," Yewki hissed. The Iwa smiled and walked over to Yewnin. His face was cut badly three times thanks to Moon. Even his eye was damaged from the strike. "Wow, they really put you in your place didn't they? I'm struggling to decide which one of you brothers is the most idiotic," Lay-Vau chuckled at the sight of him. He grabbed him by the neck and pulled him up to his feet. "Let me go at once! There's bigger things I must accomplish! More than what you can comprehend!" Yewnin panicked.

"Oh yes, you think there's gods telling you what to do, correct? I'm practically a demigod… don't you think I would know about this?"

"You don't understand".

"No, I understand everything… and I don't have time to listen to whatever knowledge or truth you think you possess," the stubborn Iwa growled. "I'm taking him to my void for an eternity of torment. I hope none of you mind," he continued. The others had no response and let him drag Yewnin back towards the drum. After a few seconds, he stopped and turned back around. "Oh, I almost forgot! I'll be taking my relic back too," he smiled whilst looking down at it. The troublesome Day Relic sat at the group's feet. None of them dared pick it up, but they didn't want the evil Iwa to be reunited with it. Yewki kicked it backwards behind them and awaited the uproar. "What do you think you're doing?" Lay-Vau said, half angrily, half with a grin due to disbelief. "I-I can't let you take it," Yewki stammered. The voodoo master released his grip on Yewnin and dropped him back down. "You're forgetting that it's mine," he growled.

"Really? Then who granted *you* responsibility?" Lumni asked.

"Foolish girl. My entity was created by the relic itself. The relic is me just as I am it," he announced. The shrouded mystery had been alleviated slightly. Although there was no new evidence regarding the relic's creator, Lay-Vau was simply a manifestation existing for the sole purpose of protecting it. "I have no time for this. I've already punished the boy, don't make me punish the rest of you," he warned.

"Your eternal life has left you tired and wanting. Perhaps at some point you were loyal and noble, but you've become evil, like time rots the fruit. You're services are no longer needed, Iwa," Yewki expressed.

"How dare you. This is a fight you will *not* win".

"You need to return to the void of voodoo and stay there, *without* the relic".

"I live *for* the relic!"

"We can't let you take it".

"The fact that you think you have the slightest chance of challenging me is amusing. Final warning," Lay-Vau grunted. Yewnin gained some distance from the brooding fight to prepare himself whilst Yewki raised his sword, trying his hardest not to tremble. "So be it," the Iwa cackled. He hovered above the floor and placed his palms together. "You remember the friend I took from you? Batehong the living fire?" he sniggered. Suddenly, a huge tornado of flames grew from the ground up as demonic roars gargled from inside. It quickly morphed into more of a body shape, until a towering fire giant stood before them, made entirely of flames. Its heat was wild and intense, causing everyone to squint from its sheer radiance. It was the return of Batehong. He'd been consumed and possessed with the only purpose of killing all that its master commanded. As a result of everyone's conflicting views, the tomb had filled up with a deadly triangle of fighters. Yewnin still stood strong and ready to attack with an uncontrollable yearning to take back his power, Lay-Vau and Batehong wanted to destroy everyone in sight to claim what was theirs, but Yewki and his team had become the true protectors of the Day Relic and it couldn't have happened in a worse situation. A three-way conflict, with only one possible victor. The true battle had begun.

"Come forth all! Dare to challenge me!" Lay-Vau screamed. The ambient drums increased in tempo to provide more tension along with the torches' flames increasing in size. Yewki scooped up the relic with his sword and flung it into the air. He yanked Seff's satchel and plopped it inside the bag to avoid anyone having to touch it. The five of them passed the bag around as they ran, dodging Batehong's huge balls of fire. They had to figure out a way to destroy the Iwa and release the trance upon the fire giant, but there was no time to think. Yewnin put aside his severe wounds and joined the fray. He jumped straight in and fought with Yewki whilst Lumni ran away with the bag. Lay-Vau advanced towards her, so she threw it over to Seff who then air blasted it over to Wick. The boy caught it as he rode on Moon's back. The two of them jumped over and weaved through the piles of rubble, but the Iwa was quickly gaining on them. He placed his right palm out towards the boy and the bear, releasing a putrid stream of black liquid, but as it travelled through the air, it hardened, turning into multiple spikes. They darted all around them like a flock of birds. A few got close but they'd managed to evade them all. Meanwhile, Batehong was swooping his large arms around in an attempt to smack both Seff and Lumni. The Wizard shielded as much as he could, but the strength of the giant knocked them over. Before he could stomp on top of them, Seff placed his hands on the floor, covering a patch of it with ice. They moved out the way to allow Batehong to step on it. After a large thud, he roared and jumped back as much as his huge body would let him. After being outsmarted, he decided to shift his focus over to Yewki and Yewnin who were still in the midst of a sword fight. They moved around as they fought to get out of Batehong's firing lines. The huge fireballs made everything harder. Even if they missed, they would explode as they hit the floor, sending out a wave of flames. The tip of Yewki's jacket caught on fire but he couldn't do anything about it whilst slashing swords together. Thankfully, Wick was passing by atop Moon and retracted the flames from his clothing. Lay-Vau was still chasing the two of them around. His patience was wearing thin, so he released twice the amount of black spikes to ensure a hit. Unfortunately, his dreams came true and one of them pierced into Moon's back leg, causing him to collapse. Wick was ejected off the bear's back then hit the ground hard, but before he could see to Moon, he launched the bag through the air to redirect their pursuer's attention. The Iwa saw the satchel flying by and went for it. His fingers were inches away but Lumni shot the bag with a fast arrow, knocking it off course and towards Seff. "Moon!" Wick cried, patting the beast's injured leg. He needed to pull the shard out before it infected Moon's blood. Luckily, the voodoo within himself allowed him to grab the spike without being harmed. He tugged it out as the bear grunted in pain, but with the adrenaline of battle, he was able to stand back up and run. Wick jumped back on and made their way towards Seff who was in the middle of casting spells at Batehong. Lay-Vau tore the bones from his body and threw them towards the bear. As the skeletal pieces fell, they somehow multiplied, until full figures landed in front of Wick and Moon. Before they could help Seff, they had to fight the group of bones blocking their way. The boy swooshed his dagger at the joints, making the skeletons break apart, all whilst Moon ran around in circles, knocking over as many as possible. Just as the last one fell, the first one built itself back up. Before long, the whole group had reconstructed and charged towards them again. Lumni appeared to ward off a handful whilst the bear carried the boy towards Seff. The other skeletons chased after them with great speed, almost grabbing hold of Moon's fur. Batehong stood in front of them, but before they could change direction, an unseen patch of ice carried them through and in between the giant's legs as he stomped. The bear slid and span, just missing a collision with the flames. The skeletons had slid also, but Batehong accidentally stepped on them. Lumni shot what arrows she had left at the remaining ones. Her quiver was quickly depleting so she picked up what arrows she could that were scattered around. Lay-Vau saw her struggle and decided to swoop down and make things worse by slamming his foot down, making a bunch of spikes shoot out from beneath the ground. Her body was trapped awkwardly in the middle of them all, unable to move and too scared to touch them. The skeletons pushed and pulled her about to try and knock her into the spikes, but she punched and hit them with her bow. The Iwa grinned and marched forward, inducing panic, but in her desperation, she came up with a last-minute idea. As he got closer, she shot another arrow, hitting a skeleton in the eye socket. The skull snapped off the neck and flung towards Lay-Vau. Whilst his attention was fixed on grabbing the flying head mid-air, she fired once more, this time at his chest. Without noticing it incoming, he was successfully struck which stopped him in his tracks momentarily. Once he'd pulled it out and looked up, Lumni had already squeezed her way out of the spikes to run towards Seff, Wick and Moon. "His physical form can be harmed!" she informed them.

"Yes, but it won't kill him," Seff panted whilst blocking Batehong's numerous attacks. Wick caught on and gasped. "But it'll slow him down," he said.

"No more!" the Iwa screamed. Suddenly, before they could hatch a plan with their new intelligence, the room around them collapsed in on itself and span around uncontrollably until everything had blurred out of reality. All was white and infinite, like they had all died and regrouped in the afterlife. "Let's see how you all fare in *my* world!" Lay-Vau announced, revealing that they'd been transported into the mysterious void of voodoo. All that was had been shifted and contained into the tiny drum, yet all was endlessly spacious. No roof, no walls, no floor, but they somehow still stood as though there was a ground beneath their feet. The Iwa's powers were amplified in his homeland, which allowed him to send out hundreds of spikes around them. They acted as cages, trapping him, Batehong and the other six closely together. "Look at you all! You're fighting is meaningless! You can't kill me so how do you expect to leave? Consider this the ultimate punishment," Lay-Vau laughed. Wick looked over to Seff and Yewki with a plan ignited from the Iwa's taunts. "You exist solely because the Day Relic exists?" Wick asked the voodoo master. Seff started to figure out what he was getting at and whispered it over to Yewki and Lumni. "So what if the relic just stopped... existing?" he concluded.

"Silence, boy!" Lay-Vau yelled. Batehong continued his attacks, making them all scatter once again, but the walls of spikes didn't leave them with much room to move. The Iwa grabbed Yewki with one hand and Yewnin with the other. His touch on their bodies was like an acidic burning sensation and no matter how much they both screamed and wriggled, there was no escape. Across from them, the fire giant slammed his fists down at the rest of the group, but Seff had created another dome of hardlight. He struggled to keep it contained as Batehong hit it over and over. Death was imminent so Wick's plan had to go into action at that very moment. Without warning, the boy grabbed the relic from inside of Seff's bag. His body dropped to the floor in agony as soon as his hand touched the device. Even though the pain was immense, he held it tightly to his own chest. The voodoo was preventing him from being completely engulfed, but the fact that he was human was counteracting it at the same time. Yewnin was strong and able to attach with the relic, but Wick's small, cursed body was minutes away from burning up. Lay-Vau sensed the use of the Day Relic and let go of the brothers. He flew over to the hardlight bubble and began smashing it himself. "Get off of it!" he screamed. Yewnin left Yewki and ran over too, to try and grab it first. Wick rolled around on the floor, letting out bright lights from his eyes. "The... the Astral Vale," he wheezed.

"What?" Seff gasped.

"Nothing exists inside of the Astral Vale!" The dome shattered and Batehong's fists were dropping down onto them. Lay-Vau and Yewnin were both scurrying over to Wick, but Seff quickly clicked on and moved himself, the boy, Moon and Lumni inside of the Vale. At the last second, Yewnin jumped in with them to fight over the relic like a rabid dog.

The relic's powerful presence made the Vale unstable which caused colourful strikes of lightning to fling in all directions. Unlike usual, there was no floor for them to stand on, forcing their bodies to fall through the infinite as their surroundings cracked and burst into radiant lights and rainbows. None of them had noticed Yewnin plummeting above them, slowly getting closer to Wick's distressed body. Back within the void of voodoo, Lay-Vau was struggling to keep upright. His legs shook and staggered around as his upper body shivered. Batehong threw rapid flames at Yewki to keep him busy. One wave of fire managed to whip his right hand, knocking him and his sword to the floor. His nose dripped with blood as he lifted himself up to look at his death-bringer. Luckily, as Lay-Vau weakened, so did the straining possession he had on Batehong, which caused the giant to pause in confusion, as though he was fighting a battle within himself. "Please, remember who you are! You're the great Batehong... a living fire... but most importantly, you're a friend. Don't let him control you," Yewki coughed.

"Don't listen to him, you dullard! You're in *my* control!" the Iwa shouted from afar, making the fire giant raise his scorching foot above Yewki. "You control yourself now. Be free. Come back, friend... please!" he begged with a tear in his eye. He looked up to him with sad, truthful eyes in hopes of convincing him. Eventually, Batehong put his foot back down by his side and began to shrink into more of a traditional shaped fire. "I-I'm sorry for what I've done, Yewki," the flames apologised.

"No! This can't be happening!" Lay-Vau screeched. Yewki nodded his head to the fire and smiled, then turned around and wiped his nose clean with his hand. "It's over, Iwa," Yewki snarled.

"How is this-".

"That boy was foolish enough to activate and transport the Day Relic into the Astral Vale, temporarily subjecting it to a world of non-existence. So for as long as he is in there, you have no purpose. All we do now is wait for you to remove yourself from all plains of existence," Yewki explained.

"But I don't want to be erased!"

"Well it seems like your body is doing that for you". Lay-Vau became more transparent like his ghostly form, but this time it was against his will. He knelt down and looked at his fading hands, absolutely dumbfounded at the fact he'd been outsmarted by mortals. Wick, Moon, Lumni, Seff and Yewnin were still falling towards nothing. The structure of the Vale at that point was critically fragile, meaning that their connection with it would soon be terminated. Wick had to hold on tight to the relic for as long as possible, not knowing how long it'd take for Lay-Vau to be completely eradicated. "Boy, look out!" Seff shouted through the strong winds blowing by their ears. He had spotted Yewnin flying down head first towards him with his hands out and eyes wide open. The Wizard prepared himself for a fire blast but Yewnin swooped to the side and entangled with him. The two of them wrestled until Seff was punched into unconsciousness. Lumni shot an arrow, leaving her with just one left. The strong gusts of air blew the arrow off its mark, but it still managed to hit Yewnin on the bottom of his shin. He gasped in pain but still focused on reaching Wick. The longer they fell, the faster their bodies dropped, making their heads feel light and dizzy. If they continued for much longer, they would all share the same fate as Seff. Yewnin was moments away from grabbing onto the boy, but Lumni twanged her final arrow, jabbing into his shoulder, but he yanked it out and kept hold of it as a weapon. Finally, after an enduring plummet, he had reached Wick's glowing body. His muscles tensed and his face scrunched up in agony. Yewnin grabbed the Day Relic and tugged but the boy refused to let go, even though it was killing him. The two of them shared the strain which allowed Wick to ease up and use more of his strength. "Let go, child! It's mine!" the mad man screamed.

"No!" Wick shouted back. They wrapped around each other and span uncontrollably. In the midst of the frantic tug of war, Moon managed to chomp down on Yewnin's left leg, causing him to screech just like he did when the bear scratched his face. The bear showed no signs of letting go. He'd had enough of seeing his friend being attacked by a grown man. Unfortunately, that grown man wasn't afraid to do something immoral to take back control of the precious relic. He stared at it as though it was calling his name. The immeasurable desire he had for it forced him to stab Wick in the chest with Lumni's arrow, leaving the boy with no choice but to let go of the relic due to the overwhelming impalement to his body. A trail of black blood pumped out into the air, which made Moon release his jaws from Yewnin's leg in sheer shock and anguish. "Wick!" Lumni cried. The bear roared with anger and sadness, but there was nothing they could do but watch him fall beside them. Yewnin engulfed the relic as though he'd been reunited with his heart and began to control his descent by flying. Instead of his eyes shining yellow and white, they glowed much more orange to convey anger. He placed his arms out, ready to finish them off with his great force, but the Vale began to brighten. After a confusing few seconds, the eternal plummet became a blinding white, indicating that they were returning back to Lay-Vau's voodoo void by force. None of them knew which direction their bodies moved in or how long they had left before they'd be back in the fight, unaware that the fight was actually over.

Yewki and Batehong stood over Lay-Vau's decomposing body, enjoying every minute of it. "What does destroying me achieve? Your brother is the real monster," the Iwa proclaimed.

"That may be true... but all trust I had for this world has depleted. No form of evil deserves a chance... and that includes you," Yewki expressed.

"So you choose to live against the current? Against the Earth you stand on... with a distrust for the people you're trying to save? And I suppose your friends are the only people you need. You're all going to save the day and protect each other. That sounds hideous".

"Why's that? You don't know what it means to be human... to have people worth fighting for when there's so much turmoil wherever you look. You're the keeper of an ancient weapon and nothing more. You served to protect it but the only thing it requires protection from is yourself. You had a choice. You could have helped keep this world safe... but instead, you contributed to its downfall".

"Don't forget your brother too. Let's say I *did* become too consumed by the relic's possession... what do you think is going to happen when Yewnin, a mere mortal, is tied to it?"

"Well we won't let that happen".

"*We*? Ha! Yes, the boy and his bear, the Wizard and his adopted daughter. That's quite some team you have there," Lay-Vau mocked. His time was over. The near-vanishing of his body was his cue to leave. "That boy may have brought my entity to an end, but I promise you... you won't be able to protect him forever. Evil will always exist and because of you, he'll always want to pursue it. The longer you bond, the harder it'll be when the day comes. Luck *always* runs out. And *that*... will be *your* punishment," the Iwa warned as his life and soul completely vanished. He was no more, just in time for Wick, Moon, Lumni, Seff and Yewnin to plop back into the void, thus making the Day Relic exist in the real world again. A moment sooner and they would have returned before Lay-Vau had disappeared entirely, which would have allowed him to remain. Yewki looked over to see Wick lifeless on the floor with the arrow still in his chest whilst Lumni and Moon shook his body from side to side. The bear couldn't stop grunting and roaring as though he was trying to say something. His large paws patted the boy's belly, but nothing seemed to wake him up. "Please don't die!" Lumni whined as she raised his head against her. Moon shoved Wick's arm with his snout and sniffled. "Wick!" Yewki panicked. He observed the arrow for a second then yanked it out the best he could. The shouting and screaming helped Seff break free from his unconsciousness, but it took him a while to rid himself of the daze and figure out where he was. "Seff! Help! Please!" Yewki pleaded.

"What? What happened?" the Wizard gasped.

"It was Yewnin. He stabbed him with my arrow!" Lumni blubbered. Seff quickly crawled across to them and placed his hand on the boy's chest. "It *just* missed his heart," he informed. Yewki was slightly relieved, but Wick was still unmoving. "Can you heal him?" he asked.

"I-I don't know". Moon shoved his wet nose in the Wizard's face as a way to implore him. Seff knew how much the boy meant to everyone, but no one came close to the love the bear had for him. "The voodoo will make it more difficult, but I'll try," the old man sighed.

"Stop wasting time you don't even have," Yewnin croaked from a distance. His body was beaten up badly. Blood poured from his leg, shoulder and face, but he still had the audacity to stand and taunt as though he was the strongest in the room. Yewki ran over and grabbed him by the collar of his robes. "This is over. You've gone too far!" he grumbled, fighting back the tears. Yewnin didn't reply and just smiled and licked the blood from his lip. He pulled the relic from behind his back and pushed it against his brother's chest, ready to release its power. Moon caught sight and quickly pulled Yewki back by this clothes as a beam of light fired where he was just stood. "That beast is becoming a nuisance!" Yewnin scorned.

"Don't you dare hurt my bear," Wick whimpered. With the help of magic, Seff had healed his wound enough for his heart to start beating again. Lumni helped him up to his feet and put his arm over her shoulder for support. "I'm going to do more than just hurt him!" the mad man cackled, unfazed by the boy's reluctance to die. "Don't try it," Lumni warned. He wasted no more time entertaining them with back chat and allowed action to speak louder than words by raising the relic at the defenceless bear. Yewki grabbed his pointed arm with both hands and pushed it upwards. The two of them pushed one another as the rays of energy streamed above their heads, both scoffing and grunting with each movement. Yewnin was able to punch him in the stomach with his free fist but Yewki refused to let go. "How do we stop him?" Lumni asked.

"We need something big," Seff answered.

"How about a house?" Wick murmured. He got to work and made a small, round Access Gate symbol with his own spilt blood on the floor, under the direction of Seff. His body was tired and frail, but he crawled around as quickly as he could. Yewki noticed them during the struggle with his brother and shadily dragged the fight towards them. "The Empyrean Energy from your blood *should* boost the spell... but I've never done it like this before!" Seff stuttered.

"If it's been attached to the Astral Vale, all you have to do is drag it through," Wick explained, not knowing if his plan would be entirely possible. He collapsed after using up whatever strength he had left, but Lumni knelt down and stayed by his side. Yewki and Yewnin had reached symbol and stood on top of it. "Now, now, do it now!" Lumni yelled. Seff panicked and did as he was told. Out of nowhere, Seff's cottage home appeared from nothing and hurtled through the air towards the two brothers like a flying spinning top. Moon tackled Yewki out of the collision zone, just ducking below the zooming house in time. It passed over their heads and crashed into Yewnin before he could react. Wood and bricks exploded into the air as the cottage rolled and crumbled. All kinds of materials mixed together to create a huge ensemble of smashing and booming sounds. The others looked on and winced until the wreckage came to a standstill. Just dust and smoke surrounded the once comfortable refuge, with no sign of Yewnin having survived. The battle felt like it'd finally come to an end, and the heaping mess signified a well-deserved sigh of relief. "You out did yourself this time, Seff. I can't believe it worked," Wick gawked.

"My beautiful home," the old man complained.

"I wouldn't stress too much about that. Not whilst we're trapped in this void," Yewki said, catching his breath after his scuffle. "I can teleport us back to the tomb, just like how we did to get there the first time," Wick answered. They looked back at the rubble, half expecting Yewnin to burst out intact. They had perfect reason to be sceptical and cautious because of how enduring he had been up until that point. "I don't feel comfortable leaving in case my brother returns," Yewki sighed.

"He's gone... he has to be," Lumni pondered.

"I can stay here inside the void. I will stand guard just in case," Batehong alerted. The group had almost forgot the fire was even there. "You can't," Yewki huffed.

"That's not up to you. I choose to stay and watch over the relic, none of you are immortal like I".

"Yes. With no way to re-enter the drum, the relic will be trapped in here forever! No one else can try and claim it," Seff agreed.

"It's the best result we could ask for," Batehong said.

"Very well, great fire. We won't forget about your deed," Yewki sighed. He bowed his head which prompted the others to do the same. "Let's leave this accursed place," Lumni scowled.

Just like last time, Seff and Wick transported them to the tomb. However, when they arrived, the room was practically demolished and near-unrecognisable. Moon licked Wick's face as Seff and Lumni hugged and patted him on the head. Even though they were stranded on Groo'ma-du Mountain, they couldn't help but rejoice a little. All except Yewki however. "I should have never brought any of you into this mess. I could have lost you all," he groaned.

"But you couldn't have done it without us," Wick explained.

"Look at you! You almost died, Wick! What makes it worse is it's not the first time either. But this time was all the more real. If it wasn't for Seff, I would have let a child die because of me".

"You can't keep going back and forth between letting us help and wanting to keep us out of it," Lumni moaned. He thought about how easily he gave in to their persuasions – right from the beginning when Wick and Moon tagged along with him. He remembered back to how he basically arrived on Seff and Lumni's doorstep with the dying boy. Everything had snowballed into what it was meant to be, but none of it felt right now that it was over. "I know I could have died but-".

"No, Wick. You shouldn't have had anything to do with this at all," Yewki interrupted.

"He destroyed an Iwa! He held the relic and fought against its power to save us," Lumni began to shout.

"Why did you have to hold it? Why couldn't you have just kept it in the bag?!"

"I noticed Lay-Vau was more heightened and his focus amplified when the relic was activated. Removing it from existence whilst it was active... I assumed it would speed up the process of the Iwa's extermination".

"He's right, brother," a voice panted. The five of them jumped and turned around to see Yewnin somehow still alive with the Day Relic still in his hand and Lay-Vau's drum in the other. "How?!" Seff barked.

"You won't believe this but... the relic, it protected me," he chuckled.

"No! Why would it?" Yewki shuddered.

"My bond with it has grown greater than such trivial factors as life and death".

"Impossible!"

"Just as I predicted a long time ago, it's protecting its host, no matter what you throw at me... even a house. Everything worked out the way I'd hoped... near enough," he scoffed whilst pointing to the large scratches across his face. "You wanted this to happen?!" Yewki shouted.

"I admit, it was a great risk... and you all fought valiantly. But I knew I'd have to be parted from the relic momentarily for its predilection towards me to intensify. Upon our reconnection, it served to protect".

"How do you know all this?"

"Because it's me just as much as I am it".

"Lay-Vau said the same thing… and look what happened to him".

"It was time for a new protector. A stronger and smarter one. That arrogant Iwa was asking for it to be stolen from him".

"What did you do to Batehong?" Wick asked.

"His flames seemed dim compared to my pure light. It didn't take long for him to perish". Without warning, he smashed the drum on the ground, breaking it into pieces. Lay-Vau's legacy was over. The only threat they had to worry about was Yewnin. "It looks like the fight isn't over," Lumni hissed.

"Look at the state of me," he exhaled, struggling to stand as blood dripped from all over. "I can't let you win. And by escaping, that means *I* win instead," he elaborated.

"Coward!"

"I could destroy you all now if I wanted".

"Then do it," Yewki snarled. The others looked at him in confusion, but he had a feeling that Yewnin was unable to use it to attack, otherwise he would have. "Why would you let us live when you could just wipe us out right now?" he continued.

"I don't have to answer to you".

"It's because you've used up its power. It needs time to heal, just like you".

"You've got me," Yewnin chuckled. "But just like my will to live, the relic still holds within it a portion of power… but I'm afraid I need that to fly away from here". He entered his glowing state again and began to float, then blew a hole in the roof which led to the peak of the mountain. "My attachment with the Day Relic is complete. Now I just need the other one," he muttered to himself before taking his leave. The whole situation had them fooled into false victory. Their triumph was torn from them before they could even call it a win. Yewki kicked what clumps of stone he could and threw his sword as far as possible. "It was all for nothing!" he roared.

"Yewki," Wick sighed.

"I almost got you killed, and it was all for nothing!"

"Compose yourself!" Seff demanded.

"None of you tell me what to do anymore. This is the last time you follow me to danger".

"And where do you propose we go?" Lumni asked sternly.

"That's no longer my concern". He sat down and drooped his head to the floor. The others didn't know what else to say. Even so, they were too scared of what his reaction would have been. Moon and Wick sat together with Lumni and Seff not far from them. They all looked up at the hole in the roof and saw the white light of day and a heavenly blue sky – so close, but yet so far away. After failing to stop Yewnin, none of them felt deserving of escaping to the surface, but unfortunately, that wasn't up to them, for after a few hours of mindless torment, a rope had been lowered down the hole. "Hello?" a female voice shouted. The five of them put aside their growing aches and pains and stood up to see who was behind the rescue. "Thene? Is… is that you?" Yewki asked.

"Yes it's me. I'm here to help. Is everyone okay? Where's Yewnin? What's happened?" she replied, bombarding them with questions. Her stolen Chuck dragon had provided her with quick access to the high mountains. She was lucky she'd interrogated Eck for infomation regarding Yewnin's whereabouts, but it was a shame she didn't arrive in time to help with the fight. "We'll explain soon. Just get us out". Seff, Yewki and Lumni were pulled up to the surface one by one, but getting Moon out was more challenging. Wick stayed down with him to tie the ropes around the bear like a harness. His only hope is that it didn't snap. Once everything was in place, he sat on Moon's back and waited to be raised. Thene, Lumni, Seff and Yewki combined still wasn't enough to lift the two of them, so the Chuck helped too, until at last, they were all safe and sound. "Thank you, Thene," Yewki said.

"So are you going to tell me what happened here?" she asked.

"We'll explain on the way home".

"And where's *home* exactly?"

"For now? With you, in the Olash villages". The six of them climbed aboard the dragon and into the large basket-like saddle, providing enough room for even the fat bear, leaving the miserable place, praying that they'd never have to return. All they wanted to do was forget that the day had ever happened, but they knew Thene would have to be informed. Reciting the events was challenging, as it forced them to relive each moment in their heads. So much effort, spilled out into one huge conflict with nothing to show for it. It was both disappointing and humiliating. It was certainly a sorrowful journey South, and the increase in snow only doubled the chills down their spines and the numbness to their bodies.

Chapter 26

Loved Ones Lost

Yewnin had always followed in his older brother's footsteps. Every thought and verdict, every action, reaction and bodily posture was absorbed from Yewki and influenced onto Yewnin for the fourteen years they lived together. They shared a small but cosy secluded home with both their Mother and Father. Neither parent was significant to the world in any way, but their children's love was all they needed, as that was what made them special in their self-contained world that only spanned across the barriers of a surrounding meadow. To keep their family happy and healthy though, both of them worked long hours on the streets of a neighbouring village, five miles away, where they'd sell various flowers grown around the fields and sit them inside of beautifully-patterned vases, which they'd make themselves. The boys would often help gather clay on busy days, but for the most part, they were left alone in the house to go about their childish mischief without the worry of being discovered. They often played with poorly made wooden weapons, which were still more stick than sword. Barrel lids worked as round shields and old buckets fitted perfectly on their heads for helmets. Living rurally with next to no exterior life meant that boredom and lack of interaction created two brotherly warriors that fought playfully against one another, inspired by stories told by their Father. After a while, the boys knew each of their fighting patterns, resulting in draws due to tiredness, as neither of them could beat the other. With no actual swordplay experience outside of the friendly brawls between themselves, it was impressive as to how skilled they'd both become. When their parents would return home after a busy day, their conversations would usually begin with questions regarding the origins of their children's cuts and bruises. Anyone would have thought the boys were regularly attacked by wild animals judging by the state of them, but it was all in good fun.

Once they were both teenagers, they were shown how to make vases with their Mother, but Yewki couldn't sculpt as well as Yewnin. He quickly became annoyed with the family trade, as he had no place being a part of it if he was useless at it. Instead, he picked flowers with his Father in the meadow, inadvertently creating a brooding rift between himself and his brother. Yewnin would be busy with his Mother sculpting vases, and Yewki would be busy taking over for her by selling their products in the village with his Father. One day in particular stood out among the rest for Yewki, which would affect his thoughts and views from then on out. He and his Father, Grinnit, sat on the floor atop a thin square sheet of cloth to protect their clothing from the dirty village floor. Their mobile shelving trolley stood at the side of them, full of amazing vases that were coated in floral patterns and graceful animal shapes. Business was slow that day, so it allowed Yewki to be alone with his thoughts for perhaps too long. "What's the point in all of this?" he asked his Father. He looked at the huge buildings above and the tiny specks of dirt below, unable to define the differences between them. Their masses couldn't have been more opposite, but to him, everything seemed the same size and held the same significance. He looked to his own being and compared its worth against the building to the side of him. He was brought into the world by his parents and lived seemingly minimalistic with not much purpose, whereas the building was constructed using a variety of materials by a handful of hard workers, with the purpose of housing many people, to provide warmth and shelter. He then looked back down to the crumbling chunks of mud and stone near his feet. Although is was small, it was once a part of something larger. It felt more a part of the Earth than he did. Inanimate objects seemed to serve a greater significance to the world, making the flower vase business that he was destined to one day take over look all the more pointless in contrast. "What's the point of what? You're going to have to be more specific, boy," his Father said.

"Everything," Yewki said. Grinnit sighed and smirked at the same time before counting the coins he'd accumulated in a sack that day. "You and your brother don't share as much time with each other as you used to, but you sound just like him according to your Mother," he replied.

"My voice is much deeper than his".

"No, I mean that you speak of the same things as he does. When your Mother and I see each other, we're amazed by the same philosophical mind-set you both have, even though neither of you influence the other. We've brought up some intelligent boys by the sounds of it".

"How does asking such broad questions make me intelligent?"

"Because they're the questions that no one ever knows the answers to," Grinnit laughed. "Most people accept the fact that not everything can be explained and move on with their lives, but you and Yewnin both keep going around in circles, asking the same things, just worded differently. You *want* to know, whereas others lack the notion to even care… and that makes you intelligent. I wish I was a clever lad growing up like you and your brother," he continued.

"You shouldn't be envious of how complex I see things. In ways, I'm the one who should be jealous of everyone else – able to get on with things without question. You may call me intelligent, but I would never have the will power to make something of myself like you did with the flower vases," Yewki moaned.

"That's because picking flowers and selling vases is easy… and you don't *do* easy. You and your brother are destined for big things, I'm sure of it".

"Oh, of course. Money barely stretches far enough as it is. We're just caught up in a looping trap, making money to stay alive to sell our goods for money to stay alive. With no excess money to go towards travelling and seeking bigger opportunities, how am I, how are *any* of us meant to reach our hands out and grab hold of better things?"

"Don't worry about your Mother and I, Yewki. We're just happy we've brought up two amazing boys. Whatever greatness that was destined for our lives is already fulfilled. You and Yewnin have the rest of your lives ahead of you".

"It's like I'm talking to you in a different language. I say all these things and you come back with forced comfort," Yewki scoffed.

"Positivity is the key!" his Father chuckled.

"I'm glad you think it's all a joke".

"Don't confuse my lack of comprehension for avoidance, boy. Do you expect me to know everything for you? I'm a simple vase merchant. So, what's the point of it all? You tell me," Grinnit said with anger, finally having enough of his son's moping. "I was asking you, Father," Yewki hissed.

"Well, I'm asking *you* now. Perhaps we can learn from each other's outlooks. You go first," he replied, lowering his tone. Yewki looked at the sea of faces passing them by, then looked to the shelves holding up all of the vases. "I see no difference between those people and those vases. I don't know what's wrong with me, but it makes me feel like an outsider," he answered.

"An outsider to what?"

"Everything… everyone". His Father noticed his son's blank stares at the shelves and put his hand on his shoulder. "So you see people as you do those vases? Well in that case, picture them as people. There's rows and rows of them, they're vibrant and colourful yet they all have the same fundamental shape. They're the same whilst being different at the same time. They can carry flowers and other beautiful things, but attachment doesn't change what the vase is. Some of them have cracks and are more susceptible to breaking, so that's why those ones are on the bottom shelf – not because they're the weakest, but because they deserve the greatest care. Most importantly though, it doesn't really matter where you are on the shelf… they're all just vases, but those who try to be on the top shelf have a greater fall if they slip.

Those that try to be the biggest and best above the others will shatter the most, and those on the bottom that fall still have the chance to get back up and fix their damages," Grinnit explained passionately. Yewki was taken back by the symbolism behind the seemingly simple sculpted pieces of clay. He realised that no matter how pointless and meaningless something looked and seemed, he would have to try and see the purpose behind something and what it represented with an emblematic point of view. With just hearing the one analogy, his mind was already eased slightly, and his surroundings were seeming significantly more beautiful. "I-I didn't expect you to be able to say such things-".

"Oh, don't doubt your old man!" his Father interrupted with a smile. "It's because I too see vases as people, but for a different reason. I've spent more time with vases and tending to them than I have people, and the more I do, the uglier I see people. This world isn't for you and that's that. You and your brother's minds don't belong around such cruelty and hardships. Your best bet is to get out there and shape it the way you want it to be, so that you're compatible with it. After all, whatever you'd transform it into would be greater than what things are like now," he continued.

"Thank you, Father," Yewki exhaled. The time had come to pack their things and head home. They pulled the wheeled shelving cart behind them and followed the long paths back to the house before night fell. The sales were the lowest they had been in a long time. Every day they hoped to return home with no vases left to carry, but the cart was pretty much full and they shook about on the rickety journey as a constant reminder. Even though the day had been a shambles, Yewki was pleased that his head was somewhat clearer, and his Father was glad he could help his oldest son. His only hope was that Yewnin was as easy to speak to.

Whilst Yewki and Grinnit were making their way home, Yewnin and his Mother, Foloria were sat together, covered in sloppy clay. They took it in turns to push the wooden pedals and turn the worn out cranks which span the turntable, whilst the other person held gently onto the blob of clay atop it to shape it into a vase with great skill and intricacy. At that moment, it was Yewnin's turn to sculpt, and his Mother was hard at work moving each of her limbs differently to get the turntable spinning. Like his Father had told Yewki, they thought of the same things usually, and seeing as though sculpting the vases was so second nature for Yewnin, he was able to ponder on his thoughts while still making an excellent piece of pottery. "What are you thinking of now?" his Mother asked. She had learned how to notice his change in character when he was alone in thought. His eyes would stare as though the world around him was transparent and his legs would no longer fidget up and down. Upon hearing her voice though, his trance was broken and he aimed his focus back towards the clay without responding. His wasn't as verbal as what he was as a young boy, which is wear him and Yewki differed. The oppressive cycle of thoughts would entrap him in his own brain for hours and hours without a moment to blink or move, whereas Yewki couldn't help but shout out and complain about things to those around him. However, neither brother knew any of that about the other, as they no longer spent enough time together anymore to realise. "I know you can hear me, Yewnin," his Mother tried again, but he kept his head down and didn't react. "How many have we made today?" she asked, as a means to make him speak. He didn't have a problem replying to questions regarding their work, or anything else for that matter, but when it came to letting out internalised feelings, he had no voice. "Twenty-six," he answered without a second of hesitation to calculate. "Brilliant," Foloria stated with a sigh of relief. She stood up slowly, full of aches and pains, then staggered over to the doorway. "Now, you're going to tell me what's been troubling you for so long," she said sternly. As soon as the words fell from her mouth, Yewnin got up to leave in a hurry, but she swung the door shut and stood in front of it, preventing his escape. He even looked to the window as a means of fleeing, but he quickly gathered common sense and sat back down as it was far too small, even for his child body. "Nothing is troubling me, Mother," he said with pain.

"Lies. I can tell something's wrong. I've heard you crying into your pillow some nights-".

"Mother!"

"No, it's heart-breaking. Do you know how useless it makes me feel being unable to help?"

"There's nothing to fix, Mother. I'm fine". He kept his head down to avoid eye contact because he knew she was staring at him, trying to depict any sort of radiant emotion coming from him. Foloria built up a rugged lump in her throat then swallowed it with great difficulty and shook her head to herself. "Can I go now?" Yewnin begged. She got out of the way of the door and let him go. The situation was nothing out of the ordinary for the two of them, as most evenings would begin with her trying to pry open her son's shell, but he'd always keep his lips sealed and get the better of her. She didn't follow after him. Instead, she stayed back in the pottery room alone, in case she started to cry. Just then, Yewki and his Father came through the front door, dragging the loud cart behind them, barley fitting it under the door frame. "Foloria?" Grinnit called through the hallway. He'd just caught the sight of Yewnin entering his bedroom above as he entered the house, which was the most he usually saw of him. Foloria wiped her eyes and nose then popped out of the pottery room to the side and greeted her husband with a loving hug. "How was it today?" she asked.

"We sold about seven. I'm sorry, we tried our best," he answered.

"Seven? Yewnin and I made twenty-six today and now you've brought back almost all of what you took with you. There's not going to be much space to keep them all soon if we keep overestimating how many we need to make," she groaned.

"How was he today?" he whispered, in regard to Yewnin. Yewki lingered about to listen in to the conversation whilst dismantling the cart of vases. "Oh, Grinnit, he's getting worse. I almost can't remember the days he was a lively young boy... it's as though he's no longer our child. He feels more and more like a stranger," she whimpered.

"My love, don't cry. We just need to think of a new approach," he suggested. Yewki thought back to his conversation with his Father and how it had helped him. He also remembered him saying how Yewnin thought similarly to him, so he assumed that there'd be a chance that Yewnin would open up if it was him. Even if he didn't feel the need to talk to his younger brother out of the good of his heart, he was curious as to just how similar the two of them thought and felt. He didn't let his parents know about the plan and made his way upstairs to Yewnin's bedroom, catching their eyes by surprise. "Can I come in, Yewnin?" he asked, letting himself in anyway before there could have even been time to respond. His brother was sat looking out of his small window at the dark night sky, seemingly continuing his deep thoughts away from everyone else. "It's been a long time since we played together isn't it?" Yewki chuckled.

"Neither of us play anymore," Yewnin answered.

"It doesn't mean we can't talk does it? We used to be really close, remember? We'd put those buckets on our heads and hit each other with sticks".

"I barely remember much of that anymore. My head's too full of more important things now".

"Oh really? Well what's more important than fun memories with your big brother?" Yewki tutted.

"A lot of things". Their parents were on the other side of the walls, with their ears against the room in hopes to listen in on the conversation. "Like what? Tell me, I'm your brother and even if it doesn't mean as much as what it used to mean, we're blood and we help each other out," Yewki assured.

"Two weeks and four days".

"What?"

"Two weeks and four days. That's how long it's been since we've said a word to each other. You said, *excuse me*, because I was in the way of the cupboard. Our last proper conversation was one month, one week and three days ago, and it was about whether or not I had seen Mother's shoes because they had gone missing". Yewki was bewildered by Yewnin's accuracy of time. He couldn't even remember the instances himself, but he took his word for it. "That's exactly why I think we should mend some broken bridges between us both".

"You won't understand," Yewnin sighed.

"Try me".

"Fine, but I doubt it'll make sense. Do you ever feel-".

"Like there's no meaning to anything? Like everything that's designed to be on a large scale seems small? You feel like all the small things have equal right to be as pointless? Why were we given life at this very moment in time? Why do you feel so segregated from the outside world the more you want to understand it?" Yewki interrupted to express that he'd been feeling the same way all along. Yewnin swung his head around from the window and ran over to Yewki for an emotional hug, forgetting about all awkward anxieties and their drifted time apart from one another. He cried into his big brother's clothing and refused to let go, revealing his dire need to be helped. Anyone could have said the same words as Yewki, but Yewnin could feel the honesty behind every word and the sense of loneliness in his eyes that he too shared. "I don't want to feel like this anymore, make it stop, please, make it stop, why can't I be like a normal boy?" he sobbed to Yewki, making his parents well up in the hallway quietly. "I promise you, when we're a little older and the vases are all sold, we'll stick together and search the world for answers! The world is too precious for people to be content for no reason".

"We should go now, we must leave now, I want to know everything," Yewnin cried.

"You're fourteen and I'm sixteen, we can't go yet!" Yewki laughed, but his brother was deadly serious and begged even more. "I've heard stories of an ancient relic that dictates and orchestrates life. If we find it, we can be in control. We won't be afraid anymore. We can ask the Shamans and we can discover all the hidden things of the world!" Yewnin stressed uncharacteristically. Yewki pushed his brother away and scowled at him confused. Just then, their eavesdropping parents barged in, overwhelmed with fear. Yewnin's suggestion didn't belong in the mind of a young boy, but he didn't share the same confusion as everyone else in the room. "How have you heard nonsense like that?" Grinnit gasped.

"I've read all sorts of things. I read stories in my head," he confessed.

"But stories in your head aren't real, Yewnin!" Yewki said.

"What's wrong with him? His imagination is far too unnatural!" Foloria stuttered and began to panic, fearing the safety of his seemingly deranged child. "I thought you said me and him think alike," Yewki said to his Father. Yewnin looked genuinely astonished at the fact that his family was staring at him like an intruding wild animal. "Stop looking at me!" he screamed.

"We want to help you!"

"You can't, just let me leave!"

"You want to leave? Fine, go and leave us all behind. Is that what you want?" Yewki hissed.

"Yes. No. I don't know! I love you all, but I just want to leave and figure everything out," Yewnin said.

"You can't figure everything out!" Yewki shouted, going back on his own beliefs. He thought that his own mind was complicated, but it was basic at the side of his younger brother's. "No child dreams of such things. This is more serious than we thought," Grinnit stuttered.

"What do we do? What's wrong with my boys?" Foloria cried.

During the evening's escalation, Yewnin's urge to leave home had grown all the more prominent, not only in his head, but also in his heart. Any other child would have feared the repercussions of packing a bag and running away at his age, but his actions were so radical and stubborn, it was like his thoughts were authorised from something powerful and unknown, as though there was no other means of advancement other than to escape the clutches of his parents. His bag was full of fruits and vegetables that had been lingering around the dining area, as well as a handful of gold coins that his parents had been stashing protectively in one of the vases in the pottery room. It stood out well seeing as though it was his Mother's most wonderful vase that she'd ever made. It was sea-blue with golden flowers spiralling from top to bottom, completely resonating with love, beauty and sophistication. It was too good for them to sell, so they used it to store their earnings. The neck of the vase was too narrow for him to get his hand in though, so he had to pour the coins into the bag, making a loud clinking sound. The noisy extraction felt twice as loud for the fact he was trying to stay silent. He squinted in cringe whilst the money plopped into the bag excruciatingly loud. Unfortunately for him, Yewki was still awake and heard Yewnin creeping around downstairs so went to investigate. Yewnin had gently placed the vase back on the shelf behind him and bent down to ignite a lantern for his dark journey ahead, but Yewki stormed in to put an end to the escapade. The door flung open, causing Yewnin to jump up and knock the shelf above him. "Be careful, you almost made me drop the lantern!" he complained, not noticing the money vase he'd just wobbled off of the shelf. Just as he finished his words, the vase smashed on the ground, shattering into a mixture of big and small shards, buried in the assortment of gold coins. "What are you doing?" Yewki shouted.

"I'm leaving to see if my ideas are true," Yewnin said.

"Wake up! Stop it, this is ridiculous". His actions were both childish and too grown up for his age. It was some sort of sickness within his mind that no one had ever seen before. "Get out of my way right now, brother!" Yewnin ordered, but Yewki refused to move and tried to restrain him. At that point, Grinnit and Foloria were charging downstairs as fast as they could after being awoken by the loud noises and shouting, all whilst the two brothers were grabbing and hitting one another. Once they entered the room, Yewnin had pushed by them with Yewki as a battering ram and fell to the floor of the hallway. He held tight onto the handle of the metal lantern and swung it across at Yewki's head, causing it to break with debris flying behind the two of them. The flame from inside remained alight, until landing in the doorway, between the hallway and the pottery room, building a barrier of fire with the brothers on one side and their parents on the other. Grinnit and Foloria were trapped inside of the pottery room, and the amount of wood and cloth around the house quickly turned into a deadly firestorm. Yewnin had snapped out of his compulsive haze upon sight of his parents in distress. He screamed and cried, but the fires had engulfed them and hid them from view. The stairs, the floor and the wooden beams above him had been coated with crackling fire, and sinister black smoke choked up the open areas, turning everything into a frantic mess of destruction. Yewki ragged his brother and pulled him away towards the main door whilst bleeding from the head. "Mother! Father! No, no, no!" Yewnin wailed.

"What have you done?!" Yewki bellowed, clambering over to a safe distance outside. He knew that the fire was too great and that his parents wouldn't be able to escape. As much as it hurt, he had to stand back and watch the house begin to crack and crumble under the scorching stress of the monstrous fire. There was no chance that Yewnin would do the same, so he had to hold him back from trying to run in. "It's my fault, it's my fault! I killed them. I killed them both!" the younger brother panted. The two of them struggled until Yewnin broke free, then wasted no time running full speed at the house, as though he was expecting to be fireproof. "No!" Yewki screamed. He watched as Yewnin showed no fear and jumped straight through the murderous yellow and orange. After a moment to ready himself and let go of all instinct telling him to stay well away from the house, he ran in to rescue his brother. The evident loss of his parents was already too much for him to come to terms to. Adding Yewnin, his only remaining family member, into the pile of charred bodies would have been too much to live with – it was then worth dying for, to save what family he had left. He moved through the flames quickly, wasting no time to feel pain. Beams had started to fall down and walls began to crumble. His home that he'd lived in his whole life had turned into a demonic ball of flames. "Yewnin!" he coughed upon hearing the cries of his brother. Yewnin had disregarded the notion and possibility of death to enter the pottery room, only to find his Mother and Father unmoving and burnt severely on the floor. The moment he spared to scar himself at the sight of their dead bodies brought with it the realization of the pain to his legs. Both his lower left and right sides had been chewed and torn by the blazes. Whilst dropping to the floor, he had the chance to peer over at the vase that had smashed earlier. Its beauty had been tarnished, but it was the closest thing he could reach for closure before his death. Luckily, Yewki was there to prevent it, and dragged him out again, this time whilst he was unconscious which made things easier. Both of them had been inflicted with lifelong scars, mentally and physically, but Yewnin was in the worst state of the two. After a nervous moment of desperation, Yewnin woke up, holding tight to a shard of the vase in his hand. Yewki looked one last time at the house with a face full of tears, then picked up his brother and slumped him onto his back. Ideally, the boys should have waited until daylight to seek help from the village, but Yewki knew that Yewnin would have been taken from him if his mind was still riddled with the strange illness. Although he had caused so much chaos and death in the matter of minutes, he was still his brother.

Weeks passed on the road. They hid in wagons and stole from markets for the most part, using trees, looming rocks and abandoned stables for shelter in the night. The distance they had travelled was unknown, and the direction they travelled in was random. They could have been wandering in large circles for all they knew. The first fortnight was the most difficult as no words were exchanged between the brothers. The sheer shock of what had happened muted their voices, and the sudden loss of their parents was so overwhelming that no reaction was produced, not even a tearful cry of despair. They were empty caskets, floating around from one pointless destination to another. It was best for them to stick to the forests, as large cities would gather unwanted attention, but the rough life of living off the bare minimum was slowly killing them. It wasn't until the first month passed that they started to talk to each other again. Yewki didn't blame Yewnin for the fire, he just wanted his brother back. Unfortunately, Yewnin felt too much guilt to bare, knowing that everything had snowballed into a giant mess, soon to get them killed just like their parents. Every cold night that passed by, he would lay and look up to the stars whilst holding the shard of vase, begging for a way to bring back his Mother and Father, or at least apologise for his wrongdoings. The distance between him and his parents was inconceivable, much like how the shard was in his hand and the stars were an endless journey away. There was no way to connect the two things, but he refused to be limited only to what was discovered. After an unhealthy amount of time alone and in silence, his inhuman yearning to find the answers to everything had returned, but he was focused primarily on possible ways of bringing back the loved ones he'd killed. There was a correlation between his guilt and his need to help and do the right thing, but such complex ideas and beliefs were distorting his innocent child mind one thought at a time. Yewki felt the same things to an extent, but his mental state was never affected by any of it. After another month's time passing by, Yewnin began to raise the notion of finding purpose and introducing the idea of mending the damage he had done. However, Yewki wanted no part of it, even though their thoughts were on the same page. They were both aware of the existence of Shamans and divination, but it would take Yewki more than just acknowledgement to let his brother loose into a world of life-changing repercussions and potential insanity. It wasn't until their encounter with a Shaman that Yewki felt the need to reconsider.

They had lost the track of days but neither of them cared anyway. All they were aware of was the rise and setting of the sun. The two of them had come to terms with the death of their parents to some degree and left behind all recollection of their home as a means to move on with what was important – surviving. They walked together through the infinite forests, hoping to find some food to steal in the upcoming miles. "I'm telling you, the Emmrin-Rashmada dragon was real!" Yewnin stressed.

"Come on, Yewnin, there are no two-headed dragons," Yewki moaned.

"Yes maybe not now, but there was. The Slayers couldn't have just constructed a god with no influence or origin".

"Or perhaps they just wanted an excuse to be savage killers, so they built a giant golden dragon sculpture as an idol. We don't even know if that much is true either. People don't use that much gold just for something ornamental".

"We'll see. I'll travel to the Slayer Kingdom one day and see for myself".

"I don't recommend that we do that".

"I didn't say, *we*. I know you wouldn't come with me so I didn't include you in the statement".

"You're sticking by my side from now on and that's that… and if you want to go all the way to Emmrin-Rashmada then tough, because I'm in charge and I plan on keeping you safe".

"Safe from what?"

"Everyone".

"Are you sure you're not actually keeping people safe from *me*?" Yewnin muttered. Yewki stopped in his tracks and turned around to look his brother in the eyes. "I'm the only one who understands you. You try telling other people about your *dreams*… your *fantasies*… they won't be kind".

"Let *me* have a go," an elderly, frail voice whimpered from a distance. Armed with only sharpened sticks for spears, they stood together and looked around, but the mysterious character wasn't even trying to hide. An old woman with strange, white stripes of paint on her face and draped gowns hobbled towards them without a care in the world, listening in to their conversation without them knowing. "Go away," Yewki commanded.

"I was here first," she laughed.

"He said go away," Yewnin echoed. Instead of doing as they told, she sat down on the ground slowly, barely able to bend her knees and lower herself. After a groan of pain, she looked back up at them and smiled. "I tell you what, if you can answer my question correctly then I'll leave you alone. Is that a deal?" she suggested.

"You've chosen the wrong brothers today, old lady. The moment you challenged our knowledge you failed. Bring forth your trivial question," Yewki sniggered.

"What's the point in all of this?" she asked.

"What?"

"Those were the exact words you used, wasn't it?" she mocked. Yewnin gained a sudden interest in the mysterious woman, even if she had just won a game against his brother. "Well, that's not fair… it's too broad. There isn't a definitive answer," Yewki blabbered.

"Wrong answer. Well it looks as though I'm staying put," she giggled.

"Fine, but we can still leave. Come on, Yewnin".

"You can leave, yes… but your brother will never get help with those dreams of his, will he?" Before the brothers could gain traction, they stopped and gawked at the wrinkled clairvoyant. "What do you know of my dreams?" Yewnin gasped.

"I know that they aren't good for your mind… but perhaps closure will help," she answered. Yewnin ran over to her and skidded onto the floor, pressing his knees into the dirt, begging to hear more from her. "Are you a Shaman?" he asked.

"Yes. My name is, Bo'jocha, and for some reason, the Earth is telling me that the two of you require knowledge". From that point on, the Shaman, Bo'jocha taught them everything she knew herself about the world, for the next eight years in the Dewhills. The near-decade of self and world discovery brought with it a distinct empathy for the Earth, however, there was a difference between the brothers, as Yewnin welcomed more and more stories and facts, while Yewki gained more of a distaste for new knowledge the more they learnt. Bo'jocha lived in the wild which gave the two of them great experience of surviving in the great outdoors. She also healed the burns on their bodies, leaving behind only painless scars. They travelled great distances and saw incredible things, but Yewnin could sense that they were being left in the dark about some aspects. He would often ask about the revival of human life, more so, a method of bringing back his parents due to the never-ending guilt he carried with him in the form of the vase fragment. Her refusal to assist in that category gradually transformed him into more of an impatient young man, topped off with the fact that he could never become a Shaman himself to help better his understanding of all life. He had an evident passion for the world, but it was ultimately rotten at its core so long as he held onto his guilt and rage. Even though the years were sometimes troubling and unfair, both their bodies had grown in size and strength, and their minds were opened on a greater scale than most humans. After the fiery tragedy, it forced them to reignite their brotherly relationship, and they worked together along with their Shaman master to help better themselves. Their childhood speciality of play fighting had evolved into actual swordplay with real weapons also. If they weren't learning with Bo'jocha, they were training their combat skills. Both teenagers had become men. Even Yewnin's intense dreams had been eased through the years of understanding, but there was still the matter of the Day Relic that was always on his mind.

The time had come for Bo'jocha to part ways with the brothers. They were like sons to her for the most part, but her intentions were solely to train and teach – not to be a parental figure. Regardless of her intentions, they were young men and had to face great crossroads of differing destinies without her – it was time for them to fly the nest and decide their fates. The three of them stood in a triangle atop a lovely cliff edge, providing them with a spectacular view of the whole of the Dewhills. A river ran down below, carrying with it a serene sound of flowing motion. It was a peaceful location that they had all grown awfully fond of, so it was a fitting place for them to go their separate ways. "Where will you go now, Bo'jocha?" Yewki asked.
"I don't know. Away from you two I hope," she joked.
"I don't understand... how can you just suddenly decide when our teachings are complete?" Yewnin sighed.

"I never said they were complete. You must merely become your own person. What use are you as individuals if you must stay beneath the wing of a Shaman?"

"It'd be helpful at least".

"All this time, you've had the opportunity to find yourself as well as your place in the grand scheme of things. Answer me this; do you think you'll ever be able to define who you are now if you don't let go of who were then?"

"I'm simply still transforming. You don't rush a caterpillar out of its cocoon".

"Of course not... but you've been wriggling unsettled in *your* cocoon for the last few years. Are you afraid of opening up and showing who you really are once you grow your wings?" she teased.

"I'm going to miss your harshness on my brother, Bo'jocha... but I think I'll miss your kindness more than anything," Yewki explained. She nodded her head and said her farewells before making her way to wherever she intended to journey. Before she could get far, Yewnin growled under his breath and stepped forward, gaining her attention and making her turn around. There was no time left for his questions to be put aside. "Oh dear, something is still troubling you, Yewnin?" she asked. He gritted his teeth and turned away from her and Yewki in anger. She and his brother looked at each other concerned. "Ever since I was a child, people have been asking me what's wrong with me... what troubles me... but I see no more use attempting to explain my feelings to the likes of those who will simply never understand," he grunted.

"Yewnin," his brother said.

"And yes, I'd be lying if I said you both haven't helped me. My eyes have been opened greatly and I can never thank you enough... but the questions in my head that I've had since a child remain unanswered. Maybe that means that only *I* can provide an answer... but to do that I must execute a means to seek it for myself".

"It's true... we'll never know the answers to absolutely everything, and fixating on something that's preventing you from becoming a greater person will be your demise," the Shaman warned.

"No, you're wrong! It's not preventing me from becoming a greater person, it's the one thing I need... to be greater than what I already am!"

"And what is that *one thing*?" she asked.

"My dreams feel like thoughts... my thoughts feel like dreams. Theories blend with proven fact and in my mind, all knowledge is accessible, everything I think and feel is out there, somewhere".

"Yewnin, enough talk of your theories. There is no all-powerful relic waiting for you to obtain. There is no hierarchy of power... we're all equal, everything must be the same and work in unison," Yewki stressed.

"Silence! You've always been holding me back, brother! Bo'jocha, confirm that the relic I speak of exists. For the sake of my sanity, at last, tell me about what I already know exists!"

"And I imagine you're going to betray your brother and I, and seek it... regardless of if I say yes or no, correct?" she asked rhetorically.

"So you finally admit it?!" he gasped.

"Bo'jocha, tell me this isn't true," Yewki begged. Yewnin was overwhelmed with a large grin as he walked excitedly towards the old Shaman, making her and Yewki nervous. "It's known as the Relic of Day. It's not for the likes of humans," she explained.

"Tell me more!" he shouted.

"It's the world's source of power, it's not a tool".

"More!" he screamed, gaining satisfaction from finally hearing about the myth he'd inflicted upon himself, as though the more he knew, the less his tormented mind had to suffer. "That's enough!" Yewki shouted, pushing Yewnin away from the defenceless woman. "If it's what you say it is, then the answers to everything must come from it. If that truly *is* the ultimatum and above all else, then I have found my goal... and my life's purpose. This is me. I shall possess the Relic of Day. Prove to you all that there is a definitive," he panted, completely disregarding that his brother was moments away from punching him in the face for his barbaric disrespect. He also felt annoyed about being left in the dark about the Day Relic, but he at least understood it was merely to protect it from desperate hands. "Yewnin, I tried to help you and this is how I am repaid? With such primitive avarice?" she huffed.

"How dare you! This is all your fault... you kept this from my brother and I when it could be the key to bringing back our parents," he exclaimed.

"That is *your* quest, not mine," Yewki interjected.

"So you would rather not save our Mother? Our Father?"

"There's nothing *to* save, Yewnin. They're dead and we must move on. Don't try and sway me with devilish manipulation".

"You'll never be happy searching for what's not yours. You'll never be able to grow whilst you refuse to let go of the guilt you carry for the death of your parents," Bo'jocha stressed. Yewnin reached into his elegant robes and pulled out the shard of vase. It had been worn through time, but he'd taken great care of it. "You want me to let go of my love? You want me to forgive myself for what I did? Anyone that has the impudence to leave behind the errors of their ways and forgive themselves is an ignorant fool! I carry the weight of my flaws because I deserve to do so," he said whilst clenching the shard slightly, cutting the palm of his hand. "Let go of it. Leave it behind along with that Relic of Day. You know it exists and that's all you should want," Yewki pleaded.

"How can you be so satisfied knowing only half of everything? Is it because you lack the comprehension, or have you lost your way?"

"Don't twist things towards me or I will put you to the floor before you can react!"

"You just cannot possibly understand how much of an awakening this is to me. I knew I wasn't wrong! But tell me... why have I had such a subconscious awareness of its existence?" he demanded to know.

"That I don't know," the Shaman confessed.

"Useless Shaman!" Yewnin shouted at her, forgetting the love and compassion she had shown him for the whole eight years. Yewki pulled out his sword and aimed it at his brother seriously for the first time, which was met with an uncaring laugh. "What? You're going to kill your own brother?"

"Put that shard down and leave Bo'jocha alone," Yewki warned. Yewnin giggled then dropped the piece of vase at his feet. "All these years, I've been looking out for you. I've been trying to help you... we both have... but nothing is ever enough. You want what you can't have and whether or not you see it, you're destroying yourself, and I can't watch you do that anymore. Your name is Yewnin, but you're no longer my little brother".

"Then leave me! You can't help me, neither of you can! The only thing that can fix things is the relic".

"If we can't help you then you have no use for us. If that *is* the case, leave us and never come back," Bo'jocha said angrily. Yewnin shook his head and walked back towards her with an even wider smile than before. He reached forward for a one-sided hug, as she had lost all respect for him and didn't want to show any affection back. Yewki watched on carefully with his sword ready, unsure if he could even strike his brother with it if the time came. As he loomed over her, he spoke in her ear. "You didn't tell us about the relic because you didn't think I was destined for it, but I'll prove you wrong... and if you're not going to tell me anything else then I'll find more Shamans. I'll climb my way to the top, no matter how long it takes" he taunted.

"We won't stand for your interrogations... it makes you no better than those Slayers," she said.

"Don't you dare compare me to those animalistic freaks! I will seek greater knowledge with or without the two of you. I will claim what I want because my purpose entitles me!"

"Word will spread".

"In that case-". Yewnin stood back slightly and pulled out his own sword with a horizontal swoop, cutting Bo'jocha's throat as it travelled across. She dropped to the floor and died almost instantly. He felt no remorse ending her life, as his mind was fixed on his end goal, so all that stood in his way seemed meaningless in comparison, just like his and Yewki's views on life. "No!" Yewki roared whilst dropping his sword and jumping onto Yewnin. They punched and kicked, but because they'd trained together, neither of them were able to gain an upper hand – exactly how it was when they were children. Unfortunately, Yewnin was prepared to kill, whereas Yewki wasn't, allowing the deranged man the ability to use his sword. Yewki refused to use his own and proceeded to dodge the blade and jab with fists whenever he got the opportunity. "Get out of my way, brother!" Yewnin yelled. They continued to fight around Bo'jocha's dead body until they both ran out of breath. "Are you actually going to kill your own brother?" Yewki said, mirroring what Yewnin had said himself earlier. "If you won't help me, then what use are you to me?" he replied. His response was sickening and sank Yewki's heart down to his stomach. "In that case, you can go ahead and kill me in cold blood, just as you did to Bo'jocha," he began to cry.

"Quiet!" Yewnin growled whilst grabbing his brother by the collar. He dragged him over near the cliff edge with ease, as Yewki lacked the will to fight back. "I kill you now, and that'll be the closing of my chapter, and the last person standing in my way," Yewnin said with a crack in his voice. "Why are you letting me do this to you? Do you lack understanding so much that you'd rather die?" he continued.

"I understand everything I need to know… and I know I shouldn't allow you kill me with your own hands. I won't give my lost brother the opportunity to kill the only person left on this Earth that loved him! So I'll do it myself," Yewki explained whilst leaning back over the cliff face. Yewnin was unable to hold on tight enough and pull without falling in himself, so he let him go after staggering dangerously close to the edge. He watched on as his loyal big brother took the fall, sparing himself from watching the corruption ensue any longer. There wasn't much emotion other than a disappointed scowl, but he tried to hold back a few tears as his brother's body dropped into the water and was carried down the deadly rapids. He watched him flow down the river for as far as he could see, then turned to pick up his treasured piece of vase, wasting no time to look over at Bo'jocha's bloody body, then left for a long time alone for reflection and to regain composure.

It had been a long and painful catalyst since he was a child, but he had finally become who he was supposedly meant to be. At the time, he assumed that the fall was the end of Yewki. In reality, he was washed up further downstream to then later join with Piea Fellow in the months ahead. After a few years apart though, the brothers were eventually destined to reunite in the sentient maze. During the time between, Yewnin travelled the land and neighbouring lands, slowly learning more and more. Interrogations were rewarded with names and locations, names and locations led to ancient ruins, and ancient ruins were homes to abundances of hieroglyphics and long-lost book scriptures, or dead languages etched into the stone tombs of old. Killing became easy very quickly, seeing as though the first people he'd encountered on his murderous path was his own brother and an elderly Shaman woman that was practically a Mother to him. The Slayers soon heard word of Yewnin through the escalating shortage of Shamans, as they also desired them as a resource for their own agendas. They quickly became a partnership once King Zamanite the Relentless heard of the powerful relic and aided him with soldiers, transport and weaponry. His brother on the other hand, stayed with Piea and helped fight for a cause, in hopes to bring balance to the evil Yewnin was creating. His philosophical mind-set had begun to leave him, and was replaced with a sense of duty, rather than a sense of personal purpose. The next few years consisted of him fixing the damage that his brother had been doing around the world, along with people like Thene, Lall and Tbrok, meeting a collection of diverse folk – one being Seffry the Wizard. Time sped up abruptly, and before anyone could compose themselves during such difficult times, the location of the Day Relic was discovered in the Veranic Ocean by both parties. On his way to the shoreline harbours to set sail, Yewki encountered the boy and his bear, and so, the events of his and Wick's journey together had fallen into place.

Chapter 27

Words Like Wildfire

Thene's dragon had lugged the injured group of warriors to her secluded Olash tribe land. The true extent of the Day Relic's abilities had prevented them from ending its reign of terror. Although Yewnin was against seven rivals, including Lay-Vau and Batehong, he hadn't lost the fight. However, there wasn't much of a victory for him either. He was lucky to escape with his life at least, and he'd certainly made an impression on anyone that dared to oppose him. Yewki started to think there was a strong possibility he was battling against things that were simply above him. A tool that held the fate of the world within it was unlike anything anyone had experience with, not just him – yet his brother was still willing to surpass the conventions of mortality, as well as morality, to prove that there was power ripe for the taking. Whether or not Yewnin was able to wield such power was the question burning in everyone's mind. As for Yewnin though, the answer was as clear as day. For him, he had all the proof he needed to convince himself that there was in fact a greater purpose before his eyes. Both sides could agree on one thing though – the extermination of Lay-Vau was needed for the sake of Earth's safety. It was just a shame that Yewnin also benefited from Wick eradicating the voodoo master's existence. So much as there was failure, there was at least a small portion of victory for them to be pleased about, but knowing that Yewnin would be somewhere continuing his schemes, the group couldn't relax. For the time being, Thene gave them a welcoming tour of her village, showing the five of them their individual places of rest. Seff had his arm swung over a fellow Olash man, helping carry his weight over to a small shack, whilst Lumni was escorted to the neighbouring hut. Everything was made of wood and thatch, which seemed somewhat primitive to say that the Olash were an intelligent race, but they had no time or concern in furthering their skills in construction, and focused their efforts into combat. The shoddy buildings were no problem for the injured visitors though. At that point, they were willing to sleep on sharp rocks like Trolls, so a bed of sorts, regardless of its comfort, was more than enough for their aching bodies. Yewki and Thene strolled to the largest of the homes, as Wick was left fast asleep atop Moon, with his chest injury on in the midst of healing. An Olash woman pointed to a secluded shack, hoping that the bear was able to acknowledge directional finger points. To her surprise, he carried the boy over to where she wanted him to go, saving her a job. He sniffed the loose door then bumped it open slowly with his nose before taking a quick look around. There were no candle lights, chairs, furniture, or anything for that matter, other than one small bed on the floor. He laid down on his fluffy belly and leaned to the side slightly, grunting at the boy to wake up for a moment. After a few more soft noises, Wick made the effort to open his eyes. He looked across at the bed that Moon was trying to slide him over onto and smiled. Still half-asleep, the boy flopped off of the bear's back and onto the bed, before closing his eyes again. Moon stayed laid down by his side and sniffed around his face for comfort, trying not to wake him back up. He'd earned a good night's rest, as did everyone else. Unfortunately for Yewki though, he had a lot to discuss before he was granted a bed.

Lall sat on a table with her legs crossed and her arms folded, with a tired and unimpressed face for Yewki and Thene to soak up the moment they entered the building. "What is *she* doing here?" he asked Thene, but before she could answer, Lall bounced to her feet and stormed towards them. She barged by the innocent Olash with her shoulder and slapped Yewki across the cheek, sending a sharp crack through the large room. Other people nearby tried not to look on at the conflict, but it was too much drama for them to resist peeking at. She moved closer, practically stepping on his feet, causing him to back up against the door he'd just entered through. "The reason for my presence here isn't what you should be asking. I don't know about anyone else but there's a much more pressing question I want answering," she jabbed.

"And what's that?" Yewki asked.

"Why are you still alive?"

"Lall!" Thene gasped.

"No, seriously... you drag a group of innocents along with you and survive a battle by the skin of your teeth. What were you thinking? What did I say? What did we *all* say?"

"This is uncalled for. Not now, Lall".

"Children, Yewki. Children! When I thought you were foolish enough having a boy by your side, you bring a girl with you on your suicide mission, along with the only person that takes care for her!"

"Seff and Lumni can handle themselves, believe me. I think the fact they're still alive proves that".

"Piea and Batehong are dead, Yewki. How many more people do you want to lose? Adding more people to the cause doesn't help us, it just increases our chances of losing people we care about".

"And how do you think we can succeed if we don't expand our numbers?"

"You think including two children and an elderly man is going to help? These are people's lives... they're not our pawns for us to control".

"You have no idea of what they're capable of. They saved my life as much as I saved theirs. We were never going to beat Yewnin, but at least we worked together to ensure we all made it out in one piece".

"Luck, Yewki. That's all it is – luck. You heal your wounds and then you leave. You never see them again".

"You seem to think I wanted them by my side in the midst of danger. They wanted to help. They wouldn't let me leave without them".

"Really? Well we both know you can be manipulative, don't we?"

"Lall".

"I can't keep doing this, Yewki. You, Thene and I are the only people who can fight against your brother… but if you're unable to keep those children away from this, I can't be a part of it anymore," she sighed, then shoved him out the way so she could leave. Yewki didn't bother chasing after her and walked towards a small stool as Thene drooped her head to the floor, keeping quiet and leaving Yewki to sit alone with his head in his hands. He'd gone from trying to push Wick away, to keeping him by his side so many times, and Lall's impressionable words were tearing both sides of his mind apart from each other. "I know she's right, Thene. I'm not a monster," he assured.

"I know, I know… you don't have to excuse yourself to me. We train our young the moment they can hold a weapon, so perhaps she thinks we're *all* monsters," Thene answered.

"I know what I must do… but I can't bring myself to do it. Not now. Not after everything we've been through. I owe them my life".

"The greatest gift you could give them would be to spare them from danger," she muttered. Yewki looked at his dirty hands, littered in cuts and scrapes. Life was uncaring for his broken body, as there was still a lot of work to be done. Thankfully, it was an opportunity for him to change topic. "Once Yewnin recuperates, his side of the story is going to spread. Showing people what he's capable of will provide him with a legion of beloved followers," he complained.

"But those that see his power as a threat will balance the divide of ideals," Thene prompted.

"Anyone that challenges him will be destroyed".

"If he's spreading his version of the truth then so can we. If we open enough people's eyes, his numbers won't mean a thing".

"You don't understand. The whole world could be on the other side of him, and he'd still have the ability to defeat them".

"Don't you think we should at least spread what word we can? If we're doomed to fail then we should at least suppress it".

"Yes... I suppose".

"I know for a fact the East won't fall for Yewnin's lies. That's a good place to start," Lall contributed whilst slithering back into the building. The sounds of Yewki using a competent mindset had won her back over, and the three of them were able to discuss proper plans. The two of them smiled at her and joined together to make a triangle. "I don't care if Yewnin can fly... my messenger birds can travel faster and for much longer," she continued. "Where else should we focus our efforts towards?"

"Elal? Torron? Magmalia?" Thene recommended.

"Not Magmalia. We keep our cause off their records for good reason. Let them continue with their efforts and I'm sure they'll hear word from someone else once it spreads," Yewki said. The three of them spent the rest of the night drawing lines on maps, discussing ideas and generally working as a team for the first time in years. Lall's disgust for Yewki was put aside in hopes that they'd eventually make emends during such dark times. After all, there were more important dilemmas that had to be resolved.

The morning after brought with it a rightful fog to emphasise their gloomy depression. The majority of Olash were unaware of what was going on and continued with their trivial lives, but a select few had been informed of the recent events by Thene, their tribe leader. A friendly woman awkwardly watched over Wick and Moon as they slept way until mid-afternoon. The moment they opened their eyes, they were greeted with a wide smile. Although it was strange and unexpected, it was just what the two of them needed. For a few seconds, they were able to forget all about their fight with Yewnin and Lay-Vau. The woman poked her head out the door to notify Thene of their awakening, which brought her over to the shack. She thanked her guard for her service and asked her to leave the three of them alone to talk. Before she spoke to Wick though, she scanned his battered body, which was covered in tight bandages and the odd stitching. Moon had also been patched up, ensuring that he was taken care of and pampered as much as the boy was. "How are you feeling?" she asked with a smile. Wick looked around on his body and sat up in the bed as he stretched his stiff joints and muscles. "Much better, thank you," he answered.

"Yewki told me you held the Day Relic for an extensive amount of time. Do you feel any pain now which feels similar to what you felt whilst holding it?"

"How's Yewki?" he barked.

"He's okay. Wick, please, we need to know if there's any lingering pain you have from holding the relic".

"I'm fine... the only thing that hurts is the voodoo".

"I wish we could fix that, but-".

"It's okay. You've done more than enough for me," he interrupted whilst standing up cautiously. His legs were weak, but he fought through it to make sure Thene was given a big hug for her help. "You rescued us and made sure Moon was okay. I can't thank you enough," he elaborated.

"I'm just glad you're all safe," she exhaled calmly. Moon raised his large body from the ground and shook off the dust and dirt. Thene then held Wick's hand and escorted him towards the rest of the group that were waiting for him, whilst the bear followed behind. Before he could even see her, Wick could hear Lumni's voice yammering on at Seff, so when he was able to see the face behind the words, his excitable grin grew twice in length. She and Seff were arguing about pointless things which was nothing out of the ordinary. Wick was just happy to see them back in their natural states. "Wick!" Lumni cheered and pointed. She hoisted over the table in the middle of the room and gave him an unexpected hug. "Ah-ha! There you go, boy... I knew you two would get close," Seff teased.

"Seff! No! He's a child!" she roared in disgust.

"Yeah! We're just friends!" Wick growled at him. The Wizard sniggered. He couldn't resist making an embarrassing remark to rile the two of them up. If he couldn't win arguments against Lumni, he could

Way of the Moon Bear

at least make sure he annoyed her at optimal level. "How are you feeling now, Seff? Any better?" Thene pestered.

"Don't listen to him, Thene... he's exploiting your care to no end. He hasn't left that bed since last night!" Lumni complained before Seff could answer for himself. The old man shook his head and scoffed at the accusation, but he knew it was true. He pulled his precious vial from the inside of his robes to make sure it'd remained intact after the rough few days they'd had. He looked at it close with a squint and smiled before stuffing back where it was. "If Wick can get out of bed, so can you!" she continued to moan.

"Not a chance. My poor bones. Perhaps you'll understand when you reach my ripe old age," Seff whimpered like a wounded dog. Yewki entered the room and ruffled Wick's hair, catching him by surprise. He then proceeded to bend down slightly to get on Moon's level to provide a thorough stroke. "If you don't get out of bed, Seff, we'll drag you," he grumbled.

"I just don't see the urgency. I'm tired, I'm old. Whatever speech you're wanting to do can be done in the comfort of this room," Seff whined. Moon clasped his mouth gently onto Seff's frail leg, making sure not to chomp down with his sharp teeth. He then proceeded to drag the Wizard out of the bed, causing the moody old bag to flop around like a fish out of water. "Alright, alright!" he huffed and puffed, pushing the bear's large head away and standing up with much remorse. Yewki and Thene led the group to the large building that they'd made their base of operations for the time being. Wick wasn't expecting to see Lall stood there waiting, and neither Seff nor Lumni knew who she was. One of her faithful hawks perched itself on the back support of a chair and stared at them as they entered. Its feathers were an elegant copper colour, with slight tinges of dark blue, and somehow shared the same stern expression as its master. "Seff, Lumni... this is Lall. She's been working hard just as we were. She's the person that notified me of Piea's death," Yewki informed.

"So she's encountered Yewnin up close?" Seff asked.

"I made his nose bleed, so he scorched the Dewhills," she answered.

"Single-handedly?" he gasped.

"Don't give her too much credit, Seff. Yewnin hadn't mastered his powers then," Yewki jabbed.

"Well he still managed to kill Piea and char an entire land in the matter of minutes," she grunted. Lumni looked ahead and noticed the crumpled maps and hundreds of messy lines drawn across them all. "What's all this for?" she said whilst taking a peek. The rest of them had a look, but the directions and markings meant nothing to them.

"We plan on spreading a message across a number of lands," Yewki explained.

"What message?" Wick asked.

"Word will fly through the air like flocks of birds. People will be given the opportunity to side with Yewnin, or side with us. It's our job to ensure we reach more civilisations than he does... but with the Slayers behind him, it's not going to be easy," Yewki replied.

"There will come a day where the world will have to make a choice... but until then, the world will remain divided, which I suppose is nothing out of the ordinary," Lall simplified. The group loomed over the plans, completely bewildered by the amount of work they had ahead of them, unaware that Yewki would soon make sure they no longer had anything to do with their affairs.

Halfway to Emmrin-Rashmada, Yewnin had flown in great pain. The merging of energy provided from the relic was essentially the only thing keeping him alive, temporarily preventing his blood from pouring out of his body so long as he was connected to it. However, his body could only take so much, so after almost a full day and night of travelling, he had no choice but to stop, though his landing was all but controlled. He plummeted into deep snow and rolled across the ground against his will, all in the midst of a blizzard. There was no way for him to figure out where he was – his mind was too busy to calculate a general location. He laid on his back, no longer fused with the relic but still holding onto it, just looking up to the white sky. Every breath blew upwards like steam, as any warmth that remained in his

Way of the Moon Bear

body slowly escaped through his gawking mouth. A minute on the ground felt like a lifetime, as his head emptied the more he refused to move, before finally conjuring the strength to nudge himself over to his hands and knees. The feeling of being a weak mortal was a sickening one, but it only gave him more willpower to fight back against the harsh environment. "I refuse to die. I refuse to die," he repeated to himself with a shivering lower jaw, as his bare hands numbed in the snow. He continued to crawl aimlessly like injured prey, not knowing what would happen. Luckily, the bright glow of the relic glimmered through the blizzard for miles, and eventually, Yewnin was found by two men covered in fur clothing. At face value, they had no reason or time to question anything and focused on saving Yewnin from his impending demise. If only they had known who he was. They wasted no time hauling him onto their large woolly steed and travelled to safety, covering him in heavy drapes to protect his skin from the icy air.

It took several hours for Yewnin to wake back up after passing out on the way to refuge. The first thing he saw was a cave roof covered in stalagmites and icicles, as he was unable to turn his head side to side. His arms and legs were stiff, but he could jiggle them slightly at least. A pathetic croak wheezed out of his mouth as he tried to talk, but it was enough to gain the attention of his saviours. The two of them walked over and dropped to their knees to get a closer look. "Try not to move," one of them said as they prodded and poked at his skin. "Where... where a-am I?" Yewnin groaned.

"Tyhappa Pass. Why are you even here? No one can survive in these elements," the other asked.

"I didn't... mean to".

"What?"

"I was on my way to Emm-".

"The Slayer Kingdom? You're a Slayer?" they both gasped, halting their healing efforts in sheer shock and disgust. Yewnin knew that if he revealed his true intentions, they would kill him there and then without hesitation. "No, no, please. I was on my way to... destroy them," he lied.

"Oh really?"

"Yes, I swear".

"And how do you plan on doing that?" one of them grumbled, having trouble believing him. Yewnin finally gained the strength to turn his neck so he could look at the two men in their eyes. "I have a... weapon. It has the ability to wipe an entire kingdom to the floor with ease," he coughed. Neither one of them replied right away and took a moment to get their heads around what Yewnin had just said before attending back to his wounds. "How long have you been out in the snow?" they asked, questioning his sanity.

"You don't believe me?"

"Not particularly," they said, looking rather repulsed as though he was crazy. Yewnin didn't like to be tested and looked around subtly for the Day Relic, but he couldn't see it. "Where is your faith?" he chuckled, after realising that it had absorbed itself into his body before the men had found him. He smirked as his eyes glowed and steamed, as the rising heat collided with the cold air. All of a sudden, he managed to sit himself up and place his palms on both of their heads, causing their eyes to roll back and boil. They couldn't even let out a whimper – the sudden heat bubbled their insides until they dropped dead to the floor, whilst smoke seeped out of their ears. Yewnin caught his breath and welcomed the unexpected replenishment of life with overwhelming gratitude. He couldn't help laughing to himself at how lucky he'd gotten. However, his body was far from healed, so there was still a way to go before being fully sustained. He took a better look around the cave the two locals had called home. It wasn't very civilised, but there was food, beds, a fire and tools, and after a brief rummage, he found enough instruments and materials to start stitching up the deep wounds. The men had searched Yewnin's body and took his possessions away to put to one side. It gave him time to reflect on what little he had, seeing as though all they had taken was a sword and an old shard of vase that he'd been carrying for more than two decades.

The ghostly howling of the outdoor wind was the only thing keeping him company as he mended what cuts he could whilst staring at his beloved piece of pottery – perhaps the only other thing he cared for as much as the relic, even though it was only a matter of time until the possessive vibrancy that radiated from the Relic of Day would make the shard seem completely meaningless in comparison. It was the only reminder of his parents and what life he once had, so he fought to make sure the memory remained intact – seemingly the only thing stopping him from being completely lost from the real world. After being able to patch himself up enough, he stole some fur clothing and left the cave to take a look around, realising that he could only see through one eye. Moon's claws had left three horrific scars on his face as well as blinding half of his vision. Physical appearance meant nothing to him fortunately, and with the relic in-hand, he didn't consider to be impaired in any way. The most thankful news of all was that the blizzard had calmed down, but it was still snowing heavily. The woolly, hoofed creature that had carried him to safety was a Chumbii, and it was looking right at him. Its horns were wide and long, and its face was lost in all the long, thick hair. If it decided to determine Yewnin as a threat then it would charge at him with great speed, which was impressive for something that large, seeing as though it was three times the size of a grizzly bear. The beast began to grunt intimidatingly, but Yewnin didn't seem the slightest bit startled. "Charge at me, see what happens," he muttered to himself. Foolishly, the Chumbii did just that, and galloped towards him, only to be blown back with a ray of light. The poor creature was left with no signs of life – killed merely for entertainment and out of spite, like target practice for Yewnin to warm up on before taking flight towards the Slayer Kingdom. There were just a few more things for him and King Zamanite to take care of before the next stage of his plan could explode into effect.

Chapter 28

Victims of Voodoo

"How was your trip to the South, Captain?" Paladin Troyori Quait asked her superior within his private quarters. They sat opposite one another in the round room, looking down to the floor. "The Gu-Ram were apprehensive to accept aid, but they swallowed their pride eventually," Captain Asieda Hockmunn replied. He had recently returned from the Southern regions to renew peace with a number of tribes. It was a difficult task, but his hard-earned success allowed him to travel home with a smile, only for the mood to be dampened by the news of Paladin Soa's death upon arrival to Magmalia. He seemed both angry and upset about Soa's recent demise, so having to discuss work whilst grief loomed over them both made their conversations too difficult to bare. "I can't believe I've lost one of my greatest Paladins. What sort of news is that to hear when returning home?" he sighed.

"I'm sorry, Captain. Perhaps we can talk another time," Quait recommended.

"What are you sorry about?" Hockmunn asked awkwardly.

"I-I don't know. Just with everything that's been happening lately-".

"It's just one heavy blow after another, and the hits keep getting stronger," Hockmunn concluded her sentence. She nodded her head and sniffled her runny nose. The Captain stood up quickly, as though he was about to scream, but instead took a deep breath and walked

Way of the Moon Bear

across to the window. His kingdom looked the same, but none of it felt right. "What's happened to our city, Troyori? Why now?" he moaned.

"The Slayers are planning something big, and they need Magmalia out of their way to succeed. We just don't know what it is," she answered.

"Well, I spoke with Paladin Shayl last night. She stumbled across a skirmish between bandits and an unknown faction. The bandits were escorting caged Shamans aboard wagons, but that's the least of it... they were accompanied by all three of the Slayer Princes".

"Who were their opposition?"

"They're not important, but Shayl said they seemed unconcerned in freeing the Shamans. Probably just out for blood – who knows what their intentions were. What's interesting is why Zamanite's sons were present. It's not like the Slayers to work with others, especially small-scale mercenaries".

"You think there's someone higher than the Slayers, pulling the strings?"

"I'm not sure. There's a strange character that keeps coming to light known as *Yewnin*, but nothing is confirmed, and we have little information about him. We don't even know if he actually exists," Hockmunn sighed before turning back from the window to face Quait. "We need to find where they're taking such a large amount of Shamans," he continued.

"Well they're already ten steps ahead of us. Access to so many soothsayers will keep them countless steps ahead now," Quait panicked. The Captain sat back down with a careless thud, causing his metal armour to clang. He seemed to have lost the will to be concerned, which was exactly what the Slayers wanted. "I think I should give you some time alone, Captain," Troyori proposed whilst standing up to hastily leave. She couldn't stand seeing Hockmunn so defeated. "The number of people I trust is depleting quickly, Quait. With most of my Paladins away in distant lands, I worry that they're meeting with the enemy behind my back. I also worry that I'll receive word of more fallen Knights every time someone knocks on my door," he said before she could grab the door handle, but she didn't know how to respond. After a pause, she turned the knob and tried to exit, only to be stopped again. "I've been wondering," the Captain said.

"About what, Sir?" she asked whilst stood in the doorway. Hockmunn clenched his fists unnervingly and looked around, avoiding all eye contact. "What if it has something to do with... *you know what*?" he said. Troyori's heart sank at such an assumption and gulped. "What does *that* have to do with all this?" she responded, with an evident tremble in her voice, looking fairly disgusted. "I know it must pain you to bare a constant reminder. Our foolishness almost got you killed," Hockmunn eluded.

"No, seriously, what does it have to do with this?" Quait snapped, which was rare for her to do in front of her Captain. "Maybe we weren't the only ones to find that, *thing*... what if they've done what we couldn't do? Only something that great could set in motion such a momentous shift," he explained.

"How would they have found it? We told no one".

"But we aren't the only ones seeking power. It was only a matter of time until someone else discovered its whereabouts". Troyori didn't respond and shut the door behind her. The conversation was too personal for her to talk about, and it was the first time they had both discussed anything remotely close to it since the dreadful days themselves.

Five Years Ago-
A more fresh-faced Troyori stood aboard a small ship in the middle of the Veranic Ocean. She wasn't wearing her usual armour, instead she was covered in light chainmail on her upper half, and cropped skin-tight trousers with bare feet. The air was chilly, causing her to shiver, but it was also a mixture of nerves at the same time, as she leant over the side to look at the harsh waves. The most refreshing feature was her lack of red spectacles as they didn't exist at the time, allowing Captain Hockmunn to appreciate her emerald green eyes as he walked over to her. "We're here," he said with a trusty smile and

nod. Quait looked ahead at a monstrous whirlpool, knowing that she'd soon be diving head first into it. "I hope you're right about this, Sir," she shuddered.

"You don't have to call me *Sir* all the time," he smiled. As they got closer, he began to look nervous for her, but he kept his own apprehensions subtle as a means to not put her off. "I don't know if I can do this, now that I'm staring right at it," she stammered.

"Just remember the plan... but most importantly, remember what this will mean if we succeed. Magmalia will be proud of you. *I'll* be proud of you," he reassured. The two looked at each other in fear. They couldn't help but come together for a hug – something they had grown accustom to doing when away from the other Paladins. Once they detached themselves from one another, they looked at each other awkwardly, knowing that they were disobeying the rules of being Paladin Knights every time they showed affection. "I believe in you," the Captain said whilst he brushed her hair behind her ear, as the howling wind blew in both their faces. For the first time aboard the ship, she managed to smile, if only for a moment. The gushing movement of the whirlpool increased in volume, and prompted the brave Paladin that it was time to jump. Hockmunn didn't have to tell her what to do next – she climbed onto the side and looked down. "This is as close as I can take the boat!" the Captain shouted. Troyori took one last look behind her then closed her eyes and dived. Months of planning and secrecy had led to that day. They only hoped that it wasn't all for nothing.

Just as Wick, Yewki and Moon had done, Quait too had ventured into the sentient maze in search of the Day Relic, but long before them. Yewki thought that they were the first people to enter, unaware that the Paladins of Magmalia had led a secret voyage five years earlier. Just like them, she journeyed through the moving labyrinth for hours, barley making it out alive. She solved the same puzzles and traversed the floating platforms, evading the huge insect creatures, showing true valour and strength through such dangerous trails whilst only wielding a dagger. By the end, her armour was torn and her arms and legs covered in cuts and bruises. She would have died on countless instances if she wasn't thinking of the Captain. The thought of returning to him with the prize was what kept her going, but her unhealthy obsession with him was making her blind to danger. The praise and acceptance from Hockmunn was something she'd been yearning for since she'd joined the Knighthood, so no matter how much pain she felt, she still pressed on. Struggling to stand, she staggered over towards the mysterious relic. It stood floating slightly above its pedestal, giving off a soothing humming noise. "It's all true," she panted to herself, barely able to breathe. Before her hands could reach out and touch it, the pedestal slid backwards as the walls engulfed it. The floor and roof folded and twisted to create an entirely different room, with Troy-ori stood in the centre, unable to escape. Lights flashed from nowhere and rubble started to crumble to the ground, followed by black crooked spikes seeping through the cracks in the bricks. She dropped to the floor and cowered in fear, unaware that such things were possible. To top it all off, the heavy beating of drums started to surround her, invading her ears. "What is this?" she screamed.

"Your punishment, thief!" the thunderous voice of Lay-Vau rumbled around the slowly-enclosing room. The drums stopped suddenly as the voodoo master's physical embodiment built from the ground up. "This relic isn't yours to take," he elaborated.

"Stay away from me, monster!" she cried. Lay-Vau snarled and pulled her towards him without even touching her. No matter how much she tried to break free, the invisible force restraining her was unbreakable. "Have you ever heard of voodoo?" he asked – the same way he would go on and ask Wick. His face grew as he smiled, and his eyes brightened as he waited for her response. "Voodoo is a myth, this isn't real, I refuse to believe!" she moaned.

"You don't believe?" he roared, releasing his hold on her, causing her body to drop to the floor. "You see all of this around you, yet you refuse to believe? This is real-".

"No!"

"Stubborn woman, I'll make you see!" he laughed whilst putting his hands on her head. "You think you're scared now... just you wait". Quait tried to wriggle out of his hands, but his grip was too tight. She yelled at the top of her voice as the curse entered her body. "Foolish humans! Let your curse be a message!" he shouted before letting go. Just then, her vision became pure white until it was unbearable, and after a few seconds of panic, her mind and body became unconscious and unmoving.

Captain Hockmunn had been waiting on board the ship for an anxious six hours with no signs of Troyori. All hope was diminishing, but he didn't know how long the trails would take, so he just had to assume she was still alive and in the midst of claiming the relic. Neither one of them knew the true power of the Day Relic, so even if she was able to take it, it would have killed her anyway. The voyage was certainly idiotic, in the sense that they didn't know what to expect or what the repercussions of failure would have been – they had journeyed foolishly towards the maze, hoping that they could use the relic for Magmalia, without considering the effects. Thankfully, not all was lost, as the clouds above the boat opened up to reveal a portal. The Captain ran to the side of the ship and looked up, not knowing what to expect, and after a dawning wait, Troyori's lifeless body plummeted from the sky towards the sea. He wasted no time to jump into the water and swim towards where she was falling. His arms and legs splashed crazily to propel himself through the rough water, keeping his eyes on Quait as she dropped. "Quait!" he screamed above. When she eventually splashed into the sea, Asieda grabbed hold of her and lifted her head up so she could breathe. "Hold onto me," he said once they got to the side of the boat. Hearing his voice brought her back to consciousness, but she was still dazed and confused. After a groan and mumble, she managed to wrap her arms around the Captain's upperbody as he climbed up a rope ladder attached to the deck. The pain of carrying her whilst clambering upwards quickly was put aside, due to his body being filled with adrenaline. Once they were on board, he laid her down and shook her shoulders, shouting her name over and over in hopes that she'd respond. Suddenly, her eyes opened as wide as they could whilst she took a deep breath and moved her head from side to side, seemingly scared as she coughed and wheezed uncontrollably. "What happened?" he gasped, relieved to see her alive, but she didn't answer. Instead, she looked around frantically at her surroundings whilst panting for air. "Troyori!" he bellowed.

"Blood! So much blood!" she let out at last. The Captain looked around the ship, but nothing seemed out of the ordinary. She looked at his face as he tried to reassure her, but she couldn't concentrate. His eyes seeped, his nose dripped and his mouth drooled, all with never-ending streams of blood. The mast and sails behind them were soaked in red and trickled down to the deck. Even the clouds above swirled unnaturally with a red hue, and as it started to rain, the harmless droplets had been swapped out for blood. She pushed Hockmunn aside and ran across the ship to look down at the water, only to see an entire ocean of red, causing her to fall back to the ground in shock, refusing to reopen her eyes. "What's wrong? Troyori, please!" he panicked whilst trembling towards her. "Blood everywhere! It's everywhere, it's everything!"

"What?"

"I see nothing but death! That's the curse – it's what he wanted me to see!" she cried uncontrollably. Asieda didn't know what to do as the rain poured down. For him, everything looked and felt normal. "It's just an illusion, it's not real!" he assured.

"It's real for me!" she wailed. Her eyesight had been corrupted by Lay-Vau, forcing her to see a blood-riddled version of the world. There was nothing either of them could do but return to Magmalia and think of ways to mend the curse. For the time being though, she clenched her eyelids closed, too scared to let the horrors of death overrun her vision, crying to herself as the Captain escorted her below deck, away from the rain.

A few weeks had gone by since the incident. Hockmunn had barely left her side since, making sure she wouldn't accidentally open her eyes and relive the overwhelming frights. They sat opposite one another at a large table, completely alone. Quait had a thick piece of cloth wrapped around her head to blind her from the world. The door to the private quarters were locked, and Troyori was kept there out of sight until they knew what to do. No other Knights had been informed of what happened, not even the royals were aware. They had kept their mission completely off the records and for good reason seeing as though they failed. The whole reason they voyaged without informing anyone was because no one would have allowed them to do so. It had all stemmed from carelessness and a need to please each other. If they had managed to retrieve the relic they would have been hailed as great heroes, but they had little knowledge of the artefact, so they were destined to fail the moment they agreed to set sail. Troyori rarely questioned the Captain, and she now felt like a fool not doing so. The affection she once had for him had vanished, as she had more important things to worry about. They rarely spoke, and when they did, their conversations wouldn't last very long. Neither of them could see a future ahead, but Hockmunn felt too much guilt to detach her from his life. He looked across the table, completely disgusted at what happened to her, noticing how pale she had gotten and how little she moved or expressed emotion. "You have to eat," he said whilst sliding a bowl of steaming soup over to her. "Troyori?" he nagged.

"I don't feel like eating, Sir," she murmured.

"But you need to. I can tell you're starving".

"Perhaps that's what I want, Sir," she said as her chin wobbled. "Perhaps that's what I deserve for being foolish enough to let this happen".

"What's foolish is letting this defeat you. You're a Paladin – the greatest Knight I've ever known".

"It's time for you to move on and let me go," she sniffled.

"No, you're still a Paladin in my eyes. You still deserve to be a part of the Knighthood".

"I didn't mean like that". Hockmunn didn't respond and walked around to her side of the table. He took the wooden spoon from the bowl and lifted it up to her mouth. "Open, come on," he prompted. Quait slowly opened her mouth and swallowed some soup. "There we go," he said, as he continued to feed her. "I know, you've given up, Quait... but I haven't. I know we've tried a lot of things and they've all failed, but I think I've finally found someone who can help".

"It's not possible," she replied in a monotone voice.

"Well it's worth a try".

"No one can fix this".

"Troyori, we *will* fix this. The other Paladins are beginning to question your whereabouts. I can't keep you a secret for much longer, they will see you eventually... but the most important thing is that you'll be able to see them".

"I don't want to see anymore," she blubbered.

That night, there was a light knock on the door. Troyori's heart started to beat frantically, worried that someone would enter and see the state she was in. "It's okay... there's someone here to help," Asieda assured. He hastily paced over to the door and opened it slightly to take a peek, making sure it was the person he was expecting. "At last... come in, friend," he exhaled, welcoming the small, thin human-like creature into the room. It was dressed somewhat professionally, with a pristine tunic and overcoat, carrying an assortment of small boxes that jingled and rattled whenever it took a step. "Greetings, Troyori Quait. How are you?" it asked with an old and withered voice. She was too humiliated to respond at first, feeling like a farm animal with an injury. "My name is Dlloyd... I'm an Imp if you couldn't tell by my voice," he joked, in an attempt to be friendly. The greenish creature scratched his hairless head, avoiding the two tiny horns on either side. The Captain noticed that Dlloyd could barely see over the table, so recommended that he take a seat. The Imp nodded and climbed up onto the chair with a smile. "I don't know how much your Captain has told you, but I'm here to help," he explained.

Way of the Moon Bear

"You can't help this," Quait groaned.

"Well I can try if you let me... but first you'll have to tell me a little more information". The room turned dead with silence. Hockmunn knew that Troyori wouldn't explain, so it would be up to him. However, he didn't want to go into too much detail. "Well, you see, there's a problem when she opens her eyes and-".

"All I see is red blood, dripping and oozing down from the walls, from people's faces, on my own body. Everything turns to death and there's nothing I can do other than close my eyes," Quait interrupted with despair in her voice, taking them by surprise. "She says its a curse, but-".

"I believe her," Dlloyd said, speaking over Hockmunn's doubts. "When you're not human, you're more open to the existence of greater power. Humans think they're higher than other species... they think they have untapped potential and that everything is in their control... so the moment they encounter something they can't explain, they refuse to believe it. If your friend Quait has said that she's been cursed, I don't expect you to comprehend it, but you should at least try and accept it," he jabbed. His enlightening words made Troyori's head tilt upwards towards him. There was little hope left inside of her, but Dlloyd was willing to do everything in his power to reach out and nurture it. "Who are you exactly?" she asked.

"Well, as you know, we Imps are usually put to work as smithy or tailor assistants. We're rarely given the opportunity to advance our skills, but thankfully I was blessed with the opportunity to work with some great tinkerers and inventors. It's rare for humans to provide such hospitality, but I suppose we inventors are all the same – open to new ideals. I've been lucky to get to where I am today, so I'm always happy to help people if I can, especially when it's for a great Knight of Magmalia," he elaborated.

"How did you know about him, Sir?" she asked Hockmunn.

"Who do you think mends our armour?" he chuckled. Quait took a moment to think about her options, or lack of, then took a deep breath. "Please help me, Imp," she begged whilst hanging her head in shame. The three of them spent the next two hours discussing Quait's situation and what could be done to fix the problem. Dlloyd was a quick thinker, but even he struggled to come up with a solution. It wasn't until he looked over to the window that an idea sparked. He thought about how the glass and its transparency allows the eyes to see straight through at the world beyond it, but if the glass was stained with a colour, then the view would be sheeted and changed into whatever colour it was. The poor-sighted were given monocles and voyagers were given telescopes – the existence of intricate glass-work was about to be advanced further, thanks to Dlloyd. He took the concept of monocles and created a sturdy golden frame that stretched across from one side of Quait's brow to the other, so that both eyes could be equipped each with a lens. The next step was to carefully cut two small circular pieces of glass, stained with a red tint as accurate to the colour of blood as possible. With the pieces together, the last challenge was to make a strap that would ensure the spectacles wouldn't fall off or break easily. It wasn't an ideal piece of apparatus to wear every day, but it was better than Quait never wanting to open her eyes ever again. Another week had passed, and Dlloyd returned with the finished product. Troyori was apprehensive to wear them, and even more so to unclench her eyelids. Eventually, she unravelled the cloth around her eyes and with a little help from Dlloyd, she attached the strange goggles to her head. "Good, good... now, try opening your eyes," the Imp said, excited yet nervous to witness the result. Hockmunn stood back against a wall, biting down on his fist anxiously. Troyori shook her head and began to panic and tremble, but Dlloyd reached over and placed his small hand on hers. "Slowly... you can do it," he assured. At last, she plucked up the courage to at least squint. Of course, her vision was completely red, but the colour of blood had blended in. With everything going well, she finally opened them properly, unable to actually see the illusions. "I can't see the blood," she gasped.

"If we couldn't mend what you see, then our only option was to alter what colours you perceive. You'll no longer be able to distinguish each and every colour, but at least the red you *don't* want to see will blend into everything and seem normal," the Imp explained.

"Wait, I-I can still see things dripping though," she huffed

"That's okay, that's okay… you can learn to disregard it, I just know it. For now, just… focus on shapes and objects I suppose," Asieda said. She looked over to the Imp, finally able to see him. He smiled at her, causing her to smile back. Hockmunn was relieved to see her lips show signs of curvature after the gruelling month of pain and turmoil. "Thank you," she said as tears ran down her face. The Imp shook his head humbly, not seeking gratitude – his happiness came from the happiness of others. "It will take some time to adjust, I'm sure… but don't lose hope. You're a Paladin and you're the strongest there is," Dlloyd said. Through the five years, she learned to live with a vision of red, slowly but surely. Just after the first year, she had returned to the Knighthood at full force. Hockmunn was happy to have his strongest and most trusted Knight back, but their relationship wasn't the same as what it once was. Both were distraught as a result of the horrific events, and it had affected how they saw each other. They still had respect for one another, but anything beyond their duties as Knights no longer existed. Every few months, Quait would travel to Dlloyd's home on the outskirts of the city to either repair or tighten any loose parts of the eye-wear. The Imp would ask more and more about what had happened that day every time she'd visit, but Quait refused to delve too deep into the events. Hockmunn had trouble believing that Lay-Vau was real, but he couldn't deny the fact she was cursed. Though, with the Captain's refusal to accept the truth, his stubbornness would brush off onto Troyori, making her question what truly happened herself. Whatever *did* happened though, they both swore never to tell anyone, as it would be treason for the two of them to disobey the commands of Kings and Queens. Their defeat was humiliating, yet there was no use for either of them to dwell on the past. Thoughts and memories would creep up on them unintentionally every now and then, but they'd learnt to put their true feelings aside. Quait had also grown used to the odd stares when walking around without her helmet on. The spectacles were a part of her, and she soon forgot that the world was once painted in more than just the colour red. There was nothing she could do but accept that her vision would always be compromised, so ensuring Magmalia's protection eventually became her only concern, and with the recent weeks bringing with it a Slayer spy, her passion for the kingdom couldn't be more essential, though her faith was diminishing the more problems and failures that arose. She prayed that the impending threats had nothing to do with the Day Relic, but Yewnin and the Slayers had no regard for people's measly prayers and hopes. Even though Lay-Vau was defeated, he had still ruined the lives of two undeserving victims. Just as Paladin Quait had done, Greenwick would need to learn to live with his curse, but with his whole body affected severely and pure voodoo taking over his bloodstream, living without hindrance was easier said than done.

Chapter 29

Detachment

Thene had invited the rest of the group for dinner on a large, round table which was usually reserved solely for the high-ranking warriors of the tribe, but there was plenty of spare seats, so Wick, Yewki, Lumni, Seff and Lall sat alongside her with a grand selection of food in the middle. Moon sat nearby, hoping for a pile of scraps to gorge through once they'd finished, trying not to look too impatient, but the drool started to swing from his mouth against his will. Everyone's arms reached and swept across the table, grabbing all sorts of fruits, vegetables and meats, except for Wick who stared at the one small piece of bread on his plate. "What's wrong, Wick?" Yewki asked with a mouthful of food. "Is it the voodoo?" he wondered. Wick nodded, feeling too embarrassed to go into detail. "The curse affects his appetite too?" Lall said, looking over at Yewki, still blaming him for what'd happened. "Don't worry Wick, you can leave if you want," Thene suggested. Moon's face dropped, hoping that the boy wouldn't abandon the table before there was leftovers, but luckily for him, Wick shook his head. "I like being a part of dinner. It makes me feel like I have a family," he explained, letting out a slight smirk. Yewki and Seff looked at each other and smiled, then returned to stuffing their faces. "So, what's next? When do we stop Yewnin?" Lumni asked.

"Lumni, not now. Can we have a peaceful meal without discussing conflict," Seff sighed.

"Why do you want to help so badly, girl?" Lall intervened.

"I just want to put an arrow in his head, that's all".

"Lumni!" Seff gasped.

"What?" she replied, clueless to how barbaric she sounded, causing the majority of the table to chuckle. Lall on the other hand glared over to her, silently judging her foolish youth mind-set. "Yes, let's discuss how to kill my brother whilst we eat," Yewki sarcastically joked, but his humour wasn't the best, as it received no laughs. "The boy hasn't had a meal like this before, just let him enjoy the atmosphere," Thene whined.

"Well, what do you want to talk about?" Lumni asked Wick, but he couldn't think of anything, so the table fell silent for a moment, amplifying the noisy clinks and scrapes of cutlery. "I know... let's talk about the bear – why is he called, *Moon*?" Thene said, having wanted to know since the first time they met. Wick looked over to his fury companion's cute round face, then threw his piece of bread for him to catch in mid-air. "You'll see why soon, don't worry," he answered vaguely, hinting at the wondrous light that came with night. "I don't understand," Lall confessed.

"Wait and see. We shouldn't ruin the surprise," Seff smiled.

"How is he so well-trained?" she pondered out loud. Wick shrugged his shoulders whilst stroking the bear on the nose. "Yewki told me you have a connection to birds. Maybe it's the same as that," Wick suggested. Just then, Lall's hawk swooped over the table to grab a chunk of meat then dropped it above Moon for him to catch in his mouth. The table fell silent with amazement at Lall's trick, as the hawk flew away and left as fast as it'd appeared. "You don't even have to tell them to do things out loud," Wick gasped.

"How do you know *you* can't do that with your bear? Maybe tha's what your necklace is for".

"That bear is already *too* strange... I think the inclusion of telepathy would push my astonishment over the edge," Seff groaned.

"You're a Wizard... you're a magician. You're the last person who should be surprised," Lumni tutted, followed by a snigger across the table. "Yes, incredible. Yewki told me how you and Wick threw a house at Yewnin?" Thene giggled in confusion.

"Well first of all, it was *my* house," Seff explained, but was cut short by a round a laughter at the thought of a teleporting house flying through the air. "Wait, with no home, where do you plan to go?" Yewki asked, only just realising that the Wizard had been made homeless. "You sacrificed your home? That's truly admirable," Thene cheered. Lumni looked over to Seff with a smirk, knowing there was a secret contingency plan he'd kept from the rest of the group. "Well, I wouldn't go so far to say I no longer have my cottage," Seff replied, reaching into his robes to pull out the small, mysterious vial he'd been carrying with him for so long. Upon closer inspection, there was a tiny ball bobbing around in the liquid. "What is that?" Yewki asked.

"It's our home," Lumni revealed. Thene and Lall leant forward to get a better look, refusing to believe a full house swam around in a container of turquoise juices. "I always have this close by, just in case anything ever happened to my cottage," Seff elaborated. Wick smiled every time the old man revealed another magical ability. It had gotten to the point where his smile hurt his cheeks. "I've always had two houses... one just happens to be miniaturised," he continued.

"How did you have time to build *one* house? Let alone two?" Lall questioned.

"Wizard construction is much faster than your usual methods. A lot less exhausting too".

"That's amazing," Wick gasped.

"All I have to do is pour it onto the ground and it'll grow – just like my vegetables, remember? Except I've made sure this will grow full-size... at least I think I did".

"You've been lucky to be taught a little magic, Wick. I don't think you'll meet any other Wizards," Yewki said, hoping the boy would thank the old man for teaching him a few things. Thene clapped her hands together like a giddy child whilst thinking of a fun idea. "Show us what you can do," she begged.

"I can't do much. I'm not very good," Wick warned.

"Nonsense! Come on!" she laughed. Seff leant over to Wick and whispered a few ideas for him to flaunt. The whole table stopped eating to watch the nervous child get up from his chair. "Okay, so... I'll try and pull the moisture in the air to make steam. That seems to be only one I'm good at," he announced before preparing himself. "No, no, no... you can do better than that. Try the air blast," Seff nagged.

"I don't know if I should try that one again".

"Come on. You'll never get better if you don't practice".

"Wait, this spell isn't dangerous is it?" Lall interrupted.

"Not necessarily," Seff muttered. Wick slowly placed his arms roughly in the right position, then readied his hands. After a deep breath, he jabbed his arms forwards and pointed his little fingers, letting out a pathetic gust of wind, sliding his body back slightly and knocking things over on the table ahead of him. He expected an angry reaction after flinging food and cutlery across the room but thankfully, everyone laughed and cheered. "Excellent! Much better than the first time you did it," Seff chuckled whilst patting Wick on the back as he sat down. "The discipline isn't so dead after all," Lall stated.

"I wish I could learn more magic, but when Yewki and I leave... I doubt Seff will want to come with us," Wick said, still thinking that his adventure would be continuing. Lall looked over to Yewki, but he was avoiding eye contact, knowing that she'd be staring at him. "Precisely. Adventures aren't for me. I've had my fill, thank you," Seff laughed.

"Good, because if Yewnin got to you and demanded the secrets of magic, you'd hand everything to him on a plate like a coward," Lumni jabbed.

"That actually is a valid point. He steals every form of power he comes across. Best not to give him the key to Wizardry," Lall said.

"I can't believe everything that's happened... everything he's done. The amount of power he possesses is unfathomable," Thene sighed.

"He can steal as much power as he wants... he'll never have what *we* have," Wick rejoiced, looking around the table of faces he'd grown to know and love. Yewki lacked the courage to correct him and tell the poor child what was really going to happen. Seeing how happy he was

Way of the Moon Bear

around everyone broke his heart. "Thank you all for looking after me and Moon so well," he continued as his eyes filled up. Yewki stood up and walked out the room before the guilt became too much, followed by Lall as everyone else watched on in confusion. Once they'd both left the room, the others awkwardly looked down at their plates, not knowing where to take the conversation.

Lall and Yewki stood outside in the village square, just as the sky began to darken to make way for night. She stood opposite him with her hands on her waist, waiting for him to say something, but he stayed quiet and kicked the rocks around on the floor. "When are you going to tell him?" she hissed.
"It's going to break his heart," he sighed.
"A broken heart will mend over time, but if he goes with you, he'll die".
"I know, I know".
"He deserves to know. If you lack courage to tell him then I will".
"No, don't. I'll tell him. Just please, let him enjoy this night". Before they could continue talking, the others barged outside, giggling as they followed the bear. "Watch what happens next," Wick said to Thene and her Olash warriors. Lall and Yewki watched on from a distance as Moon sat down and stared upwards. The group continued to laugh and discuss whilst they watched the beast frozen in time. "Just remember *why* you're leaving him. It doesn't make you a bad person," Lall said to Yewki, sounding somewhat kind for the first time in years. "Having to warn the world of my brother, or be there for the boy. I know which one I'd prefer to be doing," he exhaled.
"I'll be spreading the word soon too – you're not on your own. I think one more day here should be enough, then I'll be gone".
"I wish I could stay another day too, but it'll just make my departure harder than what it already is".
"We've both got a lot of work to do – focus on that. Our numbers need to grow if we want to stand a chance". Yewki nodded in agreement then looked over to Wick, fixated on his huge smile, imagining

how quickly it'd disappear if he knew what was going to happen in the early morning. He promised Lall that he'd tell the boy before simply leaving, but he couldn't bring himself to do so. For the time being though, he joined back with the group to make sure Wick had an enjoyable night for once. He hid his nervousness and despair behind a false smile for the remainder of the evening, all for the sake of Wick.

Like every other morning, the song birds chirped over one another as the sun raised itself slowly. Yewki was packed and ready to go, but he moved slowly and quietly, making sure no one would wake up and make things infinitely harder than what they had to be. He felt bad for toying with a child's emotions – after finally giving in and treating Wick as a rightful companion, he was changing his mind back to what it was originally. His refusal to bring the boy with him on his adventure was to avoid the very situation he was in. Never bumping into the bear in the first place would have prevented a great deal of sadness. There was no way to alter the events of the past few weeks – all he could do was close the chapter and ensure Wick never had an opportunity to reopen it. He crept out his room and walked over to the main gates, but when he gave the large doors a small shake, he realised they were locked up tight. Other than trying to barge the gates open, his only option was to clamber over the village walls, so after a moment to ready himself, he swung his bag over his shoulder then started to stealthily climb, all whilst Wick watched on from behind a well in the town square. The voodoo prevented him from sleeping that night, as though the curse knew that he was about to be dealt a great deal of pain for being up at such an early hour. Yewki dropped over to the other side, wasting no time to give the past one last look. His heart banged around quickly in his chest, thinking about how difficult his absence was going to be for everyone. All what had happened, all what they had been through together, he was prepared to leave it all behind. "Where are you going?" Wick asked, taking him by surprise just as he'd begun to look ahead to the horizon. The boy peered through a small gap in the village walls next to the gates – at long last, the two of them were separated. Yewki felt sick to the stomach, having no experience with disheartening a child's spirit. They had both grown to love each other, like Father and Son, but like any good Father, the well-being of his child was priority. Wick was too young to realise that the departure was for his own safety and considered Yewki to be simply abandoning everything he cared for. Yewki didn't want to stretch out his awkward and upsetting exit, so he continued walking away. "Yewki?" the boy shouted, with a crack in his voice, but there was no answer. He ran across to the gates and began to rattle them, but they were locked. The loud banging caught the ears of many villagers who could only watch on in confusion and pity. Moon however didn't waste any time to run over to see what the matter was. "Help me open this gate," he cried to his fury companion, but he refused, not knowing the motives behind the situation. "I said open it!" he screamed, losing all patience and treating his bear as nothing more than a tool of destruction. Moon was apprehensive, but he was frightened into pushing against the gate. "More! Push it open!" The bear kept on shoving against them, bringing more and more guards to the scene with every slam. "Come on!" One last push and the huge doors swung open. Wick ran through them without thanking or explaining to Moon, but it was made clear what his panic was for, as Yewki could be seen leaving by everyone. The boy ran as fast as he could whilst an audience gathered round the broken gateway, looking ahead at the drama. "You're just going to leave me here?" Wick panted, finally catching up. His eye started to fill with black tears as he struggled to keep up with the man's quick pace. "Leave me be, boy," Yewki finally responded, still walking ahead and lacking the decency to turn around whilst speaking. His pace quickened even more, but so did Wick's. "After everything that's happened – I thought we were all going to be a family," the boy expressed.

"Well I'm sorry that image was placed into your head. It wasn't my intention. Now go".

"I thought you were going to be my new Father!" Wick screamed. Yewki finally stopped and turned around just as Wick finished talking, revealing that his own face was dripping with tears. "I'm not your Father and I never will be!" he shouted back, grabbing the boy by the shoulders and shaking him back and forth in an overwhelming surge of emotion. Wick didn't say anything back, completely shocked by the unexpected outburst. After a moment to compose himself, Yewki let go and sighed. "I wish that was a role I could fit for you, boy... I really do. You deserve a normal life... value what innocence you still have left and forget about me," he exhaled.

"But-".

"It was a mistake. All of this – your involvement with it was a mistake... Seff, Lumni, your bear too".

"Shut up!" Wick growled as he stepped forward and punched Yewki in the chest. The man didn't react and allowed him to punch him some more, as the small fists of the child brought no pain, but with every strike he felt something much worse than pain – the expressed notion of hatred and disappointment towards him. It was something he was never able to grow used to, but he accepted that it was a verdict people deserved to have of him. Finally, the bear had reached them both to find out what was going on. It didn't take him long to figure things out, watching the boy kicking and screaming. "Take good care of him, Moon," Yewki said, holding back whatever tears he had left. "No!" Wick wailed as the bear shoved him away so that Yewki could leave. "Why are you letting him go, Moon? Why?" It pained the beast to restrain the distraught child, but he knew it had to be done. Yewki turned away and continued to leave, still lacking the decency to say goodbye, all whilst Moon pushed Wick backwards with his head. "Don't let him go, don't let him go". Thene and Lall had come to help drag the boy back to the village, but he wasn't giving up without a fight. "Come on, he's no good for you. It's better this way," Lall stressed. Thene became teary-eyed having to pry Wick away, but she knew it was the right thing to do. Seff and Lumni watched on from the village entrance in sorrow, realising how much Yewki meant to the boy. The struggle continued until Yewki could no longer be seen, thanks to the trees and tall grass in the distance. Just as he'd abruptly entered Wick's life, he was gone in the same fashion, taking with him a collection of memories that he would treasure forever.

It took two hours for Wick to calm down. By the time it was night, he was sat on Seff's bed with Moon by his side, staring down at the floor, barely blinking. He refused to move or talk, as his mind was fixated on the events of earlier and how they compared to the fun experiences he'd gathered through the past few weeks. Yewki had said a lot of reassuring words on their travels together, things that had helped Wick through difficult times, but everything was starting to feel more like lies. Nothing could be done to change things, allowing the confusion and sadness to grow into anger and hatred. "How long are we staying here?" Lumni asked Seff. He was hesitant to respond and she could see the panic in his beady eyes as he coughed and sputtered his cup of tea. "Pardon, what? What do you mean?" he stuttered.

"When are we going home?"

"Well, I thought that perhaps the two of you would be more comfortable here with Thene".

"Oh, you're planning on dumping us too?" she hissed.

"Come on, Lumni... that's unfair".

"What's unfair is that Wick and I are being tossed around without any thought as to what *we* want".

"And what *do* you want, girl?" Lall said as she let herself into the room after hearing the erupting argument from outside. "Because this world is cruel. If it were up to you, I bet you'd be out there alone with your bow and arrow, thinking you could start and finish fights for the sake of it. Do you know how much people like me wish we could be free of this life? You're just children... you have no say in anything you don't understand," she continued, apparently taking Lumni's rebellious attitude personally. "I used to be like you once, girl. I didn't join this cause because I felt a sense of duty... I joined because I thought danger was fun... but it's not. Whenever I'm on a mission I could die, and I've accepted that someday, this life will actually get me killed. If you're up for that sort of commitment then be my guest, I'll have Thene train you right now... but if you're just wanting to fight for the fun of it, then it solidifies the fact you're just a foolish little girl," she said sternly. Lumni didn't respond. It wasn't like her to feel compromised so she didn't know what to do with herself. "But surely Thene would eventually train her though, when she's old enough?" Seff asked out of interest. Lall shook her head. "If she was Olash then her training would already be underway... and I know for a fact Thene is doing everything in her power to keep the three of you away from harm, so I wouldn't count on it ever happening," she explained.

"Where's Thene now?" the Wizard muttered to Lall.

The Olash warrior stood watch atop the village walls as the gates below were being fixed. The starry sky hung over the land, providing a well-needed feeling of tranquillity through such hard times. She too felt sadness towards Yewki's departure, but for different reasons to Wick. Her lone thoughts were interrupted by grunts and the creaking of wood, as Seff struggled to climb the ladders behind her. He muttered to himself whenever he misplaced a foot during his ascent. "Only *you* could make climbing a ladder look difficult," Thene joked. She didn't know the old man too well, but it was enough time for her to realise he was a clumsy oaf. "I'm old. My agility has been and gone. I'm allowed to find physical exertion difficult now," he said out of breath, finally reaching the top. He staggered over to Thene's side, seriously in pain, but she couldn't help but smirk. "It's alright for you, Olash... my bones and muscles don't stay so fresh like yours," he moaned.

"Don't worry, I will reach old age in a few hundred years. Then I'll know what it's like to be slow," she replied, trying not to chuckle. Seff shook his head, feeling like a victim surrounded by young souls. "What brings you up here?" she asked.

"Oh, well... nothing important," he lied.

"It must have been important for you to climb that ladder".

"Alright, alright. It's the children," he confessed. Thene looked across to him with a puzzled face. She could sense a feeling of conflict hiding within his troubled eyes. "You care for them don't you?" she stated.

"But I don't want to take them home with me. They're safer here, I'm sure of it".

"Maybe so, but how long have you taken care of Lumni? How many times in those years has she gotten into trouble whilst under your watch?"

"None whatsoever".

"And the boy... he's already lost one friend".

"I just don't know if I could take care of two children".

"Lumni can take care of herself, she's not a child anymore, Seff. But the boy... the boy is a different story. He needs love and care, and if you provided that for Lumni, I'm sure you could do it again for him".

"You *want* me to take them with me?"

"Well, I was prepared to look after them here... but the more I think about it, your skill in seclusion would actually provide them with a safer life. The Slayers will find our village someday. I couldn't imagine bringing these children up just for them to be slaughtered in battle," she sighed, reaching a revelation whilst Seff scratched his head, struggling to reach a decision of his own. He pitied Wick after having to see Yewki leave, so if he left him with the Olash tribe, he'd be doing the same as him. It wouldn't have been fair for him to take Lumni without Wick either. "We all appreciate your help, Seff. Your magic is precious. We could use your help in battle... but you could help us more by making sure the generation of innocence have the life they deserve," she explained.

"Fine, fine, fine... before I change my mind," he moaned, thinking of how difficult it'd be bringing up two teenagers, but knowing it was the right thing to do. Thene smiled and bowed her head in gratitude. "I'm sure in time Wick will forget about Yewki," she said.

"Well, I don't know about that. He seemed to love him by the end. I mean, I suppose I love him to an extent, as a friend... but the more they spent time together, the more their friendship turned to family affection. It's a shame for sure".

"It really is a shame, yes. We all loved him for our separate reasons. We all had to let go of something this morning".

"And what sort of love was yours?" he asked.

"What?" Thene stuttered, realising she'd said more than what she intended to. Seff leant over to her with a smug smile and raised eyebrows. "Oh I see how it is," he murmured.

"No, it's not like that. It couldn't be. I couldn't do that to Lall. Her and Yewki had a past".

"*Past* being the operative word. I'm presuming you didn't even tell him any of this either did you?" Their conversation had changed from Seff being the uncomfortable one, to her. "I'd appreciate it if you told no one about my feelings. Remember I'm a warrior," she warned him.

"Don't worry, your secret is safe with me," he giggled before walking back over to the ladders. Although it was awkward, it was nice for her to finally tell someone about her secret admiration towards Yewki. "Thank you. And thank you again for taking care of the children. I'm sure they'll be in the best care," she smiled.

"You can count on it. I'm the master of staying out of harm's way," he bragged.

"You're such a good man for adopting Moon too". Suddenly, Seff shuddered and fell from the very top of the ladder to the hard soil below, forgetting that Wick and the bear came as a package, and there'd be no way for him to take the boy without Moon. The pain of the fall was put aside as he thought about the huge beast traipsing around his house, knocking over precious items. "No!" he cried aloud. Thene looked down in shock thinking that he was screaming in pain, when in reality, he was thinking about the inevitable troubles of owning a bear. "The bear... how could I have forgotten about the bear?" he whimpered to himself.

The day after brought with it no change in Wick's emotional state. Voodoo aside, his lack of sleep that night derived from the thought of Yewki leaving, to the point that he'd began to subconsciously compare the image of Yewki walking away to the restored memory of his Father leaving him in the forest and never returning. The curse, the lack of memory and the loss of a dear friend were damaging him all in unique ways. The mind, the heart and the body were being tormented all at once, and it was too much for a child to bare alone. Luckily, there was some good news waiting for him, Lumni and Moon, as Thene and Lall requested their presence outside. The two warriors looked at the children as they walked, knowing how important it was for them to be free from a world of danger. Lumni led the way beside Moon whilst Wick dragged his feet slowly behind. "Where's Seff?" Lumni asked.

"I'm not sure," Lall answered.

"What's this about?"

"There's no need to be vague about this – we've been discussing about you and Wick – what's the best thing, the *right* thing to do for you both," Thene said.

"And we've come to the conclusion that you'd be better off somewhere else... not here with the Olash," Lall concluded. Wick and Lumni's internal reaction was that they were being thrown away for someone else they didn't know to take care of them. At that point, they had no strength left to argue and fight for what they wanted themselves. Completely defeated, they both lowered their heads and accepted whatever came out of the adult's mouths. "It was nice meeting you all," Wick finally spoke, wiping his runny nose. Lumni's chin began to wobble, trying her hardest not to express too much emotion. "So, where is it you're sending us?" she said, struggling to maintain composure. Just then, Seff staggered out of a nearby building with a handful of sacks, food and pottery. He wobbled towards them, ever so cautiously whilst grumbling to himself, unable to prevent the majority of items from falling out of his arms. Thene and Lall both smiled at Wick and Lumni whilst they figured out what was happening. Finally, Wick's eyes opened wide, suddenly looking alive once again as he ran over to Seff. He leaped through the air and knocked down the old man, knocking Seff's things everywhere too. "Ah, Wick, be careful you nearly broke my-".

"Thank you, thank you... thank you so much," Wick blubbered. Seff was surprised by the sudden amount of affection and couldn't help but develop a lump in his throat. Lumni on the other hand still stood near Thene and Lall, too gob-smacked to move but dying to explode with happiness. Instead, she allowed a single tear to run down her face but made sure no one saw. Moon had ran to Seff as well, and started licking his face nonstop, much to the old man's displeasure. "Alright, Moon... alright," he gagged, flapping his arms around in an attempt to push the dopey beast away, all whilst Wick was still latched onto his waist. Lumni bowed her head to the two warriors and walked over to Wick and Moon to join in with the celebration. "I hope that every family can be as happy as that one day," Thene said.

"Hoping won't fix the world, Thene. It's our duty to make sure it happens... and watching those foolish children overwhelmed with happiness is the image I'll keep in my head whilst I fight. We'll be fighting for their sake," Lall responded. Seff wiped his soggy face and stood back up whilst Lumni and Wick helped pick up his things. "Thank you," he said as they handed them over to him. "We'll just need to get some walking sticks to help us with our journey," he warned.

"Oh, you're not going by foot," Thene interrupted. Lall led them over to the giant stables near the rear of the village, where dozens of dragons awaited their riders. Wick, Moon, Lumni and Seff hopped on her Colliser whilst she said her goodbyes to Thene. "Take care," she said to her as they hugged, before bowing to one another. "I'll see you when our paths cross again," Thene assured. The others waved down to her from the dragon's back, sitting comfortably in the large basket-like saddle whilst Lall was taking her seat at the front. After a few flaps, the Colliser lifted from the ground with its heavy passengers, sending gushes of wind across the village with its wings. The Olash villagers looked up to wave goodbye also, having enjoyed the rare presence of outsiders. After one last look down at Thene's waving arms, Lall whipped the ropes in her hands, commanding the dragon to fly away into the dusky horizon. It was a long journey ahead, but it allowed Greenwick to reflect on his abrupt adventure – from waking up with no recollection, forced to befriend a strange bear, to being high in the air on a winged beast, on his way to a home fuelled by magic – something he once had no knowledge about. His necklace was still a mystery to him, and so was the identity of his Mother, but more so his Father, and the burnt house that Moon had taken him to near the beginning of their adventure still lacked any significance to him. Unfortunatley, there was no use looking back. Forwards however, in the years to come, Seff would continue to properly train him, but most importantly, take care of him, which was more of a blessing than all the Empyrean Energy Wick could ever want. With Lumni by his side, he wouldn't grow up alone. He was able to learn what it was like having a sibling to grow up with. Most importantly though, the boy had Moon – the most faithful and honourable of all he'd encountered through his travels. From the very beginning, the bear was by his side – through both high and low, he was there as one half of their unbreakable bond, and it couldn't have been more appreciated, for the world was a peculiar and dangerous place – the bear was always there to show the way. The majority of Earth's inhabitants had no idea what threats were developing in the shadows, but Wick was made a part of it all and knew full well, if only for a moment in his life – though the bloody black curse of voodoo would always serve as a reminder, slowly eating away at him from the inside. He wouldn't have to face the pain alone however. No matter what hardships the future held, his bear, Seffry and Lumni would always be there to help, for that's what he deserved. It was about time he was given a safe and stable home to live in – all they had to do was wait for the cottage to actually grow, similar to how the family around them had.

Chapter 30

Girl of Importance

Lumni had always been ashamed of her past. Not even Seff knew of her origins, other than the fact she was alone and afraid when he found her. The others always had an urge to find out, but the more they asked and speculated, the tighter her lips sealed, as though she wanted to forget and pretend that her past hadn't existed at all, but soon enough, her homeland and heritage would track her down and pull her back with force. The solitary kingdom of Thrail was high and mighty in all categories, albeit not as large in scale as Magmalia. Its smaller size was compensated by its money and use of rare materials, boasting its wealth by having the majority of its structures covered in gold and silver. It was a sight that most would beg to see, but passage through the kingdom walls was reserved exclusively for the rich and powerful. If money made the world go round, the Earth would have looked as artificial and boisterous as Thrail. Just one ridiculously wealthy kingdom alone though was more than enough to rot the world. It wasn't natural in the slightest – its people fixated on golden coins that determined their fates depending on how much one happened to possess, treating money as life or death currency, as though it governed their existence like the unbreakable laws of reality. It was a sickening place to live, but its people were too far gone and their spoilt mind-sets tricked them with feelings of power and invincibility. Materialistic possessions were more important than their hopes, dreams and memories. They were aberrant machines, fuelled by their unquenchable thirst to simply own more than what they had – a vile kingdom that Lumni wanted no part of, but before she had a life with Seff, she was once among the corruption through no fault of her own, for she was born there. Her Father, Tilliphus, King of Thrail owned everything he could see from the top of his castle. He was proud of everything he had, like a magpie flaunting its collection of shiny objects. His looks and personality didn't matter, for the only thing he and others cared about were the things he owned. The well-being of his numerous wives never entered his mind whilst surrounded by so much gold, not even the well-being of his daughter – the one thing he didn't want. Having the money to sleep with who he wanted to was bound to result in a child eventually, but people like him never had to worry about consequences. He was neither a true ruler nor Father. From the day she was born to being fourteen years old, Lumni had been tossed around by maids and an assortment of the King's reluctant wives. Thankfully, her upbringing was all under one roof, but the castle was so large with hundreds of rooms that it felt like a whole world in itself. The only time she'd cross paths with Tilliphus is if she just so happened to be walking by in the halls. He had no idea how old she was – he rarely acknowledged her either. Her time alone though was an opportunity to learn archery. After stealing bows and arrows from the armoury, she'd hide in the huge gardens behind tall bushes that no one ever had the time to go near, for the majority of the garden was never visited, ensuring she'd always have some privacy to fire arrows without anyone even knowing. Once the arrows ran out, she resorted to making her own with sticks and stone until it became second nature. Her accuracy increased after every shot, until she was able to hit the mark every time. The firing range would consist of anything she could get her hands on – from mouldy fruit to priceless vases she'd taken from the castle. At first, the archery was a fun hobby to pass the time, but as she got older, it was a means to release stress and anger. As a child, she'd never realised just how neglected she was, so once it became apparent as a teenager, her hatred for Tilliphus began to grow. Sometimes she questioned if he really was her Father. It was only a matter of time until her calm and collected nature would break and metamorph into a darker range of emotions because of him.

The change in character started on a day like any other. The maids had fed and provided fresh clothes for her, then passed her on to one of the step-Mothers. It was always a mystery as to which one she'd be dragged to. That day it was with Amiliae, one of Tilliphus' more recent wives. She sat all afternoon on her balcony, watching the King's dinner guests enjoy an outdoor dance. Lumni sat in the bedroom, sliding a glass bowl across a smooth marble table from one hand back to the other. Both listened to the blissful melodies of the stringed instruments outside, feeling like they'd been forgotten. "Why aren't *you* dancing?" Lumni asked Amiliae. The sudden sound of her voice interrupted her step-Mother's daydreams and caught her by surprise. "Oh, I wasn't invited, darling," she replied.

"But why? You're his wife".

"Your Father has a lot of lovers, Lumni. Sometimes he forgets to invite them all to his parties".

"You shouldn't need an invitation".

"I suppose, but that's just the way things are. I've never been asked anything – as a woman we should be obligated to abide without question," she explained with disappointment in her voice. Lumni got up and walked over to the balcony to peer down at the fun time below with envy. "The rules aren't fair," she said.

"What's not fair is you not being grateful for what you have," Amiliae snapped, but she knew in her own heart that Lumni was right. The women were expected to lead by example and never to disobey those above them. Their wealth and livelihood was at stake whenever they dared to oppose what the King wanted and expected of them. "It just doesn't seem right. Why doesn't my Father speak to me?"

"That's what Fathers are like. I rarely spoke to *my* Father. As soon as I was old enough, he sent me here to be a part of this kingdom and to marry *your* Father".

Way of the Moon Bear

"What is he like?" Lumni pestered. Amiliae hesitated before coming up with a vague answer. She didn't want to shine the King in a bad light whilst under his roof, nor did she want to ignite a hatred inside of his daughter. "Well, we don't talk a lot ourselves. We only see one another every few... nights, when he wants to see me. He's a very busy man... taking care of this entire kingdom for you and I," she stuttered.

"If he's busy then how does he have time to dance with those strangers?"

"That's enough, Lumni. Why don't you go to the kitchen and see what the cooks are making tonight?" she huffed in an attempt to get rid of her. Lumni stormed out, knowing when she was no longer wanted. The countless corridors would have made anyone confused, but she was used to walking around them for the majority of her days, to the point where she could traverse them blindfolded if she wanted to. Access to the kitchen was on the ground floor, which meant numerous slides down the many staircase banisters. Eventually, she reached the bottom half of the castle, unbeknown to her that the King's dinner guests were done dancing and were making their way through the garden doorway, which just so happened to be right next to the kitchen. Just as the doors were in her sights, the crowd of inebriated party snobs waltzed back inside, stampeding straight by her before she had a chance to move. Most of them were unaware of her presence, but the ones that did looked down at her face and snarled, then turned up their noses, treating her like an outcast or nothing more than a parasite. She heard whispers and muttering whilst attempting to cut through the crowd to get to the kitchen, and it wasn't long until a large, pompous man deliberately shoved her aside. "Get out of the way," he moaned.

"Don't push me... you fat lump," Lumni growled instinctively, followed by instant regret. The rich people didn't care for anything others said, unless it was an insult. A number of witnesses gasped and stood still in dismay, as though Lumni's temper was the worst thing they'd encountered in their privileged lives. "How dare you, little girl! Know your place, maid," the man grumbled as he raised the back of his hand towards her. "I'm not a maid, I'm the Princess," she said as an actual maid grabbed hold and pulled her back to avoid the man's impending slap. "How outrageous! The King *has* no children. Guards, guards, control your maids. This is ludicrous," a snooty woman scorned. Tilliphus could hear the commotion ahead, fearing the slightest displeasure from his guests. "What's going on here?" he erupted out of nowhere, looking down at his daughter and the maid. He wore an elegant dark blue jacket, covered in golden buttons, and a necklace dangled as he leant forward slightly, glimmering in the light. A ruby red jewel swung from the centre of the chain, gathering the attention of anyone that got close to him. "*She* claims to be a Princess!" the woman laughed and pointed. It took the King a while to realise that the girl in question was actually Lumni, only having a vague memory of what she looked like. "Nonsense, I have no daughters. I think the maids have been helping themselves to our wine," he lied with a nervous chuckle. The crowd laughed along with him, as they always did, even when the jokes weren't funny. He gave Lumni a deathly stare then escorted his guests to the ballroom, accompanied with armed guards that carried a mixture of swords, spears and bows. "What were you thinking?" the maid panted at Lumni, before dragging her over to the kitchen.

The stoves, spit-roasts and cauldrons were functioning at full force. Full pigs span with apples in their mouths, glistening as they dripped in grease. Various stews brewed and bubbled, with steam rising to the roof with nowhere to escape to. One day in the frantic kitchen was enough to drive a person mad, but its staff had transcended beyond madness and cooked the food like mindless slaves. Lumni zoned out from the overlapping voices and sounds, gazing at the poor dead pigs, finding some form of resemblance to her Father in their fat, dead faces. Her encounter with him was perhaps the closest the two of them had ever gotten, but it meant nothing, especially when he openly disregarded her existence. The thought of his blood being a part of her made her sick the more she thought about it. She didn't even know which one of the wives was her actual Mother, or if one of them even was.

For all she knew, given her Father's reputation, her Mother could have been one of the maids or cooks. The manic atmosphere in the kitchen was fitting semblance for how she was feeling inside. A part of her wanted to march into the ballroom and demand answers, but realistically, all she really wanted was to be alone and cry. The only person who could've possibly lifted some weight from her shoulders was one of Tilliphus' oldest wives, Melinor. Perhaps one of the nicest of the step-Mothers, Melinor always made sure Lumni was happy and entertained when under her care. Having experienced the longest amount of stress whilst living in the castle, her hair had greyed fairly early, and lack of contact with the sun meant that her skin was pale and rather withered, and as a result, the King had lost all interest. Her bedroom had been moved to the very top of the castle to make way for the younger, fresher women that took over the lower levels. Lumni wasn't put off by the seemingly endless flights of stairs though, and visited Melinor rather frequently. Her visit that night however was very different. The troubled girl knocked on the bedroom door, waiting for Melinor to answer. "Ah, darling! Come in, come in," the woman beckoned before shutting the door behind her. Lumni ran over and jumped on the comfy bed like usual then watched as Melinor walked over to sit in the tall armchair like she always did. "What's wrong? I can tell something's bothering you," she asked. "Come on, spit it out," she nagged jokingly.

"Why doesn't my Father love me?" Lumni said, unable to stop a stream of tears from seeping out. Melinor ran over and wrapped her arms around Lumni. It pained her to see the innocent girl in such a sad state. "Oh, dearie," she moaned.

"I don't feel like I belong here". Melinor looked at her and thought for a moment before reopening her mouth. It was clear to see there was something she was dying to say and express, but she knew once the words were said, there was no going back. After letting out a stress-filled sigh, she knelt down in front of the bed to be on the same eye level as Lumni. "There's something you should know – something I've been wanting to tell you for a long, long time... but I've wanted to wait until you were old enough to understand".

"I'm old enough. Tell me, please," Lumni gasped, hungry for information, not taking into account that the news could potentially make her feel worse. "Your Father is an evil, evil man. All he cares for is wealth and power. I've seen him talking to a strange man about... relics and artefacts? His stature has polluted his mind and money just isn't enough for him now," she explained in a nervous tone as her heart rate increased. She looked around on the off-chance someone was spying on them, which showed Lumni how dangerous the conversation was. "I don't want to live here anymore," Lumni blubbered.

"You sound just like your Mother," Melinor said with a crack in her voice before standing up to pace back and forth, folding her arms to stop her hands from trembling. "Where *is* my Mother?" Lumni murmured, apprehensive about the response, but needing to know. "She tried to run away time and time again... but Tilliphus would catch her – not because he cared for her, but because she was his possession, as we all are. He showed no interest in her until she tried to escape. She took care of herself, even when she was pregnant, and when you were born, he took you away from her".

"Why?"

"He couldn't bear to see someone else with more than him. You see, he had the most possessions, but he lacked any love or affection. He was unable to feel such things, so he made sure no one else could. One night, she tried to run away with you, but the guards had grown impatient with her reluctance... she had you in her arms... and they just... they just killed her," Melinor sniffled. Lumni sat up straight as her eyes grew wide. Her stomach began to churn and her skin turned slightly pale. She could feel the sheer shock and disgust explode from her heart, sending a wave of cold energy through her body. "I'm so sorry, Lumni... but it's time – we can try and run away, but we have to be smart. Your Mother lacked rationality," her step-Mother exclaimed. "We need to make sure we're ready. I know it's a lot to take in but-". Before she could stress any further, Lumni got out of the bed and clenched her fists, seeing a world of dark red hatred. Years of feeling confused, unable to fully release her emotions – it was time for her to finally explode. "Lumni, you need to calm down," Melinor begged, but it was too late. The rage-filled teenager lunged over to the fire place and grabbed the metal fire poker without having to think, then ragged the door open. Nearby maids shuddered in fright at the sound of the door slamming behind her. None of them had an opportunity to comprehend what was happening as the manic child ran down the stairs as fast as she could towards her so-called Father. Tilliphus was in the ballroom, entertaining his fake friends with fine dining and music, enjoying his temporary happiness the best he could. Before Lumni could barge in and put an end to it though, two guards stood in her way. They charged at her at the same time, but her small body allowed her to roll between their legs. As she passed through, she stole one of the bows from them then pushed open the heavy ballroom doors. The loud clanging of the doors had gotten the attention of the entire room. Even the musicians had stopped playing to see what all the fuss was about. She wasted no time to arm the bow with the fire poker and launched it across the room as though it was an arrow. The aggression could be felt across the room by the amount of energy she exerted to raise the bow and pull back the string without hesitation. The metal rod whizzed through the air and pinned Tilliphus by his jacket against the stone pillar behind him. The crowd screamed and panicked, escaping from any exit they could find whilst guards flooded into the room, not expecting to see a mere child causing so much chaos.

The King grunted in shock, but once he realised the rod hadn't actually touched his body, he attempted to rip and wriggle out of the jacket. "Who do you think you are?!" he bellowed.

"I thought I was your daughter! But not anymore!" she screamed, as a handful of guards restrained her. Just then, Melinor barged in after running down after Lumni. "Leave her alone!" she wailed.

"Melinor, what is this?" Tilliphus roared, finally breaking free from the humiliation, with his jacket still stuck in the pillar by the rod.

His necklace was more noticeable without the overcoat, and swayed side to side as he marched forward. "You killed my Mother!" Lumni screeched.

"Do you know what you have done? Do you know who you're talking to?" the King yelled.

"Do you know who *you're* talking to? Do you even know my name? Do you even remember my Mother's name? Because I don't – you stole her from me!"

"You somehow have the audacity to come in here, attempt to kill me and spit lies about things you know nothing about. You have no right to be in this castle. Everything within these walls carries some form of importance… all expect you. You are meaningless… pointless! You were nothing more than a mistake. Now, be gone! Guards, get rid of her!" Tilliphus shouted.

"Don't hurt an innocent child, you coward!" Melinor demanded, standing up for herself for the first time in her life. "I told her everything, it was me. She deserved to know how much of a vile person you are!" she continued. The King yanked a sword from one of the guard's hands and stabbed Melinor through the chest. He leant in and put his mouth to her ear as she gasped for air. "How foolish of me. Thinking it was worth keeping such an ugly wench in my home. You never showed me gratitude. This is exactly what you deserve," he told her before pulling the sword back out. Lumni screamed and cried at the sight of Melinor's life leaving her body, but before she flopped to the floor, she conjured the strength to reach forward and tug the King's jewel from his neck. Using the distraction to her advantage, Lumni bit down on the guard's hand and broke free from his clutches. With a face full of tears, she ran over to swipe the ruby red necklace before Tilliphus could. If shiny objects were all he cared for, then stealing his prized possession was the perfect final blow to enact before making an escape. The large and sluggish stature of the guards allowed the small girl to duck and weave between them until there was an open door leading to the huge garden. She knew the outdoor area better than anyone else in the castle, so it wasn't hard to lose her pursuers. After catching her breath in the tall bushes, she headed for the pointy fences – the last obstacle between her and the city. By that point, bells from the watchtowers were chiming loudly to alert the surrounding area of the escapee. Before the kingdom would fill with too many guards, she climbed over the fence, cutting her leg on the spikes as she dropped to the other side. Most of her life had been spent inside the castle, so navigating the large city was near-impossible. Thankfully, the dark of night allowed her to stay undetected as she scurried through the narrow alleyways, but the deep slash to her leg eventually forced her to stop. With a moment to reflect on what'd just happened, she cried quietly, curled up tight on the floor, all alone in the shadows of the cold city.

Footsteps of armoured soldiers crunched back and forth till the morning, but there was no sign of her. The King carried too much pride to give up though, so the search continued through the day with triple security throughout the kingdom. Unfortunately for him, she'd managed to climb in the back of a cart in the middle of the night, providing safe passage through the heavily guarded city walls. She stayed hidden under a mound of hay at the back of the wagon, only peeking out every few hours. Once she'd travelled a significant distance, she leaped out much to the driver's surprise and confusion. Having no experience in the great outdoors, the poor girl spent the following four days starving, thirsty and deprived of proper sleep, roaming aimlessly with the stolen ruby necklace gripped tightly in her hand. The blissful wild felt sombre and mundane in comparison to Thrail's elegant and shiny appearance, but she wouldn't have had it any other way. Her only connection to the kingdom at that point was her Father's jewel – no longer carrying any value. Finally, she came across a peaceful pond. The water tasted strange, but there were no other options. It at least served as a good way to dispose of the necklace and all the pain and torment it symbolised. After throwing it into the pond, her past and heritage sank down with it, hopefully never able to be brought back to the surface. With the past out the way, only the future remained, but the thought of not knowing what to do or where to go brought her to tears. Unexpectedly, the noise of the jewel splashing in the water had gained the attention of the passing Wizard. Seffry looked on at the crying girl, not knowing the best way to make himself known as he crept closer, but his clumsy footsteps eventually ruined his stealth, and Lumni turned to look. "Oh, hello. I was just coming to see if you were okay," he stammered. She wiped her tears – allowing a stranger to see her cry made her feel weak. "What brings you all the way out here, little one? Have you lost your parents?" he asked softly.

"I don't have any parents," she muttered.

"Ah, oh dear... I see. What happened? Where did you come from?"

"None of your business".

"Oh... well, am I allowed to know your name?"

"Lumni".

By the time two years had passed, Seff and Lumni could consider themselves a comfortable family, and with the inclusion of Wick and Moon, the household had doubled. Her name was quickly forgotten at Thrail, except for the step-Mothers and maids who remembered her as the only person to successfully escape the dreadful castle, and Tilliphus, who remembered her as the only person to tarnish his reputation. Whispering tales of the King's neglect to his unwanted daughter spread across the kingdom, rightfully painting him as the savage he was. His image wasn't the only thing to pain him however – the loss off his precious necklace meant more than anyone could have imagined. Feeling ashamed without it, he spent most of his days alone in his private quarters, no longer enjoying the company of guests. The only outsider he welcomed into his castle at that point was Yewnin. The two of them had been working together on rare occasions since just before Lumni was born, but given the change in situations and the possession of the Day Relic, their meetings had become much more frequent. Just after visiting Emmrin-Rashmada, after almost dying in the blizzard due to battle wounds, he travelled to Thrail to talk with the pompous King, excited to hopefully hear some good news. Tilliphus' room was dimly lit, but his eyes were closed so it didn't matter. A heavy night of drinking alone had drowned his sorrows momentarily, but the pain in his skull made him question if the wine was worth it. Yewnin had recently entered the room and was surprised the King hadn't realised. He shook his head in disappointment then coughed to announce his presence. Tilliphus almost jumped out of his arm chair in response to the unexpected noise, then scowled across to him. "Oh, so I take it you heard the news then?" he asked with a groan as he rubbed his weary eyes. "Remarkable isn't it?"

"Yet you drink as though it pains you to live," Yewnin jabbed.

"Come on, Yewnin".

"You used to be a very different man, Tilliphus. I dread to think what drove you down this path, but I'd be lying if I said I cared".

"You're in a cheery mood. Did your Day Relic plan work?"

"Lay-Vau is gone and my connection to the relic is stronger than ever, and I've successfully imprisoned all the Shamans I could ever need".

"It doesn't look like it was an easy scuffle," the King gagged, looking at the scars on Yewnin's face left behind by Moon's claws. "Simply prices I'm expected to pay," Yewnin replied.

"Speaking of payment... you're here for some incredibly crucial information. Don't think I'm telling you before you give me the amount we agreed upon". Yewnin sniggered at the King's desperate craving for golden coins, considering him a simple, closed-minded fool. "Tilliphus, do you ever get bored of wanting more and more money?" he sighed.

"What's your point?"

"You must think that the more you get, the less you need... but it's a void that you can never fill. Surely you should set your mind on more important things?"

"Well there's a lot of things I wish I had... but what makes you suddenly think you can trade more than gold with me?" the King scoffed. Just as he finished talking, the three Slayer Princes stepped out from the shadows, causing him to tense up with nerves. "Want something greater than money? The Slayers will happily steal for you.

Want something that was stolen from you? The Slayers will happily take it back," Yewnin teased. The amount of murderous talent in the room was unprecedented, for Tilliphus at least. He leant forward and thought about his long lost necklace – the jewel passed down from ruler to ruler, representing unparalleled power and wealth. Without it, he felt worthless, regardless of the money around him. Suddenly, he looked up with a wide smile. "The girl. I want the girl," he demanded.

"You'll have to be more specific," Yewnin grumbled.

"A foul girl... technically my daughter but-".

"Oh I see... you want her back as heir to the throne".

"Don't be preposterous. She stole my pendant, the wretched minx. If she doesn't have it anymore then she'll at least know where it is".

"Name?"

"Lumni," he growled as he gritted his teeth. Yewnin was shocked to hear the name. He had no idea he'd been fighting with the King's unwanted daughter of all people. "Extraordinary. Would you believe me if I told you I've encountered her before? She was working with my brother".

"Nonsense, she's a foolish little brat".

"We shouldn't rule out the possibility. He's been gathering a few peculiar characters lately. A Wizard, a boy and a bear, and by the sounds of it, your daughter. If my brother continues to get in the way of my plans then I'm sure her path will cross with mine once again, and if I know my interfering brother, you can consider it done". Tilliphus stood up to shake his hand, but Yewnin didn't move. "I need the information you have," Yewnin stressed. The King sat back down and smiled, knowing that Yewnin was going to love what he'd discovered. "*The Undying Beas*t, *created by the world* – you told me that's what the Shaman said to you. Well, my mining colony to the East had been searching for gold and... well," Tilliphus began to explain.

"Enough subtlety. Was the *other one* there or not?"

"Oh yes, Yewnin... the Earth Relic... we've found it".

End of Book 1

Printed by Amazon Italia Logistica S.r.l.
Torrazza Piemonte (TO), Italy